Fly Again, Phoenix

Stephanie Cho & Paul Jeon

Editor: Bronwyn Harris

Cover Design: Karine Makartichan, US Illustrations

Formatter: Elijah Feyisayo

ISBN: 9798862020007

www.flyagainphoenix.com

Dedicated to God, who saved us and made our lives so beautiful; to our loving family and friends; and to all the young people out there in need of hope and light.

Journal #1

The seawater rushed in toward me, and, giggling, I ran away. But at that moment, Dad scooped me up from behind and he waded into the water, letting my small feet, ankles, and legs rest in the foaming, salty water.

"Her jeans will get wet! She'll catch a cold!" Mom yelled from the sand.

But Dad and I were too busy laughing.

"Dad, let's catch sand crabs," I asked him.

He carried me back to the shore and my feet met the moist, accepting earth once again.

I looked up, knowing I'd see that warm smile of his that made all my doubts fly away. For a moment, I admired his jet black hair that was always swept to the left side and the dimples above his smiling lips.

Just then, a wave came in and we both peered at the sand at our feet, scanning for bubbles that sand crabs made as they burrowed deep into the earth.

"Right here, Dad!" I yelled, pointing down at a spot with a dozen tiny bubbles popping above the sand.

Dad started pawing away at the moist sand like a dog, sand flying everywhere, and I stood, guffawing.

"Gabby, help me dig," he said quickly without looking up.

Together, we pawed away, not caring that brown sand was getting inside our fingernails. After a few seconds, I felt tiny legs scratching, tickling the flesh on my fingers.

"Dad! I felt one!"

"Great job, Gabby!" Dad was always full of compliments for me.

Soon, we had made a gaping hole in the earth, and all that was left to do was to wait for water to fill it up.

A huge wave rolled in.

"Whoa! Whoa! Whoa!" we yelled together over the roar of the wave.

As water rushed over our hole, we quickly put our hands into the hole, feeling for the little critters.

Eight sand crabs floated to the surface, and we victoriously scooped them up using both hands. Before the sea creatures could crawl off our hands and fall to the ground, we ran over to the empty glass kimchi jar that we always brought and deposited them safely inside.

Dad reached over to me and gave me a big high five, his large palm dotted with sand.

I smiled at him, thinking I'd be with him forever. Best friends forever.

~

My dad left for the war in Afghanistan when I was twelve years old. Dressed in his military uniform, his warm smile was gone and his furrowed brow now radiated tension. Though I could grasp onto his hands, coarse and tired, he was already far away, fighting a battle not yet waged against enemies not yet faced. I watched as my mother rubbed his now shaven head, her eyes covered with a thin veil of courage in a time of so much uncertainty. Rubbing his head back and forth, back and forth, she hummed a wistful melody.

2:00 A.M. The time of his departure had arrived. My heart kept fluttering like a strange animal in my chest. At the terminal, ticket in hand, Dad knelt down with both knees to the floor so that he could look up into my eyes. He looked at the floor for a second, and then looked up at me. Tears thinly veiled his kind brown eyes as he swallowed his tears, his Adam's apple moving. "Gabby, Gabby. I'm going to go away for some time, but I will see you soon. I love you. I love you." I stood as strong as a redwood tree, with its roots reaching deep into the ground, promising myself I wouldn't lose my composure and cry like a child. His strong arms wrapped around me and soon, I was enveloped in that moment, his words swirling around me. "I'm going to go away. I love you. I love you." Muffled in his shoulder, I pleaded, "Daddy, don't go," but it was lost in the moment. My tears left two dark dots on his uniform.

Dad slowly stood up and saw Mom. Her face exuded an aura of strength and stoicism, but her delicate hands softly trembled. Now, face to face with Dad, her eyes, glistening, told no lies. I didn't know at the time, but she was scared; her mind was racing through all the possibilities of the worst outcomes, all the consequences, all the alternatives. My parents embraced one another, knowing full well that it could be their last time. As they let go of one another, my dad mustered a meek smile, his eyes glued upon my mom, who was the most beautiful woman to him. My mother's stoic face wavered, as she cupped her mouth, stifling a loud sob that briefly came forth from her throat. I quickly grabbed my father's right hand.

"When are you coming back?" My hand almost refused to ever let his hand go.

Thoughts washed over his face as to how to explain the situation, but before he could answer, his name rang out throughout the terminal gate.

"Lance Choi. Lance Choi. Proceed to the gate."

My father's face turned to the gate and then quickly to us.

"I love you," he said hurriedly, as he turned to the gate, releasing my small hand.

"I love you," my mom and I both called out after him. This is when my body started trembling, an earthquake shaking the foundation of that strong redwood tree. My face grew hot and tears streamed down my cheeks.

After handing over his ticket, he, in his army fatigues, turned back, paused, and waved at us. His large doe eyes, longingly looking toward me and Mom, are forever imprinted in my mind. My father walked through the gates and soon, he was gone.

Five years passed since her dad had left for Afghanistan, and Gabby was beginning her senior year of high school. Opening her eyes slowly one Saturday morning, she squinted as the powerful rays from the sun pierced through her eyelids. She let out a brief, quiet yawn, shaking away the tiredness of staying up late writing an essay for AP English Lit. Her keen eyes then noticed something new: luxurious red rose blossoms peeping through her two windows. She quickly stood up from her bed and scanned the roses, admiring their full shape and crimson tones.

"Dad would've liked that," she said aloud, her sweet voice ringing crisply in the air. Her dad's deep voice faintly rang in her ears, "Gabby, look at those flowers," as he would point at newly blossoming flowers wherever they went.

Gabby quickly changed from her blue pajama bottoms to some black basketball shorts, and then she made her way into the garden. The cool ocean breeze characteristic of her town, Toccoa, California, kissed her bare arms; the trees and shrubs surrounding her quivered with life and vitality. But as she watched the red roses in silence, she couldn't help but feel they were a weak embodiment of her dad. A hollowness crept into her chest and pounded against her heart like a cold, merciless bell.

Walking a little further, she stood upon the little grass lawn where her dad had often practiced his golf.

"Watch this chip, Gabby," he would say with a playful grin. Gabby envisioned his focused eyes as he made his pendulum-like swing, the little white ball flying across the yard in an arc to his target spot. She would cheer and clap for him, and he would smile with that loving twinkle in his eyes. For a moment, she was so lost in the vision of him that when the memory ended, she was startled to find that she was standing alone in her yard.

Tilting her head up to look at the vast and cloudless blanket of blue, she spotted a single plane flying high in the sky. She wished her heart could soar like that plane full of hope. But at the same time she was afraid to wish because it might not come true after all. For all these years she had taught herself to not dwell on the fact that she missed her dad, but how much longer? She was already seventeen. Just then, the thought hit her: Would he even make it to her high school graduation?

A flood of sadness crept up to her throat from her chest. To keep herself from feeling it all, she quickly walked back to her bedroom. Peeling back her flowery covers, she slid inside her cool bed and put the covers over her head. For some moments, she just lay still, but after a couple seconds, warm tears started slowly sliding down her cheeks. She wasn't a crier so she realized she had been holding the tears down for some time now. She reached her hand out from under her blanket to grab a tissue from the tissue box on her desk, but instead, her fingers hit thick paper. Gabby peeped out from beneath her blankets and saw that it was the most recent card that her father had sent her. She had almost memorized it word for word.

~

My darling Gabby,

I miss your cheerful smile and your bright laugh. I miss hitting balls with you at the golf range. How I wish I could watch you play on your girls' golf team. I'm so proud of how you not only excel in your classes, but also in sports, in your voice lessons, and in everything else. Remember to rest, too. You only have one life to live. I am well so don't worry about me. Hoping to see your face soon.

Love,

Your Dad

~

She wiped the wetness off her cheeks as she read her dad's slanted, sophisticated handwriting across the page. With her slender fingertips, she gently grazed his handwriting in blue ink, as if her dad's presence would magically flow from it. For a moment, a pang of resentment filled her heart, because when her dad did get a chance to come home, it was only for a week, before he would head off to be a drill sergeant for younger soldiers in basic training. But she wanted to believe her dad loved her, and that he wasn't putting work before her. Gabby swiftly put her bed covers over her head and buried herself inside her blankets, trying to drown out the pounding feeling of missing the one person who had made her world feel all right.

When she emerged from her bed thirty minutes later, she quickly ran over to her full-length mirror to check her face, hoping her eyes weren't puffy so that her mom wouldn't ask her why she was crying. Her gentle, clear, brown almond eyes and lovely double eyelids were intact. She breathed in and out, her chest rising and falling rapidly, glad to be feeling a bit better.

Cautiously walking into the kitchen, she noticed that her mom was placing food on the countertop. Gabby's stomach grumbled as she looked upon the plates of creamy mac 'n' cheese and tangy, sweet Chinese chicken salad. But though her stomach automatically reacted to the food, she felt no desire to eat.

"Why do you look so tired? You slept so much," her mom questioned her sharply without looking up from the plates she was placing on the table.

"I had a bad dream," Gabby lied.

Her mom's rapid movements made the ceramic plates clatter against the cold, glass dining table.

"You have your voice lesson on Tuesday. Make sure you practice today. You didn't practice yesterday, did you?" She spoke with that shrill, accusing tone that Gabby was so used to but still made a chill run down her spine.

Gabby gulped. Her mom was always telling her to practice.

"Okay," she briefly replied, staring at the heat rising from the yellow mac 'n' cheese.

Soon she and her mom were seated at the dining table, and Gabby looked up at the empty seat across from her where her father had once sat.

She shook her head and buried her fork into her salad, eating obediently.

"You're going to be late for choir practice. Eat more quickly, Gabby."

"Okay, Mom," she quickly replied, her anxiety rising by the second.

At choir rehearsal, Gabby got lost in the excitement of being surrounded by her friends and scores of other young people her age. They were preparing for their winter concert, so they rehearsed lively Christmas and Hanukkah music all morning long. The children's cheery voices ringing throughout the large rehearsal room put Gabby in good spirits. She felt like doing the choreographed motions that went along with the songs and wearing fuzzy brown reindeer antlers for "Rudolph the Red-Nosed Reindeer" was a little childish, but she still got a laugh out of it. At least she didn't have to wear a big red nose.

At break time, she rushed out the door to meet up with her good friends, Mikayla, Denielle, and Dennis.

"I got asked out to Homecoming!" Denielle squealed in her loud, assertive voice. Gabby studied Denielle's perfectly straight-permed long black hair and the tight pink top she was wearing that revealed her belly button.

"Already? By who? School just started!" Mikayla blurted out in her sweet, bubbly voice.

Mikayla, Gabby, and Dennis burst out in laughter. Denielle was very attractive and always had no problem getting guys to like her. Gabby smiled at the surprising but not so surprising situation as Denielle continued to glow and beam.

Dennis had a secret crush on Denielle that only Gabby knew about so she observed how he crossed his arms and tried to look happy for Denielle with a wry grin. Gabby stifled a little laugh and kept watching Dennis, hoping he wasn't too sad.

Mikayla then oozed with excitement about a crush she had on a new boy at school, and how she was hoping to get close to him so they could go to Homecoming together. Gabby imagined what the cute surfer boy, Jordan Piper, looked like. She imagined a boy with luxurious, wavy blond hair swept to the side and mesmerizing blue eyes.

"Your mom isn't going to let you go to Homecoming, right?" Denielle asked Gabby in her frank manner.

"Yeah, only Prom!" Gabby replied, feeling embarrassed that she wasn't allowed to go to any high school dances except Prom.

"Aww…" Mikayla said compassionately, shaking her caramel-blonde head.

"Break time is over!" the choir moms exclaimed loudly as they rang a large golden bell.

All the kids in their bright red uniforms flooded into the rehearsal rooms again.

They were now practicing "The Last Farewell," the final song they sang at every concert. The slow, beautiful melody was full of longing and always felt so poignant to Gabby's young heart.

I'm going away at eventide

Across the wild and the rolling sea

I bid you stay,

Here by my side

And share a last farewell with me

Through snow-clad mountains, proud and tall

Or a thousand miles 'cross the burning sand

Our last farewell, then will I recall

When I'm alone in a far-off land

A wandering song is all I know

Yet I love you more, more than words can tell

I hear that call, and I'm bound to roam

I leave you now, with a last farewell

I leave you now, with a last farewell

Suddenly, Gabby heard her phone vibrating on the empty chair next to her. She looked at the screen. It was Mom. Wondering what it could be, she grabbed her phone and swiftly made her way to the bathroom.

"Hello?" Gabby asked urgently as soon as the bathroom door closed with a creak.

"Gabby…" her mom choked out in between her sobs.

Gabby's mind raced, carrying her heart to her worst possible fear. Did something happen to Dad?

"Your dad's coming home," her mom finally announced with great joy.

That's when huge tear droplets started coming out of Gabby's eyes as if they had been waiting for all the years her father had been gone. Her head and back bobbed up and down as uncontrollable crying came over her in waves. Her cries sounded like the yelping of a small puppy, and they echoed and bounced off the dark grey walls of the small bathroom. She cupped her mouth, trying not to be too loud.

"When?" she asked urgently, with snot now forming in her nose.

"Tomorrow," her mom replied.

"Oh my gosh Mom!" Gabby cried, wiping the tears from beneath her nose. Giggles bubbled up from her spirit and her mom started guffawing loudly, too. The mother and daughter laughed together for a few moments.

"Okay, I gotta go back inside now," Gabby said excitedly. "See you later!"

Holding her phone, Gabby elatedly walked out of the bathroom. As she sat back down in the choir room, Mikayla asked, "Did something happen?"

Gabby grinned widely while still looking attentively at their choir director.

She whispered back to her, "My dad's coming home."

"What?" Mikayla gasped in her childlike voice.

They looked at each other and smiled ear to ear. Gabby felt as if her heart would explode like a million fireworks in the sky.

Back at home, Gabby's mother handed her the written notice of her father's discharge. Gabby held the letter in her hands, her hands softly trembling. All the times they cried because they missed him. All the birthdays and milestones they celebrated without him. All the worrying about whether he was well and safe. It had all led to this day. Her heart fluttered wildly as she beamed a wide toothy grin, a happiness overtaking the weariness she had held for so many years, as she scanned his name again and again just to make sure: Lance Choi. Lance Choi. Lance Choi.

The next morning, Gabby ran over to her mom's bedroom, eager for what the day would bring.

"Mom, what should we get Dad as a welcome home present?" Gabby asked joyfully, feeling tingly all over with excitement. She did a little jig as she waited for her mom to respond.

"Hmm, I don't know," she replied, applying some plum-colored lipstick in front of the mirror on her vanity.

Suddenly, Gabby lit up with an idea.

"Can we get him yellow roses?"

13

"Sure!" her mom quickly said. Gabby was amazed her mom actually said yes to something she suggested.

The flowers would be a signal to her dad of the love that they shared. He had brought Gabby a bouquet of yellow roses every single year at her voice recital. She loved running over to her dad after her performance. He would hug her warmly and tell her she did a great job and hand her the biggest, most fragrant bouquet that she could imagine. Gabby would feel like the most loved daughter in the room.

~

At the airport, Gabby clutched her bouquet that they had wrapped in lovely lilac-colored paper and a purple ribbon in her sweaty hands as she looked this way and that above the adults in front of her. They were all awaiting loved ones who had gone to Afghanistan. Seeing a little opening between an elderly gentleman and lady, she scooted between them and stood in front of them.

Her mom, who had gone to the bathroom, found Gabby and stood behind her. They looked at each other for a moment and grinned.

Gabby smelled the roses one last time, making sure again that they smelled sweet. She twirled the bouquet in her hands with nervous excitement, eager to give her dad the sentimental present.

A group of soldiers emerged, and her heart started to race. She scanned the men's and women's faces. Every single face looked unfamiliar to her and her head started to spin; she feared her father had not come for some reason. A spell of dizziness overtook her as the soldiers' faces looked blurred. No Dad. "He was supposed to come. He has to be here," she thought with misery.

Just then, she caught the sight of a familiar set of kind brown eyes and a prominent square jawline. Her eyes grew large and tears of relief welled up in her eyes. It was him. Dad.

"Lance!" her mom yelled.

Her dad looked in their direction and smiled. But immediately Gabby could sense something was off. It wasn't his normal genuine smile that made his eyes sparkle and light up. It was as if he forced it.

Puzzled, Gabby still ran toward her father and hugged him.

"My beautiful girls," he said brightly as he hugged her and her mom at the same time.

Gabby noticed that the wrinkles by his eyes had deepened and that slight creases had formed around his mouth. His skin had tanned from being in the Middle East, and dark brown freckles peppered his cheeks.

Gabby wrapped her arms around her dad and rubbed her face against his warm chest. She held onto him and cried and giggled, cried and giggled. Gabby's mom wept upon his shoulder for a long while and kissed him on the cheek with her wet face, repeatedly saying, "I missed you so much." For some long moments, the three hugged each other. Relief and comfort she hadn't felt in years flooded Gabby's soul as rain upon a parched desert.

But when Gabby looked up at her dad's face, he was just smiling that plastered-on smile, not shedding a single tear. She also noticed his eyes flitting from here to there and even behind him. He seemed tense and nervous.

Gabby's mom was so busy wiping away her tears that she didn't seem to have noticed all this.

Gabby gulped and shed a few more tears, upset at this change in her father. She had expected to see his old self.

"Dad, I got these for you," Gabby said, handing him the bouquet.

Lance looked down at the roses and for a moment, a knowing expression filled his eyes; he hugged Gabby tightly and rubbed her head quickly, just like the old days.

Gabby's heart jumped and tears squirted out of her eyes. It was Dad after all.

"Thank you. They're yellow roses," he said warmly.

Soon, the whole family had piled into the car and they were on their way home.

"Dad, want to go play golf this weekend?" Gabby asked eagerly, wanting to make him happy.

"Sure!" he replied chirpily. But once again, it had that artificial tone.

In the back seat, Gabby frowned to herself.

"Darling, what do you want to eat for dinner? How's Chinese? Your favorite?" her mom asked, squeezing his shoulder with her free hand as she drove with the other.

Suddenly, Lance grew quiet and did not answer.

Rubbing his forehead back and forth, he replied, "I'm really tired. I think I'll skip dinner today."

Gabby and her mom looked at each other in the rearview mirror, but Gabby's mom made a face to Gabby signaling that they should just be accommodating.

"Okay, Dad!" Gabby replied with kindness.

Gabby's father put his head back against the seat and closed his eyes and said no more for the rest of the drive home.

Journal #2

I remember when I was young, Dad would come into my room every night when I was studying and say, "Great job, Gabby. Good night!" His legs would trudge heavily up the staircase to his room and I'd smile to myself, my heart warmed by his gesture.

Dad's Army friends told me he was so friendly and peaceful amidst the chaos, so everyone wanted to be around him. They called him their "home away from home." When he came back in September, he received the Medal of Honor for saving two of his men's lives. But I'll never forget his face as he stood on the stage at the award ceremony. His face was like hardened plaster—with no expression, dull, cold. I wondered who that man standing there was. Where had my dad, Lance Choi, gone? I ran out of the ceremony because my stomach started hurting and sat on the toilet until the end of the ceremony.

18

My dad was gone. The dad that I knew has been lost in the ravages of war.

I was hoping he would return to his normal self over the next few weeks, but he still hasn't.

I can tell that he tries to be the same dad as he used to be. He puts on a smile and chats with me, but I can tell he's not truly happy. When we go to hit balls at the golf range, I look up after hitting a ball to check if Dad is proud of me, but he seems lost in thought. It's as if he's there, but not there. Nowadays, he's been changing even more. His face is usually downcast and dark, his brow crinkled, and his mouth in a deep pout. He walks from this room to that, slamming shut closet doors, finding dissatisfaction in everything.

"Who moved my shoes like that?" he'd yell.

"Who left my closet door open?"

"Why are you purposely doing these things to upset me?"

"We're not!" Mom and I would wail.

His paranoia is escalating by the minute.

Post-traumatic stress disorder, or PTSD, is what they call this illness that many soldiers come home with. I wish Dad would get therapy for it, but he got mad at us for telling him he needs therapy. I feel even more on edge these days because he's been drinking every night–a lot. He never once touched alcohol before he went to Afghanistan, but now…he can't live without it. Mom doesn't want him to drink and grabs the bottles out of his hands, but I sometimes wonder to myself if it could be good for Dad to get away sometimes. Maybe he needs some alcohol to forget–to forget the things that scare him. Once or twice a month, I hear him screaming in the middle of the night from a nightmare. Mom told me not to tell Dad that she told me this, but he sometimes wakes up from a dream wailing and he cries in her arms, his whole body trembling, until he falls asleep exhausted. We think he might be remembering friends he lost in the war, but we don't mention it to him because it could make him feel worse.

I couldn't sleep last night, so I finally realized I needed to do something. I can't just watch him progressively get worse. To create a therapeutic environment for him at home, I decided to redecorate his room. I opened up the white curtains and held them back with nice white velvet ribbons I bought from Joann's. I dusted off his bookshelf and desk, which he no longer sits at, except when he's frustrated and feels like breaking an object on his desk. Dad likes a clean house. I filled up a glass vase with fresh water and stuck some bright orange tulips in there from our garden, which is bursting with color.

I ran around the house setting a few more vases–in the living room and dining room, and one in the corridor as well.

I waited expectantly as I heard Dad come in and make his way toward his room.

He brusquely ripped his golf glove off his hand and threw it down on his desk but made no comment on the nice changes I had made. I sighed.

"Dad!" I said chirpily, clearing my throat, a little intimidated. "How was golf today?"

Normally he would've shown me his score card and given me a lengthy methodical explanation of his golf game with a wry grin, but today, he just grunted and left the room, and me just standing there in my cleaning apron.

I was at a loss for words.

"I just have to do better next time," I thought, trying to muster up some confidence.

Spotting a picture frame of me and my dad on his desk, my throat grew tight and I tried hard not to be sad. My dad had raised me not to cry. Tired, I sank into his cold leather chair, the plush leather so comforting...compared to someone's presence.

~

Touching the worn guitar that her father had played for her at this very beach when her family would go camping every summer, Gabby felt tears forming in her eyes. Her eyelashes fluttering, a single warm drop fell into her palm, when just then, it began to rain. Gabby just sat there, as the rainwater collected in the sound hole of the guitar. She almost enjoyed the sound that the drops made, and she did not care what was happening to this once cherished instrument of her father's. A few seconds later, suddenly realizing that she wanted to save it, she snatched up the guitar like it was a small child and quickly scurried to the nearest lifeguard post. Standing there on the unmanned lifeguard post with the guitar strapped around her shoulder, Gabby wondered where her lifeguard, her hero, was. Though this wooden guitar was now decaying, she silently hoped that her family wasn't.

As she turned around to leave, an enormous rainbow spanning the horizon made her stop in her tracks. Her stormy heart became completely still as it became filled with an inexpressible and sure hope. Something good was coming.

Something, or someone, who would change everything.

A half mile away from Gabby sat a boy on the beach. He stood up to skip some rocks. A sense of frustration and emptiness nagged at him and he couldn't shake it off.

"If only Mom were here," he thought aloud.

The rain beat upon his dark grey hoodie and he let it drench him and his thoughts and take hold of his mood, his being...

Just then, Trevor saw the sky clear up, and the brightest, most vivid rainbow stretched across the sky. His heart stopped, and he sucked his breath in. It was like a smile from heaven.

Feeling a nudge of comfort against his chest, he lingered in the wondrous moment.

G

The chill in the air filled her bones and Gabby hugged her body tighter, her thin brown sweater not enough to protect her from the wind. Slowly trudging toward the maple tree in front of the school band room, where her friends always met for lunch, she observed the tree was now donning a lovely suit of bright yellow leaves. The changing colors of the leaves and the seemingly endless days of her father's illness before her made her heart plunge heavy like a stone sinking into the depths of a lake.

Gabby's friends were all in marching band except for her. To support them, she would go to their field shows and cheer in the bleachers alone like a band mom. She would observe her friends closely as they'd march earnestly in configuration. Though they considered themselves mere "band geeks," Gabby was truly proud of them.

Her eyes were fixated on the black asphalt as she walked, but her daze was interrupted by her best friend, Rochelle Liu.

"Hey! What's up?" Rochelle asked in her cheerful voice.

Gabby looked up and smiled. She noticed that Rochelle was just finishing up one of her "Rochelle dances," where she would wiggle her whole body, especially her long, slender arms, like an octopus, all while making a goofy expression with her eyes. She did this signature dance when she was supremely happy. All their friends were roaring with laughter and some were cupping their mouths so that food wouldn't fall out. Gabby actually found herself giggling a little, too.

Gabby instinctively hugged Rochelle, reaching for some comfort. But after a moment in her warm embrace, she quickly drew back, not wanting anyone to know that she was troubled over her dad.

"Hey," she said, smiling into Rochelle's lean, pretty face. She breathed a little easier, surrounded by her loving friends.

"Hey Alicia! Hey Janet!" Gabby said to her other friends. They were seated on the wooden bench in front of the tree, voraciously eating sandwiches and dumplings lovingly prepared by their moms out of cute, colorful Asian plastic lunch containers.

Gabby continued to smile and catch up with her friends, concealing the sadness in her heart. She gently put down her black Jansport backpack on the bench, sat down, and let out a deep sigh. The weight of her family sat like a boulder upon her thin frame. For a moment she felt the fear creep in again, but then she collected her thoughts. Rochelle quickly sat down next to her.

"I'm having a sleepover this Friday. Can you come?" she asked Gabby, showing her pretty white smile despite her purple braces that she recently got. Rochelle was the event planner of the group.

24

Gabby's heart fell. She got ready to tell Rochelle one of her mom's age-old rules: that she could only go to one sleepover a year. But at the same time, she didn't really feel like going. If she went, all she would be thinking about was Dad anyway.

Gabby looked at the ground, then looked at Rochelle. She looked into her reflective brown eyes, feeling a sense of comfort.

"Sorry, my mom only lets me go to one sleepover a year. I went to Alicia's sleepover for her birthday, so…" she said apologetically.

"Aww man…" Rochelle replied in her good-natured voice.

She slung her arm over Gabby's shoulder and said, "We'll make up for it. We'll do something else that's not a sleepover."

Gabby smiled at Rochelle's sweetness as she took out her lunch from her dark green thermal lunch box. She saw that there was cut up mango in one container. Though her favorite food in the whole world, it, for some reason, looked so unappetizing.

But knowing her mom would be mad if she didn't eat it, she took her fork and jabbed at a chunk and placed it in her mouth, the tanginess jolting her tongue.

Rochelle chatted in her lively tone about the boy she had a crush on, Yuta Hatsukade, and how she hoped he'd ask her to Homecoming. Yuta was the marching band president, suave, charming, yet sincere, with voluptuous raven black hair. Gabby usually had a crush on someone, too, but there was no room in her heart or mind for boys at the moment.

Gabby just smiled and nodded. She wished she could feel as thrilled about life as Rochelle did.

When Gabby got home that evening after track practice, she stood in her ever-darkening room in front of her full-length mirror. She stared into her face. As night closed in, she wondered about her fate. Her dad was so unpredictable. She felt she was standing upon the ledge of a cliff, with strong winds buffeting against her. But Gabby shook the thought away. She knew she had to stay strong for her mom, and for her future. She had to stay focused on school and getting good grades.

Just then, she heard the front door swing open downstairs and her mom's voice. It trembled with anger.

"Where are you going?" she questioned Dad.

"To the market."

"To buy more alcohol?" her mom interrogated fiercely.

"Don't tell me what to do," Gabby's dad firmly said before slamming the door shut and walking out to the driveway. His footsteps echoed from the pavement and slowly died away.

Gabby sat upon her bed, now in her blackened bedroom and hoped her family wasn't spiraling down like water down the kitchen drain.

She instinctually reached for her phone to text Rochelle but she remembered her mom's stern words: "Don't tell anyone about your dad."

As the darkness permeated her being, she lay down on her cold bed. But hating the sinking feeling deep in her chest, she turned to her side and flicked on the small Snoopy lamp next to her bed. On the table lay her Bible. Engraved upon the shiny leather cover was her name in small gold letters: Gabrielle Choi. She grabbed the book and flipped through the pages. She went to her favorite chapter: Psalm 23.

"The Lord is my shepherd. I shall not be in want," she began reading softly to herself.

"Even though I walk through the darkest valley, I will fear no evil, for you are with me; your rod and your staff, they comfort me."

She envisioned Jesus with a shepherd's staff, and him walking next to her to protect her and guide her. This image helped her breathe a little easier.

She held her Bible against her stomach and spoke to God out loud.

"God, please protect my family. Please let Dad get better."

Curling up on her side and hugging her arms, she fell asleep, escaping the nightmare in which she lived.

Meanwhile, Lance had returned from Ralph's and he sat upon the cold black leather couch in the living room, about to pour himself some vodka. His vision adjusted to the darkness and his eyes darted across the room, seeing if there was any perceived danger. His uneven breathing broke the silence and his brow felt wet as his anxiety built up more and more.

He shook his head, telling himself it's okay, that he was just at home. Memories of Afghanistan started to flood into his mind like seawater but he pushed them back by clearing his throat loudly to distract himself. As he took a sip of vodka, his gaze fell upon the picture frames on the wall next to the T.V. They were snapshots of his family–his old wedding photo, a picture of Gabby's first time at the beach as an infant, their family on their annual camping trip. The people in the photos looked so joyful and the photos possessed a magical warmth which his family was now devoid of.

"Those times feel like millions of years ago," he thought.

He tried to recreate those feelings of love within himself, but he failed at his attempts. All he felt was a hollow coldness in his heart, as if it were an empty cave.

"A black cave," he said aloud to himself as he continued looking at the picture frames.

He gulped down the strong liquid, which filled his cavernous self. The burning in his throat felt almost cathartic. He wanted to feel something that told him he was alive. He also wanted to feel punished for not being the normal Lance that his family needed. Filling shot glass after shot glass, he drank deep into the night, until the room started to look blurry and he needed to rush to the bathroom to vomit. The bathroom was much too far and he made it to the kitchen sink. Holding onto the metallic edge of the sink to keep balanced, he finally sank to the ground and lay on the beige linoleum floor. He knew he was about to faint but he welcomed it. At least for a little while he could escape the fear–the fear of his past, but more than that, the fear of the person he had become.

A little while later, Carol Choi got up from bed, unable to fall asleep, and searched the home for her husband. She entered the kitchen and saw him lying on the floor. She stood still at the mouth of the kitchen and watched him as he slept. She studied the even rise and fall of his chest. His grey and maroon plaid shirt had remnants of his vomit here and there. Quickly grabbing a kitchen towel, Carol knelt to the ground and gently rubbed away the vomit while staring into her husband's face. At least while he was sleeping, he looked peaceful. She stroked his soft brown hair, which felt so familiar to her. Everything about him was familiar except the war that raged within him. She slowly got up and walked to the cabinets in the hallway, grabbed some blankets and a pillow, and headed back to the kitchen. He was still sleeping soundly. She gently tucked the pillow underneath his head which was wet with sweat, and laid the blankets over his body. For a moment, she considered going back to the bedroom to sleep, but then she lay down next to him. Holding his hand in hers, she studied his handsome face in the still dimness of night.

~

The following night, Carol wandered around Macy's, the place that was her sole escape. But though she was surrounded by brilliant, colorful, appealing clothes, all she could see was images of her husband: his stoic face, his angered face, him drinking and drinking. Her head spun just thinking about it all.

"Five years," she thought. For five years she had waited for her husband's return, but now that he was here, he was not at all like he used to be. She felt as if her life had been stolen from her.

Tears left Carol's eyes, as her heart hardened even further at the unfairness of it all. She felt hatred, she felt sorrow, she felt grief, but she had no one to turn to for comfort. On top of that, she had to stay strong for Gabby so that her daughter could grow up to be successful, unlike her.

At that moment, a stunning, bright red dress hanging on the front of a rack caught her eye. For a moment, she admired the dress, as it took her back to holiday parties of the past when she would dance with Lance and everyone around them would cheer because of their sweet, vibrant connection. For a moment, she was in a trance thinking about her husband's winsome smile and magnetic brown eyes. She woke up from her trance and studied the red dress again, thinking she could wear it for a holiday party in a few months, but then the hard reality sank in that there would be no celebration with her husband being like that. She grabbed the hanger, tempted to buy it just because, but then she shook the thought away, wanting to save money for Gabby and her future.

She clutched her purse and ran out of Macy's, holding back her sobs that came over her in waves. Quickly turning the lock on her car door, she sat in the driver's seat and, putting her head against the steering wheel, she cried and cried. Her cries rang loudly throughout her car, but nobody on the outside could hear them. As she sat alone in the dark parking lot, her heart felt an endlessness to her sorrow. Her heart was forever broken, and there was nothing that could fix it.

Journal #3

Today I have my voice recital. I have a feeling Dad won't show up, not that I want him to. I don't want anyone to see him in one of his moods. But a part of me misses how he used to come to all of my voice recitals when I was young. He would be smiling behind his tripod and he would record the entire show–even all the other students' songs. I loved seeing him in the audience because he made me feel calm and comforted despite my nervousness. But right now, Dad isn't "here."

Gabby started singing the Whitney Houston song softly to herself, "There can be miracles when you believe...Though hope is frail, it's hard to kill." She slowly walked down the stairs, trying to be strong and positive. Just then, she heard an angry outburst from her parents' room as her father came out holding her mom's favorite turquoise vase. He threw it across the living room, the vase crashing through the bay window.

Gabby froze in her tracks, her entire body tense.

"Lance!" her mom screamed, grabbing for his arm. Shoving her in fury, he stormed out of the house and zoomed wildly away in his truck.

Gabby's mom started wailing on the floor, her permed hair a mess.

"M-mom...What happened?" Gabby asked, shaking.

She moved a little closer to where her mom was hunched over in the living room and, kneeling down, held her shoulders. Her heart seemed like it would race out of her chest like her father's truck just did out of the driveway.

"I told your father he needs to stop drinking, and he suddenly be-came--vio-lent," she said, her voice shaking, between sobs. She broke out into a wail.

Gabby's heart twisted inside her as she looked out the window into the black night.

With her protective instinct, Gabby put her arm around her mom.

She did not know that someone else was watching this scene through the shattered window, peering into the cracks in her life.

The power went out in Trevor's house. The light of his cell phone blinded his eyes as he peered into its luminescence. His eyes squinted as they tried to adjust between the darkness and the brilliant, blinding light.

"Trev, the lights are out!" his dad shouted from the other room as if Trevor did not notice.

Trevor did not reply. He was too busy trying to adjust, adapt to his present condition. He wondered how he would do as one of those cave dwelling creatures with very small pupils. They lived in the dark and rarely knew the light. They grew adaptations to survive, to live in their profound darkness. Did they know what light was?

He closed his phone. The dark corners of his room ran to fill space that the light no longer assumed. He could hear his dad fumbling through the dressers, opening and closing, rummaging through them like a raccoon through last week's refuse.

"Trevor," his dad shouted from the other room. "Go get some batteries for the flashlight. It's not working."

Graciously, his father gave Trevor an excuse to leave his room. He shouted back some assortment of words that signaled an acceptable reply.

He grabbed his house keys and wallet and headed out into the night. It greeted him with a cool, autumn hello. Holding his keys and wallet in his hands, he reached down to find his shorts' pockets, but he could not find them. He sighed, bowing to his laziness, and opened the mouth of his sock. He stuffed his keys and wallet down the sock's throat and closed it. His new appearance made him look like he had an ankle monitor on, but Trevor did not care.

He rode on his bike often. The cool breeze as he passed through the suburbs reminded him of a television show. He imagined himself as one of those sitcom children, rushing home to be greeted by a lovely mother and father. The perfect child would always throw their bike on the grass, just for anyone to steal, and run inside the house to announce his plot-starting entrance. To Trevor, the bike rides were freeing. They allowed his life a rhythm, a constant. He saw sights he had never seen before even in places that he had passed multiple times. In motion, the convenience store, the school, the houses no longer stood still in time. They changed. They moved as he moved. Would they move when they were no longer in sight? Possibly, but Trevor was not there to see their motions.

The convenience store was about five miles from Trevor's house. It had been run by the same family for quite some time, even before Trevor's father even lived in the town. The father ran the convenience store for most of the day and the son took over at night. The father, grey-haired with glasses that sat on the bridge of his nose, knew everyone in the town—and all their vices. The son, black-haired with blue contact lenses, knew nothing about anything and was content to practice all vices. Trevor biked in the darkness of the neighborhood, occasionally passing streetlights overhead. He wondered about the cave dwelling salamander again.

A cave salamander lives in the recesses of caves and dwells in the watery limestone depths. The salamander is pale, his skin void of any pigmentation. It knows no light, yet it maneuvers through the cave's pool as deftly as an Olympic swimmer. Clown-like pink protrusions characterize the pale creature, serving as its signifying characteristic: its ability to adeptly hear the vibrations and sounds of the water for the most minute disturbance. A silly look for such a necessary adaptation in a pitch-black world.

Trevor finally reached the convenience store. Sweat ran down his forehead as he entered. The son greeted him with a glazed look like that of one of the old donuts on the counter. Trevor browsed the candy aisle and the chip aisle, perhaps looking for a treat that may satisfy him. Nothing interested him and he soon relinquished his search and grabbed the batteries his father sought.

He placed the batteries on the counter and looked up at the convenience store owner's son. The son's eyes were red, bloodshot from the long hours or something else. Trevor reached down and grabbed money from his sock. The clerk paid him no mind. Trevor smiled and passed the batteries and money to him. Without a word, the goods and currency were exchanged, and the transaction was completed. Trevor opened the door and the night greeted him with a cool, autumn hello.

"Weird," he chuckled to himself. He hopped on his bike and pedaled home. His mind soon thought of the amphibian once more.

The cave salamander. What does it know? Can it differentiate friend from food, or food from friend? Can it sense the water drops of the limestone stalactites and recognize the drumbeats as the music of its very world? Can it recognize the brilliance of precious gems, unearthed by the ever-present moisture, as worthy, as beautiful, as wondrous? Trevor biked through the suburbs, swimming through the dark.

Just ahead of him, a concussive crash cracked the night of steady sound. Like a falling stony column meeting the cave's floor, the sound echoed throughout the suburbs. A large, ornamental vase lay on the green lawn of an off-white house. The bay window was shattered as shards of glass littered the small, fading flowers underneath it. Angry shouts poured out from the window and could be heard from the street.

Trevor stopped his bike parallel from the house on the opposite sidewalk. The door suddenly and violently opened, slamming closed just as quickly, as a figure hurried out of the house and into the large truck. The truck, startled from its slumber, coughed fumes and backed out of the driveway and into the night. Even from afar, Trevor could see the remains of the pieces of the home. The light of the living room sat upon the lawn, upon the neighboring trees, and onto the grey sidewalk. Trevor's eyes followed the light, from the sidewalk, to the trees, to the lawn, and finally into the room. The light revealed a lone, familiar figure standing in the midst of broken glass and living room decorations strewn about. He recognized her as the girl who knew everything in class, the girl who smiled to those without glee, the girl that had joy. Her face was wet from tears and made her eyes sparkle like gems in the light. Gabby stood tall in the living room, peering into the space between her hunched over mother and the place where her father once stood. The space was infinite.

Trevor, stuck in time, gazed at Gabby through the broken bay window as the light shone and illuminated the street.

Something pierced Trevor's heart, as if a shard of glass was lodged into it. For some reason, he couldn't get himself to leave. He stayed where he was, watching Gabby's family. Knowing Gabby Choi, she probably wouldn't have told anyone about her dad. She was private. Trevor felt a sudden storm of frustration rising in his chest. There was nothing he could do.

Back at his room, he flicked on a flashlight and, exasperated, spun it around his ceiling, illuminating random things. The circle of light landed on the constellation of glow-in-the-dark stars he had placed above his bed in middle school.

Middle school. The worst years of his life. He felt he was suffering alone, then.

Like–Gabby was now.

His memory took him back to when his twelve-year-old self carefully placed the collection of green glow-in-the-dark stars on the ceiling because he was afraid of the dark. His fear of the dark had become heightened after his mom passed away. Looking at the stars' friendly glow gave his younger self a sense of comfort and made him feel less alone, less hollow.

Trevor flicked off the flashlight and for a moment lay still on his bed in the cool darkness.

He couldn't believe it. He could've never imagined Gabby Choi to have the kind of family problems that she did. Ever since elementary school, she looked like someone who had the best life and everything going for her. He pictured Gabby on the blacktop of their school, grinning from ear to ear with that smile of hers that was as radiant as the afternoon sun. Now and then, they would play tetherball together at recess, and she would always beat him. But she'd always smile humbly and compliment him anyway.

Trevor held the flashlight against his chest and tried to think of what could've helped him in his middle school years when he was grieving the loss of his mom. He jumped out of bed, sat at his desk, and began scribbling intently on a sheet of paper, scratching his head now and then. Something so strong stirred in Trevor that night, an ardent urgency he had never felt before.

~

Gabby lay awake, unable to close her eyes.

G

Gabby lay awake, her heart beating wildly out of control, yet unable to breathe or make a sound. She frantically looked this way and that around her room, as if something was about to lunge at her. Yet there was nothing. Just the image of her dad pushing her mom hard and throwing her mom's favorite vase and her mom's hair in a mess and tears, tears, tears.

She wanted to cry, but she was afraid her dad might come. She knew he wouldn't come back tonight but still she was so afraid. The trembling convulsed her entire body and it would not stop.

She lay rigid like a statue under her covers, yet trembling, all her senses heightened, for what seemed like hours. She wanted to stay vigilant just in case. She wished she had a lock on her door. Somehow, all the fatigue carried her to sleep and she awoke the next morning, not remembering what had happened the night before.

"Gabby," a gentle voice said. It was her mom, seated at her bed, asking her to wake up. Gabby opened her eyes and rubbed them; they were puffy from tears. Something must've happened the night before. She couldn't remember.

Her mom embraced her, her strong floral perfume filling Gabby's nose. This was strange. Her mom rarely ever showed physical affection. Her mom started crying on Gabby's shoulder, her back moving up and down. Startled, Gabby asked, "What's wrong?"

Her mom suddenly grew stiff in Gabby's arms and she looked up slowly.

"What do you mean? You don't remember?" Her mom stared deeply into Gabby's eyes, concerned.

Gabby searched her memory, but it felt black. She remembered yesterday was the day of her voice recital...But she didn't remember going.

"Umm…," Gabby replied.

Gabby's mom had this quizzical, sad, torn look on her face.

Her mom hugged her once more, with a deep sigh of relief that seemed to come from somewhere else other than her own small body.

"It's better this way," she said, with more calmness.

Wiping away her tears, Gabby's mother fixed her brown wavy hair that was always perfectly permed.

"Her hair…," thought Gabby.

Suddenly, the memories came flooding back. Her mom's hair a mess. On the floor crumpled up. Moaning and wailing…

"That was all real?" Gabby thought.

"Mom!" she said. "Mom!" Tears sprung from her eyes then. "Are you okay? Are you hurt?"

Then, she remembered her dad storming away and driving in his unstable state.

"Where's Dad? Is he okay?" she asked, her tears streaming now like a steady waterfall down her cheeks. The events of last night made a chasm as wide as a canyon in Gabby's heart. She couldn't believe it had happened to her family.

"Your dad texted an hour ago. He'll be back by dinner today." Her mom spoke with kindness in her dark brown eyes.

It was all strange. Her mom never was this gentle and calm and warm before. Gabby supposed her mom felt she needed to be the best parent she could be to Gabby since Dad was like that.

Gabby grabbed her mom's arms and looked at them one by one, scanning them like a doctor for cuts or bruises, any sign of injury. She didn't see anything. But her hair yesterday…it was…it was too hard to think about.

"Mom, what happened?" Gabby moaned. "Why was Dad…so mad?"

Gabby gazed into her mother's eyes, and she could see an immense tiredness overtake her.

"I told him to stop drinking. And he asked if I understood how he felt. How it felt to cope with what he copes with."

41

"But still, Mom…" Gabby cried. "Not this…"

Just then the front door swung open downstairs and loud footsteps entered the hallway.

Gabby's body tensed up and she stopped talking. She grabbed her mom by the shoulders and pushed her toward her closet doors, telling her with her eyes to hide.

Gabby sat on her bed, not knowing where to go.

She quickly undressed and jumped in the shower, knowing her dad wouldn't enter the bathroom with her in there. She shivered under the sudden deluge of cold water. She'd be safe, yet her heart beat wildly like she was an animal of prey.

Meanwhile, her mom cupped her mouth in the closet, holding back the sobs that she had suppressed.

~

The next day, Gabby's legs seemed to carry her to school, but she was somewhere else. In a daze, she didn't even notice kids were running past her to school, hitting her shoulders because the bell had already rung. She held her arms, not knowing what to think, what to do…

Period after period passed by; her teachers' voices sounded like background noise or muffled sounds, as if she were underwater. Finally, it was three o'clock and Gabby picked up her books and dragged herself to her locker. She felt as if her mind were in a state of paralysis. She didn't know what to do. She silently stood before her locker, staring at the rusty beige back wall of her locker, as if there was something shiny there hypnotizing her.

Trevor, whose locker bay was across from Gabby's, stopped what he was doing and watched her. His heart sank. He grabbed his books and slammed his locker door shut extra hard.

"**A**t each turn, you have to make a decision. There are many characters in this game and depending on what you choose, you'll get a different ending." Toad's engrossed left thumb moved the controller's joystick as he smashed the circular buttons with his right thumb.

"That's why I like this game. There are so many decisions you can make, you know? Like everything has a choice and a consequence. Like life."

Trevor laughed. For Toad, that was probably the most profound sentence he had ever said. "That's deep."

The two were seated on a small loveseat sofa in Toad's living room. The room's decor was very 70s chic…according to Trevor's limited knowledge of the 70s: littered with pastel browns, oranges, greens, and yellows. A brown throw-blanket here, an orange woven rug there, a green sofa pillow over there. It felt very cozy and yet so sentimental.

Toad's eyes were glued to the television screen. Trevor has known Toad all his life and for most of it, Toad and Trevor had spent their time inside playing Toad's various video games. Fighting games, role-playing games, strategy games, shooting games, any game really. When they were younger, they would play from night to morning, their eyes bloodshot from the constant visual fiesta of vibrant colors and motion. Tonight was no different.

"I like this guy the most." Trevor's longtime friend pointed at the screen in the direction of an anthropomorphic frog with a gold breastplate, blue gloves, and a long green cloak. "Dude's awesome. He is so strong for this part of the game. One slash and dead." Trevor wondered if the similarities between the frog character and Toad were lost upon his good friend.

Trevor reached into a bag of beef jerky on the coffee table and watched the characters as they slashed and hacked each horde of monsters to pieces.

"Mayhap a hidden door lurks nigh? Let us search the environs," Frog croaked.

Toad's thumb vigorously mashed the X button to skip the dialogue. "Cid should be here soon. He had detention today."

Cid was a wiry eighteen-year-old. His hair was a deep dark brown and he had a penchant for talking back to people he did not respect. He must have done that today.

"Detention? On a Friday? Who gives detention on a Friday?" Without even a glance at each other, Trevor and Toad both knew.

"Mrs. Batista." They laughed, knowing that Cid probably stared at his phone the whole class and once confronted, probably dismissed her with a curt, insulting line of wit. Trevor looked forward to Cid's arrival.

Friday afternoons were usually the moments of escape for Trevor. He would usually go to Toad's house and lie around eating various snacks while the hours flew by. Toad's parents did not come home until later in the evening so Toad, Trevor, and occasionally, Cid, would make the living room their own. Shoes, socks, and candy wrappers would be thrown here and there as they lounged, usually watching Toad play his game of the week.

This was all so familiar to him, yet today, something felt amiss. Something scratched upon the door of his conscience, leaving small prints upon the wooden door, insisting to be let in. A small cat in the cold. A child left outside for far too long. Gabrielle Choi in her dark grey hoodie.

Early in English class, Trevor saw Gabby slumped over on her desk, staring into the nothingness of the whiteboard. Mr. Durbin droned on about the political climate of the 1950's and how it influenced Ginsberg. He prompted the class with an innocuous question, yet the usually ever-ready Gabby did not raise her hand. Mr. Durbin proceeded to throw many other softball questions out and Gabby lay still upon her desk, frozen in a moment far away. He had never seen her like that. He had rarely seen anyone like that except his father when his mother received her diagnosis.

The broken glass. The turquoise vase strewn on the lawn. The gaping, shattered hole in the bay window.

Frog: "I must ponder this turn of events. You may remain for the night." The noble frog croaked his dialogue as eloquently as an anthropomorphic frog could. Toad, with his right hand, grabbed a strip of beef jerky from the table and chewed it vigorously, masticating the dried meat into a fine putty in his mouth.

Today, Gabby had sat that way for each class he had seen her in. Mr. Hawkins, the math teacher, tried to talk to her after class, but was met with a shrug and a nod. He probably gave her that "Gabby, what's wrong? You have to pay attention in class" lecture that Trevor knew all too well. The vase still lay on the grass, visibly cracked.

"Why don't these dudes go away! God, these random fights are so annoying after the first 1000 times." Toad began furiously mashing the buttons to complete the battles, finding himself devoid of joy in his once pleasing game.

Trevor often saw Gabby in snapshots of his life. She was always there. In his elementary school. At birthday parties of a mutual friend. At the Ralph's on Main. Although he thought of her as somewhat unremarkable at first–deep dark brown hair, thin frame, delicate hands, angelic voice, intensely sharp wit, chocolate brown eyes–Trevor began paying closer attention to her later in his life. Despite all these seemingly unremarkable qualities that he remembered in vivid detail, Trevor always liked her smile.

The glass from the bay window lay shattered and scattered upon the green lawn. The roar of the pickup echoed from the end of the street as the sobs of a woman pulsated through his mind, pounding his temple over and over again. Neighboring lights turned on. Pursuant eyes peeked out of windows. Murmurs littered the quiet street. Dissidence in suburbia. The white house quickly turned black, the vase shards upon the green lawn darkened into indistinguishable, silent stones. To Trevor, the sobs never stopped.

Trevor had ridden his bike past the house the next morning. The window was still a fresh wound, but the dewy grass was free of any glass.

"Run, Glenn. I will hold them off." Stuck in a memory, Frog froze in time as he remembered his dear friend's parting words.

"This part is sad." Toad took a momentary reprieve to soak in the story.

"Cyrus!" Frog screamed upon the clifftops as his friend lay, defeated by Magus, an otherworldly terror. The hero's sword was broken, shattered in irreparable pieces of useless metal. Frog kneeled helpless before the sheer immensity of power.

"Slimy creature. I will give you a more fitting form!" the mage cackled. Frog woke from his memory, his webbed hands shaking from the all-too-real fright. The hero's sword lay before him, a masterwork of mythical metal and magic.

Back in the classroom, Gabby, hooded in her all-too-familiar grey sweatshirt, sat motionless. The bell rang and she was gone. Trevor quickly gathered his things and ran behind her. She walked straight, bumping into shoulders and bearing irritated looks. After her sixth shoulder bump, she dropped a clutched textbook and it butterflied upon the floor. Trevor quickly moved to grab it for her and as he looked up, it was snatched from his fingers without a word. "Did he see her face?" he wondered. Gabby turned and disappeared into the torrential sea of backpacks and body odor.

The back door of Toad's house opened and closed quickly. Cid threw his backpack on the floor and immediately buried his hand into a bag of tortilla chips. Trevor and Toad greeted him in grunts, and he returned the favor. After gorging himself on chips, Cid crackled a sentence of almost incomprehension.

"What game is this?" In reply, Toad, in the quickest motion of the whole night, turned to him with delight.

"This game is…" Toad's voice seemingly trailed off as Trevor began to munch on more beef jerky as his mind drifted back.

He shook his head. He wanted to stay in this moment, watching Toad play games. His mind went back to the hallway. The book lay butterflied upon the floor. He grabbed it within seconds and as he looked up to give it to her, he remembered her face. He finally remembered her face. Pale. Tears veiling her brown eyes. Lips quivering. She quickly took the textbook from his hand and melded into the crowd. Her face did not leave him. He did not sleep for the rest of the night.

"Now, watch this," Toad said excitedly.

"Handeth over the Masamune," the knight croaked.

Frog clutched the hilt of the fabled blade, his webbed hands steady as he lifted the blade for the first time.

"Mine name is Glenn. Cyrus' hopes and dreams and now the Masamune, these will become my burden! Forthwith I will slay Magus and restore honor!"

Responding to the knight's conviction, the blade reverberated with mythical power, tearing the sky asunder with a bright blue beam.

With a sudden urge, Trevor stood up from the loveseat, his impression firmly within its cushions. Toad and Cid turned to him, startled by his abrupt actions. Trevor quickly grabbed his backpack and what sock he could find.

"I've got to do something." Without another word, Trevor quickly headed out of Toad's all-too-familiar living room as his friends, somewhat bewildered, shrugged and continued their tradition. He was greeted by the cool air of the evening. He quickly rode his bike down Toad's street and met the off-white house once more. The driveway was empty and the house dim. Trevor jumped off his bike and walked by the house, examining it in detail. Upon his inspection, a bright turquoise shard on the sidewalk called to him. He carefully grasped it within his palm.

In that moment, a singular, shimmering thought lay upon the floor of his mind.

"I have to help Gabby."

It was the following Monday. Second period, AP Biology. Gabby could not remember how she arrived there, seated on one of the many wooden stools around the room, in front of a hardtop lab table. Mr. Nguyen droned on about cellular respiration as Gabby's mind phased in and out of class. One moment, she looked around the room and saw familiar faces and in the next, her eyes glazed over as she stared dead-center at the surface of the black table into the empty spaces between the atomic particles that she could not fully see. As soon as the bell rang, Gabby snapped out of her haze, quickly grabbed her books, and rushed out the door, her chest tightening. She didn't want to be seen. She was afraid that somehow, someone would find out about what was happening at home.

Finally reaching her locker, Gabby let out a big sigh after holding her breath for so long. She finally had a chance to look down at what she was wearing: grey sweatpants, black hooded sweater, and some bright blue flip-flops that slapped on the

51

concrete wherever she went. She couldn't remember what she was thinking when she had put on her clothes that morning. As her focus traveled from her own appearance to the locker, her eyes grew wide in stunning surprise. Three long-stem daisies were stuck in the crack of her locker, their white petals shining bright as the sun. Gabby stood there, confused and mesmerized at the same time. She turned her head surreptitiously to see if someone had left the mysterious gift. Everyone around her was bustling, rushing to their lockers so they could go to their next class.

Gabby smiled the slightest smile and gently pulled the flowers from the gap between her locker and the next one. Flowers in one hand, she used her other hand to carefully run her fingers across the petals, contouring each petal to make sure they were as real as they seemed.

"What is this? Who would do this?" she wondered. Her mind quickly recited a list of possible names: Rochelle, Alicia, or Janet. Then her mind wandered to other high school possibilities: boys. "Does someone have a crush on me?" she thought playfully. However, that thought was quickly dashed when she remembered her glum expression and poorly matching, unflattering outfit that morning.

"Nah," she said out loud. She quickly opened her locker, took out the next period's books, and slammed the locker door shut.

Gabby walked to Mr. Durbin's English class, with the daisies gently tucked in her arms along with her literature anthology. The desks in Mr. Durbin's class were arranged in pods of four to promote group discussion and Gabby sat in the pod nearest to Mr. Durbin's desk. The veteran English teacher dressed in a light blue button-up shirt and khaki pants lifted his eyes from his laptop and spotted the flowers on his top student's desk.

"Nice flowers, Gabby. Who are they from? A secret admirer?" Mr. Durbin teased, walking past her on the way to the podium upfront. The girl in the grey sweatpants and black hoodie could not help but blush as the now-attentive and curious eyes of her peers looked at the flowers, looked at Gabby, then looked at each other in amusement, chuckling to themselves about the possibilities of who would like Gabby Choi. In those brief seconds, Gabby felt more alone than she ever felt before, but at the same time, more alive in knowing someone cared enough to give her something beautiful in what she thought was such an ugly life.

Mr. Durbin quickly called attention to the class and the curious eyes looked to the front. Gabby took that moment to brush her long, soft brown hair through her fingers. She did not know who may have given her the flowers; they could be in this very class. Curiously, she scanned the room, analyzing who might have left her the daisies and if they showed any signs of doing so. She amused herself with the thought that if she had left something so lovely for another person in her class, she would not have been able to hide her interest in seeing whether they liked the gift or not.

Though it was only the first month of English class, she had known many of these people for most of her teenage life. In the pod of tables farthest from her, situated in the corner of the room next to the large display of student-made posters about Oscar Wilde's short stories, there were four boys with their heads down. However, the boys were not sleeping, but rather looking down at their phones, scrolling through social media, trying their best to be as inconspicuous as possible. Mr. Durbin, still in the middle of his introductory lecture, strolled to their pod and lingered there as each of the boys quickly straightened up, at attention. None of those boys paid any extra attention to Gabby nor to her flowers.

The young woman's eyes continued scanning across the room, but she could not find the clues she was hoping for. Studying the gentle white petals and yellow centers of her flowers, she was content with the fact that she had received them.

After the bell rang, Gabby gently stuck her flowers beneath her arm and once again rushed out of the classroom, breathlessly hoping nobody was staring at her and her flowers in the hallway. As the cool Toccoa wind rippled through the hallway and against her hair, she found herself smiling shyly to herself. For some moments, she had even forgotten about the ache in her heart.

~

Walking home that day, Gabby had a lightness in her step. She started humming quietly.

"Hmm...What should I do with these daisies..." she wondered.

Before her father had changed, her hobby had been to arrange flowers every weekend at her neighbor Bella's flower shop with Bella's leftover plants and decorate the house with them. Her mom would always light up and snap photos of them and show all her friends.

With a spontaneity that overcame her, Gabby decided to swing by Bella's shop and ask for some leftover baby's breath. She thankfully took the flowers that had been carefully wrapped in crisp brown paper and ran home to arrange them in a vase.

Quietly in her neat but dim room, Gabby placed the baby's breath and three daisies next to a slender, green sea glass vase she found lying around at home. Washing the dusty vase vigorously with warm water and soap in the bathroom sink, she smiled, realizing she was actually doing something active. Ever since the "incident", she had felt like a zombie, not doing anything she used to feel passionate about. She sat at her desk and snipped and trimmed away. When she was done, Gabby looked at the bright yellows and soft whites among the cloud of baby's breath and smiled a gleaming smile.

She actually felt happy.

More than that, someone was caring about her.

And as the flowers lit up her dim, simple room, a small light shone in her heart and gave her comfort.

Filing into fourth period art class the next day, Trevor sniffed the air, the familiar scent of his art teacher's jasmine incense filling his nostrils. He then noticed that Mrs. Parlait had placed colorful tri-folded name tags on all the desks. She must've wanted to change up the seating chart for a special activity. He scanned the classroom and found his seat…and Gabby's side-by-side! His heart began to race. "I hope she doesn't notice anything…" he thought. He quickly scanned the room to see if Gabby had come yet. He let out a deep sigh, relieved she wasn't there yet.

Sweeping his hand through his thick, curly brown hair, Trevor nervously looked around as he sat in his seat. He sat tall, trying to be confident. Gabby soon approached him and he felt a swoosh of air as she sat down beside him. The smell of her shampoo lingered in his nostrils. He turned to say hi but Gabby had already opened her mouth to greet Trevor.

"Hey, Trevor," she said in a friendly tone. "It's been a while!"

Gabby was always so nice.

"Hey!" Trevor said, trying not to sound nervous or awkward. "It's so good to see you in art class!" He thought to himself, "Shoot, that sounded weird." For a moment he studied her face, noticing she looked a little happier than yesterday. "I wonder if it's because of the flowers I gave her," he pondered.

Luckily, Mrs. Parlait liked to get to work right away and announced the first project of the semester: Abstract Art. "Class, I'd like you to use either pastels or paint to make an abstract work that illustrates your current state of mind." With a dramatic flourish of her hand, she uncovered a sample abstract piece of her own that had been covered by a beige cloth on her easel at the front of the class. The students eagerly craned their necks to get a look at the mystery art piece they had been yearning to behold. The canvas had a strange assortment of purple circles, triangles, and lines, as well as black and white faces that resembled Picasso's. They weren't full faces, they were half faces with white chalky skin and big, round, black eyes, making them look like mimes. She let the class gaze at her work in puzzlement and she sat down at her desk, humming a strange little tune.

Several students turned to their friends to whisper, "She's so weird," while others giggled. Mrs. Parlait fidgeted with her ancient record player and played her favorite music–Beethoven.

"Abstract art to show my state of mind...So deep," Trevor muttered under his breath, and quickly grabbed some light blues and orange from the pastel tray.

Gabby sat still in her chair and would not move. Then, she hesitantly reached for the black, dark blue, and purple pieces of pastel from their shared pastel set. She nonchalantly and silently made strokes across her page without hesitation.

Trevor peeked at her paper now and then, and noticed how different his art was from hers. He had drawn shapes resembling a seascape with a bright orange sun, while Gabby's paper was filled with geometric shapes filled in with obscure colors. He couldn't make out what it was. It was just a mass of darkness. His heart sank. He searched his mind for what he could say.

"Gabby, what does your abstract art represent?" Trevor asked gently.

"Mm…it's just…nothing. I don't know," she answered quietly.

Perceiving that was a picture of her heart, he then said, "It looks beautiful."

She smiled slightly and just kept looking at the swirl of black, purple, and blue.

He continued, "It's like…a storm at sea…but the dawn is coming and all will be still again."

Gabby beamed and her face lit up like the dawn. Trevor smiled. "Yes!" he thought to himself.

Gabby grabbed a single yellow pastel stick and put one streak at the top right of her page, in an arc, then sighed a little, contentedly. Trevor was amazed at the change in her face. She looked a little more at peace.

Just then, Mrs. Parlait swung by their desk and looked at both of their works. "Hmm.." she said with approval. "Both very beautiful portrayals of the sea," she noted.

~

Sitting before the sea after school that day, Gabby wondered where it had all gone.

Her loving family.

Her parents' happy marriage.

Her motivation in school.

Even her looks.

She didn't care about anything anymore.

She didn't even feel like talking to her friends.

She reached for the sand hoping to feel the feeling of comfort it had always given her but half expecting to be left with that same hollow emptiness. She was right. The soft, moist sand no longer lent any comfort.

She squished her toes further into the mud.

Gabby just felt cold, and alone.

Trevor watched from afar, having come to the beach to walk his dog. He couldn't believe it was Gabby sitting there on the shore. He rubbed his eyes with his cold, pale hands. His heart beat fast again, something that was happening more often these days ever since he decided to help Gabby Choi.

She looked so lonely. He wanted to go up to her and start a conversation but that would be weird.

"Funny," he thought. "I used to come here all the time when I thought about Mom."

He put on the hood of his yellow parka and kept looking out at the sea, as if he were a watchman for Gabby. Gabby's small figure was a single black dot on the landscape of sea and sand. Her sweater didn't look too thick. The wind was gusty and frigid.

"What the heck," Trevor finally thought, and releasing his dog from the car, he decided to approach Gabby. He also brought with him an extra jacket.

Gabby shed a tear and turned to go home. Just then, a huge German Shepherd bounded up to her, licking her face. She liked dogs and suddenly laughed as it licked her tears off her face.

"Jesse!" Trevor yelled, grabbing his leash.

Gabby noticed Trevor, and suddenly looked down, wiping her face and matting down her wind-whipped, salty hair.

Sensing she was embarrassed, Trevor exclaimed, "Oh, hey Gabby! What are you doing here?"

Gabby looked up and smiled through wet eyes, but didn't say anything. She just realized she had been alone all afternoon and missed being around people.

Trevor just stood there and smiled. She peered at his face. His pale skin was rosy in the cold air and his light brown hair had been blown by the wind but still handsomely sat on his head. His smile was white, big, and genuine.

To break her nervous silence, Trevor boomed, "Do you like dogs? This is Jesse!" and together they petted the friendly dog.

Trevor admired Gabby's smile, which he almost never saw anymore at school. It was a shy smile, pure, and full of secrets.

Remembering he had brought an extra jacket, he nervously handed it to Gabby.

"Wear this. Your sweater is so thin," he said quickly.

Her eyes grew big. She stood silently, not knowing what to do, because she had never worn a guy's jacket.

But remembering her manners, she took the big black jacket and slowly put it on. She instantly felt warmth spread over her back, arms, and stomach. She felt good. She looked at the immensely long sleeves, one by one, and laughed. She didn't expect to feel comfort today.

"Thank you," she said, smiling again through new tears. It was an intermingling of gratefulness, sadness, and happiness.

"No prob!" Trevor exclaimed, always so heartily. Then he suggested, "Why don't we go to the Starbucks nearby and get something hot to drink?" "I have a gift card," he added.

"Sure," she said quickly and a bit more confidently, to her surprise. She wanted to spend time with someone, especially someone nice and comforting like Trevor.

At Starbucks, they sat opposite a round table, the color of mahogany. Gabby looked down at her steaming cocoa. She had started to feel self-conscious amidst crowds. Her extra long sleeves didn't help.

Trevor couldn't believe how much Gabby Choi had changed in such a short period of time. He thought he was the shy guy that she always said hi to first in her bubbly, joyful voice.

"Gabby, remember the time in middle school when we were both in Student Council and we sold hot cocoa as a fundraiser?" He wanted to conjure up better times.

She smiled brightly. "Yeah, that was a lot of fun! They disappeared in like five minutes!" She thought back to how she had been student body president…And now she was…ugh. She looked down at her cup in shame. She took a quick sip of the cocoa, the creamy sweetness hitting her taste buds unexpectedly. She quickly wiped the bubbly foam off her mouth.

"Gabby, is there something you want to talk about?" Trevor asked.

Gabby was startled at how forward he was.

She pursed her lips, her gaze still staring down, heart racing. She couldn't believe she was saying the words as they came out but they did: "It's my family…"

Gabby suddenly recalled how Trevor had been absent in middle school for a month because his mom had passed away. Maybe, just maybe, he might understand…

"My dad came back from Afghanistan…and you know…the war…it changed him."

Trevor nearly choked on his cocoa. Gabby actually told him!

He looked across at the frame on the wall, trying to look composed. Then he looked into her brown expectant eyes. They looked like a frightened doe's. "I see. I'm sorry to hear that, Gabby. I was wondering why you looked so down these days," he said quietly.

Gabby's heart felt like it had been punched, but in a good way. No one had asked her why she didn't smile like she used to, or why she had gotten a lot quieter.

Trevor and Gabby sat in silence.

Everything was the same, but everything had changed.

Her heart felt a faint glimmer of hope. It flickered like the single flame on a lighter. The cocoa had warmed her body, and now her heart was warmed. It felt something it hadn't in a long time. Comfort…and like she wasn't alone anymore. Alone in the pain. Alone in the knowledge that her dad was no longer himself.

Gabby looked down at her cup again, which was still mostly full. Trevor, not wanting her to feel uncomfortable after telling him her secret, asked, "Want to head out?"

Gabby looked up at him and smiled. She wanted to say thank you but she could only smile. They held each other's gaze for a moment.

"Yeah," she finally said.

Gabby slowly got up out of her seat and followed Trevor, but Trevor quickly grabbed the jacket off her chair that she had forgotten and gave it to her again for her to wear.

"Thank you," she said, feeling that lighter flick on in her heart again.

On a notably cloudy and grey October day, Trevor headed out of his house. His black Toyota Corolla churned with one, two, three turns of his keys before the engine finally ignited. Out of the familiar neighborhood and into the Toccoa streets, the car glided like a phantom, switching from lane to lane, side to side. Green, red, green, red, green. At each stop down the Pacific Coast Highway, the familiar sights and sounds of his beloved hometown–the old haunts, the distant memories, the times gone–danced upon the car windows like shadows on a wall. The old car settled to a halt at a red light. On his left, the Chinese food restaurant, with tan stucco walls and a faded red neon sign saying Seafood Town, wafted its smell of pork shumai and Mongolian beef. On rare Sundays after church, Trevor's family would be allured by the enchanting scents, sit at one of those round tables with the spinning serving wheels, and eat their fill of all that was sweet, savory, salty, and delicious.

Nervously tapping the steering wheel of his worn-down car, Trevor approached the entrance gates of a large estate. With rolling green and golden yellow hills and flowers adorning the grass, a large sign overhead read "Green Hills Memorial Park." The guard at the gate, about his father's age with eyes that had long lost their luster, motioned for him to roll down the window and state his purpose.

Trevor cleared his throat and answered, "I'm here to see my mom." Without much of a word, the guard handed him a pass and ushered him to move forward, through the gates and into the lush green land.

The old Toyota Corolla lurched up the hills, ascending higher and higher up the estate. About half-way up, the car spouted a guttural noise, a desperate noise, a noise akin to a fat man trying to do his first and only sit-up. Fearing for his and his car's safety, the young man pulled his car over and parked. Before leaving his car, Trevor carefully unbuckled a bouquet of purple irises from his passenger's seat.

He longed to reach his mother's grave, but at the same time, his steps seemed to slow down for he did not want to face her grave, the silent reminder of her absence. Walking between rows and rows of tombstones put Trevor in a philosophical mood. For all of his life it seemed, he had lived without a distinct goal or purpose. A wave of shame overwhelmed his soul, and he wished he had lived differently. But how? He didn't know what he was good at, if he was good at anything at all. Finally, he reached his mom's grave and he smiled, relieved to be liberated from his anxious thoughts.

Her metal plaque shone with a steely grey glint and he was glad that someone had maintained it recently. He abruptly sat upon the fresh, green grass and read the plaque aloud as he always did: Miranda Song. Kind and Compassionate Mother, Daughter, and Wife who Loved Christ.

A trickle of warm tears suddenly left both of Trevor's eyes as he quickly placed the lovely irises over her grave, as if this act would somehow bring him and his mom peace. Frustrated that there was no way to get to his mother, he wished he could be transported to heaven for a moment to talk to her face to face for once. But since that was impossible, talking to her grave would have to do.

"Mom," Trevor spoke, choking back tears.

A breeze ruffled the delicate flowers, and Trevor feared that this sacred moment, longed-for connection with his mother, might be lost. He quickly gathered his thoughts and spoke again.

"I hope you're doing well." He imagined his mom in heaven, where there were no tears, no heartache, no brokenness, and he wished he could be there, too.

"Dad's doing good. He still doesn't read his mystery books like he used to, but he started doing carpentry, and he enjoys it a lot. He made a couple stools for me and him to eat at the kitchen counter."

Another breeze passed by Trevor's ear and he listened for his mom's reply in the wind, though he knew he would not actually hear anything.

"I'm–the same as usual. I go to Toad's house everyday after school…to play…games." He giggled and wiped his forehead, imagining his mom's disapproving but playful, kind look. She always understood him.

"Mom, I have to apply for college soon but I don't—I have no idea what to major in, what to do."

He paused. What would his mom have him do?

"Follow your heart," said her warm voice in his heart. She had said this to him many times as he was growing up. Trevor could picture her compassionate brown eyes that seemed to embrace all of who he was, faults and all, never accusing him, always loving him. He remembered how he would drop his backpack and run to his mom to hug her after school when he was young, after a hard day at school where he was bullied for being the fat kid. She would hold him until he felt relief and until he could feel love for himself again.

Trevor shifted his gaze to her grave again and he was slapped in the face with the cold reality that her face was just inside his memory and she, herself, was gone. A different kind of outpouring of tears came forth from him, his heart aching physically, tangibly. It was then that he realized just how much he had been missing her.

Wiping a couple big droplets of tears that had fallen over her plaque, Trevor tried to stop the trembling that took over his entire body. Without his mom, he felt so much self-hatred and self-rejection. Her love had beaten those things down so that he could let love in. But now, without her, he felt small and insignificant again.

For a moment, Trevor lay down next to his mom's grave, his face facing the blindingly blue sky. The bright sun pierced his vision and he covered his face with his palm. Closing his eyes, he wished with all his heart to disappear. At that moment, he saw a memory: the vision of Gabby Choi standing inside her living room that night. Her father's car rushing rapidly out of the driveway. The crash of the vase against the window rang in Trevor's ears. Gabby had basically lost her father, the father she had known. The aching in Trevor's chest dulled a little and the pulsating inside his head slowed down. He then remembered her tear-streaked face in the hallway when he picked up her book for her.

Without getting up from where he lay, Trevor spoke again to his mom.

"Mom, there's a girl at my school named Gabby. She's really lost...like me. I want to help her. Help me to help her."

His nose filled up with snot from all the crying but he didn't care what he looked like, since he was alone for miles all around.

"God, help me to help her," he thought, as he drifted off to an exhausted slumber.

Journal #4

Dear God,

There's a boy at my school named Trevor Song. He's been really friendly and kind to me. I even told him about Dad a little bit. And I feel better, like a big weight has been taken off of my heart. Thank you for helping carry my burden, God. Please be with my dad. He seems so distressed and anxious and troubled and there's nothing I can do to help him. Please, please heal him and our family.

-Gabby

G&T

Two weeks later, Gabby was in her AP Environmental Science class, when Mrs. McAlister started handing back their exams from the previous Friday. Gabby eyed her teacher nervously as she swiftly made her way around the room, her long pink-gold skirt swishing between the desks. Gabby studied her teacher's bright red-framed glasses, pointy nose, and stern gaze and gulped. She had haphazardly read over the lecture slides but didn't have the energy or motivation to memorize them diligently like she used to. Finally, she smelled the familiar strong wine-like scent of Mrs. McAlister's perfume as she walked past Gabby's desk, dropping her exam in front of her. Gabby's heart fell as her worst fear came true. Circled at the top of her exam was a letter that she had never seen in all her high school career—a bright orange D.

Her mind began to race. "If I got a D on the test, and I turned in my project late, what do I have in the class?"

Suddenly her weeks of apathy snowballed and crashed into her face.

She realized she could have a C on her report card, forever ruining her high school career.

"What is Mom gonna say?" she suddenly panicked. Her face grew hot and she felt she had been given the death sentence.

Trevor, a couple rows away and diagonal from her, watched her from his seat. He could read the consternation on her face. His hand tightened into a fist upon his desk. "Gabby's the smartest girl in our grade. And because of her dad now she might not get into the college of her dreams. This is not fair! I have to do something," he thought, anger and misery welling in his chest.

As soon as the bell rang, Trevor mustered up his courage, and making sure that everyone had exited the room, ran up to Mrs. McAlister, who stood by the door ready to turn off the lights and go to lunch.

"Mrs. McAlister," he said breathlessly. "I know I haven't been the best student in your class, but I have a request."

"Trevor, what do you mean?" she asked, slightly alarmed, slightly annoyed because it was lunchtime. Her hand rested upon the light switch and she held her hip with her other hand.

"It's about Gabby Choi. I–I can't tell you in detail but she's going through something terrible, so she can't focus well in school and she hasn't been herself." He couldn't believe he somehow put the right words together. "Please give her another chance. Or a boost of extra credit–or something. She did well all her life in school. She deserves to go to a great college."

Mrs. McAlister listened intently with her lips pursed. She adjusted her bright red glasses on the bridge of her nose. Pausing to think for a moment, she studied Trevor's desperate, sincere look in his eyes. She was surprised that such a quiet student could have so much conviction.

After what seemed like forever, she responded. "Okay, I will have a talk with her and arrange something. Thank you, Trevor, for having the kindness to point that out."

He couldn't believe it. "Thank you! Thank you so much, Mrs. McAlister."

Smiling, he scooped up his books and quickly sped out the door. Then, he remembered that Gabby would still be feeling bad.

"It's lunchtime…That means…She's probably at her locker right now," he thought aloud, and proceeded to race down the empty hallway toward her locker bay.

"Gabby!" He caught her just as she shut her locker door weakly. She looked faint. Fear emanated from her gaze. Trevor couldn't know that she had been imagining her mom's reaction to her grades over and over again in her head a thousand times. She looked away.

"Hi," she said in the kindest voice she could muster.

"I did so bad on my Environmental test," Trevor said. "But guess what? I heard Mrs. McAlister is giving out tons of extra credit!" Spontaneously and out of sheer nervousness he tossed his papers up into the air as if in celebration.

"YEAH!" he yelled by himself in triumph.

Gabby just stood there not quite knowing how to react. Looking down she let it sink in. Then, a smile appeared across her mouth. A light appeared in her big, brown eyes.

"Really?" she asked brightly. "She's really giving extra credit?"

"Yeah!" he exclaimed, smiling broadly then. "Isn't it great?" He felt like a total loony being so enthusiastic in front of Gabby but he knew it was worth it.

"Wow...thanks for telling me Trevor," Gabby smiled weakly, blinking back tears. "Do you know how much extra credit?"

Trevor's heart swelled as Gabby kept asking him for more information, her hope rising by the second.

"As much as you need, Gabby," he said in the sincerest, most charming voice. Not expecting to see the level of ecstasy on Gabby's face, Trevor laughed and caught himself tearing up as well. Wanting to hug her but knowing that would be too much, he gave her the biggest high-five. She returned it gladly.

"Where are you going now?" Trevor asked.

"To lunch...in front of the band room. That's where my friends hang out," Gabby answered, her appetite returning to her.

Seeing the color come back into her cheeks, Trevor knew that his job was done, and parted ways.

"Awesome! See you tomorrow!" he waved as he walked quickly away.

"Seeya!" Gabby said, her voice bubbly again.

G&T

Three days later, Gabby arrived home from school, when she heard the sound of quiet guitar playing coming from her dad's study. Her heart leapt with joy and she quickly strode toward his room, amazed that her dad was doing something he once really enjoyed. She approached his door that was slightly open and looked curiously through the crack. When she was a little girl, her father would put his legs up on his desk and cradle his beloved guitar that he had inherited from his uncle, and sing with his warm, melodic voice. But as Gabby peered into the room, her heart fell.

A half empty bottle of alcohol sat at his desk and as her dad strummed, his gaze was staring at nothing. He was completely spaced out. Gabby sighed, the term, "dissociation", arising in her mind from her hours of reading about PTSD. Though her head knew that her dad was spaced out because his reality and his memories were too hard to bear, her heart couldn't help but feel disappointed about her absent father.

She trudged upstairs to her room, tossed her backpack nonchalantly on her bed, and grabbed her laptop as was her custom to look up the next movie she could watch. Sitting with her back against the headboard, she watched movie after movie until her room began to dim with the approaching evening.

"Dinnertime!" her mom called from downstairs.

"I have a project to do. I'll eat later!" Gabby lied. If it had anything to do with academics, her mom would be fine.

She continued to watch *You've Got Mail* for the second time.   As long as she could stay away from her parents, everything was okay.

But as the darkness continued to permeate her room, she felt a sinking feeling in her stomach. How long would she continue this? Could she avoid her parents forever? Would she really let her grades continue to drop?

Just then, a person's face rested upon the top of her mind: Trevor Song. For a moment, her mind lingered on his gesture at Starbucks, when he quickly grabbed the jacket off her chair and gave it to her to wear.

Gabby found herself looking up his Facebook so she could muster up the courage to Facebook message him.

For a moment, she just stared at his Facebook profile and couldn't budge. She felt this would only lead to disappointment.

But then her fingers typed.

"Hey!"

A few seconds passed. Gabby let out a big sigh and tossed her laptop onto her bed covers.

Just then she heard a cheery "ding!" as a message came in.

She quickly grabbed her laptop, beaming.

"Hey!" he had said.

"How are you?" he added.

"I'm…" she thought of how to answer. "I'm okay," she responded, surprised at her own frankness. Normally, she would tell her friends, "Good."

"I was wondering…did you tell any of your friends about what's going on at home?" Trevor asked.

Gabby paused. "Why is he asking this?" she thought. She looked up from her screen and went over their time at the beach in her mind. He was kind. He was genuine. He could be trusted.

"No, I didn't. Why?" she replied.

"Just wondering. Just wondering how I can help," he answered so frankly.

"Trevor Song…" she thought in her mind. "He's a breath of fresh air."

"Thanks," she answered, not knowing what else she could add to that.

Wanting to be alone she thought of just exiting Facebook but a part of her didn't let her leave the conversation. Something inside of her told her that Trevor was a good person and someone she could confide in, for once.

"How can I help?" he asked again.

"Is he serious?" she thought. "Why does he want to help me?"

"Umm…well someone put flowers on my locker. Wanna find out who that is for me?" she half-joked.

"What? You have a secret admirer!" Trevor responded, wanting to make her smile.

She smiled.

"I guess so," she played along. This was fun, a lot more fun than watching movies all by herself, 24/7.

"What are you up to?" Gabby asked spontaneously.

"I was about to walk my dog–you probably remember him–at Wilson Park."

"Oh…fun!" Gabby tried to sound enthusiastic.

"Wanna come?" he asked.

The cursor blinked for a few seconds.

Gabby finally decided she wanted to go, but first she had to think of an excuse she could make to her mom. She would never approve of her meeting a guy alone. She would tell her she needed exercise. That would make her happy.

"Okay!"

"See you there in 15 minutes," he answered.

"Seeya."

Wilson Park was bustling with people and light was streaming into the expansive soccer fields. Scanning the front of the park, she spotted Trevor in his bright yellow parka, bending down to tie his shoes. Gabby found herself quickly walking up to him.

"Hi!" she exclaimed, finding herself happy and excited for once.

"Hey!" he looked up from his shoe and gave her his huge lightning grin. Grabbing Jesse's leash, he said into the cold air, "Let's go!"

It was nice to be outside, and nice to be around someone other than her own family.

"I came to this park everyday since I was five," Trevor shared.

Gabby looked over at his face to check if he was serious. "You're kidding."

He smiled. "Nope," he said semi-proudly. "Jesse is my sibling, you know. Gotta treat him right."

"Family-oriented," Gabby made a mental note.

"Do you like exercising? Sports?" Trevor changed the subject.

Gabby scanned her mind for the last time she exercised. Wanting to look good, she answered, "I used to play basketball when I was young...I used to play with my...dad."

"Oh, nice!" he answered, sounding natural.

"Trevor is so...mature for his age," Gabby thought.

For a while, they both walked quickly in silence.

"What did you do today after school?" Trevor finally asked.

"I watched *You've Got Mail*," Gabby admitted. She normally never watched movies during the weekdays. She had only focused on her academics and extracurriculars.

Trevor chuckled. "Are you a fan of rom-coms?" he teased.

"No," Gabby quickly retorted, but then changed her mind. "Well, yes...Yeah I love romantic comedies. I guess I've watched a lot of them."

"Which romcom do you like the most?"

"*What a Girl Wants.*"

"With Amanda Bynes?"

"Yeah, she's awesome. So funny," Gabby said, smiling. This felt natural, so far.

"Why do you like that movie so much?"

"I like how she goes to London to find her dad who she's never met. And she also meets a really cute guy who is a musician. I love guys who can sing."

Gabby realized she had said too much.

"Hahaha!" Trevor laughed again. "Ooh...maybe the locker boy is cute and sings very well...You never know Gabby!" he teased.

"Stop it," she said, playfully.

It almost felt like they were good friends already.

Becoming defensive, Gabby added, "Well, I liked that movie before my dad ever became…you know. Thinking about it, I never thought I'd have a dad problem. He was like…" Then, not wanting to reveal too much, Gabby paused. "I don't know why I'm telling you so much. I just met you. Sorry."

Trevor laughed in his good-natured way that Gabby was getting used to. "Gabby, I knew you since elementary school."

"Still, we weren't, like, friends, you know."

Gabby wasn't sure what was so funny about what she was saying but Trevor kept laughing, this time, really loudly.

"What?" she finally asked, flabbergasted.

"Whenever I'd walk down the hallways, you'd wave and smile at me like I was your best friend or something."

"I did not!" Gabby answered, then starting to laugh as well. "Actually…I did…I did to everyone."

Looking over at Trevor, Gabby felt as if she were talking to a brother. It felt natural, and right.

She was thankful that Trevor reached out to her in her time of need, when no one else had bothered to ask her what was wrong.

They walked around the perimeter of Wilson Park three more times, and not wanting to reveal things about her family, Gabby asked Trevor questions about him being on the basketball team and about his dog. Time flew by and Gabby found herself smiling the whole time.

~

Walking back into her house, Gabby couldn't help but beam because of her time spent with Trevor. She stooped down to untie her shoelaces on her black and pink running shoes, when her mom stood before her with her arms crossed.

"Why were you gone for a whole hour?" she demanded.

Gabby's heart started racing.

"I was exercising," she replied. She hoped with all her might that her mom wouldn't find out she had been with Trevor.

"You exercised for a whole hour?"

"Yeah," Gabby said. "I gained a lot of weight so I needed it," she lied.

"Who did you meet, Gabby?" her mom demanded again.

"No one." Gabby hoped her eyes weren't betraying her and showing her fear.

Her mom's eyes flared up like two flames of fire.

Gabby shuddered.

"Give me your phone," she said.

"No!" Gabby automatically replied. She started to feel angry. "Just trust me!" she exclaimed at her mom.

"Do you have a secret boyfriend?" her mom shrieked.

Gabby ran up the stairs to her room and shut her door and locked it.

Her mom banged on the door and wrestled with the doorknob but Gabby went under her covers and tried to drown out the sound.

After what felt like forever, she could hear her mom's footsteps retreating angrily down the stairs.

Gabby's heart, which had been racing, steadily slowed down, and she lay awake for hours thinking about her life.

Her mind traveled back to her childhood, when she was too young to realize that the way her mom treated her was unfair, and that she was possibly using her to satisfy her own ambitions.

~

Growing up, Gabby liked to spend time in quietude, writing stories or playing with little animals that visited her backyard. She fed squirrels, followed lizards, and communicated with the pair of mourning doves that visited her house by making cooing sounds just like them: "Ooo, Oooooo." One day, she was walking along the stone path that ran across the center of her lush, green backyard when she spotted a small, round object inching slowly in front of her. She crept closer to study the unidentified creature. Her mouth dropped as she discovered it was a small turtle! For a moment, the young girl marveled at the intricate brown and yellow designs upon its round shell. At first, she looked around, not knowing what to do, but then she ran back into her house and sprinted into the kitchen where her mom was.

"Mom! Mom!" she yelled and shrieked with utter delight. "I found a turtle! Can we keep it?" Her little feet pitter-pattered upon the kitchen's linoleum floor tiles. Mrs. Choi, donned in an apron, busily stirred a pot while simultaneously checking on another. Always busy, she tended to be constantly preparing for something for some reason whether it was a community function, church congregational bake sale, or a parent-teacher conference; Mrs. Choi was a mover.

"Sure." Mrs. Choi, without averting her gaze from the assorted whistling pots on the stove, agreed to Gabby's request, much to the young girl's surprise. "Go into the garage and find an empty shoebox. Don't use any of my shoeboxes. There also should be some lettuce in the drawer in the fridge."

Immediately, Gabby scurried through the kitchen and into the dim garage. Mrs. Choi, though very busy with her various projects, never took the time to organize her garage. An unadmitted packrat, Gabby's mother kept everything that had any tangential and possible use to her in the future. Gabby, in search of a shoebox, had to go through a hula doll, pink sunglasses, and a series of old books before she found her first box: a shoebox from her brief stint as a ballerina. After her first lesson, Gabby realized it was not for her.

Quickly, Gabby ran back into her kitchen, dug through the various produce in her refrigerator, and tore off a sizable chunk of romaine lettuce before her mother could shout a word about how she took too much. The turtle had not moved from where she left it.

At first, Gabby tenderly fed the turtle a piece of bright green lettuce, trying to coax it into the box; however, after repeated failed attempts, Gabby ever-so-gently picked up the turtle by its shell and placed it in the box. The little girl crossed her legs on the dirt of her backyard and stared at the turtle, reveling in the slightest move of the little reptile. Observing her delighted daughter and done with her cooking, Gabby's mom thought this was the opportune moment to ask her daughter something she had been thinking about.

"Gabby, why don't you run for sixth grade class president? You know, when you were in first grade, Miss Funatsu said you never spoke in class. Isn't it time that you go out and try something like this?" Mrs. Choi cajoled with a sly grin.

With a squeamish look upon her face, Gabby, turtle box in her lap, squirmed in response to her mom's suggestion, abruptly shaking the poor turtle into the recesses of its shell. Public speaking made her stomach curl up, bounce against her rib cage like a pinball, then settle in the bed of knots that were her small intestines. If she needed to pass up a paper in class, she could barely tell her neighbor to take it from her. Her "psst!" sounds were whisper-quiet and the usual gentle tapping of the paper that other students did to receive attention was too intrusive for the shy Gabby. Often, her left arm would just hold the paper out in front of her until someone finally noticed.

"I heard from Sarah's mom that Sarah is going to try out for it."

In her group of friends, there were three girls: Allison, Sarah, and Gabby. Allison wore glasses, had jet-black hair, and often did not say a word unless she really needed to. Sarah was bold and fierce. Nothing scared her. In class, if a question was asked, Sarah's hand would shoot up first, waving around like a flagpole on a windy day. Sarah's nostrils would flare and her cute button nose would twitch whenever she knew the answer to a question. Her answer would flow out like golden honey: sweet in tone, pure in quality, and always correct. In Gabby's opinion, there was no way that she could compete with Sarah. As the shy girl in the front corner of the classroom, Gabby thought she could not compare to her friend. Often when asked a question, her words would rush out, with no elegance or eloquence, like a group of school children running out their classroom through one narrow doorway at the start of recess. Just the thought of going against Sarah summoned the twin demons of doubt and dismay. She shook her head in an attempt to dispel the notion of being sixth grade president.

"Mom, I don't want to say a speech in front of the entire school," Gabby finally said, her stomach tightening. Those darn words, those school kids that rushed out to the playground, escaped, and there was no way to bring them back in. Gabby would have to live with the consequential rebuttal from the ever sharp Carol Choi.

Gabby didn't notice it, but her mother's eyes didn't blink at the words of dissension. They focused on Gabby, the gaze squeezing through the pores of her skin, through her skull, into the soft developing brain matter of her gifted daughter's brain, and into her thoughts, in an attempt to squash any doubt. Carol had a knack for convincing people to do what she wanted, and Gabby was no exception. The shrewd mother knew her daughter and her tendencies. Carol understood why Gabby did not want to run for sixth grade president and it did not matter. The ambitious mother had already pegged Gabby for greatness from day one and she would not lose to Sarah, Sarah's perfect mom, or anyone else.

"I'll help you write your speech. We can practice it together." Her mom gave Gabby that look, the look that made the walls start closing in and the oxygen even when outside start to feel thin. The only way to free herself was to succumb to the pressure. The young girl could only nod her head in agreement.

"Good, we'll start in an hour." Carol walked into the house, leaving her daughter with her turtle, speechless. The turtle stayed withdrawn in its shell and Gabby wished she could have crawled right in there with it.

Gabby went to her bedroom and sat at her desk, wondering what she would want to say in her speech if she did run for president. She suddenly remembered how she had written in her journal recently that she wanted to help people fulfill their potential. She flipped open her pink Hello Kitty journal to that page and smiled at the big letters written in her favorite purple pen. "Maybe I do have something to offer people," she thought in her heart.

Tentatively, she got out a piece of lined paper from her drawer and started to write down her first words of her speech.

Within a week, word got out to Gabby's artistic Aunt Lauren that she would be running for class president, and her aunt graciously volunteered to make her campaign posters. When Gabby's mom delivered the finished product into Gabby's hands, Gabby smiled in awe. Her aunt had cut out each letter of her name in bubble letters on fluorescent green, orange, pink, and yellow paper. She had even decorated the posters with little colorful smiley face stickers. The posters were bold, eye-catching, and beyond Gabby's wildest imagination.

"I have a chance to win," she thought quietly to herself, smiling down at the flashy posters.

The three weeks leading up to her speech flew by, and before she knew it, Gabby was standing before three hundred pairs of bright, beady eyes in her school auditorium. The room was warm from the body heat of young kids packed together in close proximity. The air smelled funny—musty plus sweaty combined. Six other candidates for class president were sitting behind her on the stage, already having delivered their speeches–poised, confident, and smart for kids their age. Now it was her turn to convince her peers and sweep them off their feet. For some odd reason, Gabby felt comfortable as she stood before the mic in front of the audience, as if she was meant to be standing there at that exact moment in time.

"Hi, my name is Gabby Choi and I am running for sixth grade class president. I've always had the desire to help many different people. That is why I am currently studying five languages."

Murmurs rippled across the room as kids faced each other to discuss what they just heard.

For months after that day, random kids would come up to Gabby at recess and ask, "You're learning five languages? Which languages?" with huge eyes that seemed to bulge out of their sockets. Gabby would smile and almost laugh, seeing their avid curiosity. Then, she would kindly and humbly say, "Korean, Spanish, Chinese, Japanese, and English."

Her genuinely helpful heart, her intelligence, and her cheerful smile won her school over and, out of seven candidates, Gabby won with a landslide victory. For the first time, Gabby's confidence soared through the blue sky and her heart felt light like the clouds.

In eighth grade, she ran for student council again, but this time for student body president. She won and led her entire school joyfully and confidently. Gabby did not quite feel it at the time, but she was growing into a young woman of boldness who was gaining the trust and favor of her peers.

~

Gabby's thudding heart gradually slowed down as her mom retreated down the stairs. Her mom's angry outburst left her brain feeling numb and she felt a weariness overtake her entire being. Her eyes glazed over, she lay awake until 2 a.m., wondering if she'd ever be able to get away from this life.

A month had passed since Trevor and Gabby's first hangout at the park. Gabby still felt burdened by her father's sickness, but she also felt encouraged by the random acts of kindness done by the mysterious stranger at school. At least there was something nice to look forward to the next day. If it weren't for that person, she would've been mired in a hole of hopelessness. Though she didn't know the identity of this benevolent person, she secretly hoped she would meet them one day.

Meanwhile, Trevor and Gabby started talking almost everyday at school and after school, too. Though they were becoming close friends, Gabby was still mostly private and didn't discuss her family in detail.

Fall turned to winter, and Gabby worried about her college applications. She had many left to do but she just felt exhausted and unmotivated when she would sit at her desk to start on them. She was crippled by the fact that her grades had dropped this semester and could threaten her chances of getting into the top schools. She dealt with all her stress and anxiety by herself, afraid to tell her mom about her grades.

One November morning, Gabby woke up with a sore throat and sniffles. Burying her head in her pillow, she thought, "Good excuse to not go to school." But she knew Mom wouldn't buy it. Still, she tried.

Tiptoeing downstairs to the kitchen where her mom was busily whipping up some vegan waffles, Gabby asked timidly, "Mom, I feel really sick. Can I stay home?" Glancing at her once, Mrs. Choi said automatically, "Nope, you're not that sick. Go to school."

Gabby sighed and, trudging back upstairs, dutifully started getting dressed for school.

She gave each class period her all, giving each of her teachers her total attention, ignoring the pain all over her body. After school, the frigid November winds enveloped her body and Gabby shivered beneath her thick black coat. Coughing, she felt hot and cold at the same time and her body ached all over. Sighing, she wished her mom had let her stay home for once.

Upon reaching her doorstep, Gabby had so many thoughts swirling in her mind. "What if Mom gets mad at me for getting sicker? She might think I wasn't wearing my coat. She always blames me when I'm sick." At that depressing moment, she noticed the glint of stainless steel in her field of vision. A large pot sat there in front of her on her porch.

Puzzled, Gabby lifted the lid of the pot tentatively with her mittened hand. A warm cloud of steam flew up toward her face. It was a huge pot of chicken noodle soup! Chunks of celery and carrots and pasta bobbed up and down in the yellow grease. The white pieces of chicken breast here and there looked so juicy and fresh. Gabby nearly drooled. She gazed in wonder at the lovely concoction, then looked up and down the sidewalk, mind-boggled even after experiencing these kind gestures many times.

Lifting up the heavy pot, she ran through the door excitedly. Sitting in the empty kitchen darkened by the cloud cover, Gabby took her first taste straight from the pot. It was perfect!

"Wow!" she said aloud. She grinned, her face gleaming for the first time that day, her happiness literally melting away the sickness from her body.

"How did they know I love chicken noodle soup…" she said aloud, then chuckled.

"I hope she likes chicken noodle soup," Trevor thoughtfully pondered at home as he washed the dishes and looked out the window.

Gabby dug into her bowl of soup, shoving spoonfuls of pasta and chicken into her mouth, not caring she looked like a hooligan that was starving on an island.

Right after eating as much as she wanted, Gabby Facebook messaged Trevor, who she always went to first with exciting news.

"Guess what? Today, the angel stalker person left chicken noodle soup at my door! I mean, how did they know I was sick and how did they make the soup so fast?" Gabby spoke so fast when she was excited.

"HAHAH," Trevor replied.

"What's so funny," Gabby said.

"Nothing, that dude is really nice," Trevor typed, with a satisfied grin.

"I really want to find out who it is soon," Gabby said dreamily. "What if it turns out to be some creepy guy though," she said in disgust.

Trevor paused and, smiling, cleared his throat. He started feeling uneasy about keeping it a secret from Gabby.

Resting her chin on her laptop, Gabby waited for Trevor's response.

"Gabby, what are you doing on Saturday?" Trevor changed the subject.

"Nothing," Gabby answered. "Why?"

"My friends are watching Spider-Man. Wanna come with us?"

"I love Spider-Man! Sure! I'm down."

Trevor smiled his bright, genuine smile again, amazed at how Gabby was so lively when she talked to him, compared to the hollow look in her eyes when she walked around school.

"Okay! See you at 3:20 in front of AMC Rolling Hills 20."

"YAY!" Gabby replied.

Lying back on his bed, Trevor sighed, glad he could make someone happier; he felt honored.

Satisfied with his work for the day, he turned off the lamp and drifted off to sleep as he brainstormed future surprises for Gabby.

"Angel stalker guy," he muttered with his eyes shut, and then chuckled heartily.

On the last day of November, the first quarter report cards were mailed home from school. All day long, Gabby had trouble focusing in her classes and she kept checking the clock for when she could race home. As soon as the bell rang at 3:08, Gabby drove speedily home, leapt out of her car, and sprinted to her old black rusty mailbox. She swung open the mailbox door and peered inside. The mailbox was empty. Her heart fell and twisted within her. Her mind raced and vacillated between getting back into her car and getting away or going inside her house and having to face her mom.

Before she could make up her mind, the front door opened quickly. Her mom made her way toward her swiftly, her body rigid with anger. She was holding a small, folded paper in her hand. It was Gabby's report card.

"Gabby! What is this?" she demanded.

Gabby flinched. She stood in her driveway, frozen.

Her mom came right up to her face, her face contorted with rage.

"You got three B's!"

Gabby's heart seemed like it would beat out of her chest.

Her mom crumpled up the report card and threw it at Gabby's chest. The crumpled report card bounced off her chest and onto the cement driveway in front of Gabby's feet. Gabby looked down at the little ball in front of her, her cheeks getting hot.

"How are you going to go to Harvard!" her mom screeched. "How could you do this to me?"

Her mom grabbed Gabby's wrist and dragged her into the house where she could continue screaming at her behind closed doors.

Gabby numbly stood in front of her mom in the hallway, tears bulging out of her eyes and running down her cheeks. She wiped away the wetness quickly with her hands.

Just then, her dad passed by holding a newspaper, but he glanced only once at them and then went into his room, closing the door behind him.

"What about Harvard!" her mom kept screaming.

Finally, even though Gabby knew her voice would not be heard, she opened her mouth and yelled back.

"I couldn't focus on my studies because Dad's like that! I was depressed! Didn't you know?"

"Depressed? Why were you depressed? Your job is to be a good student!" her mom kept shouting, flames flickering in her eyes.

Gabby ran out the door and kept running until she reached the small park in their neighborhood.

Her mom screamed after her. "Where are you going? Come back here right now!"

Gabby hid in the corner of the park behind some large bushes. Huddled there, she hugged her arms, shuddering from the cold because she didn't bring out a jacket and trembling from fear and anger.

Hours passed by but Gabby stayed hunched over on the ground, her eyes glazed over. She had nowhere to go.

Gabby sat there numbly, spacing out, when suddenly a Bible verse entered her mind: "Though my father and mother forsake me, the Lord will receive me." As she thought about this Bible verse, the love and comfort of God flooded into her heart and soothed her weary soul.

As the blue sky slowly darkened to grey and then dark purple, she realized she should go back home because her mom would get more upset if she came after dinner was prepared. She had nowhere else to go anyway. With no other choice, Gabby slowly walked toward her house, hugging her arms and numbly looking straight ahead.

When she opened the front door, she could see her mom in the kitchen opening and closing drawers, each time slamming them shut as she swiftly moved about the kitchen.

Seeing Gabby timidly standing there, her mom glared and said angrily, "You ruined your life."

Then, after a pause, "Do you know what I sacrificed to get you to where you are now?"

Gabby felt as if she had been hit in the face, although her mom was a couple yards away from her.

Her legs carried her slowly up to her bedroom, and she sat upon her bed in the dark, not able to think anything else for hours.

Although in the following days her mom acted as she always did, Gabby walked about her home like a shadow, as if half of her were missing. She peered at her mom's face at times, wondering how she felt about her. All she knew was that she had disappointed her mother and that it would be impossible to make her mom feel proud of her again. She timidly kept her distance, speaking quietly to her only when she absolutely needed to.

G&T

"Trevor, can you go get the Christmas lights from the attic?" his dad boomed from downstairs, as Trevor lay on his bed watching YouTube videos.

"Sure, Dad!" Trevor replied, and quickly putting down his phone, he walked to the attic. It had been a while since they had dusted the attic, so he let out a big sneeze that echoed through the cavernous room.

His eyes darted around, looking for the box labeled "Christmas," which they took out every year to decorate their tree. But Trevor couldn't help but notice his mom's desk, bringing to mind all the times he noticed her sitting there, reading her cherished Bible or praying quietly.

Walking toward the big cardboard box labeled "Christmas" with thick red Sharpie, he opened it, and a jolt of happiness seized his heart as he saw his mom's old holiday candles in there.

Excitedly, he ran downstairs with the box so that he could quickly light the candles with his dad.

~

Looking at the colorful twinkling lights on the houses, Gabby wished for Christmases past. She recalled how her dad had always spent an entire half day putting lights on outside, to make her and her mom's piano students happy. He always did it without complaining, so cheerfully. Reaching her house, she saw that it was all dark, on the outside and the inside. Standing there in front of the fixed bay window, she couldn't get her feet to move. She turned around and walked swiftly away toward the street corner.

Without hesitation or second thought she just kept walking and walking, her red and white mittens digging deeper into her grey wool coat pocket. She didn't stop until she reached Trevor's house. His house was dark on the outside except for a glowing red reindeer beside his front door. "Maybe it's Rudolph," she thought, and peered into his living room window. At that exact moment, Trevor's dad was decorating their Christmas tree, placing a string of lights on the highest branches. Gabby swallowed her tears and just watched. Just then, Trevor appeared in the living room with a box, perhaps full of ornaments, and shot a glance at Gabby standing outside. He quickly put down the box and ran outside.

"Gabby," he said breathlessly in the cold. "Come on in. We're just decorating the tree."

She just stood silently, not knowing what to do. He took her arm and gently drew her into his house.

The house smelled of cinnamon and sugar, almost like snickerdoodles. Gabby sniffed the air and remarked aloud, "I didn't expect a house where two men live to smell so sweet!"

Hanging Gabby's coat, Trevor said happily, "We like to light my mom's favorite candles. She loved sugar and spice."

Trevor's dad got up from fixing the base of the tree, and, slapping the dust off his hands, embraced Gabby. He was warm like Trevor.

"I've heard a lot of great things about you, Gabby." His voice was deep and manly, but very warm and reassuring.

"Want to help us decorate the tree?" Trevor asked. "Look at this ornament I made in first grade," he laughed, showing her a bright yellow and gold ball ornament. A colorful mess of glitter glue sprawled all around it, and at the center was a picture of Trevor with a missing tooth in front.

Gabby smiled and burst out laughing. "It's cute," she said. "Thank you guys for having me," she told them sincerely, and grabbed a red ball ornament from the cardboard box.

With such kind and welcoming people like Trevor and his dad around her, she felt like she was part of a family, a good family.

"Rudolph, the red-nosed reindeer," she started singing quietly.

"Gabby! You have a great voice!" boomed Trevor's dad.

"Yea, Dad. She takes voice lessons and even sang at competitions!" Trevor added.

"Wow! Please sing louder. My wife was the singer. Not me or Trevor. We–" he trailed off.

"You don't want to hear us sing," Trevor finished.

"Haha," Gabby laughed. At least she could add something to this family.

For a moment, she worried for her mom, about whether her mom was happy at this moment, but then she shook the thought away and thought, "For now, I have to be happy. I want to be happy." She said a prayer for her mom in her heart and kept decorating the increasingly vibrant tree, finding herself giggling out loud as Trevor continually made her laugh.

December turned into the New Year, and pretty soon it was the time of year the whole high school buzzed about–Valentine's Day. Gabby knew that this year, she was not going to get anything from anyone. Almost every other Valentine's Day since she was young, she would receive presents from admirers that she didn't know existed until the day of. In sixth grade, Sean Kalita had handed her a huge bag of seven dolls (His parents owned a toy shop). She had never talked to him before. He even did it again in seventh grade. This year, Gabby felt unattractive, boring, and gloomy.

"At least I have the random acts of kindness person," she thought with some positivity.

Trevor decided this would be the last random act of kindness before he revealed himself to Gabby. He felt it was going on for too long and he felt uneasy. He wanted to be one hundred percent honest with her.

"Valentine's Day...Valentine's Day…" Trevor said to himself as he paced around his room. "What can I give her so that it doesn't seem like I like her?" he questioned, as he rubbed his curly brown hair, making it a mess. "Well, she doesn't know who it is anyway…" he speculated. "Well, she really loved that chicken noodle soup last year. Maybe I'll make her something...bake something?"

Finally, he decided to make a batch of red velvet and white chocolate chip cookies.

"Perfect," he thought. "Red and white...and not too romantic."

Remembering that Gabby went to voice lessons every Tuesday, Trevor timed his delivery for Tuesday afternoon.

Placing the basket of warm cookies carefully on her doorstep, Trevor turned around and swiftly started walking back home, putting his hood over his head, as was his custom.

He did not know that Gabby's voice lesson was cancelled that day.

As Gabby's mom opened the door to go teach piano, she called for Gabby to come and see the surprise, but Gabby quickly ran past her mom and out the door. Looking both ways down the street, she saw a small male figure at the end of the street, just about to turn the corner. He was wearing a white hoodie and faded light blue jeans.

Sprinting down the road as if she were in an action movie chasing down a criminal, Gabby caught up to the unknowing, nonchalant Trevor, who had placed earbuds in.

Gabby grabbing his shoulders from behind, Trevor jolted with a look of alarm in his large brown eyes, meeting Gabby's shocked ones.

She heaved heavily from the sprint, and could barely form the word, "Trevor," which she mouthed silently.

Trevor stood there, frozen. Gabby didn't know that he saw the cracked window, the vase, the shoving, the tears. He had pretended all along, to protect her.

"How….Why?" Gabby said, knowing the random acts of kindness had begun before she had told Trevor about her family. The random acts of kindness had begun the day after her dad…" It all started coming together in her head.

"Did you see…? That night! Did you…see that?"

Trevor just stood still, searching her eyes, not sure what to say to make sure he did not shatter Gabby, and their friendship. But honest as he was, he admitted quietly, "Yes."

Gabby felt as if someone had slapped her across the face.

Anger and embarrassment mounting inside of her, she asked, "Why didn't you tell me," and started walking away, wanting to run away and hide from Trevor, hide from the world that now knew her worst secret.

"Gabby," he exclaimed, walking toward her and holding her arm gently. "Listen to me!"

"No," Gabby said without looking back; she kept running all the way home.

Three days passed without Gabby returning any of Trevor's texts, earnest as they were. Finally, after nine missed phone calls, Gabby actually picked up, agreeing to meet him at the nearby diner. Trevor, beaming, headed to the diner like lightning.

When Trevor saw Gabby's face, his heart fell. It was streaked with anger and resentment and she no longer smiled youthfully as she had begun to in recent months. She looked as if she had been battling on her own the past few days, and appeared much older, her friendly cheerfulness and calm demeanor absent. Trevor did not know what to do. The silence between them was painful.

"Why didn't you tell me it was you?" Gabby asked angrily, her lips quivering despite her trying to control them. "No one was supposed to know about my dad. No one."

"Gabby, I was just passing by your house. It just happened. I–I was just trying to help," Trevor stammered, startled at the hardness that had overcome the sweet Gabby Choi.

Grabbing her purse, Gabby ran out of the cafe, just like she had run away on Valentine's Day, a sight that had crushed Trevor even though Gabby could not see his pain then, blinded by her own.

This time, Trevor would not let her go off alone.

It had begun to rain and her new orange-brown dress was beginning to get soaked, but Gabby did not care. She just wanted to get away as fast as she could. She drove toward the Palos Verdes cliffs, where she always went when she wanted to be alone.

Knowing she wanted to be by herself but afraid for her safety, Trevor parked a distance away.

Gabby sat on a large rock and began to weep in the rain, the coastal landscape becoming blurry through her tears. She was glad no one could hear her sobs, which she had held inside until now.

Though she didn't talk to God at all anymore, suddenly, words formed in her mouth that surprised even her by their honesty.

"God! Why did Trevor have to find out? Why didn't you help me keep it a secret? I thought you were a good God! Isn't it enough that my dad is like that? And doesn't even care about me anymore? I don't even know if he's ever gonna come back!"

All her fears, disappointments, and rage lay bare between her and God, a spiritual chasm that made her feel even more alone.

"Gabby," a tender whisper suddenly filled her heart. "Trevor loves you. He will protect you."

Gabby blinked twice. It was the first time Gabby heard God's voice so she wasn't sure what to think, but it was unmistakable. At that moment, her heart grew quiet and she felt a peace pervade her entire soul. Wiping the rain from her face she got up and slowly made her way back to her car, walking around the large brown puddles created by the rain.

Suddenly, she was filled with remorse over her behavior toward Trevor. He never did anything to hurt her. He was just trying to be helpful all along.

Just then, she looked up and saw a rainbow-colored umbrella, opened and pointed toward her. It was Trevor, handing it to her. Hot tears streamed down her face again and her cheeks got hot. She was embarrassed and sorry. She stood before Trevor, feeling naked.

"Gabs, let's go home," he said, kindness in his tired eyes.

Suddenly exhausted by the crying and the cold, Gabby just collapsed into his arms and just held onto him, weeping overwhelming her body and coming in waves as the stormy ocean. Despite her being utterly vulnerable and snot forming in her nose, the dryness of Trevor's plaid shirt and warmth emanating from his chest felt good and comforting.

"Thank you," she wanted to say. But she was too overwhelmed and exhausted. She had carried around so much weight for so long she was tired to the bone. The only thing that gave her energy to keep standing was Trevor's presence. For the first time, Gabby could relax, as herself, with someone else. And that someone was the sweetest, most thoughtful person around– Trevor Song. Despite the pain, Gabby felt a profound peace, as if she glimpsed the tip of a miracle, as the figure of a small white sailboat in a misty sea.

Trevor, who was expressive with his emotions, found tears escaping his eyes as well, realizing then just how much Gabby had been hurting. He knew, somehow, he had been chosen to help her, and he felt almost a sense of relief.

Still holding Gabby in his arms, through the fog he made out the figure of the lighthouse, its light still flashing on time. Like that lighthouse, he wanted to be steady, strong, and comforting for this lost little girl, who had seemed so strong all his life like that lighthouse, up until now.

Standing under the umbrella together for what seemed like thirty minutes, Trevor sensed Gabby had stopped crying on his chest. Bewildered, he did not know what to expect. Would she run off again? Would she be upset with him? Rubbing her eyes, and cupping her nose because it had been running, Gabby looked up at Trevor and smiled with her eyes, a light shining once more in them because her lighthouse stood in front of her—an 18-year-old holding an old rainbow umbrella.

Trevor searched her eyes, amazed at the change, and at the same time, his mind raced. "How will I care for her? Am I able to do this?" But behind all those questions was a resounding sureness. Sureness that he was going to stay. That he was going to be with Gabby Choi in this moment in her life. Clasping her cold wet hand, Trevor led her to his car so he could drive her safely home.

~

Ever since that day, Gabby felt a peaceful reassurance, because she wasn't alone anymore. Trevor stopped his random acts of kindness, but instead he walked with her through the school hallways and talked with her after school at Yami Teahouse, on the swings at Wilson Park, and via text. Gabby's smile returned, but still, Trevor noticed that she was fragile and in need of tender care and constant watchfulness on his part. But he didn't just carry her burden. Instead, he found out that the true Gabby was still in there— the one that laughed readily, the one that asked questions because she truly cared, the one that saw the best in others. Trevor started looking forward to every moment he could spend with her, but Gabby still felt she was a burden and tried not to discuss her problems too much.

Trevor found himself thinking about her all the time, wondering how she was feeling, whether she felt good enough to do her homework and study, whether she'd get into the colleges of her dreams. He hoped that Gabby would keep getting brighter and that she would accomplish all that she had worked her whole life for.

But as life often does, Trevor and Gabby's life would take an unexpected turn.

G&T

For a few months, Gabby's father had been quieter and calmer, though he still walked around with a darkened face and did not say much to his family. But on March 2, the anniversary of his friend Chad Remayne's death, he relapsed, shaking the family's foundation to the core.

"Blown into bits," he said while eating his Honey Bunches of Oats cereal.

"Huh?" Gabby asked, feeling tense at her father's random statement.

"Blown into bits!!" he yelled, suddenly standing up and slamming his fists on the counter.

Gabby leapt up, holding her father's shoulders to calm him down. "Dad!" she exclaimed. "What's wrong?"

It looked as if her dad wanted to cry but he was never one to show his tears in front of his family. Instead his sadness turned into anger.

Sensing in her chest that he was going to grab and throw something, Gabby took a few steps away from him, still keeping her eye on her dad.

But it was too late. The blue ceramic cereal bowl that he had thrown against the counter exploded into bits and one shard flew into Gabby's face.

Always highly resistant to pain and brave, Gabby stood still, relatively calmly touching her cheek. Looking at her hand, Gabby's eyes grew wide at the bright red blood. Finally, the pain sank in and she flinched. No one else was home, so she just ran to the upstairs bathroom to quickly wash herself and bandage the wound.

She stood tall and strangely rigid in front of the clean bathroom mirror, staring for a long time at her reflection. Her whole body felt numb; her heart felt numb and feelingless. Her heart mourned a loss, but she was mentally too drained to process what kind of loss.

She lay still on her bed curled up into a u-shape. She said nothing, did nothing, ate nothing until nine that night.

"Gabby, whatsup?" a text illuminated her dark bed.

She knew it was Trevor. She could hear his cheerful exuberance.

She lay still, still staring off into the distance.

She didn't answer him.

After many hours, Gabby finally decided something. She would not stay in this house any longer. She would get on the Greyhound the next day to her Aunt Marie's house six hours away.

At dawn, Gabby slowly packed a backpack and gently slung it over her back. She carefully made her way down the stairs, her body lighter from not having eaten; the steps didn't creak. Checking her backpack one more time to make sure she had her cell phone and charger, she opened the front door slowly and closed it with a click.

It all felt dreamlike–driving to the Greyhound bus station on Fifth, getting out of her car, and then getting in line in front of the enormous vehicle. Before she placed her right foot on the first step of the bus, she paused and reflected. But the pain in her cheek moved her legs and she found herself on the bus, paying the Black bus driver who smelled strongly of cigarettes and mint gum.

Sensing something was wrong, Trevor was at Gabby's house at 5 a.m., just as her bus left the terminal. He stood before her empty driveway, his mind searching for an answer for where she could be at this hour.

As Gabby leaned her uninjured right cheek against the cool glass of the bus, the freshly sprayed Windex odor kept her awake and her mind arrived at the thought of Trevor. Once again, she had left him without notice. She reached for her phone in the front flap of her backpack and called him, not realizing it was so early in the morning.

He immediately answered and she said in a dazed voice, "Trev, sorry."

Trevor's heart raced and he started to panic.

"Where are you?"

112

"Trev, don't worry about me. I'll be fine. I'm going to Aunt Marie's."

"The one up north?"

"Yeah."

"For how long?"

Gabby rested for a little while. She felt weak from the blood loss and the fact that she was running away.

"Don't tell anyone. I'll miss you," she said, still in her dreamlike state. "Sorry, I wanna sleep," she said, concluding their call.

"Gabby! Are you running away?" Trevor was always so quick to sense things.

Gabby smiled faintly.

"Gabby, don't hang up. Don't run away. Come back!"

"I—can't...anymore," Gabby replied.

Trevor hung up and zoomed toward the Greyhound station, not believing Gabby was running away.

Later that day on the bus, Gabby called Trevor again, feeling she owed him an explanation.

When Trevor found out what happened, he cried.

"Why didn't you tell me?" Misery swelled in his chest because he couldn't be there for her.

"Is it still bleeding? Does it hurt a lot?"

113

"No," Gabby automatically answered, to not worry him. She smiled for the first time since it happened.

"Where is Aunt Marie's house?" Trevor asked, trying to sound nonchalant.

"Why? You're gonna follow me?" Gabby half-joked.

"No...yes."

"What?"

Gabby stifled a laugh of glee. "That would be fun," she thought.

"Trevor, don't miss school."

"You don't miss school."

Trevor always knew how to keep things lighthearted.

They hung up and Trevor sat in his room, thinking.

He decided Gabby needed him most right now.

Immediately, Trevor hurriedly packed his blue backpack with as many necessities as possible, not really caring though what he packed. He just had to get to Gabby.

"Trev, where do you think you're going?" his father said at his doorway, hands on his hips. He had overheard their conversation.

"I'm going to go help Gabby," he replied resolutely.

"Why. How about school?"

"Dad, it's Spring Break next week."

114

"I know that. How long are you going to stay with her?"

Trevor paused.

"I don't know. But as long as she needs me, Dad."

He continued to stuff his backpack.

"It's time to focus on your studies, young man, not go after a girl."

"I don't have feelings for Gabby in that way. She's my friend. I'm the only one who's taking care of her."

Grabbing his son's arm, Trevor's father looked into Trevor's eyes. "How about college?"

Trevor dropped his backpack on his bed, and looked his father in the eye, fiercely resolute yet respectful.

"Dad, I can make up the work later. I can even do this semester over again. But Gabby is not going to make it if I don't do something."

After a long pause, Mr. Song rubbed his head and said, "Trevor, I'm proud that you want to help your friend that badly, but please keep your future in mind."

"Okay, Dad," Trevor answered, tears forming in his eyes.

~

Gabby knew she was getting nearer to Aunt Marie's cottage when she passed by the small redwood forest just in front of her house. Gabby looked out the window, excited for the first time the whole trip, wanting to get a peek at the expansive lake in front of her aunt's property. Its placid waters shone and flickered in the afternoon sun like a dark blue sapphire, and rows and rows of great redwoods lined its shore majestically.

Gabby smiled a gleaming smile and sighed, happy to be away for once.

Aunt Marie, who was Gabby's mom's younger sister, used to live in Toccoa near Gabby's house. She had been Gabby's babysitter and ride-giver when Gabby was younger, so she felt like a second mom. She got the call from Gabby and immediately agreed to let her stay for a few weeks.

When Gabby arrived at the station, she quickly spotted Aunt Marie's always vividly bright colored clothing and fun jewelry around her neck; today, she had chosen neon green and dark orange. Running to her, Gabby fully embraced her. Gabby felt more comfortable with her than her own mom, though she didn't fully realize it then.

"Gabby sweetie," Aunt Marie murmured, Gabby drinking in her fragrance–Clinique Happy. Though she did not have any children, Aunt Marie was very much maternal, warm, and compassionate, a lover of people and animals.

In Aunt Marie's hand was a Carl's Jr. bag, and Gabby, a foodie and starving as she was, asked what it was. It was just as she had hoped.

"You know me so well," Gabby said sweetly, smiling up at Aunt Marie. She reached for the Loaded Breakfast Burrito inside the paper bag, but just then, Aunt Marie gently held her face and stared at the bandage Gabby had applied.

"You didn't tell me…Gabby what happened?" Aunt Marie asked, her voice slightly trembling.

116

Gabby smiled it off, just glad to be here. Biting into the burrito, she kept smiling, but tears formed in her eyes and quickly betrayed her smile, showing Aunt Marie and herself how she was truly feeling inside.

Aunt Marie quickly responded, "I'll take you to my doctor first thing tomorrow morning to get it checked out," and held her shoulder, leading them to her red 1969 El Camino.

In the car, Aunt Marie immediately turned on the country radio station and started talking happily, asking Gabby about school, about her friends, about the boys, and filling her in on her hobbies--gardening, archery, and baking. Gabby found herself smiling comfortably and feeling at ease, feelings she rarely had back in Toccoa.

Meanwhile, Trevor was following close behind, thinking of Gabby every step of the way. As a single parent, Trevor's father was always busy and so the two of them had not been on a vacation since his mother's passing. Trevor soon saw the same sight as Gabby–the redwood forest. Towering above him, the great ancient trees with grooved, red-brown bark amazed Trevor and he found himself grinning ear to ear all of a sudden; he had always had a fondness for nature. "I wonder what animals are in that forest," he thought. Once again his mind returned to Gabby and he checked his watch, wishing to arrive faster.

Gabby had once described Aunt Marie's lake house to him, a light in her eyes as she avidly described the pier on the lake, a path leading down to a forest in front, the second-story porch that went all the way around, the fire pit with logs where she sat when she was little and made s'mores for the first time, and where Aunt Marie would tell spooky stories to the cousins, dressed as a ghost, wearing white sheets with two holes for her eyes. Trevor remembered everything Gabby told him, and so he knew exactly where to go. "Right after the Cambridge Redwood Forest," Trevor thought. "Almost there Gabby," he whispered to himself. He ate the last Cheeto in the snack-sized bag he had stuffed in his backpack and rested his head against the back of the seat for the last leg of the trip.

Meanwhile, Gabby was getting situated in Aunt Marie's cottage. Her excitement to see Aunt Marie quickly faded and she realized how alone she would be here, without her friends, without school...without Trevor, the one who she always talked to these days. She stared at her phone, sad that he hadn't texted in a while.

Meanwhile, Trevor woke up from his nap and checked his phone. Gabby had texted. He leapt up in his seat, his brow furrowed in concentration. Just then, the bus came to a sudden halt and Trevor's heart jumped in elation and excitement.

Running down the middle of the bus and forgetting his manners, he got off first, jumping off the second-to-last step, his backpack bouncing against his body.

Gabby sat on her bed as Aunt Marie cooked, wishing things hadn't turned out this way. She felt she should check on her bandage but then she felt too emotionally tired to try.

Just then, she got a text and she smiled reaching for the phone, as she always did when Trevor texted.

"Gabs, I express-mailed a package to you," Trevor said.

"Trevor's always up to something weird and funny..." Gabby thought, but excitedly hopped off her bed and ran to the front door.

She opened the door but nothing was there. She decided to call Trevor. She felt lonely anyhow. Walking down the path toward the forest, she waited for him to respond.

"Hello?" Trevor asked from behind a tree nearby. He watched Gabby carefully. She looked kind of disconcerted, a high schooler being in the woods instead of at school.

He leaned against the tree and waited, wondering what to do to maximize her happiness.

"I don't see a package," Gabby said sincerely, huffing and puffing as she kept walking down the trail.

"Where are you going?" Trevor asked.

"To the forest."

Before Gabby could process what Trevor had just asked, Trevor said, "Gabby, I'm here." Trevor couldn't wait any longer.

Just then, Gabby stopped in her tracks and Trevor continued to watch her from behind.

Slowly turning around, her heart beat faster. "No...way..." she said into the phone, mostly to herself.

There next to the tallest redwood's trunk stood Trevor Song in real, human form. His pale face and arms almost made him look like a friendly ghost that was visiting her at Aunt Marie's cottage.

With abandon, Gabby ran towards Trevor and hugged him. Trevor chuckled. Gabby had gotten more expressive with him.

"Trevor!" she exclaimed. Pulling back from his embrace, she said with joyful but concerned eyes, "What are you doing here?"

119

"Came to see you," he said, quite suavely for Trevor.

"I know...but how about school…" Gabby said, elongating the vowels in "school."

Trevor shrugged. "I felt that you were of utmost importance," he said, giving a chivalrous bow.

When he raised himself up, he noticed Gabby was about to cry, but she smiled through the tears. She was so relieved that he was here. She was feeling so alone. She hugged him once more in relief, sensing his back with her palms and realizing that he was actually there, in the woods, with her.

"Trevor, you must be tired. What time did you leave?" Gabby asked another ten questions after that, becoming a total chatterbox.

Trevor smiled, knowing a chatty Gabby meant a happy Gabby. They talked about his trip and the cool sights they both saw all the way up to the front door where Aunt Marie stood, gaping.

"Gabby, don't tell me...your friend came all the way here for you?" She eyed Trevor, observing him closely, truly startled.

"Hello ma'am, my name is Trevor," Trevor said chivalrously once again, shaking Aunt Marie's hand firmly.

Aunt Marie noticed the kindness in his gaze and the way he smiled genuinely at Gabby.

"Is it okay for you to be missing school?" Aunt Marie asked Trevor just like Gabby did a few seconds ago.

Trevor smiled, not quite sure knowing what to say. They wouldn't understand why school wasn't the biggest priority for him like it was to Gabby.

"I'll do make-up work," he said to smooth things over.

"Are you sure?" Gabby asked sincerely, feeling guilty, staring at Trevor's face with her big brown eyes.

"It's all under control," Trevor reassured her, half lying to make her feel okay.

"Oh," Gabby said quietly, looking down at the ground.

"Gabby, show me around!" Trevor said in his booming voice, the voice he used to reenergize Gabby.

Gabby smiled, excitement mounting in her lean face. Trevor noticed the bandage but decided not to discuss it at the moment so she wouldn't get sad again.

"Come here!" she said, quickly walking into the cottage to show Trevor around.

"I hope you don't mind if I stay for a bit, Aunt Marie," Trevor said. "I was just...really worried for Gabby."

Once again awestruck at his sweetness and sincerity, Aunt Marie flashed a wide grin and motioned with her manicured hand, "Come on in!"

She felt surprised that someone had been looking after Gabby.

After a quick tour of the house, Gabby led Trevor outside to the shore of the lake, which was the "best part."

Seeing that she was exhausted from running around so much, Trevor finally made her sit down to rest. A cool breeze traveled across the deep blue waters, ruffled their hair, and licked their young faces.

121

For a while, they both silently gazed off into the distance, realizing they were indeed very far away from home and what they were used to, amidst the quiet lake and vast forest surrounding them.

"I never thought I'd be here," Gabby admitted. "I–I thought I'd do very well in high school until the end and get into the school of my dreams."

"You still have a chance," Trevor reassured her. "You'll be able to make up what you missed and graduate with a great GPA." Trevor was always so positive when it came to other people.

"Trevor, why did you come?"

"I don't have much to lose."

"You do. A lot."

She turned to look at him, his brown eyes looking back at hers.

Suddenly feeling alone so far from home for the first time, Gabby hugged her bare legs. Sensing her loneliness, Trevor gave her a side hug. Suddenly, she started to cry, her sobs convulsing her thin frame. She missed them. No. She missed...herself. Where had she gone? How did she end up here? Trevor, empathetic as he was, teared up, too.

"Gabs, everyone feels lost sometimes. Everyone. But it doesn't mean you actually are."

Somehow, the conviction in his words resounded in her mixed up heart.

"What do you mean?" she beseeched like a little child.

"What I mean is…" he began like an older brother, "I'm here for you, and God is watching over you, like the stars," he said awkwardly, pointing up at the sunlit sky.

Gabby laughed a little and wiped her tears with her baggy sweater sleeves.

"Let's do something fun," Trevor said, a reassuring look on his face. Gabby wasn't used to having "fun" but Trevor only knew that. Walking into Aunt Marie's cottage, Trevor smiled at Aunt Marie.

"Aunt Marie, may we borrow your kitchen today?" Trevor asked cheerfully.

"Sure, my sweeties! I'll be working in the garden this afternoon. It's all yours."

Gabby looked at the both of them, confused yet excited about the plan they had hatched.

"Today, we are making mini strawberry pies from SCRATCH!" Trevor boomed heartily.

With a quizzical brow plus the biggest grin, Gabby wondered how he had known she liked strawberry pies.

"A little bird told me," Trevor added.

Aunt Marie handed them a box of baking supplies and fresh ingredients. "Trevor asked me while you were in the bathroom a while ago, so I ran to the store and got the ingredients!" She winked at Gabby and smiled widely, looking from Trevor to Gabby, Gabby to Trevor. "Have an awesome time! Ask me if you need any help."

Gabby was overwhelmed by their cute surprise. She bubbled up with excitement for the first time since she got there.

Looking at Trevor putting on an apron swiftly and washing his hands at the kitchen sink, Gabby felt she didn't deserve it all. At the same time, she thought about her parents, and how she shouldn't feel so happy when her mom...and dad...were still suffering back at home. At that moment, Trevor started singing Michael Jackson's "Thriller" really loudly and Gabby found herself laughing freely and forgetting her labyrinthine worries as she joined him at the counter.

After three hours of throwing flour at each other's faces and eating their miniature strawberry creations scrumptiously, the two headed outside to look up at the famous starlit sky above Aunt Marie's cottage. They stood silently at the edge of the small, old pier. Night was falling, and the first stars began to appear, glimmering with an otherworldly, angelic sheen. Gabby looked up at them in wonder, as if it were her first time seeing them. Trevor could tell she felt at peace. Trevor looked up, too, wondering if he could count all the thousands of stars.

He started to hum a tune, "Mm mm mm..." to the melody of "There Can be Miracles When You Believe."

Gabby turned to him with a start. "How'd you know that? No one knows that song."

Trevor smiled and quietly said his late mother had often sung that song.

"Oh…" Gabby said sweetly but quietly.

"It's okay," Trevor quickly said, his voice a little stronger. "She's up there, now," he smiled and looked up at the stars again, which were now as multitudinous as the sand on the seashore.

This made Gabby think about God. He felt so far away.

As if he knew what she was thinking, Trevor turned to Gabby and said, "God cares for you a lot, Gabby. That's why I'm here. I'll be...your little guardian angel."

"Do you believe in God?" Gabby asked shyly.

"Now I do," Trevor answered right away, even to his surprise.

"Why?" Gabby asked, staring at his brown curly hair as he looked to the dark velvety sky.

"I believe," Trevor paused, "because I witnessed my first miracle. I found a reason to live," he admitted, with surprising courage and honesty.

Gabby looked up at Trevor's face as he watched the moon, and through his eyes traveled the places he'd been. Looking down again, she wondered where he had been and what had led him to where he was now.

"Trevor, thanks for coming," Gabby spoke genuinely. "I–I don't deserve it."

Trevor looked straight at her then and said, "Gabby, you're worthy."

Startled by his words that seemed to somehow always move her heart so, Gabby looked into his two lovely, true eyes, searching them. There was a lot more to Trevor Song than she thought. No one had ever told her those words, except the pastor at church. Gabby never felt worthy, she realized then.

Despite the courage she saw in Trevor's eyes as he said that statement, Gabby sensed a vague emptiness in him and decided to encourage him, too, which she was good at.

"Trevor, you deserve the best things in life. Really...I'll never forget what you've done. I'll always be indebted to you."

"Don't say indebted," Trevor said. Then, forming a fist he reached forward for a fist pump. "We're friends," he spoke warmly and reassuringly.

Trevor wanted to say, "You're the best friend I've ever had," but he just thought it and looked away toward the black lake shining in the moonlight.

A strong, frigid gust of wind enveloped Gabby and she quickly wrapped her arms around herself firmly. Even with those few words Trevor had spoken, Gabby Choi was changing. Protectively leading her toward the cottage, Trevor offered his own jacket, which Gabby declined, but once again, she felt a love she had never felt before, healing her mind and soul.

~

After saying good night to Gabby, Trevor followed Aunt Marie down the hallway of the lodge. Old photos lined the walls, documenting Marie's personal history. There were photos of her friends, family, and her life adventures. She had lived quite a full life. One photograph stuck out to him the most: a photo of Aunt Marie helping a young Gabby on a red tricycle. Trevor stopped to look at Gabby's face.

"She's cute, huh? Look at those cheeks!" Crinkling her eyes, Marie made a pinching motion with her thumb and index finger against the photo.

"So cute. I looked better then too! Like wow! I had it going on." Marie smiled and let out a hearty laugh. Aunt Marie was a pleasant woman with a kind smile.

She stopped at the end of the hallway in front of a very small room at the back of the house. It only had a single twin bed with not much floor space, but it looked comfortable. A thickly curtained, small window on the right side of the room overlooked the bed. The sheets and the pillow case matched, both a worn bubblegum pink with white frills along the edges. Aunt Marie and Trevor both peered around the room, from the left to the right, as if they were inspecting a crime scene.

Aunt Marie turned to him, "Well, this was the best I could do on such short notice. Next time, if you come here again, I'll set you up with a better room with some better sheets!" She laughed her hearty laugh as she grabbed the sheets. "This is all I had, but they're comfortable! And plus, you can be a princess for a night!" She laughed again, chuckling to herself as she stepped out the room. "Good night, Trevor! Thank you for coming to help Gabby. You are so sweet." She closed the door behind her and finally, Trevor was alone.

He sighed and thought to himself, "What am I doing here?" His matted, dark hair rested upon the pink pillows for just a moment and soon, he was fast asleep.

G&T

The next day after lunch, as Trevor grabbed some fishing gear from Aunt Marie, Gabby sat alone on a log on the shore of the lake. It was Sunday and she realized she wouldn't be attending church now that she was at Aunt Marie's. Ever since she became depressed, she didn't feel like going to church but her mom would fling the blankets off her bed and make her wake up for church. Gabby couldn't believe she had come this far away from God. She used to love God so much. She used to be so excited to go to church and was the one who told her friends about Jesus. Now, her Bible lay next to her bed at home, its pages untouched, the cover probably gathering dust by now. She felt guilty but also didn't know what to do about it.

"God is probably disappointed," she thought.

Gabby grabbed a small white rock next to her shoe and threw it forcefully into the lake, not knowing how to skip rocks.

A few moments later, Trevor trotted toward her with a fishing rod they borrowed from Aunt Marie.

"What are you thinking about, Gabs?" he asked, his eyes squinting at the bright sun rays.

"Nothing. Well, I just feel bad for not praying or reading the Bible much these days."

Trevor sat down next to her on the old, scratched up log.

"You know what…I used to think that way too. I haven't gone to church since middle school." He continued, "But…it seems like God still showed up in my life."

This piqued Gabby's interest. "Really?"

Trevor just smiled a wry smile, and began preparing his fishing gear.

Gabby sighed a sigh of relief. Looking over at Trevor working on the fishing rod, she felt some of her bitterness melt away. Intently focused on fixing the fishing rod, Trevor looked like such a smart guy. And yet he was here, hundreds of miles away from school, away from home, just to help her feel better. That was a miracle.

"Trevor's so deep. I wonder what Trevor's life was like," Gabby mused.

"Do you like fishing?" Trevor broke into her thoughts.

"I always thought it was boring," Gabby admitted. She started giggling. "One time my uncle took me and my cousins fishing at a manmade lake, and we caught absolutely nothing. We were just stung by the bees there. My cousin Janice accidentally squeezed a bee under her armpit. She ran around screaming her head off for like thirty minutes."

"Wow," Trevor said, picturing that image with a half-chuckle.

Finally, Trevor had fixed the rod and he sat patiently. He looked like a veteran fisherman, sixty years of age, with his old, sun-bleached, beige fisherman's hat he had borrowed from Aunt Marie.

Minutes passed.

"You're so patient," Gabby observed, staring at the navy blue glint of the fishing rod, her chin resting against her hand.

"Life is about waiting," Trevor said semi-heartily while throwing out the line a little farther.

They both laughed at how adult-like his comment just sounded.

Finally looking away from the water, Trevor looked straight into Gabby's eyes, his brow furrowed. For a moment he looked so mature, and looked like he had arrived at a moment of great clarity, though Gabby could not decide where the clarity had come from.

"I know it's hard for you, Gabby," Trevor spoke with weight. "But there's gonna be a light at the end of this tunnel. Just you watch."

He said it with this absolute certainty, as if he had heard it straight from God.

Gabby shuddered a little, disbelieving what had just occurred.

"How do you know?" she asked.

"Mm-m-mm," Trevor shrugged. But his eyes said that he just knew; he felt this conviction beyond human reason.

Gabby pondered his words, wondering if God was speaking to her through Trevor.

Her chin cupped in her palm, she mulled over their conversation in silence, thinking life was so weird, being here with Trevor, whom she didn't know at all just months ago.

"Let's catch a bunch of fish and fry one for dinner!" she exclaimed, feeling more positive and energized all of a sudden. She held her hand out, suggesting she wanted to give fishing a try, too.

Trevor looked over at Gabby, amazed at how resilient she was. Indeed, there was a lot more to her than met the eye. He admired her strength, and her hopefulness blew a fresh wind against the bitter and old parts of his own soul.

G&T

The next morning, in the cool of dawn, Trevor awoke. He felt at peace, with a calm in his heart he didn't even feel at home.

"Funny," he thought, moving his legs beneath the thin pink blanket to the side of the bed.

Trying not to make the floorboards creak so as not to wake anyone, he stepped into the long hallway which smelled of oak and cedar. The wooden floor was old yet shining golden yellow in the morning light, probably due to Aunt Marie's vigorous scrubbing.

Passing by Gabby's door, Trevor stopped for a second and took one step back. Looking at the delicate, pink dried flowers hanging upside down on the creamy white door, Trevor felt a pang of pain in his heart. He stayed in front of Gabby's door and closed his eyes, getting ready to briefly pray for her.

"Dear God, please heal and comfort Gabby's heart. Let her not feel so alone. Help me to help her in the way that you would."

As he searched his mind for anything else to say, the door swung open and he was met with Gabby's alarmed doe eyes.

"Oh, good morning!" she said, still looking shocked.

"Hi," Trevor stammered. He quickly brushed his fingers through his curly brown bedhead mess of hair.

Gabby grinned, observing the strands of hair pointing this way and that on top of his head. Trevor was usually so well-kempt at school, looking cool in his basketball clothes.

Trevor smiled back, awkwardly, and Gabby noticed how cute he was.

"I have to go to the bathroom," Gabby said, striding swiftly away down the hall.

"Gabby," Trevor called out after her.

"Yeah?" Gabby asked, expectantly. Anything to break the stifling monotony of spending her days at Aunt Marie's cottage.

"Want to go...look for animals?" Trevor asked, suddenly remembering she liked animals.

"Sure!" Gabby did a little jig then, still facing her back to him, and Trevor laughed, since he had thought Gabby Choi was only a very calm and demure girl.

"Okay, I'll meet you outside in five," Trevor said, trying to sound cool.

Gabby looked back one last time in front of the bathroom door and smiled an awkward and funny smile, grateful for his sweet offer.

Brushing her teeth vigorously, Gabby wondered where Trevor was going to take her. At least there was something to do today. Spitting out a wad of minty toothpaste foam, Gabby looked at it and grinned, feeling happy and light, not knowing that Trevor had prayed for her just moments ago.

Trevor was hungry but he knew he had to chart out a hiking course. He sat at the front steps of the cottage scratching his head, when Aunt Marie came up the path with a basket full of wild berries that resembled raspberries.

"Trevor, are you hungry?" Aunt Marie asked in her friendly manner, seeing him eye the basket of berries with a famished look on his pale face.

Not to be rude, he nodded once slightly.

Reading the hungry boy's face, with a snort, Aunt Marie jubilantly exclaimed, "I am going to make you a pile of my original three berries pancakes as tall as the Leaning Tower of Pisa with some fresh cream on top."

Trevor's face gleamed at the thought of such a meal.

"Thank you," he responded warmly and sincerely, full of appreciation.

"Aunt Marie is always so happy and generous," he thought.

"How long will it take? I was planning to chart a hiking course for me and Gabby. Is it okay if I come back in fifteen minutes?"

"Sure!" Aunt Marie's shining smile could parallel the bright morning sun.

"What an impressive kid," she muttered to herself as she made her way up the front steps.

Turning back once more, she approvingly watched Trevor trotting with purpose and conviction into the woods.

Gabby flew down the stairs and onto the porch, almost bumping into Aunt Marie.

"Where is he going?" she asked, only able to see Trevor.

"He said he's going to chart a course for you guys," Aunt Marie replied, wiping sweat from her brow. "He's great," she added.

Gabby stood silently on the porch, quietly watching Trevor's back as his figure grew smaller and smaller. Something in her heart began questioning, "Why is he doing this?" Something in her heart told her that no one else had made her feel cared for in this way.

Later at breakfast, steam kept rising from Gabby's delectable dish of moist pancakes, drizzled with syrup and melted butter, her favorite, but all she could see was Trevor.

She sat motionless, staring at him as he scarfed down his food. He ate like a man who had worked in the field all day. She couldn't figure him out. She wanted to ask why he was here, but didn't feel comfortable. Instead, she tried to act natural.

"Trevor, you know our Senior Project is due next week right?"

"Yea," he answered matter-of-factly, still looking down at his food.

"What did you write yours on?"

"I didn't do it yet."

"Are you going to?"

"Uh, we'll see," he answered, to Gabby's utter disbelief. "We'll see?" she thought. "Does he not care?"

"Oh," she said quietly.

"Did you do yours?" Trevor asked, finally looking up as he took a gulp of milk. A look of nonchalance yet insecurity filled his eyes, but he didn't know Gabby could see it.

Wanting to change the subject, Gabby said, "I did work on it, but now I'm here." She had only done fifty percent of the project because she didn't feel the motivation to complete it.

"Don't talk about school," Gabby made a mental note, as Trevor got up to put the plates away.

After breakfast, they got some hiking gear from Aunt Marie: hats to shade themselves from the sun and water thermoses. They then set off on their first hike into the woods.

"How often did you come to Aunt Marie's growing up?" Trevor asked in his friendly, relaxed way.

"Mmm...every other summer?" Gabby replied. "Aunt Marie is like my second mom to me. She babysat me when I was a baby and gave me rides to school in elementary school."

"Oh," Trevor answered.

"How about you? Are you close with your extended family?"

"Nope. It's just me and my pops. All my other relatives live in Korea and I've never met them," he answered, swinging his arms at his sides as they huffed down the downward sloping forest trail.

"Trevor," Gabby suddenly spoke, a weightiness and sincerity in her voice. She stood in her tracks, facing him.

"Why did you come?" she asked, not believing that she asked him.

Trevor stopped walking and caught his breath, his hands on his knees.

Gabby didn't realize how tiring his journey had been until then. She took a step back, even more sorry.

His breaths getting calmer, Trevor looked up at the fresh green pine boughs and patch of blue sky overhead and said almost to himself, "It was what I felt was the right thing to do."

Once again, Gabby felt that hush. The hush that came over her heart earlier that morning as she saw him disappear down the path. "Why?" her heart kept questioning. "How?" it also asked.

Blinking her eyes a few times, Gabby was at a loss for words. No one had made her feel this way before.

Trevor smiled, pointing at a limb overhead. "That's called the Elegant Trogon. I didn't expect to see one here. They're usually in Arizona or Texas."

Gabby spotted the brilliant red and green hues on the stately bird a few trees away. She stood amazed at its wonderful, shiny, majestic plumage.

"Wow, that's gorgeous," she said between breaths. "I never saw one before." They stood beholding the natural wonder for some moments.

"When I was little, I had bunnies," Gabby said excitedly. "But my parents didn't buy them from a pet shop. They took me to this old man's house. When we got to his backyard, there were hundreds of bunnies running around everywhere! There were dirt holes all over the ground," Gabby explained with joyous nostalgia.

Trevor grinned, imagining the picture Gabby painted for him.

She continued.

"I picked one white bunny and one brown bunny, but I didn't know they were boy and girl, and they started having babies every two months--seven or eight babies every time!"

Trevor guffawed, clapping his hands once. Gabby looked at him and laughed at his laugh. She felt comfortable, like she was with a brother. Smiling widely, Gabby genuinely began enjoying herself and forgot all the reasons she had to come to Aunt Marie's.

Soon they came across the firepit where Aunt Marie had dressed up as a ghost and told spooky stories to Gabby and her cousins when they were young children. The firepit was surrounded by six huge logs where people could sit around the fire. Trevor stood on top of one of the logs and pretended he was a knight, wielding his imaginary sword in front of him in a noble gesture. Gabby laughed and laughed at this new playful side that came out of him. Gabby pretended she was holding a sword too. "Let's have a sword fight. Actually, let's use branches as our swords," she said eagerly, between giggles.

They scurried around looking for some nice, long, thick branches. When they each found one, they started sword fighting, saying "Hiyah! Hiyah!" and giggling.

After their sword fight Gabby was thirsty and went toward her red metallic thermos bottle lying on a log, when a raccoon appeared and grabbed it.

"Oh my gosh!" Gabby yelped.

It stood in between her and Trevor and would not let go of the thermos bottle it was clutching.

Just then, Gabby remembered that raccoons like shiny objects.

"Raccoons like shiny objects, huh?" she asked Trevor.

"Yeah. I wonder how we can get it back…"

Trevor dug around his pockets for something shinier than the bottle. He found some shiny candy wrappers that he had stuffed in his pockets on his journey to Aunt Marie's.

Trevor held out the wrappers in his palm and lowered his hand toward the ground. The raccoon actually eyed the wrappers and started to slowly make his way toward Trevor.

"What if he bites you!" Gabby exclaimed. "Don't raccoons have rabies?" she asked, letting out a nervous giggle.

Trevor was intensely focused and did not answer. He held out his other hand in a signal to Gabby to stay quiet.

When the raccoon was right in front of his hand, Trevor dropped the candy wrappers on the ground, and the raccoon let go of the bottle to grab the wrappers. Trevor quickly grabbed the bottle from the ground and handed it to Gabby. The raccoon was still busily looking at its shiny new toys. The two teenagers laughed at the critter.

"Let's go," Gabby said as she grabbed Trevor's shoulder, motioning to him that they should get away from the raccoon.

They started running down the hill together, exhilaration filling their lungs. When they reached a flat area of the forest ground, Gabby began looking carefully at the tree bark and the ground to see if there were any insects.

"When I was little I liked to play with roly polys," Gabby said as she kept studying the reddish-brown bark of the great redwood tree in front of her.

"Me too!" Trevor exclaimed.

"Did you play with earthworms too?" she asked excitedly.

"Yeah! I would lift up this cinderblock in my backyard and look at all the insects underneath it."

"I did too! And after it rained, I would dig up the mud and look for earthworms deep in the ground."

They laughed together, realizing they had parallel childhoods.

Trevor went toward a bush and peered here and there, studying the huge, wispy, white spider webs.

"What are you doing?" asked Gabby.

"I'm looking for spiders."

"Spiders?" A chill went up Gabby's spine. "You like spiders?"

140

"Yea, I'd play with them all the time when I was little."

"Are you Spider-Man?" Gabby asked.

Trevor smiled. "I wish."

As Trevor kept searching for spiders, Gabby peered at the thick, furry green moss growing on the sides of the tall, stately trees.

"Moss grows on the north side of trees right?" Gabby asked Trevor.

"Yea, it's because the north side of trees is shadier and damper," Trevor replied.

"You're so knowledgeable," Gabby noted.

"Nah," Trevor replied. "It's from watching a lot of Youtube."

After walking all the way to the train tracks, which was the last point in Trevor's itinerary, Gabby was exhausted and she slumped down on a boulder. Her cheeks were flushed a bright pink.

Trevor, alarmed, checked her temperature by placing his hand on her forehead.

Gabby giggled, a little embarrassed.

"Sorry for making you walk so much," Trevor said quickly.

He quickly opened up his thermos and held it in front of his friend. He then took off his fisherman's hat and started fanning Gabby's face with it. She smiled at the refreshing coolness that spread across her face.

"It's okay," Gabby said. "Thank you."

"Let's rest before we go back to Aunt Marie's cabin," Trevor said. "Sorry, Gabby."

"It's okay, Trevor!" Gabby said reassuringly.

Gabby thought to herself that Trevor was really sweet.

By the time they returned to the front steps of Aunt Marie's cottage, it was twilight. Looking up at the ever-darkening sapphire sky and feeling and smelling the crisp, fragrant air of the forest all around, Gabby smiled, realizing she had spent the entire day well.

"The day went by really fast today," she said in her sweet, soft voice. She beamed with thankfulness at Trevor, whose hair was matted against his forehead from sweating so much.

Trevor stared into each of her big, twinkling eyes, one after the other. He studied them to study her heart. Gabby's eyes were full of strength, contentment, and jubilation–emotions that Trevor had not seen in her earlier at the breakfast table.

A feeling of satisfaction surged inside of Trevor, wondering how he managed to transform this girl's disposition.

Gabby kept smiling angelically into the night, her eyes content. Her magnetic smile drew Trevor in. Realizing he was staring at her face, Trevor shook himself awake and offered Gabby his hand to help her up the steep steps.

"It was a lot of fun," Trevor fumbled over his words, suddenly nervous.

Although they were with each other only a day, it felt like a lifetime.

Gabby smiled a genuinely grateful smile once more at Trevor before skipping inside.

Trevor, gently closing the screen door behind him, looked down and smiled.

"To change a life," he thought meditatively.

"Dinnertime!" Aunt Marie's shrill voice cut through the still evening air.

"Whatever adventure this is or will turn out to be...I like it," Trevor ruminated alone.

Plunging down on the soft mattress in his room, he knew he was not there in vain.

Gabby, too, sat on her bed, looking into the dresser mirror opposite her bed in the ever-darkening room, not realizing that her life had just taken a turn–a turn down the road of lasting and beautiful blessings. A turn in her life God had planned long ago.

Later that night, Gabby lay awake in her bed, feeling less empty than the night before, when she had cried herself to sleep. Undoing the strap on her soft, tan leatherbound journal from Aunt Marie, she wrote on a page.

～

Dear Trevor,

Thank you. You make me feel happy and loved. I'm so glad you're here.

- Gabby

～

A circle of yellow light shining down from the small blue desk lamp adjacent to her bed emitted heat on her hand. Gabby then envisioned Trevor as a circle of warm, bright light on this dark and lonesome chapter in her life. Feeling safe and secure, Gabby restfully lay herself down to sleep.

That night, Gabby dreamt a strange dream.

She saw a great pink rose, with large, supple petals. It was the largest rose she had ever seen, and it was flourishing and awesome to behold. Suddenly, large thick vines traveled up the rose stem and started choking the blossom. Soon, the rose was tied up and shrank under the weight of the net of vines. In her dream, Gabby began desperately praying and the rose's vine captors started breaking apart, the rose becoming free and quickly regaining its original size and splendor. Suddenly, Trevor was holding the now whole rose, and he gave it to Gabby, happy tears in his eyes.

Gabby jolted awake, her heart rapidly beating. She sat up in her bed, trying to make sense of the dream. For some odd reason, she knew without a shadow of a doubt that the rose represented Trevor Song.

G&T

Early the next morning, even before the dawn broke through the darkness that shades the land, Trevor awoke to a slight rapping sound on his window. At first, it sounded like a small bird tapping against the glass, but as Trevor slumbered, the rapping became louder and louder and soon, it sounded like a giant eagle slamming its powerful beak against the fragile glass. Trevor quickly awoke and pulled the curtains open. His eyes squinted, he looked outside amidst the morning dimness, scanning across the yard to see what the noise was. Suddenly, a head adorned with brown hair arose from below. Stunning eyes peered through the frosty glass. With a fright, Trevor's heart jumped and his body followed as he crashed onto the floor with the pink sheets draped over his legs. Now on the floor and staring at the stucco ceiling, Trevor continued to hear a loud knocking on his window. He quickly pressed his face against the glass and scanned for this intruder of sleep. He did not see stunning eyes anymore, but a slim, dark figure.

"Trevor, come out." She spoke in a soft whisper that, in the morning stillness, sounded so close to him. It was Gabby. Trevor pressed down his sleep-wrinkled clothes with his hands and scurried down the hallway and through the sliding doors. He was met with the brisk cold and a shiver traveled down his spine to his feet. His feet danced for just a moment. He was wearing the same clothes he wore the day before.

"Finally! You're here," Gabby whispered with excitement. "Come, follow me. I want to show you something." She pranced across the field next to the lodge and into the underbrush. Trevor, still half-stunned by the cold and the sudden awakening, looked around. The horizon was slowly unveiling the face of the sun. It must have been nearing five-thirty. He quickly scurried after Gabby into the thicket.

Trevor traveled close behind Gabby in the small glimmers of the ever-growing light. The small branches of bushes grazed his shins and feet. Luckily, he was wearing the same jeans he had slept in. His feet crunched the undergrowth's remnants of twigs and fallen leaves. Their steps echoed through the trees. Gabby did not bother to look behind her as she walked. She walked with the most assurance and confidence that Trevor had ever seen from her.

Soon, the path started to widen and the trees seemed to have grown farther and farther apart. The trail welcomed them to a large opening where a fallen tree trunk lay in its final resting place. It no longer stretched its arms to the clear blue sky, but rested upon the dark brown, accepting dirt. Small sprigs of other vegetation embraced the tree in gratitude for their new sprung life. The neighboring trees wore bright green suits of moss upon their bark in remembrance.

They stood in silence as the sun continued to touch the patient plants that awaited its arrival all night. Finally, Gabby ran to a nearby rock, jumped upon it and placed her hands on her hips. She breathed in a deep breath as if she were trying to contain all the morning air in her lungs. Her shoulders and arms moved with her emphatic breath. With a grace and speed that Trevor had never seen from the usual calm, demure girl, Gabby leaped from the rock and ran to the largest tree: a red fir. She touched its ancient bark, moving her hands across its coarse grooves. Her hands were seemingly moving through time as they moved further and further up the tree trunk. Trevor, half amused and half shocked by this new girl that stood before him, smiled. Finally awake from its deep slumber, the sun greeted the two through the tree leaves and rested upon Gabby.

"I used to come here all the time." Gabby broke the morning silence. "These forests, they are all so familiar to me. I used to run through this place as a kid." She smiled. "I remember I used to turn over those rocks over there to see the bugs scurry away." She kicked over a small rock and found a grey pill bug. In her fingers, it rolled into a small sphere. Gabby rolled the bug between her fingers, back and forth, back and forth. She gently placed it under a neighboring rock and chuckled to herself. She pointed to the fallen tree. "Last time I came here, this tree…it was still standing." She directed Trevor to the remaining splintered tree stump.

"A lot has changed since I last came here." Gabby's smile slowly disappeared and her eyes glazed over for just a moment as if she had just traveled some place afar. Trevor was about to speak, as if to bring her back, but just as suddenly as her spirit seemed to leave, she came back to him. "I want to show you one more thing." Without another word, Gabby began to hike up an ascending trail. The trail hugged a steep slope, having been carved into the terrain by other more intrepid hikers. One careless step would lead to a

147

week of bumps and bruises into the bushes below. The trail continued to carve up the hill, further and further up. The trees that once towered over them began to clear and soon, Gabby's steps slowed.

Trevor, with great heaving breaths, caught up to her. Hands on his knees, he looked up at Gabby. The sun, new in the east, rested upon Gabby as the sweat on her brow glistened. "Gabs, where are we going?" Trevor heaved. He couldn't advance one more step. All his cross country training and biking hadn't prepared him for such a hike.

"Gabs, where are we going?" Trevor repeated.

Gabby lifted her arms and exhaled. "We are here." Her eyes panned to a clearing on top of the hill. The clearing was covered with long grass, bright yellow mustard plants, and brilliantly vibrant poppy flowers. In the newly rising sun and the gentle breeze, the field was brushed with gentle yellows, royal purples, and fresh greens. It was all new, all in time, all sun-kissed. Gabby smiled. The corners of her mouth seemed to touch the very tips of her ears. It was the biggest smile Trevor had ever seen. They began walking through the long grass. Their hands grazed the tips of the grass, each blade sliding through their fingers. There were no footpaths set before them. Gabby, still smiling, started to hop through the grass. She was alive again. Trevor, still panting, began to smile too.

"Gabs, you're crazy." He chuckled as he chased after her. Catching a second wind, he caught up to the frolicking Gabby. Without skipping a beat, they began to skip across the field. Their laughter echoed down the field, into the familiar forest, and into the very azure sky. They picked some poppies and tumbled into the tall grass, creating a nest of vegetation below them. They sighed with great relief. For once in their life, they felt at home.

They lay there in the grass for what seemed like several passing days. The sky rotated like a kaleidoscope full of effervescent clouds. After a few moments of hearing the wind whistle through the waves of grass, Gabby pointed at the passing clouds. As the clouds hovered above them, they looked like graceful, white brushstrokes upon a sea of blue canvas. Oh how beautiful they were. Yet Gabby knew that these wonderful, God given clouds were here today and gone tomorrow and she felt a tinge of sadness seep into her soul. The sadness did not overcome her though. She no longer would bow before that throne. In this moment where beauty was finite and happiness fleeting, she did not lay her head low. Gabby realized that she did not have time to be sad by the disappearance of beauty. She only had enough time to revel in the fading seconds of such marvelous, God-made strokes upon the world.

Gabby smiled and Trevor must have noticed her happiness emanate from her. Lying in the grass, he turned his body toward her.

"What's so funny?" he asked. It was one of those questions boys ask when they know nothing.

Gabby turned to him, her happiness still emanating from her spirit.

"I just thought about how those clouds up there look like a painting. It is like God painted those clouds himself."

Trevor lay back down and stared into the clouds. Gabby was sure that a mind like Trevor's was trying to think of the most witty line about the clouds. "God must have been a fan of impressionism." or "God sure does love blue and white." That made her happy to think about. Trevor always tried to make her happy.

149

"That one looks like a dog." He smiled. He turned to her and his eyes appeared as large as she had ever seen them. She smiled in return, letting out a small chuckle. Trevor still surprised her even now. The clouds continued to pass as if nothing had changed.

"I have one last thing to show you before we go." Gabby sprang up and ran down the slope. She did not turn around as she ran through the blades of grass, but she heard Trevor quickly behind her. Soon, he was beside her in a steady trot. He jogged so effortlessly, his hair tousled in the wind, going here and there across his face. As the field declined into a level, flat ground, Gabby, nearly out of breath, began to slow her pace and stopped in the middle of the flat field. Trevor brushed back his brown hair and stopped right next to her.

"Man, I am tired. You're pretty fast. You should join the cross-country team." He put his hands to his knees even though he did not break a sweat. Gabby guffawed.

"Not even in my wildest dreams." She caught herself breathing heavily from the run. It was exhilarating. She inhaled deeply so her chest rose heavily and let out a loud yell. It echoed up the field and resonated into the very clouds.

The hairs on Trevor's skin rose and he jumped with a fright.

"What the…what was that for?" Trevor stared at Gabby. Gabby felt relieved.

"Now that felt good! Now I am ready!" Gabby shook her whole body, making sure to loosen any dead spots that remained about her. Trevor still stared at her, awaiting her answer. Just as suddenly as her deafening shout, she began to sing. Her voice came out effortlessly and cleanly. It was the best singing voice she'd had in a long time. She felt free from her troubles, from her woes, from her discontent, and her voice clearly echoed her new attitude.

"The hills are alive with the sound of music! With songs they have sung for a thousand years! The hills fill my heart with the sound of music. My heart wants to sing every song it hears!" Gabby sang with an unparalleled joy as her lovely voice echoed through the green grass, through the timeless trees, and through the steady winds into the picturesque sky.

Trevor's stare changed, from one of sheer bewilderment to one of sheer happiness.

"Gabby, that was amazing. You had me scared for a second with that scream, but man that was amazing! You definitely are one of a kind." He laughed and smiled at her.

Gabby smiled.

Gabby was free.

G&T

L ate that night, Gabby got a phone call from home. It was her mom.

Immediately as she answered the phone, her body tensed up and her heartbeat sped up at the fury raging in her mom's voice.

"Gabby, come home right now! How could you miss school for three days? How could you do this to me?"

"I don't want to be at home."

"What is wrong with you? Why not?"

"Why not? Because of Dad!"

"So what? What's the big deal?"

Gabby couldn't believe Mom couldn't see how Dad being like that was bothering Gabby. Her mom continued to scream into the phone.

"You come back home right now. You have to get good grades! You have to get into Harvard."

"Do you only care about me getting into Harvard?"

Her mom continued to shriek nonsensical things in her high-pitched, screeching tone.

Angry tears flooding from her eyes, Gabby finally hung up the phone, in disbelief that Mom could not even see what she might be going through.

Hearing the ruckus in the room next door, Trevor sat rigid on his bed, alert and tense. He searched his mind for what he could do. He decided to wait until Gabby felt comfortable talking about it with someone. Thirty minutes passed. Gabby's room was noiseless.

Finally, he decided to go outside and throw a pebble at Gabby's window because he knew that always made her smile. Also, he did not want to wake Aunt Marie.

In the gnawing silence of her room, Gabby sat on her bed, holding her arms, still resentful and bitter. "Why do I have to deal with a mom like that all my life?" she thought, though she didn't form the words. Suddenly, a light object hit her window, shattering the silence.

Immediately, Gabby smiled a slight smile, welcoming Trevor's presence. Opening the window, she looked down and saw Trevor smiling up at her in his yellow parka that she had grown to love since that day at the beach.

Running down the stairs, she jumped off the last step and quickly grabbed her jacket off the coat rack as she exited the house in her leather flip flops.

153

Trevor was waiting at the swings, where he knew Gabby felt comfortable talking and liked a lot.

Gabby approached him quickly, smiling, but still holding her arms as if trying to shield herself still from her mom, who was 350 miles away.

"Hey!" she said brightly, but quietly.

Trevor wordlessly came up to her and softly hugged his friend. "I didn't mean to but I heard your conversation with your mom. Well, not the words you said but yeah, the tone of it...all."

Gabby looked up, thankful in a way that someone had heard. She had always wanted a witness.

"Yea?" she asked hopefully.

"Are you okay?"

Gabby swallowed, trying to prevent the tears from coming. It was the first time. No one had been there for her when her mom screamed at her constantly for no reason, not even Dad. Dad just stayed in his study, not bothering to intervene. Gabby realized then, that no one had defended her all this time.

Looking at Trevor, she felt a rush of emotion overwhelm her soul and she hugged him again.

She was silent, her mind thinking a thousand things but saying nothing.

Trevor stood calmly and let her hug him.

Looking into Gabby's two eyes, Trevor reflected her sorrow in his own two doe eyes.

Gabby stepped back, startled. "Why do you feel sad for me?" she was about to mouth.

And then she realized–she had never imagined that anyone would care. Since her mom didn't care about her feelings, she didn't expect anyone else would. Her feelings were trampled on repeatedly.

Feeling uncomfortable and awkward, Gabby looked down. "Trevor, let's talk about something else," she said quickly.

Trevor's mind flashed back to all the times Gabby ran away from him, ran away from facing the pain that was so present in her heart. Then, he knew–she was afraid to feel everything because it might be too much for her.

"Gabby," he said clearly but with tears in his throat.

Gabby turned to look at him.

For what seemed like an eternity, they stood, five feet apart, just looking at each other. It was as if the universe were spinning and they stood still in time.

Gabby felt afraid to face the truth but in Trevor's gaze she felt a safety and a courage to do so–to simply be herself for the first time.

At that moment, tears started running from her eyes in steady streams, trickling down at different rates down her two cheeks. She quickly wiped them away, leaving cool wetness on her hands in the cold night air.

"Let's go inside," she said, ashamed.

Trevor did not let her go this time.

"Gabby, your mom should not treat you like that," he said in a surprisingly deep, mature-sounding voice.

Gabby stood still in her tracks, her back to him.

She looked down, sorrowful and feeling naked.

The words didn't even sink in because she had been hit so many times; she had heard the opposite message for so many years.

Once again he called into her heart.

"Is that how it's always been?"

"Yeah," Gabby said, resentment in her voice. "For as long as I could remember."

She grew more honest. "That's why I'm here. Because after my dad became like that, I–Both of my parents were...yea, you know the rest."

Suddenly the truth hit Trevor and it startled him. Trevor always felt he was missing one of his parents, but here was Gabby, who had both of her parents alive, and yet they couldn't be relied on. She was basically alone, fending for herself all this time.

Gabby looked at the ground for a second, a look of discomfort on her young face, now furrowed. She felt found out. Her family secret was out. What if it got back to her mom? What would she do?

"Don't tell anyone," she wanted to tell Trevor. But she was too tired to move her lips and form the words. Instead, she walked down the path toward the forest to be alone.

"Gabby, it's dangerous. I'll go with you," Trevor called out after her.

Gabby stopped and stared into the black forest that felt more welcoming than the thought of her own parents. Motioning to Trevor, she let him come along, and he quickly ran to accompany her into the dark, which he usually was afraid of. Clutching her arm, he walked courageously into the dark, not even turning on his flashlight, wanting to let Gabby hide herself and her story in the dark.

A single wolf howled a mournful tune to the yellow of the moon in the distance.

~

After their nighttime walk, Trevor lay awake, thinking of all his childhood memories growing up. His dad's warm, easy smile. The way his dad hugged him when he got home from work and said "My son" with a light in his eyes. The way his parents waltzed and laughed across their small living room floor. His mom's lovely face and the smile creases by her mouth and eyes from years of blessing people with her warmth and joyful presence. Her easy laugh. Endless baking of cookies during the holidays to satisfy Trevor's sweet tooth.

He lifted up his life and Gabby's side by side like he was looking at two photographs next to each other. One appeared vivid and bright like the glow of colorful Christmas light bulbs. Gabby's photograph appeared like a blank grey photograph that was developed wrong.

Rubbing his face with one hand, Trevor lay with his eyes closed, trying to process everything he just learned about Gabby Choi's life. Turning to his side and lying still as a statue under the covers, Trevor recalled Gabby in middle school and how she walked confidently around school as eighth grade student body

157

president. On spirit days, she wore their class color, bright red, from head to toe, even with red shoelaces tying her braided hair. She always went all out, for everything. She was the leader that others looked up to. It looked like she had everything going for her.

In the first few years of high school she was always waving at people in the hallways with her caring smile. When Trevor would watch her lead California Scholarship Federation meetings in front of a hundred students, he could never have perceived that she had this brokenness in her life.

At that moment, in the stillness of his cool room, slanted streaks of moonlight shining across his covers, Trevor remembered Gabby's faith. She talked about God to almost everyone.

"Maybe that's what made her so confident, and joyful," Trevor thought quietly. "How else could she live the way she did?"

Meanwhile, Gabby, drenched in the fatigue which she always felt after one of Mom's tirades, lay in her bed. She used to read the Bible whenever her mom screamed at her. God was her comfort. She hadn't called on God in so long. For the first time in forever, she actually wanted to talk to God. Trevor's friendship and love had opened her heart and made her realize that God still loved her, even though her life felt like a wreck...that he was still with her, even now during this dark time.

"God?" she said, surprised at the timidity in her own voice. She sank a little bit beneath the old covers pulled up to her chin, shy and unsure because she hadn't prayed in so long. She cleared her throat a little, her voice ringing like a bell in the cool, crisp air of the night.

"I'm sorry I didn't...pray to you in so long. Hi," Gabby said, with a little chuckle. "Please forgive me," she added, feeling guilty for abandoning God for so long.

"I was–really upset. I was upset at you, mad at you, actually, because of Dad." Great tears bulged in Gabby's eyes, surprising her, making her wonder where they had come from.

Then, she cried before God.

And the same comfort that she had always felt with Him came, even in her bed all the way in Aunt Marie's cabin, and she felt safe, as if she were a baby being rocked in the arms of God himself.

She cried like a baby.

He watched, and listened, and spoke into her heart. "I love you, Gabby. I love you. It's okay. I'm not mad at you. I love you."

And that was all it took for her to feel better. Her eyes closed, Gabby let her head sink into the softness of her pillow and she glided into a deep and peaceful slumber, her heart having been comforted by her Father.

G&T

Having read that exercise is good for people with depression, Trevor decided to teach Gabby a little bit of basketball every day. He loved basketball anyway, and Gabby had told him she wanted to get better at it.

One afternoon, they decided to play a game of one-on-one basketball for the first time. Gabby spread her arms apart and her right hand shadowed the ball at all times. Her eyes were glued to the ball, and she tried to hit the ball out of Trevor's hands at every chance she could get. She would not let him get past her. Trevor chuckled loudly at this competitiveness he had never seen before in her. He upped his intensity, too. Trevor dribbled extra low to the ground so that Gabby couldn't get her hands on the ball, his back bent forward almost ninety degrees. It was a close game, but finally, Trevor made the game-winning shot, and Gabby just stared at him in amazement. He smiled as bulging droplets of sweat fell from the tips of his soaked hair.

Grabbing his water bottle off the ground, Trevor poured all the cool water onto his head as he leaned forward. Gabby giggled loudly as he vigorously shook his head several times, water droplets flying off his curly bed of hair in all directions. Gabby thought to herself that he looked like a dog that had just taken a bath and was drying itself.

Gabby took a gulp of her water and neatly wiped the sweat off her forehead and the sides of her lean face.

"Trevor, I never watched you play on our school team," Gabby huffed, "but you must've been really good." A feeling of guilt crept into Gabby just then. "He's here with me, missing out on school, and basketball," she thought.

"Trevor, aren't you worried about school? Are you sure you don't want to go back?" Gabby vocalized her thoughts.

"No, I'm fine," Trevor replied quickly with a hint of cynicism. Gabby thought for a second before she spoke again. She couldn't understand why this smart guy was so nonchalant about his grades.

"Trevor, where do you see yourself in ten years?" Gabby asked, sounding a lot like her father, who loved to ask her that question. Trevor looked extremely uncomfortable for a second.

"I don't know. I really don't know," he stammered, rolling the basketball toward the corner of the court where they kept it.

Gabby's face fell but she quickly tried to fix it with a hopeful smile. Just then she felt something deep within her soul. She knew there was something broken inside of this wonderful person she had come to know. He was smart, ingenious, brilliant, and on top of that, so caring and personable. Something wasn't right. Once more, she thought outside of her own sphere of

161

troubles and, looking over at Trevor, sought to know the world from which he came.

As Trevor went to use the restroom, Gabby sat in the treehouse, where she could think privately away from view. She thought long and hard about what Trevor was like in the past. In elementary school, he was so cute. He was the one happy boy with those half-moon smiling eyes that would be singing loudly as he walked onto the playground. He was cheery and bright. It struck Gabby then that in middle school, something shifted. Trevor would walk around with his hood on, hands in his pockets, not saying anything. Gabby could still see that faded greenish grey jacket he'd always be wearing. She was never close to Trevor so she hadn't thought deeply about why he had changed. She just supposed he was going through the sulky period of puberty.

Empathetic as she was, Gabby thought of Trevor's mom's death and how that might've impacted him. "Hmm…if one of my parents had died in middle school…" she imagined. It would've felt as if half of her was gone.

Just then, she heard Trevor's footsteps crunching on twigs and she quickly wrapped up her musings. Looking up into his eyes, Gabby smiled brightly.

Later that night, Gabby lay awake in her bed, unable to sleep. She thought about how strange her life was, being here, not at home. Turning onto her side, she stared at the tan leather journal that lay on her nightstand. Feeling the smooth cover with one hand, she remembered the one journal entry she had written about Trevor. Lying on her back, she stared up at the old-fashioned white ceiling that looked like it had tiny craters in it and thought about Trevor, who was so kind to come all the way here for her, and be so gracious. Suddenly her heart went from cold to warm, thinking about him. She wanted to give back to him for all he had done and was doing for her. She wished she could help him.

Trevor also lay awake, as he usually did. He stared off at nothing, wondering where his life was headed. All he saw was a dense cloud of vagueness–but then he remembered Gabby and the passion that had sprung up inside of him that fueled him to come this far to help her. It made him feel alive, but still, he was worried. The only thing he was interested in was writing, but how could he make a living out of that? What direction would he head in after high school? Everyone else seemed so sure, so passionate, so talented, in something. Everyone except him.

In their uncertainties, the two youths fitfully fell asleep, unaware that they were headed toward the very thing that they were searching for all of their lives.

G&T

Two days later, around ten in the morning, Gabby was in the middle of a good dream. She and Trevor were at the beach, playing by the waves and laughing and splashing each other. The late morning sun shone across her bed and over her eyes, making her squint. She yawned and stretched in her bed like a baby squirrel. Her eyes closed, she smiled, nestling again into her bed. As soon as she thought of sleeping some more, the thought of hanging out with Trevor filled her mind and her eyes opened wide with glee. She hopped out of bed and ran out the door, not caring if he saw her mismatched purple and blue checkered pajamas that she had borrowed from Aunt Marie. She ran all around the house in her baggy, overly long pajama pants with a silly grin on her face, but Trevor was nowhere to be found.

Peeking outside the living room window, she knew Trevor wouldn't go far without her. He was too thoughtful. Sure enough, he was seated at the treehouse entrance, scratching his head and doing something with great scrutiny and concentration. Running

164

upstairs and slapping on her outdoor clothes, Gabby ran out the front door, but began walking calmly as she approached the treehouse so she could peek on what he was doing and also maybe not look so excited to see him.

Trevor didn't even notice her approaching. A small black notebook the size of a palm lay in the center of his lap, and he rubbed his head as he peered down at the open notebook.

"HEEY!" Gabby said joyfully and breathlessly.

Trevor jumped and looked extremely startled.

"What?" Gabby responded, smiling and looking very free in her spirit.

A smile formed across Trevor's face, which was pale and slightly haggard, as if he had woken up very early.

"Hey Gabby!" Trevor exclaimed politely and warmly with a growing grin.

"Whatcha doing?" Gabby asked, continuing to be playful.

"Nothing," Trevor quickly said, turning to put his notebook behind him inside the treehouse.

Gabby snatched the book from behind his back and wiggled it in triumph. She giggled with a toothsome smile crinkling up her face, but did not open the notebook.

"Hey," Trevor moaned. "Give it."

"Why?" Gabby got more curious. "Is it your diary?" she teased.

"No," Trevor replied quickly with an embarrassed smile.

She stared in wonder and curiosity at the smooth, hard front cover of the tiny notebook, bound by a single thin black elastic band. She looked at the back. It was a Moleskine notebook. "Fancy," she thought. Gabby paused for a second in silence, to be polite and to respect his privacy.

Trevor looked as if he were becoming more open to the idea of showing Gabby, so, reading his face, Gabby asked sweetly, "Can I please read a little part?"

Trevor laughed shyly with a half-contrived look of shock on his face and scratched his head.

"All right," he gave in. Like a wizened, expert author, he took the notebook carefully and studied the pages in order to open the notebook up to the exact page he wanted Gabby to read.

"Are you a writer? Do you write?" Gabby asked, excitement running through her body.

"I guess you can say that," Trevor replied.

"So am I!" Gabby replied, shocked they shared this in common. "I've loved writing stories since I was little!" she added, wide-eyed and grinning ear to ear. She had never met another friend who was into writing for fun.

Gabby then caught her breath and began to read Trevor's small, slender, thoughtful-looking handwriting across the page. Gabby got into her literary analysis mode, like the English nerd she was, and she detected that Trevor's writing had a passive, calm, dismal mood. She then noticed tiny jagged pieces of paper protruding from the center of the notebook; he had ripped some pages completely out.

"Why'd you rip them out?" she asked, her curiosity in full expression.

"I rip out my writing if I read it over and I don't like it."

"Why?" Gabby asked, totally mind-boggled. "I would never do that," Gabby thought to herself.

Trevor smiled weakly at the barrage of questions. He had always kept his writing private and did not want anyone to see his product until he deemed it perfect and worthy.

Trevor smiled tentatively as Gabby began reading his selected page in silence.

"Oooh." Gabby suddenly interrupted his mute introspection. "This part! I like it!" Her eyes were peering laser beams at the lines as if it were a great treasure she had never seen before.

Trevor laughed but did not say a word.

"I've never seen writing like this!" Gabby frankly observed. "You should keep writing, Trevor," she said, finally looking up at him from the pages.

"Nah," Trevor replied, thinking Gabby was just being nice.

"I'm serious!" Gabby said, much like an older sister.

Trevor observed how much brighter and stronger Gabby had grown. He didn't pay any mind to his writing. Caring for Gabby came first to him.

Gabby read Trevor's facial expressions and could tell he didn't think much of his writing. She reread a portion. She looked up at Trevor's face, studying it cautiously. In that moment, Gabby got a sense deep inside her heart from the tone of his writing and from his appearance that he was stuck somehow, like a stream that had met some rocks and could not flow forward. She continued to peer at his face, young, yet simultaneously appearing old. Gabby then noticed how Trevor's broad shoulders were always hunched forward a little. He seemed as if he were carrying a weight, a weight he had carried for a very long time. In studying him for those long but short moments, Gabby's heart knew things that Trevor had never told anyone.

Trevor looked quietly at Gabby as she smiled at the pages of his Moleskine. His heart had moved in that moment when she told him she liked his writing. She was filled with this infectious hopefulness despite the darkness of this period in her life. Her kindness filled his heart with hope like a dry well with water.

"Thanks, Gabby," Trevor said, clearing his throat.

A light filled Gabby's eyes, glad that she had encouraged him a little. "Keep writing, Trev," she said again warmly and honestly.

"What did you like to write about?" Trevor asked, changing the subject, offering Gabby the orange homemade cushion he had been sitting on since the floor of the treehouse was hard.

"No, it's okay," Gabby said quickly, but Trevor insisted, and placed the cushion on the floor next to Gabby like a genuine gentleman. Not knowing what to do in response to this act of service, she just smiled and sat gratefully on top of the soft cushion, thanking Trevor.

"I liked writing stories about imaginary places. Like, the character would encounter a magical object that would take them to another realm. One time, I wrote about my family's trip to

Canada—we saw so many animals there—and gave the essay I wrote to my fifth grade teacher on the first day of school, even though she didn't even ask for it." Gabby's eyes wandered back to her child self and they lit up. "I was weird," she added with a chuckle.

Trevor, his chin resting in his right palm, leaned against his elbow and watched Gabby as she avidly described everything. She had gotten more talkative during their stay at Aunt Marie's. He saw that she was becoming happier, and freer. And he learned that the true Gabby Choi was still in there, beneath the weight of her chains. He hoped he could help her stay free and become freer with time.

Gabby, meanwhile, continued to stare into Trevor's face, trying to pick up clues to who he was, to his past—the parts of him that he didn't talk about.

The two sat in the tree house, smelling the pine in the air, feeling very much at home with each other. Though Gabby had very little going for her, in this moment with Trevor she felt complete. She felt like she had everything.

Trevor, who was still looking into her face, felt the same.

They spent the entire afternoon in the treehouse, writing short stories, swapping them, giggling, and ooh-ing and ah-ing at each other's work. After making spaghetti for dinner with Aunt Marie, they were back at the treehouse, because Gabby wanted to "see the full moon above the treetops." Gabby got two mugs of cocoa for them, wanting to give back to Trevor for all he had done.

Gabby looked down at the two white marshmallow morsels bobbing up and down in their chocolatey bathtub, suddenly feeling the intimacy of being in the ever-darkening treehouse alone with Trevor. She cleared her throat, and kept looking down at her cocoa.

"Trevor," Gabby said softly, her voice suddenly full of shyness. "Thank you for coming for me." She looked up at him. Her voice grew a little stronger and was full of sincerity. "Thank you for skipping school and staying with me."

This caught Trevor's attention. Putting down his mug, he peered at Gabby's face.

It was full of serenity, wonder, and love. It had a warm glow that wasn't there when he first came. She looked almost like a cherub.

"You know, when I got here, I felt really lost and like my life was all a mess…but you somehow put it back into order again…piece by piece…like the Kelly Clarkson song." She giggled at the Kelly Clarkson reference.

Trevor smiled widely. "I didn't do anything, really," he said, as usual.

"No, you helped me tremendously. And Trevor, don't say you didn't do anything, anymore. Just like you helped me, I know, you're gonna help and strengthen so many other people."

No one had ever said something like that to Trevor, but somehow, deep inside, it rang true in him.

"Thanks, Gabs," he replied with a flattered grin.

With a sudden surge of energy, Trevor got up and boomed, "Wanna shoot some hoops?"

Gabby laughed, seeing the spurt of confidence in him. It was new and refreshing.

"Sure," she replied gleefully.

The two scurried down from the treehouse, and Trevor quickly grabbed the ball. Grabbing the ball that he tossed at her, Gabby spontaneously went for a three, which swooshed effortlessly. Clapping her hands together once loudly, she laughed and laughed, utterly surprised.

"Gabby…You are getting better than your basketball coach!" Trevor said in a playfully menacing voice.

Throwing the ball at Trevor with power, Gabby laughed, "Now you try, Coach!" Looking at the hoop with his signature sideways glance, Trevor aimed from the farthest corner of the court. Despite the low chances that both of them would make threes, Trevor made a perfect shot.

"Oh my gosh!" Gabby shouted and started laughing, and the two hugged each other, giggling.

Looking at Gabby, Trevor felt something new grow inside his heart. But he quickly looked away from her and picked up the ball again to play basketball. Gabby continued to look at him admiringly. She couldn't stop smiling when she was with Trevor Song.

~

The next day was the three-week mark since they had arrived at Aunt Marie's. Gabby wondered if she felt ready to go back to Toccoa. She wasn't sure why or how, but perhaps Trevor made her feel stronger. He kept telling her that God was there for her and that she could trust in Him. Trevor promised that God was going to help her family, and Gabby was starting to believe.

171

When Gabby told Trevor the news that she was ready to go back, he imagined how it would be to be back home, back at school. His heart fell with a vague emptiness. Rubbing his head, he realized he had gotten so used to spending time with Gabby everyday. She was the first person he'd see in the morning and the last face he'd see at night. He didn't want to go back to the way things were.

In the midnight hour of the last night at Aunt Marie's, Trevor lay awake counting the minutes till morning. Time seemed to run its own pace, abandoning its God-given pacing and laws. Minutes were hours. Hours were seconds. No matter the time, Trevor lay awake knowing the imminence of the situation. He had to tell Gabby that he, in his youth, in his heart, in his very being, loved her.

He ran the timeline of their relationship through his mind. The broken window. The flowers in the locker. The chicken soup. The walks through the forest and fields. All moments. They were once so vivid before, but these memories were being sieved through the gray of time. In the darkness, he attempted to paint the lines of the memories again, carefully going through details to make sure they were right, just like he remembered them, but these new strokes were too new. They lacked the details of a time lived in the moment, the feeling of breathed in, breathed out reality.

Yet, he remembered her face. He always remembered her. The look of unparalleled anguish, anger, sadness, and grief through the broken window. The bewildered wonder at the flowers from a mysterious admirer. The betrayal of a trust broken and the struggle for a trust renewed. The laughter. The look of a person now whole again. In the midnight hour, Trevor saw her, Gabby Choi.

Trevor's father, Steve, was a practical man with many idioms. "Actions are louder than words, Trev." In his friendship with Gabby, Trevor made sure that his actions spoke, but he still remained unsure, unsure in her knowledge of his heart for her.

"She has to know that I like her, right?" The thought scattered in the thick darkness of the room.

"There is a power in an utterance." Trevor remembered the pastor of his father's church coughing into the microphone. "God created the whole universe in an utterance."

"'Let there be light!'" The pastor theatrically threw out his right hand in the air, as if commanding the very divine powers that brought forth all being.

Trevor drew his hands from beneath his blankets and threw them in the air.

"She has to know!" he silently exclaimed in his thoughts.

His mind went back to that memory of leaving the flowers in her locker. In his memories, the flowers dimmed in comparison to Gabby's radiant face. Her face shined when she saw the flowers. The illuminating glow, as sadness and grief bowed to the brief happiness of being cherished, stayed with him. He wanted her to feel that way all the time with him.

"I have to tell her," Trevor whispered into the night. The words bounced off the wall and echoed into his ear.

"I have to tell her."

Gabby, in the early morning, slept fitfully as she dreamt a recurring dream. She went from this door to that, looking for Trevor; she dialed his phone number, but he was nowhere to be found. When she did find him, it seemed as if he did not know her, and he just smiled a mocking smile as if he were laughing at her. The image of him would disappear, and then once again, she'd be out looking for him, dialing his number, knocking on doors, but no Trevor, just figments, distortions of him.

Gabby awoke, feeling a numbness in her head, and placed her purple-socked feet on the ground to get out of bed. She didn't realize how hollow she felt.

Meanwhile, Trevor was lying in bed, smiling, rehearsing what he was going to say to Gabby that morning. He jumped out of bed and stood before his closet, rummaging for the best clothes he had brought to Aunt Marie's, sniffing this shirt and that to see if it smelled okay. He laid out his clothes on his bed and studied them like an artist.

Gabby stood at her mirror for a passing moment, gazing at her reflection for just a fleeting second, not realizing she did not like what she was seeing.

Just overnight, through her series of nightmares, she had been reduced to the former Gabby, the smaller Gabby. The Gabby that did not feel like anybody, that felt smaller than a somebody. Her dreams were a reflection of the Gabby that didn't feel she was loved.

Gabby, in her grey crewneck sweater and faded jeans, slowly closed her bedroom door and walked down the dimly lit hallway to the living room. As she passed, the photos of Aunt Marie's memories followed her, their smiles riding her shadow. The clatter of bowls and silverware echoed from the kitchen. Trevor rummaged through the kitchen, trying to find cereal when he finally saw Gabby standing at the mouth of the kitchen.

"Good morning, Gabby." His eyes shone with delight as he knew what he planned for today.

She weakly smiled and sat down at the table. Gabby ran her thumb across the inside of her fingers. She didn't notice Trevor sitting down in front of her, his gaze firmly affixed on her.

"Do you want some cereal?" He pushed the box towards her, but she shook her head as a response.

A panic started to descend upon Trevor. His young mind ran through the alerts. "She's not eating. She's not talking. She looks tired, but I can't say that to her. She must have had a bad dream. Just be kind."

Trevor flashed a comically big grin and opened the box of cereal, filling his bowl with cereal and the two-percent milk. Before his first bite, he looked at Gabby. She stared through the kitchen window to the forests that surrounded Aunt Marie's cabin.

"Where are you?" he wondered.

The first bite of the overly sweet cereal shocked his taste buds. He quickly gulped it down to rid his mouth of the flavor.

"So, what do you want to do today?" Trevor scooped another spoonful of cereal.

"I don't know," Gabby softly uttered, her voice barely louder than a whisper.

"She spoke!" Trevor's mind jumped at her words. He quickly stirred his spoon through his cereal.

"I was thinking, because we may have to leave soon, we could explore the forests one last time and maybe even have a bonfire." He lifted his gaze from the cereal bowl to gauge her response.

Gabby continued to stare out of the window as if his words were carried by the wind and taken far away.

"Dumb idea, Trevor. She hates bonfires. No one likes fires." Trevor scrambled to call her back. "Or we could do anything you want to do, Gabby." His words fell short at the doorstep of Gabby's mind.

In her mind, Gabby ran her fingers across the white walls of her room back at her house. Around the room, mementos littered the floor. Photographs of her family memories allured her with familiarity. She reached for a familiar photo of her and her parents at the beach. Her parents lifted her between them as her feet dangled in the air. She danced amongst the incoming waves along the seashore and giggled a song. After hours of play, her father carried her on his back and her mother kissed her forehead. Gabby remembered how she felt that day. Immeasurably happy. As quickly as it came, the memories dissolved, leaving an empty frame.

"Gabby." Trevor called to her for the third time. The cereal in his bowl was unrecognizable mush and his mind rummaged through the drawers hoping to find an answer to Gabby's condition.

She finally turned to him and her gaze was silent.

Trevor stared into her eyes for what seemed like an hour: searching, calling, running.

"I might as well give it to her now. That will cheer her up." Trevor quickly grabbed the paper on the counter and passed it to Gabby.

"I wrote this for you." The words tumbled out of his mouth. His hands slightly trembled and his heartbeat thumped against his rib cage.

Gabby's eyes fell upon the paper.

~

His fingers shook. He had been begging for hours and not one soul paid him any mind. A well-known craftsman, now out of work, out of trade, and out of time. His eyes fell, crestfallen. His hands attempted to steady the wooden bowl, the same bowl he had crafted, as the few coins jingled against one another. Ting. Ting. Ting.

As the sun cast looming shadows, the man retreated from the sun's gaze. He recalled the old adage. "For the eye of the universe judges all." Would he be judged for what he had done? Would he be judged for what he did not do? What would he do? The man pondered as a presence stepped before him.

The man's eye steadily rose from the jangle of coins and squinted at the sight. The sun stood beyond the figure's shoulder, defiant to the eyes. The figure leaned down, entering the shadow realm, and her face was bright as day. She smiled and laid a resplendent yellow-and-white daisy upon the wooden bowl. She had many flowers like that in a basket she carried. Before he could speak, the flower woman was gone. No trail of petals, but her presence remained.

Her flower lay within the bowl. The petals ran white at the edges to a golden center. Radiant. The beauty cracked the man's sun-glazed visage. A smile appeared on his face. He let out a chuckle underneath his worn breath. In his swiftest movements, the man stood up, his aching bones alive anew. The bowl turned over. The coins chattered upon the sidewalk. In resolute passion, the man bellowed to the waning sun. "I must thank the woman for her kind deed."

In a haste, the man went from person to person asking about the woman with flowers. Most met him with peculiar looks, judging stares, and dismissals with a wave of their hands, yet he persisted. Soon, a woman pointed him to a path that the woman with flowers walked every day. In his tattered and dirt-ridden clothes, he thanked her and hurried down the unfamiliar road.

Step. Step. Step. Step. The man hurried as the sun hung low. The roadside, barren at first, started to show life, as young seedlings took root. As he continued, the roadside greened, the seedlings flourishing into lush arrays. Greens turned to brilliant hues of yellow and white, their majesty leading him closer to the woman with flowers. The flowers sang a chorus to the gratitude he held in his heart. The joy beat in his chest as he turned the corner as the road bent.

He was met with ashes as the flowers were no more. What were once raucous colors of green, white, and gold were mute. Ashes rained from the trees as their timber fingertips cindered. Sitting in the rain, the woman with flowers stilled, her basket now empty. She stared at the burnt remains of a house once her own, the stone walls charred, the wood incinerated. The craftsman, unable to move, uttered in a near inaudible whisper.

"We will rebuild."

The wind began to blow the ashes from their settlements. The woman did not stir. The man's heart beat against his throat. Even louder, the words fell.

"We will rebuild. I will help you."

The man, with an ounce of courage and flower in hand, moved and gently placed the flower into the empty basket. As the ashes touched the petals, the woman grabbed the basket and stood up. Her actions were deliberate and measured, to hold her emotions in. Carefully, she smiled.

"Let's rebuild."

~

Trevor anxiously sat across from Gabby as she read the story. He tried not to stare at her, but he found his eyes wandering around the kitchen yet they always went back to her. He made mental notes of her every single detail and shuffled through the words that he wanted to say, waiting for the best moment to say what was on his mind. After his eighth time of reading the cereal's nutrition facts, he noticed Gabby, still holding the paper in her hands, was staring through the kitchen window again. Expressionless.

"Now is the moment." Trevor gathered his resolve.

"Gabby." As the word left his mouth, it rattled his teeth and fell on the table like a 50 pound barbell. She turned to him for the first time in the long morning.

"You and I have been through a lot." Trevor stared into his cereal as he stirred the disintegrated bits and tried his best to collect his thoughts. "I know the past has been difficult and so has the present, but I want to help you build a better future." He looked up from the bowl to see her eyes, stunningly brown, stare back at him.

The words beat in his chest. The words balled up their fists and knocked on his bones and shook every muscle fiber. As the words rallied into resolve and his resolve led to action, Trevor's eyes focused upon her and her stunningly brown eyes. He knew what he wanted to say all along.

"I will be there for you. I always want to be with you. Wherever you go, I will go. I am yours."

Gabby's eyes read the story with her mind, but her heart did not move. It wouldn't engage. It was just yesterday when she couldn't sleep because she was excited over the growing romance between her and Trevor. She weakly held the paper in her hand, standing up rigidly. It was as if her entire being had turned into wood. Gabby felt it all over, but she couldn't and wouldn't explain it to Trevor. But when she looked at Trevor's eyes she felt a flicker of something in her heart that was once there before, like a glimmer of a memory—a glimmer of light, beauty, hope. Where had it all gone? It felt like a thousand years ago. Without even realizing it, Gabby returned the paper to Trevor and she spoke without emotion, "Thanks Trevor, but I–I'm not ready for a relationship." That was the nicest thing she could produce at the moment. Trevor's sad puppy eyes held her gaze, as if pleading to Gabby. Gabby turned her head away from Trevor and she awkwardly looked toward the lake and the forest, the frigid wind blowing from the window straight through her heart.

Trevor could not understand what had overcome the sweet Gabby.

"Gabby!" he cried out finally in desperation, as Gabby left through the kitchen door and started walking down the forest trail.

But she was resigned to her fate–the fate of being alone.

Trevor helplessly stood there, his heart in the form of paper still in his hand, torn and in anguish, conflicted more than ever.

But Trevor did not cry until he found out from Aunt Marie that Gabby had left for home first, alone.

Texts from Trevor to Gabby:

Dear Gabby,

I just wanted to let you know that I'm here for you if you want to talk. It's okay if you want to stay friends. I just want to make sure you're okay. I'm here for you if you need anything.

~

Gabby,

You're worthy. You're beloved. You're the daughter of the King. He is with you.

~

Gabby,

Did you get home safely?

~

Gabby knew something was wrong with her heart; she just didn't feel. But she couldn't change it. Her self-hatred was so deep she couldn't see it was keeping her from feeling love. And when she felt this way, she couldn't let anyone in.

When Gabby arrived home, she felt grateful when she saw no one was home, and, laying her backpack next to the piano chair, she played an improvised melody. The songs that her fingers produced were always reflections of her heart, and God used to communicate with her during this intimate time of reflection in the past. She was thinking of nothing at all, when suddenly an image came into her mind: It was Trevor, carrying her out of a burning building, his face blackened by the flames. Gabby's heart stilled, and, shocked, she stopped playing on the keys. She knew the vision was from God. It was about what Trevor did for her. Gabby's heart raced and the emotion came flooding back into her heart like warm water over one's hands under a sink faucet. "Trevor saved me," she realized. Then, the harder realization sank in: "Trevor loves me." All her memories of him returned to her like an old-fashioned film reel: him dropping off chicken noodle soup at her doorstep when she was sick; him hugging her whenever she was crying; him coming all the way to Aunt Marie's; him talking to her about God...Suddenly, Gabby awoke from what had felt like a stupor and she abruptly stood up. Cupping her mouth with both hands, she could not believe what she had done.

"Oh my God, oh my God!" she said quietly and then more loudly as she paced the living room.

Grabbing her phone, she reread Trevor's last text and realized that she had ignored him for an entire day.

Tears emerging in her eyes, she called Trevor, but his phone was off.

On the bus, Trevor was fast asleep and his phone had died in his palm.

Gabby searched her living room, wildly wishing she had done things differently.

Meanwhile, Trevor awoke from a stressful sleep, not knowing that Gabby had called. Something in his heart told him that it had more to do with Gabby than him, but so many other voices haunted him, saying that he deserved to be rejected. He tried to drown out these voices but they were too powerful. He succumbed, and his heart grew slowly hardened against Gabby and opening his heart to her again. His story lay in his backpack, the impact of the story not having been felt yet, the magic lingering in between the words.

As time passed, what Gabby had done sank in for her even more and she couldn't bring herself to talk to Trevor. She felt so guilty and she didn't feel she deserved a second chance. But then she couldn't do anything else but think about him. She wanted to be with him. She wanted to be with him all the time.

They missed each other, but in silence.

Gabby could barely sleep that night, tossing, turning, ruminating about Trevor, and woke up at 6:02 just as the sun was beginning to rise. She sat up in bed, her bare soles against the hardwood floor, all her feelings of missing Trevor coming back to her like floodwaters. She abruptly stood up. She knew she had to do something.

183

"Do I confess to him?" She lit up at the idea, a smile spreading across her sleep-deprived face. Her heart started to race. This was what she wanted to do. She sat at her desk, full of fiery conviction. Taking out her treasured journal, she quickly wrote down everything she wanted to say to him. Meanwhile, she earnestly prayed to God, asking if Trevor was "the One," the one she had been waiting to meet her whole life. And she felt that God was saying yes. God told her the word, "Cornerstone," which Gabby interpreted to mean that their love would be built on the solid foundation of God's love.

After asking Trevor if she could visit him later that afternoon, Gabby excitedly opened her closet and rummaged for the prettiest dress she owned. It was a navy blue spring dress with tiny flowers of various bright pastel colors that came down to her knees. As afternoon approached, she put some mascara on, which she never did, and made sure her hair was smooth, shiny, and flawless. After applying a rose tinted lip gloss to her lips to make a subtle, feminine look, she looked over herself for the hundredth time in the mirror, then swiftly left home for Trevor's house.

Gabby parked in front of his place and breathlessly made it to the front of his house. She arrived at the steps of cracked, faded pink paint and looked down at her feet for a second. Looking up, she shook away her doubt and got ready for the big moment. A slight breeze ruffled her hair and she smoothed out her hair once more and cleared her throat.

She reached for the doorbell and pressed it quickly to overcome her jitters. In a couple of long moments, the door opened and Gabby's heart felt a shock as she came face to face with Trevor. He had a smile, but an uncomfortable smile, like the "I'm happy to see you but I don't know what to think" kind of smile.

He didn't know what to make of two days of silence from Gabby.

"Have a seat," Trevor quickly said, motioning to the familiar living room armchair Gabby had often sat on.

Suddenly, Gabby felt overcome with fear, and she followed Trevor a little into the kitchen where he was about to reach for some orange juice to give to his guest.

In the voice of a small mouse, Gabby asked timidly, "Can we drive somewhere? Like to Rocketship Park?"

Trevor's confident, easy smile concealed his thudding heart.

"Sure," he said briskly and curtly and closed the refrigerator door promptly.

Driving over to the park, the two mulled over everything in silence and Trevor, sensing Gabby's uneasiness, cranked up the country radio station. Gabby breathed a little better and smiled slightly out the window.

"I wonder what she's thinking of," Trevor thought as he glimpsed Gabby looking out the passenger window. He knew she always did that when she was in deep reflection over something.

When Trevor parked in front of Rocketship Park it was just as the sun was sinking below the sea and its hues drenched the bright green hills with its last burst of golden hues. Some of the orange golden light shimmered on Gabby's lush brown locks and on the tips of her eyelashes.

Trevor turned his body toward Gabby to face her and study her visage, but Gabby continued to stare out the right top corner of the windshield and continued thinking.

Just as Trevor was about to wonder if Gabby was going to stay silent forever, Gabby spoke in a clear, sure voice.

"Trevor, when you told me you liked me, I didn't feel ready for it." She kept looking out the corner of the windshield.

"I was a mess. My family was a mess. I had no idea where I was headed. And you liking me just didn't make sense to me. I had nothing to give you but these fractured pieces of my life."

A single tear emerged from Gabby's eyes but she quickly and confidently brushed it away.

"I didn't feel–lovable, so I was scared that someone would like me. But the thing is–you're the best thing that ever happened to my life. Sometimes, I feel afraid because you're too good to be true in a way. All I ever knew was the wrong kind of people. I'm sorry I didn't talk to you for the past few days…"

"It's okay, Gabby," Trevor interjected.

"I really like you," Gabby said, looking at Trevor with her doe eyes sparkling with a veil of tears. Trevor looked at her and smiled widely in disbelief and shock. "I like everything about you." Gabby laughed, smearing her mascara a little as she wiped away her tears. It was as if a huge load had been lifted off her chest finally.

It was the first time anyone had ever said that to Trevor. His heart felt as if it had expanded three thousand times its size, and completely captured by her in that moment, he turned to face Gabby.

She smiled a bright, genuine smile and studied his eyes, wondering how someone like him existed, and that he loved her.

Trevor did the same, looking down shyly, and then looking up again with a great sheepish grin and tears in his crystal clear, loving brown eyes.

Trevor brought her in for an embrace suddenly and stroked the back of her head protectively, knowing it took a lot out of Gabby to say those words and so relieved that she had.

"I was almost afraid you would never talk to me again," Trevor admitted weakly.

Gabby laughed, seeing Trevor be so honest in this way. She smiled, nudging her face against his cheek and holding his shoulders.

Holding each other like that for what seemed like an eternity, it finally washed over them–the truth that they were now together, and that they were really, really happy.

~

Journal #5

OMG I TOLD TREVOR I LIKE HIM. I CAN'T BELIEVE IT.

TREVOR IS MY BOYFRIEND NOW! I AM SOOOO HAPPY!!!! :) :) :)

God, thank you so much for bringing us together. Thank you for sending Trevor into my life. I love you so much!!!

~

That night, Gabby sat at her piano, her fingers resting upon the cool, soft keys. She recalled that day that Trevor confessed his feelings to her and how her heart had gone numb. A grin spread across her face as she remembered the fiery conviction that had overcome her and led her to confess her feelings to him. Sighing a happy sigh, she felt inspired to play a song, but then she suddenly got the idea to create an original song for Trevor. Her heart fluttering wildly, she grabbed her phone and pressed record on the recording app. Sitting tall on the piano chair, she smiled excitedly as she got ready to play. Her fingers began to dance across the keys in sync with her heart. The song overflowed with the appreciation she felt for Trevor for all he had done for her. When she was done, she played the song and was shocked at what she heard. It actually reflected their journey together. She decided to name the song "Trevor in Gabby's Wanderings."

~

Listen to "Trevor in Gabby's Wanderings" on Gabby's blog here: www.gabbysmelody.com

Trevor's black Toyota Corolla sighed as it relaxed into the all-too-familiar curbside parking spot in front of his house. Trevor turned off the car and sat in the front seat, recollecting all that had happened to his life since he met Gabby. Like pages in his favorite book, he revisited a moment again: her smile when she received those flowers. He had driven to several different grocery stores and florists to find the right bouquet. He picked up, smelled, and put down more flowers than he ever thought he would in his lifetime. It was all worth it, though, because he would do it all again to see Gabby Choi smile again.

Trevor tapped the top of his steering wheel with his left palm and chuckled to himself, the night's darkness embracing the suburban neighborhood as lights from houses spotlighted the street. He flipped to a different moment, the mental ink on the page still wet, fresh, and so real. "I really like you. I like everything about you." Gabby's soft, brown eyes resolutely shined a determination

189

that only love can flame and in that fiery light, Trevor basked in the glow, the irreplaceable warmth of being loved and loving someone.

He opened the middle compartment of his car and on top of all the folded Jack in the Box and Carl's Jr. coupons, the turquoise vase shard glimmered in the street lights. Carefully, he picked up the shard with his thumb and index finger and placed it on his left palm. He ran his right index finger across its edges, its sharpness summoning the surreal shine of Gabby's living room once again. In his memory, Trevor imagined walking across the street and onto the front lawn of Gabby's house, peering into the shattered bay window. Gabby, still, sat on the couch, her head in her hands. Her silhouette, once shadowed by the living room's halogen lamp's brightness, filled with color and life as the surrounding arraying hues dimmed. He reached out to her, but as soon as he attempted, the memory faded, the book closed, and he was greeted by the night's darkness again.

There, in that old Toyota Corolla, in front of the house he always lived in, he tightly folded his hands together, closed his eyes, and let out a new prayer.

"God, I know I don't talk to you much, but please love Gabby. Renew her family. Revive the dead places and bring them to life, once again. Amen."

He opened his eyes. The street lights still spotlighted the streets and the neighbors in their homes stirred, busily shuffling between activities before sleep caught up to them. Unfurling his tightly folded hands, the turquoise shard left deep imprints upon his palm. Trevor carefully lifted it and placed it back on top of the coupons in the middle compartment.

"I like you." The words rang in his head once again. Trevor could not believe that the whole city of Toccoa did not shake after those words. He took out his phone to text Gabby once more before he went into his all too familiar home.

"What should I say?" Trevor thought. "A thank you?" He shook his head. What words can follow the ones that Gabby had uttered to create a new life in him? Trevor smiled and turned on his phone's camera.

To commemorate the moment, like fresh ink on the page, Trevor sent a text to Gabby. "To remember the night." The text was christened with a smiling photo of Trevor in the front seat of his black Toyota Corolla in front of the all-too-familiar house as the lights of the neighborhood spotlighted upon him.

The lights seemed to follow him, every step, to the front door of his house. The young man turned around and saw that the neighborhood was as it always was, but that he was the one that was new.

S tanding before Mirror Lake High School the next day for the first time in three weeks, Gabby felt a sense of relief, like a coming home. She looked expectantly at the gates painted a dark bronze, which had always welcomed the star student and filled her with anticipation. But as she kept staring at her beloved school, her mind traveled to all of the missteps she had made during the past school year. A dread overcame her soul, and she suddenly turned around, her back to the school.

At that moment Trevor found her hand and held it in his. Gabby jumped a little because this was the first time they were holding hands. Electricity traveled up and down her body. Looking down at the ground, she felt her heart all aflutter like feathers blowing in the wind, and she smiled shyly and bashfully.

"It's the first time a guy is holding my hand," she whispered to her new boyfriend, while still looking down at the sidewalk.

Courteously, Trevor let go of her hand immediately.

"No, I like it," Gabby said with a growing grin.

Trevor meekly held her hand again.

Gabby felt this new sensation of his soft palm against hers. They smiled brightly together, neither believing they were holding hands. They lingered in the moment in a magical silence. Trevor quickly rubbed the back of his head with his left hand and grinned, his heart racing like wild mustangs.

Just then, the school's morning bell rang. Gabby looked at her peers quickly and dutifully shuffling to their classes, clutching piles of books tightly against their chests. She felt she should hurry up to her classes, too, but her feet felt glued to the pavement. She felt herself shrinking smaller and smaller.

Looking up and gazing into Trevor's lovely brown eyes, she was startled that they were full of conviction and belief in her. In his eyes aglow with love, Gabby seemed to find herself again more fully after being lost in her ruminations, regrets, and fears.

Sensing her feelings, Trevor spoke. "Gabby, you are the greatest student of Mirror Lake High School. Even though you had some struggles, it wasn't your fault. You are going to do awesome and finish off this year victoriously."

Gabby looked down at her feet.

"Gabby," Trevor spoke again, as if he were trying to awaken the real Gabby Choi.

She suddenly looked up, a look of resoluteness in her fiery eyes. "I think you're right," she said. "No more. No more dwelling in the wrong places. I'm ready to move out."

193

Trevor laughed suddenly, surprised by her boldness.

"It wasn't my fault I had to miss school," Gabby added quietly but with power in her voice.

Trevor smiled admiringly at his girlfriend's confidence.

"What?" she asked playfully, a fire in her eyes.

Her fire almost singed the shirt on Trevor's body. It was electric. It made him feel tingly with excitement. "Gabby Choi…" he thought in his head.

"Nothing," he said, smiling.

"Let's go," Gabby said, taking Trevor's hand and striding into school as if she owned it. Her dignity was felt and echoed through the hallways of Mirror Lake High School.

Trevor grinned. Gabby always surprised him in the most unexpected and wild ways, and he was glad for the adventure.

~

It was third period, when Gabby and Trevor had the same class. As they neared their English classroom, the cool Toccoa breeze traveled down the hallway and sent a shiver up their spines. Gabby mustered up a playful smile and reached for Trevor's hand and held it for a moment, her eyes twinkling with love. Trevor grinned a boyish grin and gave her hand a brief, reassuring squeeze. Then, they both took a deep breath, and stepped into their classroom.

Gabby and Trevor were met with shocked eyes and whispers amongst many of their classmates.

"Where were they for two weeks?" they heard the school gossip, Charlotte Thornburn, whisper a little too loudly to her seat partner, her green eyes flashing at them like lightning.

Gabby's cheeks turned red like tomatoes, and her heart grew wooden inside of her, but Trevor gave her a comforting grin and she smiled, feeling a little better.

The young couple gave all their attention to their knowledgeable, friendly teacher as he lectured on Aristotle's rhetorical devices, ethos, pathos, and logos. They took careful notes of his slides presentation. Now and then they would look across the rows of seats at each other. If Gabby looked worried, Trevor made silly expressions with his face to make her smile. Gabby stifled her giggles and tried to keep a straight face and keep looking at her favorite teacher.

After class, Gabby gathered her books and looked over at Trevor. She beamed at her new handsome boyfriend, recalling how they had held hands that morning. He smiled back a winsome, youthful grin. She nodded at him once to signal to him that now was their time to talk to their teacher.

But Mr. Durbin was already right behind the two with his arms crossed across his broad chest and a look of grim sincerity.

"Gabby and Trevor, I'd like to speak with you two," his deep voice rang close to their ears.

Trevor and Gabby looked at each other with alarm. They stood side by side in front of Mr. Durbin's cluttered desk as their aged teacher sat upon his chair with difficulty. Trevor's eyes scanned the piles of assignments scattered across his desk, and wondered if there was some meaning in the mess. Gabby stared at his protruding belly through his purple t-shirt and wondered if his weight made it hard for him to move around.

"Gabby, Trevor, you missed two weeks of school with no notice to the school. Were you on an extended spring break? Did you travel somewhere?" Mr. Durbin asked with that deep crease of his across his freckled forehead.

"No, sir," Trevor replied quickly for the both of them.

Gabby looked down, but she remembered what Trevor had told her earlier in front of the school and stood tall, knowing it wasn't her fault she had to miss school.

Gabby cleared her throat and spoke clearly and intelligently.

"I had a family emergency, Mr. Durbin, and Trevor was just helping me get through it...because I couldn't do it alone."

Mr. Durbin looked at Gabby with a look of startled amazement.

"Mr. Durbin, we're very sorry," added Trevor. "Is there any way we can make up the work we missed?"

Gabby looked at Trevor and smiled at how he always said the right words at the right time, and with sincerity and courtesy, too.

Mr. Durbin didn't speak for some moments, overcome by the change in the pair.

"If that's the case, I will write up an email with the assignments you missed and send it to both of you by tonight. Next time, if something comes up, remember to notify your teachers," he said with more softness.

"Okay, Mr. Durbin," they answered at the same time.

"Thank you so much," Trevor added politely.

"Thank you, Mr. Durbin," Gabby said genuinely.

Leaving the room and being met by an empty hallway, Gabby quickly rushed into Trevor's arms for an embrace. He stroked the back of her head softly.

"Are you okay?" he asked.

"Yeah," Gabby answered.

"You were awesome," Trevor said warmly.

"Thank you, Trevor. You too," Gabby said in her little-girl voice that she only used with him. She continued to hug him and feel the comfort of his chest.

After school that day, Gabby jumped upon her bed and lay in the mass of light purple blankets on her unmade bed. "I have so much makeup work to do," she groaned, her head buried in her blankets. But then she excitedly got up to text Trevor. Just then, she heard a knock on her door. Her heart stopped.

It was her mom. She came in and sat upon Gabby's bed.

"I heard from Aunt Marie that a boy was with you at her cabin," she said abruptly. She paused to let Gabby fill her in.

Gabby froze. "What should I say to her?" her mind raced.

She slowly got up and sat upon her bed next to her mom. She considered not telling her that she was dating Trevor, but also, she didn't feel like lying. She drew in a deep breath.

"Mom, I started dating. Trevor–is a really good person. He's very pure at heart," Gabby said, knowing her mom was very conservative, the words tumbling out of her mouth, like a two-year-old emptying a box of Legos.

For a few moments, her mom said nothing, but crossed her arms. Gabby searched her mom's eyes rapidly to detect any rage or anger.

Gabby did not know that while she was at her aunt's house, her mom had a talk with Aunt Marie and started doing some self-reflection. She didn't want to hurt her daughter, realizing that she was going through a hard time because of her father. Most of all, she didn't want her to run away again.

"What's his name? How did you meet?" her mother asked with a forced kindness in her voice.

Gabby grinned a crooked grin, surprised that her mom was actually being calm.

"His name's Trevor. Remember the person who kept giving me gifts? Remember the chicken noodle soup? He was doing that. Not to be creepy or anything. To help me get out of my depression because of Dad."

Gabby's mom raised her thin, brown, penciled-in eyebrows.

Her daughter searched her mom's face. Her mom's crinkled brow loosened and she seemed curious.

Gabby smiled a huge, dreamy smile. Her mom was startled at the brightness that seemed to radiate from Gabby's face like the very sun. She hadn't seen her daughter look so happy in many months.

"He sounds like a very kindhearted person," her mom said, a look of thoughtful seriousness on her face. For a few moments, she seemed lost in deep thought.

"I'll let you meet him," Gabby said quickly, before her mom could say something negative about them dating.

"That sounds like a good plan," her mom replied. Gabby smiled in awe.

Her mom got up from the bed and straightened her floral dress, and made her way toward the door. Turning around, she added with more sternness, "Make sure you diligently do your makeup work, Gabby."

"I will!" Gabby replied chirpily.

As soon as her mom shut the door, Gabby fell upon her bed, back first, an ecstatic grin on her face.

"Mom is actually letting me date!" she squealed by herself, kicking her blankets. "I can't believe it!"

As Carol Choi opened the turquoise-blue front door of her house, the sun filtered through the shamrock-green leaves of the large shrub in front of their house. Tiny white flowers with yellow centers dotted the shrub here and there and danced in the breeze as they were kissed by the sun. She stared at the lovely sight with new eyes, letting out a small, happy sigh.

"I'm going to piano lessons!" she exclaimed joyfully, as she shut the door quickly behind her. In actuality, she was going to a therapy session. Getting into her blue Honda Pilot, she reflected on the therapy sessions of the past. She did not know it at the time, but her heart was feeling lighter because of therapy. She started going when Gabby had run away from home. Aunt Marie had called her sister multiple times and urged her to try therapy, knowing that Gabby's relationship with her mother was strained.

For several days, she was adamant about not going and was even offended at her younger sister's advice.

"I don't have a problem!" she had snapped at her wise younger sister.

But as the days passed and she heard no word from Gabby, her hardened heart began to change. She felt cornered; her husband was not himself and Gabby was wanting to have nothing to do with them. She needed a way out of the mess, to find the light at the end of the tunnel she was in. She finally picked up her phone and contacted a female therapist through her health insurance provider.

Carol smiled as she pictured her therapist Shirley's wide grin and cheery face that greeted her with such warmth and love every time she saw her. Even though Shirley was at least ten years younger than her, Carol felt nurtured and cared for by her genuine spirit.

"I love you for who you are," she had told Carol at one of their sessions.

Carol had always been hard on herself for as long as she could remember, since that was how she was raised. Hearing those words were like balm and aloe to her weary and harried soul.

Grabbing her light pinkish-ivory leather purse, she got out of her car and strode toward the clinic. The fresh Toccoa breeze ruffled her curly brown hair, as she found herself smiling to herself.

She checked in at the front desk with the always kind and professional Latina receptionist Joanna, and she sat down waiting for Shirley to appear at the hallway to usher her in.

After three minutes, Shirley enthusiastically called her name as she always did: "Hey Carol!"

Grinning like a little girl, Carol gathered her belongings and stood up, excited to be with her therapist who had become like a sister and a friend. She noticed Shirley was wearing a cute bright red halter-top and beige, form-fitting pants, with gold high heels.

"Different look today," she noted mentally.

As soon as they sat down in Shirley's room, her nose picked up the familiar peppermint candle scent. The small room was dimly lit and she noticed that new, colorful, encouraging posters had been put up on the walls.

"I like your red shirt," Carol told Shirley.

"It was my birthday a few days ago, and I wanted to embrace the newness of this year by wearing something different and new!" she replied with her childlike enthusiasm.

A radiant glow seemed to emanate from Shirley's face as she described her new adventure. Carol smiled a smile that reflected Shirley's youthful vibe.

Putting her hair behind her ear, Carol looked down at the old jeans and white polka dotted long-sleeve black blouse she always wore and wondered if she should try wearing something new, too.

"Well, how was your week?" Shirley asked, her kind brown eyes looking deeply into Carol's.

Even though Shirley asked her this question every time, it still touched her heart. She realized no one truly knew how her week was. Driving Gabby to Girl Scouts, voice lessons, choir rehearsal. Teaching her piano students up in Palos Verdes. Playing piano for church. Cooking every meal. Washing every load of laundry. Making sure Gabby had healthy snacks right when she got home from school. Taking care of her two younger sisters when they needed help or life advice. Taking care of Lance. The list went on…

For a moment, Carol just sighed and smiled, realizing she couldn't explain it all to Shirley. But she tried anyway.

"It was hectic. I didn't have any time for myself, really…" She reflected on how Shirley had taught her to make time and space for herself.

Shirley listened compassionately and kept her gaze fixed on her. "Was there anything that lifted your mood or made you smile this past week?"

Carol scanned her mind and thought quietly for a few seconds.

"This morning when I woke up, Lance was reading the newspaper in the living room. That used to be his habit before he went to Afghanistan. These days, as you know, he has been sleeping most of the day, so it was nice to see him doing something leisurely bright and early in the morning. Maybe it means he's getting better? I wish."

Shirley beamed. She was always bursting with positivity.

"That is something to be celebrated!!" She continued looking at Carol with a warm smile.

Carol looked down at her worn purse.

"Yea, maybe…" she admitted hesitantly. "He's been so up and down. Like yesterday, I made eggplant parmigiana, which is his favorite food, and served it to him with his favorite extra-ginger ginger ale, and he just looked at it and walked by." Her lip trembled for a moment. Warm tears welled up in her eyes. She wanted to say, "It really broke my heart," but she remained silent.

Shirley's warm presence and acknowledgement of her suffering eased the pain a little bit.

Carol sighed. "I guess I just have to try harder."

"Mmm...Interesting what you just said. You just have to try harder. From what I've heard, you have been trying your best, day in and day out, all this time. You can tell yourself, "Good job," instead. It's not easy, what you do."

Carol mulled over what Shirley just said, and more hot tears rushed out of her tear ducts as she felt seen and recognized for all she had been doing.

"Also, how Lance responds is outside of your control. You can't control how he feels on a given day, so give yourself compassion."

Carol lit up and wondered how Shirley always knew exactly what to say to help her feel better.

"Is there anything else you'd like to discuss?" her lovely therapist asked curiously and warmly.

"I've been thinking more about what you asked me last time. Whether there was something in my past that made me the strict parent I am today..."

The memories that had surfaced throughout the past week emerged at the forefront of her mind, and the emotions of those memories made Gabby's mother feel a physical pain in the center of her chest. But she knew she had to process them so she could be a better mother to Gabby.

"I never complained about my father, because I always tried to respect him, honor him. But now that he's passed away, I guess I can share about him."

She gulped, feeling vulnerable about sharing this story that had been buried and hidden for all her life.

"When I was six, my family was really poor, but one day, my dad came up to me and said I would be starting piano lessons. I was so excited since no one at my school knew how to play piano. It was something that only the wealthy families of Korea could afford. When I was thirteen, my dad said I would be the church pianist, but I didn't know I'd have to be the pianist for Sunday worship services, the church choir rehearsals, holiday concert rehearsals...so many rehearsals throughout the week. I was only in middle school. I barely had time and energy to do all my homework because of so much piano playing to do for my dad's church. Since my dad was a pastor, I always thought you were supposed to give your whole life to God, so even when I was tired, I told myself that I should feel honored that I could do something for God."

Carol paused to think.

"My dad was kind and respectful toward his church members, but at home, he often got angry. He had a really traumatic and sad family life growing up, maybe that's why. He ran away from North Korea during the Korean War all by himself, and as punishment, the North Korean government executed his brother. My dad probably carried that pain all his life. He would be really controlling and angry toward us five kids. I didn't tell anyone this until now, though, since he was a pastor. I wanted to protect him."

Shirley kept a steady gaze and nodded at her to keep sharing.

"When I was a senior in high school, I came home late one night–around eleven–after discussing church logistics with a guy my age. We were just planning a church outing. When I got home, my dad was furious that I had been out late with a guy and he grabbed a door that was in our garage and hit me with it as soon as he saw me."

Looking up, she noticed that Shirley's eyes were gleaming with tears.

Suddenly, an immense, enormous storm of sadness flooded Carol's soul and she cried for her child self.

Shirley quickly grabbed a tissue from her Kleenex box and handed it to her.

Dabbing her eyes, she sat in the truth. The truth that she was physically harmed by her father.

Shirley gave her space to just be, to just feel. She noticed her client was looking at something with a vacant stare. She sensed a great emptiness about Carol.

"How are you feeling right now?" she asked with respect and gentleness.

Carol felt it wouldn't hurt to be even more honest.

"I feel...empty. It's a feeling I often have, but I never knew why I felt this way."

Suddenly, a revelation overtook Carol's heart.

"Maybe...I lost my sense of self-worth after that night."

Shirley handed her one more tissue.

Then, sitting up in her chair with a look of great sincerity, she spoke into Carol's hurting heart: "You are worthy. You are worthy of the best kind of love. You didn't deserve what your dad did that night. You deserved and still deserve protection."

"And, no one can take away your inherent worth," she added quietly.

Although Shirley usually gave Carol a hug at the end of each therapy session, she felt moved to get up out of her chair and hug Carol now.

Carol held onto Shirley's back and she cried softly, like a child with her nurturing mother. She realized no one had been there to comfort her that night those thirty years ago.

Leaving the clinic, Carol felt physically tired from the overflow of emotions, but she also felt a lightness in her spirit. The heavy iron chains around her spirit had been broken, and she walked in the new truth of Shirley's words: "No one can take away your inherent worth." The words rang through her mind like the clear sound of a bell. As she walked to her car, she walked, not with the discouragement of a victim, but the confidence of a victor. Her therapist's love wrapped around her heart like a warm embrace and she felt free to love herself.

Getting into her old blue Honda Pilot, she cranked up the country radio station instead of the usual classical and smiled, hearing her favorite song come on at just that moment: "In Case You Didn't Know" by Brett Young.

"In case you didn't know / Baby, I'm crazy 'bout ya / I would be lying if I said that I could live this life without ya," she sang enthusiastically with her newfound joy.

At that moment, she heard God whisper, "I'm crazy about you." Through gleaming eyes, she smiled.

"Thank you," she whispered back to God, and she zoomed down Pacific Coast Highway toward the beach to catch the last glimpses of the strawberry pink sunset sky.

~

A couple days later, Carol found herself at the women's clothing store, Talbots. She had usually gone to the Salvation Army to buy her clothes, but that morning, she opened her closet and stared at her collection of clothing and saw that it was a motley, old bunch. "I want something fresh and new," she said to herself. The image of Shirley walking confidently in her bright red top, tight beige pants, and golden high heels shimmered in her mind, and she wanted to try something new, too. Talbots showcased a lot of bright and bold-colored clothing, and Carol felt this was exactly what she wanted.

As she walked down the aisles of the expensive shop, she felt her breaths becoming a little shallow as she felt a little overwhelmed and self-conscious. She felt she was a little too old and old-fashioned for the style of Talbots. Her eyes lingered on a rack of light yellow blouses and dresses, and she felt they were a little too bright. Then, she passed by a navy blue dress that looked simple and smart, and she reached for it, but then she pulled her hand back because this was the style she had always gone for in the past. At that moment, an employee walked up to her and greeted her. She was about ten years older than Carol, with wrinkles around her eyes. She was wearing glossy raspberry-pink lipstick and a form-fitting white dress on her shapely figure with a bright red beaded necklace around her neck.

"Are you looking for something in particular?" the sophisticated lady asked.

"Um...I'm going out on a dinner date with my husband and I just wanted to impress him," Carol said, a little embarrassed.

The lady smiled reassuringly and walked over to the left side wall, as if she had already been watching Carol and inferring what she would like. There hung a dark green dress. Carol's heart skipped a beat. It was exactly what she would want to wear. It was a one-shoulder dress that was about knee-length, with a few rose-shaped blossoms on the shoulder. It was feminine, classic, and elegant. She couldn't wait to try it on.

The lady, whose name tag read "Janelle," nodded as she admired the dress with her.

"That's a beauty. Perfect for a romantic date night with hubby," she said warmly. "What size would you like?" she asked as she grabbed the metal stick which reached clothing hanging high up.

"I'm a size 6 petite," Carol replied with a sweet, excited grin.

Holding her newfound treasure, she walked into the spacious, clean fitting room with wood panels and mirrors on two walls.

Slipping on the dress, she felt the cool silkiness of the inside of the dress run across her slim body. In the warm glow of the well-lit fitting room, her jaw dropped at how perfectly and stunningly the green regal dress hugged her every curve. The little girl inside of her squealed, excited to show her husband that very evening.

Holding her red and white Talbots bag close to her side so that her husband wouldn't peek inside the bag, Carol joyfully approached her husband, who was watching TV on the couch.

Placing her hand on his arm, she breathlessly asked, "Honey, want to go out to Gaetano's tonight?"

Gaetano's was their favorite Italian spot in Toccoa. It had an outdoor patio with stringed lights and trees all around that created a romantic ambience.

Lance looked up at his wife and then looked at the TV screen for a couple moments. His eyes looked as if he were seriously contemplating going.

"Sure," he replied, and then continued gazing at the penguins gathered on the polar ice cap on the TV screen.

Carol gave him a quick peck on the cheek.

"Great," she said with an excited smile. "How's 6:30?"

"6:30 is good," he replied to her surprise in his deep, warm voice.

Carol went into her room and sat in front of her dresser mirror. She envisioned wearing her new dress with the pearl earrings her husband had bought her on their fifth wedding anniversary. Sighing, she felt happy for once.

As the clock struck 5:30, Carol found her mind racing, as it often did as of late.

"What if he changed his mind?" she thought to herself.

She eyed the emerald green dress hanging upon the door, her breathing becoming fast and uneven.

Just then, her husband entered their bedroom and gave a crooked smile to his wife.

Her heart jumped and she found herself grinning back at him. That brief moment in time made her feel like she was twenty-four again, when they had first met and fallen in love.

"Have you seen my cologne?" Lance asked, as he went to and fro around their room.

"The one I gave you when you came back from...Afghanistan?" she asked, hope rising in her chest.

"Yea, that one. Smells great," he muttered as he kept searching the room.

She reached among her collection of perfumes on the vanity and held up his sleek, black bottle of cologne, the smell which she loved.

"Thanks," he said, and she fixed her gaze upon his eyes, hoping to make an emotional connection like a few moments ago.

Lance instead sprayed his wrist with the cologne and then rubbed the side of his neck with his wrist. The smell pervaded the room and Carol found herself smiling like a young girl again.

She spontaneously stood up and embraced him. His arms wrapped around her waist and they held each other for a long time. She couldn't remember the last time she had taken the chance and done this with him.

Like the old days, she clasped his hand and wordlessly invited him to slow dance with her. His body remembered and followed her movements across their bedroom carpet.

She leaned her head against his chest, but then he suddenly drew back, feeling triggered by a distant memory...

Tears emerged from Carol's eyes but she hoped he didn't see. She hugged him again, to let him know it was okay. But she didn't feel okay.

"Are you okay honey?" she asked sweetly, looking up at his face.

He was frowning that frown that meant he was deep in thought, but then he shook his head to shake away the fear.

"I'm okay," he said, and then he kissed her mouth deeply.

Carol's heart beat at the speed of racehorses as she melted into his kiss.

When he drew his face away, she felt as if her legs had turned to jello and might sink to the floor.

Lance stared into her eyes with twinkling eyes and smiled a boyish grin she hadn't seen in years. Carol started giggling and giggling. Lance held her gaze.

"Are you gonna wear that dress?" he asked with a wry grin.

Carol quickly ran over to the dress to cover it from his view.

"It's a surprise!" she squealed.

Lance winked and quickly left the room so she could hide her surprise from him.

Carol jumped on her bed, and lay, staring up at the ceiling, dazed, with a gleaming grin. She couldn't believe he kissed her.

~

Holding hands, Carol and Lance walked toward Gaetano's and although they had been there many times, they gasped at the lovely bright lights that hung over the patio. As Carol told the restaurant host about their reservation, Lance kept staring at his radiant wife. Her cheeks shimmered a rose-pink in the moonlight and the fire in the outdoor fireplace danced in her chocolate-brown eyes. Carol looked at her husband and smiled a girly grin.

The patio was full of guests and bustling with waiters who went to and fro between the snug rows of tables that were just a foot apart from each other. The guests were donning fine clothing and were mostly in their fifties and sixties. Waiters refilled wine glasses and everyone was engaged in lively conversation.

Lance and Carol were shown their table and they eagerly sat down. Lance kept smiling at his wife and Carol finally asked, "What?" in a playful voice.

"You look amazing, so beautiful tonight," he said, stumbling over his words, which he never did.

Carol beamed, so glad that her husband delighted in her and her new dress. Just then, her husband did something that made her giggle with joy. Lance took out his phone to take a photo of her.

"Look at me," he said with a thoughtful look on his face as he focused on the shot.

Carol smiled femininely and confidently. She wasn't sure if she was allowed to feel so good.

Lance showed her the photo.

213

"That dress was made just for you," he complimented her sincerely, warmly.

He looked down at the photo like a boy with his beloved red fire truck.

Carol propped her elbow against the table and leaned her face against her hand, admiring her husband's good looks and just taking in the moment.

"What should we eat? I'm starving," Carol said, handing Lance a menu.

"Eggplant parmigiana," he said immediately.

Carol laughed at how simple her husband was at times. He always stuck with his favorite dishes. But she couldn't help but feel a bittersweetness since the last time she had cooked that for him, he had rejected it. She shook the feeling away, wanting to enjoy the night.

Carol reached for her husband's hand and they stared into each other's eyes for some long moments, smiling.

"It's great to be out here," Lance said. "It takes me back to the first time we came...when we were first married, before Gabby was born!"

Carol chuckled.

"We were so young and carefree," she said. "After Gabby was born, it was so hard to do date nights, but we tried our best and most weekends we did!" she added, finding herself enjoying herself.

Lance thought back to those sweet times they had shared and how their love had always been so passionate. His heart broke a little, thinking about how, because of him, things had gotten hard for Carol…

"Have you decided what you would like tonight?" the waiter asked the couple. He looked college-aged, with curly brown hair and sincere, respectful eyes.

"Yes, we'd both like the eggplant parmigiana," Carol responded for the both of them.

Lance stared at his lovely wife's face, admiring how strong she had been for their whole family. He held her hand over the table again, and then brought her hand up to his mouth and kissed it once.

"I'm so excited to eat," Carol said, looking around at all the other tables covered with delectable looking dishes.

Feeling tired from hunger, Carol looked down at the table and her mind retreated back to the reality–that her husband was ill. But she fought the feeling.

"Honey, what was your favorite memory that we shared?" she asked him.

Lance scanned his library of memories, a library as rich and full as the library in Beauty and the Beast. He felt tempted to choose a couple memories, but then he looked across the table at his stunning wife, and he responded, "I love today, right now." And then after a pause, he added, "I appreciate you so much, honey."

Carol felt tears of relief squirt out of her eyes.

"I know it hasn't been easy for you," he continued, his brown eyes looking into hers with sincerity.

His wife looked down, feeling like she was responsible for making him feel happy. She didn't want him to feel bad.

"It's okay, sweetie, you don't have to say that."

Lance searched his mind, but he couldn't find an appropriate answer. He didn't know what to do in response to his wife's feelings.

"Where did you buy your dress?" he asked, grabbing a piece of bread and dipping it in the olive oil and balsamic vinegar mixture in the middle of the table.

Carol beamed widely, light seeming to shine from her calm face.

"I got it from Talbot's. You know the store that I always wanted to try but was too scared to? 'Cause the clothes are so bright...and bold?"

"Yeah, you told me before," Lance replied as he munched on the moist bread.

"This lady named Janelle helped me and she knew exactly my style somehow!" she squealed. "I couldn't believe how lucky I was in finding this," she said as she looked down at her outfit.

Lance smiled admiringly at his wife. He was always proud of her.

Carol smiled again, shyly, not used to dressing up. Her heart felt fluttery, feeling like she was dating her husband again.

"Two eggplant parmigianas," the waiter cheerfully exclaimed.

Carol grinned. Food always made her instantly ecstatic. Heat rose from their dishes as the mozzarella cheese looked so gooey and mouth-wateringly delicious. They dug into their plates immediately.

Being in a fancy restaurant with his wife made Lance reminisce about their youth when they first started going on dates.

"Remember our first date? Oh my gosh...I can't believe I did that," Lance said playfully, with a belly chuckle.

"Oh my gosh...That was so funny," Carol remarked as she stuffed her face with a big chunk of parmigiana.

"I was so confident I could skate well, and after just about two strides, I fell on the ice right smack on my butt," Lance shook his head as he grinned at his young, silly self.

"And then I quickly gave you my sweater to cover up the rip in your pants," Carol snorted loudly.

"It was cute, though," she added, smiling with a twinkle in her eyes. They held each other's gaze, smiling into the night.

"You can admit that I was a total buffoon," Lance joked with his wife.

Carol giggled. "I liked it. It made me like you more," she admitted.

Carol remembered how her then-boyfriend's face had gotten red like a ripe cherry after his accident.

"You got so red after," she laughed loudly like her younger self.

"I was so surprised you asked me for a second date," Lance reminisced.

Carol rested her face in her hand again, her eyes gleaming and her smile radiating pure joy, remembering the sweetness of their love. She marveled at how they connected almost instantly.

"And then you held my hand, first," Lance teased his wife.

"I didn't want you to fall again!" she said with an embarrassed smile, remembering that moment she took his hand on the ice rink, and how her heart had fluttered so wildly.

"I wanted to hold your hand, too," he said, looking intently into his wife's eyes.

They held hands over the table, almost forgetting that their food was getting cold.

"You know, Gabby grew up to be just like you," Lance said as he cut himself another piece of parmigiana and methodically put it in his mouth.

"Why do you say that?" Carol asked coyly.

Lance thought for a moment as he chewed the cheesy goodness in his mouth.

"She's ambitious, smart, funny, and beautiful," he said as he smiled into the night, thinking about his beloved, wonderful daughter.

Carol beamed at his compliment.

"And she's humble like her father," she noted as she poured some of her water into his empty glass, knowing he loved his water.

"I'm so proud of who she's become," they said at the same time. They both giggled.

"Remember when she was little, she hardly ever spoke and was a pensive little girl? Now, she's president of clubs and speaks in front of hundreds of her peers!" Lance said enthusiastically.

Carol reflected upon her daughter and how much she had grown up and become the leader she always saw in her.

"I wonder what she'll be when she grows up," Lance said with thoughtful curiosity upon his face.

Carol held his hand warmly. "I hope she becomes great like you."

Lance stared into his beloved wife's kind face, feeling so much love for her.

"Want to take a walk in the park where we had our first kiss after dinner?" he asked warmly, with a sudden spontaneity that was unlike him.

Carol giggled, looking down at her plate. She looked up and smiled at him as a "yes."

Just then, a waiter walking with a plate of food bumped into a guest that abruptly stood up, and the waiter bumped into Lance. As the young man fell toward Lance's chest, Lance's memory suddenly transported him to when an explosion had gone off and his fellow soldier and close friend, Ben Younger, had fallen in the same way toward his chest. His hand started to tremble, and he tried to make it stop. Lance had felt so much anger toward himself after that incident. He wished it was he who had been injured, not the young Ben. He should have protected him better.

A sudden fury overcame Lance and he abruptly stood up.

"I'm gonna go to the bathroom," he gruffly told Carol.

A mix of emotions overwhelmed her as she searched for an answer in her husband's eyes that looked like two flames, so different from the sweet gaze he had just held her in a minute ago.

She observed him as he made his way toward the men's restroom. He walked in that strange gait that he walked in when he was agitated.

Carol breathed deeply in and out, telling herself, "This too shall pass," but she couldn't stop shivering, which is what sometimes happened when she was fearful and nervous.

In the bathroom, Lance went into the largest stall, and he tried to distract his mind from the image of Ben Younger with his left leg amputated and both eyes now blind. The sorrow wracked his brain, and he wanted to sob but no tears came out. It was as if his body were reflecting who he felt he was: an evil sergeant who failed to protect his soldier. Just then, he heard a man entering the bathroom, so Lance quickly left the stall and went out back to his wife.

Carol was sitting with a far-off look in her eyes, but she shook away the daze she was in so she could be present for her husband. She reached out to touch his arm reassuringly. He looked like a lost young boy; he refused to look up at her eyes.

"Honey, do you want to talk about it, or no?" she asked cautiously, but with warmth, reaching her hand out to gently touch his arm.

Lance kept staring into space with his far-off look in his kind brown eyes.

"I'm okay," he finally said, his voice a little more calm.

Carol breathed a little easier.

She sliced her eggplant parmigiana and kept eating, to create a mood of normalcy for them.

Lance looked down at his food, but he thought in his mind, "I can eat this great-looking food just fine, but Ben is blind, Ben is blind…"

"Ben is blind" kept repeating in his head, the relentless voice not letting him rest.

Lance held his cloth napkin and clenched his fist.

Carol held her breath.

Suddenly, everything–the stringed lights, the outdoor fireplace, the guests in gaudy necklaces and fine clothing–all the beautiful things that Ben couldn't see, felt suffocating to Lance. He couldn't shake off the anger he felt against himself, and he couldn't stand being at Gaetano's anymore.

Lance abruptly stood up again.

Carol's heart stopped.

"Let's go," Lance said hoarsely, and taking Carol's hand, he stormed out of the patio.

Carol held back tears, as she followed her husband out to the parking lot, trying to keep up with his pace.

"I have to pay," she said.

He didn't look back and kept walking.

"I have to pay," she said again more loudly, her voice trembling with sadness.

Lance looked back at his wife, a wild fury in his usually kind eyes.

Seeing that his wife looked distraught, he covered his face with his hands and then rubbed his forehead with his hand.

He looked around and up at the sky, not knowing what to do with himself.

After taking a few deep breaths, it seemed he was coming back to himself.

"I'm sorry, darling," he said, his tone still serious.

"I'll go pay, and apologize," he said, walking toward the restaurant again.

"No, it's okay. I'll do it," Carol said quickly, and she ran toward the restaurant, sobs coming over her in waves, hoping her husband couldn't see.

Lance watched her from behind, feeling helpless and weaker than ever before in his life.

Carol wordlessly drove them home, which is what she did whenever her husband seemed to not be in a good condition, so that he could rest. Lance looked out the window, searching his mind for an answer to his condition, but the miserable answer always came: none. He felt lost in a rough, black sea, with no one around him for miles and miles. No one could help him. No one could rescue him. How sorely he wanted to see the light.

Once they got home, Lance quickly walked into the bedroom, and Carol followed. They wordlessly changed into their pajamas, both tired from what had happened.

In her lilac-colored silk pajamas, Carol sat upon their bed. Lance observed this, and wondered why his wife wasn't going to sleep, which was the norm.

Lance sat at the edge of the bed and took off his grey socks, and placed them in the laundry basket next to their bed. He was about to lie down, when Carol faced him, still seated cross-legged.

She hesitated for a second or two.

"What can I do to help you?" she asked in the silent, still darkness.

Her voice came to him, soothing, gentle, with a hint of desperation.

Tired from his inner battles, Lance let out a deep sigh.

For a moment Carol feared that he would avoid the question and just want to go to sleep, but then he spoke.

"I don't think there's anything you can do, darling," he said with resignation. He rubbed his head.

What he wanted to say was, "I feel like I failed you and Gabby. I feel like I'm drowning. I'm scared. I feel scared and alone."

Carol hugged him, the part of him which she knew about.

He stayed in her embrace, hoping the fear wouldn't consume him.

G&T

Going to school was suddenly exciting for the two lovebirds because Gabby would run to meet Trevor between each class period and they would hug each other tight, talk, and giggle before going off to their next class. People noticed Gabby Choi no longer looking glum but instead smiling her bright smile once more and laughing loudly in class. Trevor used to dread going to school, but he, too, had a new vigor and tried harder in his classes to impress Gabby. Before, his life was an endless series of déjà vus, one day exactly like the next, but now that he was with her, every day felt fresh and new.

"Trevor, I heard there's gonna be a meteor shower today! Let's go on top of Palos Verdes to watch it!" Gabby squealed through the phone exactly two weeks into their dating. Palos Verdes was the hill overlooking the ocean adjacent to Toccoa.

"Let's do it!" Trevor responded enthusiastically.

But as their car approached the top of the hill, they noticed the sky was thickly quilted with clouds and so no meteor shower would be in view.

"Hm...what should we do?" Gabby asked quietly as they stood overlooking the blackness of the ocean, knowing that something good would come out of this. Nothing could stifle the joy Gabby felt when she was with Trevor. Putting her arms over his shoulders, she said with a gleeful smile, "Let's dance."

Trevor then took out his phone and played a song on Youtube and placed his phone in his front shirt pocket. It was the very romantic song from the '90s, "Back at One," by Brian McKnight.

Gabby's eyes grew wide. "OH MY GOSH, THAT IS SUCH A GREAT IDEA!" she shrieked, laughing ecstatically.

Swaying with Trevor in a quiet wooded area before the ocean in the dark made Gabby feel giddy and she asked Trevor to play fast music so they could actually dance. Trevor played "Uptown Funk" and they started to dance faster. Gabby had never danced in public before so this was a big deal. It helped that it was dark, and she was wearing a big, flowy white shirt so Trevor couldn't see her every movement.

While still standing apart from Gabby, Trevor lightly placed his hands on her hips at one point and Gabby felt self-conscious about her body at the time but it didn't really matter. She was too busy enjoying this time with Trevor. She turned 360 degrees to the beat of the music. She giggled, slightly embarrassed that it came out a little awkward.

"You dance so cute! And you have so much rhythm!" Trevor exclaimed with a surprised grin.

225

"NO!" Gabby retorted cutely.

Song after song passed. They got so lost in their dancing that Gabby didn't even notice the several passersby walking their dogs and staring at the pair, though Trevor did.

When they stopped dancing, they were dripping with sweat from their sudden outburst of joy that had lasted thirty minutes straight. Trevor and Gabby laughed into the night sky. Though the sky held no moon or stars, the two had lit the night on fire in a kaleidoscope of bliss and celebration.

"I bet the people who passed by were jealous," Gabby said with a sneaky grin of satisfaction, after Trevor told her about the gawking passersby.

Some moments later, the fact that she had just danced in public, and in front of Trevor, sank in. Gabby started freaking out inside, but she was glad it meant that she felt so comfortable around Trevor.

As the two walked hand in hand along the sidewalk, Gabby suddenly yelled to Trevor, "You ARE a noodle in the wind!!" Trevor laughed, embarrassment in his voice. Trevor had once told Gabby that his childhood friend Thomas called him a "noodle in the wind," because he was so fluid in his movements when he danced.

"I'm not!" he said.

"Yeah! You are!"

They burst out laughing, their laughs echoing through the dim, quiet neighborhood.

Trevor drew Gabby in for a hug and she buried her face into his soft shirt that smelled like sweet, clean soap. She thought to herself that Trevor smelled like babies do. Holding him close, she suddenly remembered how in a book she read about Christian dating relationships, the author said to voice your physical boundaries early on in dating.

Gabby studied Trevor's face to see if this was a good time to talk about it. He looked calm and at ease.

"Trev, I have something I want to talk about with you," she started, gently, studying his dashing face.

"Yeah?" he gazed at her, giving her his full attention.

"How about we wait to kiss until the perfect moment?" Gabby asked breathlessly.

"Sounds good," Trevor quickly replied.

"Really?" Gabby thought inside. "That was simple."

Trevor studied Gabby's face—her huge, inquisitive eyes, her dainty nose, her pointed chin—wondering how a girl so young could be so mature and wise. She smiled back at his kind expression, her chest unburdened and feeling relieved after saying what she wanted to say. Gabby embraced Trevor again and sighed a happy sigh, her heart at perfect peace. Trevor held her gently like a protective older brother, vowing to do anything he had to to guard and cherish Gabby and to honor God.

Clasping his hand with hers, Gabby began swaying, inviting Trevor to waltz with her. He chuckled into the frigid night air and Gabby realized this was the perfect time to show Trevor the piano song she had made for him the night they had gotten together.

"Trev, I made you something," Gabby said breathlessly as she opened her purse and eagerly grabbed her phone.

"What is it?" Trevor asked with a curious sparkle in his eyes.

"I made you a song–on the piano," Gabby said with growing excitement. "It's called 'Trevor in Gabby's Wanderings.'"

She pressed play, hoping with all her heart he'd like it.

~

Listen to "Trevor in Gabby's Wanderings" again on Gabby's blog here: www.gabbysmelody.com

~

Trevor's eyes became glazed over, first with wonder and then elation. He listened very carefully the entire time as Gabby curiously studied his face. As soon as the song ended, Trevor replayed the song, and then, grabbing Gabby's hand with his, started dancing to the rhythm of Gabby's song, closing his eyes and smiling as he hummed along. He looked so silly that Gabby burst out giggling, but she played along with him, swaying and laughing intermittently.

As they slowly came to a stop, Trevor softly put his forehead against her forehead and quietly said, "Gabby, that was amazing." In that moment of closeness with Trevor, Gabby felt enveloped by a wonderful comfort. She closed her eyes gently as he closed his.

"Thank you so much," Trevor said with utmost sincerity. "That was the best gift I've ever received."

Gabby smiled a gleaming smile.

It was almost nine o'clock and Gabby's mom would want her in early, so they made their way back to Trevor's car. On their way home, Trevor listened to Gabby's song three more times.

"Gabby, you're really talented," he said, to Gabby's surprise and pleasure.

"Nah," Gabby replied.

"You're extremely talented," Trevor said genuinely.

This made Gabby grin widely.

"Thanks," she replied sweetly as she nestled her head against Trevor's strong arm that rested against the center compartment.

When they got to her house, Trevor walked Gabby all the way to her front door as was his custom. A single light was on, the light that shone over the two front steps.

"Good night, Trevor," Gabby said lovingly as she hugged him with longing, already missing him.

Trevor looked into her eyes, and meaning each word, said warmly, "I adore you."

Gabby sucked in her breath a little, having heard these three words for the first time. She looked up at his beautiful, shining eyes which were full of sincerity, feeling so much love flow out of her heart for him. After a pause, she said shyly but while looking straight into his eyes, "I adore you."

229

They smiled as they embraced each other once again for the last time for the night. Wrapped up in Trevor's arms, Gabby felt utterly safe and completely loved. Trevor felt the same way.

"Good night," Gabby said and waved as her boyfriend turned around to walk to his car.

Still looking at Gabby in the face, Trevor waved and said, "Good night!" Gabby continued to watch him walk away, and he turned back two more times and smiled and waved.

Gabby smiled a new kind of smile that she never smiled before. Her night, her life, was complete.

G&T

A few days later on Friday night, Trevor and Gabby met up after dinner to run around their school track together. After jogging a couple laps around the track, Gabby suggested that they do a sprint race across one straightaway. Gabby and Trevor flew across the track, laughing and giggling as it was their first race. They were surprisingly equally fast, and ended up being tied.

"You're so competitive!" Trevor remarked, huffing and puffing, stooped over with his hands on his knees. "It reminds me of when we played one-on-one basketball at Aunt Marie's."

Gabby laughed, pleased with herself and glad she could show her boyfriend her athletic side. After their spurt of energy, they headed to the bleachers to drink some water and rest.

On the walls of the large gymnasium of Mirror Lake High School, a majestic bronze mustang was emblazoned on the red brick walls with the word, "Mustangs" in grand, bold gold letters. After sipping from her water bottle, Gabby wiped her mouth and stared at the large testament to student success, a monument to academia and her life for so many years. Her thoughts traveled from those hallowed gold letters, down the red brick walls through the outside corridors, past the lockers, over the lunch tables, and finally into the classrooms where she spent so many of her formative years. Her mind entered the classrooms and she envisioned the rows of empty seats now filled with students eager to learn.

"My dream is to be a teacher," Gabby said breathlessly, grabbing her red jacket and pulling it closer around her body as they looked out at the stadium. She reached for Trevor's hand and felt its plush softness against her own palm.

Her eyes glistened as she scanned the empty football field, the lights shining brilliantly across the fluorescent, perfect green grass. Her eyes looked excitedly at the field, as if she could see her future students standing there before her eyes.

Trevor half-grinned, happy for Gabby yet wondering what it feels like to have such certainty about the future.

"In sixth grade, I wrote in my journal that I want to help people fulfill their potential," Gabby continued, giggling at her young self's maturity.

"You already do, Gabby," Trevor spoke with such sweetness. Gabby sighed and looked straight ahead. The vision of her students upon the field disappeared as fear crept into her heart.

Trevor saw the discomfort in her eyes.

"What's wrong?" he asked, searching her face.

After a pause, Gabby admitted something that shocked Trevor. "The future sometimes feels uncertain...and honestly, scary at times...after all I've been through. It was all...really intense for me."

Trevor, concerned, looked at the field again, where his school's football team had many moments of great glory. Shifting his feet beneath the bleachers, he sat in silence, letting her remain in silence, and mulling over what she said.

The cool air from the Pacific Ocean blessed Toccoa with a crisp, evening breeze that revived tired lungs. Gabby took a deep breath, letting the air linger and course through her veins, before releasing it back into the beach town's atmosphere. Her next words stumbled out.

"But I don't think my mom would even let me be a teacher. She's always wanted me to be a politician, some great leader in society. If I tell her I want to become a teacher, I can already imagine what she would say." Gabby lamented at the idea of another unwinnable argument against her mother. The weight of her mother and father's troubles lay heavy upon the young woman on the bleachers.

"I think I could be a great teacher. I mean, I've been tutoring since I was twelve years old and everyone tells me I'm great at teaching. But still...I'm afraid."

Suddenly, Gabby leaned her head against Trevor's shoulder and spoke dreamily into the night sky, "Trev, I like how I can say anything in front of you...and you won't judge me." Her boyfriend looked into Gabby's twinkling brown eyes, concerned for her. She had once been so confident, so sure. Gabby Choi. Everyone thought she could do anything.

"Gabby," he finally spoke. "I don't know what to do either."

Gabby paused at the weight of what Trevor said. She felt the heaviness of his admittance like a stone sitting in her own soul. She hugged him warmly and, looking into his worried face, sighed with a hopeful smile and mustered up her courage.

"Trev, I see your future in your eyes. It's written all over your face that you will have a great future." She emphasized the word "great." Pointing toward the bright stadium lights overhead, she kept looking into Trevor's eyes. "You are the brightest light I've ever seen," Gabby added sincerely.

Trevor squeezed Gabby's hand, realizing the blessing that he now held. The brisk air had cooled any sweat from their tiring run and the couple sat still, relishing in the night's abode.

"You know, Gabby, I recently saw something that made me think of you. It may seem a bit nerdy but bear with me."

The young woman quizzically looked at Trevor Song. Though they had been through so much together throughout their short time this year, she felt that she had known Trevor for much of her life. What would he say in response to her apprehensions, to her future endeavors? In anticipation, her eyes gleamed under the bright track lights, waiting for the young man to speak.

"So, I was watching this movie with my dad the other day."

Gabby imagined Trevor lounging in his living room with Steve Song. Trevor's legs were propped up on the couch's arm and he contentedly lounged, taking up the length of the sofa.

"*Lord of the Rings*. It was one of my favorite parts of the movie. Aragorn, one of the main characters, struggles with who he is throughout the story. Born the son of a king, heir to a vast kingdom yet he wears worn-out, old clothes throughout his journey. He fights his destiny again and again and again, but he always seeks to do good." Trevor's brilliant eyes gleamed as he recalled his favorite tale. Gabby sat on the bleachers, trying to connect the threads together.

"In the scene, Aragorn is about to go into battle against his enemies and he is severely outnumbered, outmatched, and he is doubting himself again. Can he do it?" Trevor's eyes turned to Gabby to see if she was still paying attention. She attentively and kindly nodded in acknowledgement. He continued.

"Out comes this hooded figure. He slowly lowers his hood and reveals himself to be Elrond, the king of the elves! Actually, one of the kings, but I won't get into the details." Trevor chuckled to himself, waving off the idea of telling Gabby the deep and storied lore of the franchise. "Sorry if I am boring you, but this story will have a point."

Gabby sweetly nodded and smiled. Though she was struggling to see where this story was headed, she had never seen Trevor so enraptured. The young woman admired this spark of passion, the fire that burned within him to tell stories.

Trevor joyfully continued, "So here is the point. Elrond confronts Aragorn and says that Aragorn's fate is doomed to fail unless he becomes who he is meant to be. The elven king brings out a legendary sword and tells the lost ranger to, 'Be who you were meant to be.' So Gabby, after this long-winded story, I am telling you the same thing. 'Be who you were meant to be.' Don't worry about what your mom will think or what your dad will do. Just pursue your own dreams and do what makes you happy."

The smile on the young man's face rivaled the lights above the track field. He spoke with such conviction, a conviction that would not have been possible a few months ago when Gabby had first met Trevor. Something had changed about him; an indispensable, unconquerable fire burned within him. Gabby Choi's bright brown eyes appeared a hazelnut brown color as the track lights shone against them. They were transfixed on Trevor Song, this young man that had changed her life.

Deep within her spirit, a wick of light, a spark, lit up the once-cavernous, unending, seething, uncertain darkness. It retreated in response to the light. The simple story with a simple message said with a simple love had created such a profound passion within her.

"You will be the most phenomenal and life-changing teacher. You changed my life, and you will change many other people's lives for the better." Trevor confidently grinned and his hand gently squeezed Gabby's, yet she felt like her entire body, mind, and soul were being embraced, loved, and treasured by him. Her heart jolted at those words and she smiled with a twinkle in her eyes. She just stared into her boyfriend's deep, kind eyes. She put her arms around his neck and hugged him tightly.

"Thanks, Trevor," she said near his ear. "I don't know where I would have been without you," she added softly. Gabby nestled her face into Trevor's cheek, feeling the softness of his skin and breathing in his sweet, clean scent.

Soon, she was asleep. Startled, Trevor realized how exhausting everything had been for Gabby. Sitting as still as possible so as not to wake her, he held her securely in his arms, keeping her warm. He searched the stadium lights overhead, hoping he had told her what she needed to hear.

There was a singular bookcase in Trevor's house. It was about four feet high and three feet long and it housed the many novels that belonged to Trevor's father. Trevor's father had a sizable collection of crime novels that occupied the top shelf of the bookcase. Then he had his miscellaneous books on the second shelf. The second shelf was half empty; a collection of old cookbooks, magazines, and Trevor's required school literature collected dust between the wood panels. His father, Steve, would often sit upon the recliner and enjoy reading crime novels during his free time. His brow remained furrowed as he went page by page, often licking the top of his thumb to ease the flipping of the pages. Trevor's mother would not bother him during those times of literary reverence, for once allowing the patriarch of the family a time on his throne.

As a child, Trevor imitated his father's reading. On more than one occasion, he grabbed a crime novel from his father's collection, opened it to a random page, and scrunched his face into a pained expression, doing this all the while next to his father. Once, his mother saw his impression as she walked out of the kitchen, resulting in her holding her stomach as she bent over laughing. Her laughter startled Steve Song so much, his stern gaze searched the room for an answer to his wife's guffaws. It went from the book to her to their son, who stared at the novel with the most wrinkled face. Like a good detective, the crime novel enthusiast connected the dots and Steve Song's brow loosened. He tousled his young son's hair and let out a chuckle.

"You little rascal." Steve smiled and then looked at his wife. "You sure do enjoy his impression."

Wiping a single tear, she responded with a smile and a nod. Trevor remembered how his dad rose from his throne and gently grasped his mother's hands, interlacing his fingers with hers. His cheek pressed against hers, he began to hum a familiar tune: "Bring your sweet loving, bring it on home to me." Steve Song brought his lovely wife close as her eyes relaxed and rested upon his, perfectly in the moment, in the stillness of the night.

Though a calm and calculated man, Steve loved the gripping tension of crime novels, appreciating how the writer could fabricate compelling conflict and story with just a few words. He often spent time on his precious weekends to find another novel to read. He ran his hands across the shelved books in the bookstore in search of the right book. He read the back of the book for a quick synopsis and analyzed the first page to see how the writer introduced the narrative. If he found a book with a good first impression, he would nod to himself in the aisles, reading the book as he walked to the counter to pay. Steve would ponder the premise of the story as he drove home, and upon arriving, he would quickly tuck the book away in the respective first shelf, not cracking it open until the proper, designated recliner time.

However, his trips to the bookstores stopped after his wife's death. The books upon the first shelf rarely were opened and when they were, Trevor was the one peering into these tomes to see what his father liked about them.

Now, Steve and Trevor spent their nights in the living room watching television, thumbing through the channels.

"200 channels and nothing to watch." Steve continued to flick through each channel, giving each digit a second to explain their case before he was onto the next one. Trevor paid little attention to the quick succession of images passing across the screen. The television finally stopped at a home makeover show on network television.

"Move that truck!" the wide-eyed, perky host shouted as the anxious family stood next to him. A large diesel truck panned away as an even larger, monumental house was revealed. The family crumpled to their knees and thanked the heavens for their newly renovated house. More Hail Mary's and utterances of Jesus echoed through the house as the overly smiling host introduced them to their new home.

"Maybe we can be on that show, Trev." Steve Song's eyes peered away from the television screen for a moment to his son. Trevor sat on the adjacent grey couch with one knee up and one knee down, a peculiar position that Steve did not bother to understand. Trevor's eyes momentarily looked up from his phone and saw the father figure of the television family run through the renovated man-cave with a jaw-dropping display of happiness.

"No chance." Trevor scoffed as he looked back at his phone to see if Toad, Cid, or better yet, Gabby had texted him.

239

The television suddenly shut off. To Trevor's surprise, his father was staring at him, his brow furrowed. Before the teen could speak, Steve went to the bookcase and brought out two novels to read. He tossed one upon his son's lap. Trevor glanced at the cover. The title read *The Pacification* and the book cover had a picture of a bullet hole in it, a rather dramatic cover for a book entitled *The Pacification*.

"We are going to do something new for once." Steve paused. "Or I guess, something old. Something we haven't done in a long time."

Trevor looked at his father in the normal way teens supposedly do: an unmoving blank expression with blank eyes. Putting down the book, Trevor tried to execute his quick escape.

"Dad, I think I will go to Toad's. He is going to have pizza." Before Trevor could fully stand, his father's eyes, with a powerful gaze, commanded him to sit.

"Just this once, Trev. Let's read together. We haven't done this in a while." The corner of Steve's lips curled up ever so slightly. Trevor did not remember the last time his father wanted to read. The teen opened the book and read the first page. It was one of his father's crime novels.

"I really liked that one when I read it the first time. I think I read that one soon after I met your mother for our first date." His father let out a chuckle, albeit brief.

The story opened with a detective in his dingy office. Old lettering of the old detective's name was on the crystalline glass window. The writer described the office in depth, going from the bookcases to scattered paperwork to finally resting upon the grizzled, savvy veteran detective. He was equipped with a five o'clock shadow at 2:00PM.

Trevor glanced at his father who reclined in the all-too-familiar position on the recliner. Steve Song's brow furrowed as he excavated the pages, quickly turning them in mere seconds.

Trevor's dad, unlike Trevor, was an avid reader. Soon after his wife passed, Steve wanted to impart that love for reading onto his son as an attempt to connect with his growing boy. He even enrolled Trevor in a speed-reading course. Trevor remembered those sessions well. The classes were held in an office-turned-classroom on the second floor of a small plaza next to a liquor store. Three long tables, each with three chairs, lined both sides of the classroom and there was nothing else in the room. In the long aisle down the middle of the class, the teacher paced back and forth, repeating the same instructions over and over. Each session, Trevor had to scan pages and pages of dots. Several hundred dots in several dozen rows. One after the other.

"Scan the dots. This is training for your eyes. Scan the dots."

On those days, whenever Trevor slept, he would see the rows of dots moving across his inner eyelid. He once even woke up from a dot-related dream. With those thoughts in mind, Trevor accelerated his reading pace, making his eyes pan across the pages like a motor boat across tranquil water.

"The detective's squalor shattered as the damsel swung open the door. Her hair shone with a radiance of a thousand suns and yet her eyes were even more blinding: a piercing green of the finest, most precious jade."

Steve Song looked up from his book to look at his son. "This is nice. No noisy television. No dumb shows. Just two guys reading two good books. We should do this more often." Trevor looked up and nodded, acknowledging his father, because that was what his father wanted.

"You know, you may not remember this, but we would do this often when you were younger." Mr. Song put his book down, his eyes requesting his son to do the same. "I loved reading these crime novels back then. They were my escape. They put me into a world of drama, of uncertainty. I would sit on this armchair and read for hours at a time, just taken by these stories."

"And when I read, I would look angry, but I really wasn't. I just was really into the book. You would imitate me too." Trevor's father furrowed his brow humorously, imitating his son imitating him.

"Your mother loved your imitations. You would even imitate a conductor during church choirs too. She would laugh every single time even though the other moms would give her dirty looks." Trevor's father looked down upon the cover of the book and then at his son once again.

"She really loved you, Trevor." Steve Song's eyes shone with a fine veneer in the halogen living room light.

Trevor placed his book down upon his right thigh and nodded. "I know and we loved her." A silence fell over the room as they let the spirit of that phrase drift from corner to corner of the room. Trevor picked up the butterflied book and continued to read as the writer crafted his intricate web of plot points, each subplot intertwined in more subplots underneath the cadence of a noir main plot. Trevor turned the book over and glanced at the list of books attributed to the writer. Over ten books were listed.

"I will never be this successful," Trevor muttered under his breath, just loud enough for his father to hear.

His father's brow furrowed once more. His figurative paternal switch had been proverbially flipped. "Don't think that way. That is why you must do your best. You have to try."

His father's voice began to grow distant in the teenager's mind, a déjà vu of a past conversation. Trevor heard the story before. The teen nodded in acknowledgment to the words of advice. "I know, Dad." Trevor's head gazed down at the book, not focusing on a word.

Trevor's father was a man of routine for much of his life. He woke, worked, ate, and slept, each activity always at the same time. When asked how he did it, he shrugged his shoulders and said, "I'm an engineer. That's what I do." There was a precise intensity to every single task he did. From what Trevor could remember, and what his father told him, his mother threw a wrench into that. She was a woman of spontaneity. According to Steve Song, he would quite frequently find Trevor's mother upon the beach, wandering upon the sand, enjoying the cool shore breeze and the sun's warm embrace. Steve Song loved that about her. He loved her.

During their dates, Steve would do things to match her spontaneity like buying her flowers for no occasion or singing her songs that he made from the three guitar chords he knew. Her lips greeted him with a pink levity, with joy, with gladness.

Sensing his son's dejection over the future, Steve Song sat up from his armchair and moved toward his son. Gently grabbing his son's forearm, Steve cleared his throat.

"I've been meaning to tell you this for a long time. Seeing you not live to your full potential has given me so much heartache.

My son, you have so much potential." He stared at Trevor, who did not return his glance, rather opting to stare at the book for a little while.

"Trevor, I watch you go to and back from Toad's house almost every single day. As soon as you get home, you close your door and sleep. When are you going to focus on your studies? I'm sure you don't do it at Toad's house."

Trevor looked up and shook his head. He knew he was in this lecture for the long haul. He might as well bear it.

"When are you going to get it together? You have so much potential. You know, when I first met your mother, I was pretty aimless myself, but your mother, bless her, encouraged me to pursue a profession that can last for a long time. A technique. And that was engineering for me. You have to find a technique too."

The teen nodded his head.

"Look at your cousin, Michael. He has his mind set on being a doctor. He has already interned at hospitals and worked under doctors and nurses. He's focused. He's ambitious. He is out there working toward his future."

Michael Chon, beloved son of Steve Song's sister, Sandra Chon, always served as the gold standard in topics of exemplar offspring in the Song family tree. Always tall for his age and with defined cheekbones and broad shoulders, Michael captured attention wherever he went. For much of his youth, Trevor was compared to Michael. Before the Chons moved out of Toccoa and to Northern California, Trevor used to see Michael often at the speed reading course. Married to a successful lawyer, Sandra Chon often boasted of her accomplishments which included Michael and his accomplishments, no matter how small. Even his reading speed required its own standing ovation. That is where Steve was inspired by the idea of enrolling Trevor in the same class.

Though Michael received all the acclaim, Trevor never disliked his cousin. It was impossible to hate him. After class, Michael and Trevor often ventured downstairs to the neighboring liquor store. There, Trevor would dig through his pockets for whatever he could find that would amount to a dollar so he could buy some Hot Cheetos. If he had no money, he would longingly stare at the bag of chips before leaving the store. Michael would always saunter out later with Hot Cheetos in hand and shared the deliciously crimson artificial goodness with him.

Though he tried his best to not show it to his father, the comparison to Michael pained Trevor every time Steve mentioned it. To Trevor, Steve Song chiseled a colossal homage of Michael and Trevor dwelled in its shadow. It highlighted the parts that Trevor was not: his lack, his deficiencies, his shortcomings.

Trevor knew he had squandered many of his teen years on neither flights of fancy nor dreams of grandeur, but in the dirt of the everyday. He did not capitalize on his time. He was not in the Model United Nations club or a part of the student council. He had nothing to boast about in his transcripts or extracurriculars. What had he done until now? Was he a failure? Obviously in comparison to the many others around the world, in his class, in his recent memory, he sure was. His eyes continued to stare down at the butterflied book in his lap.

"If you need any help, Trevor, you can ask me. I am always here for you." Trevor's father's eyes softened and rested upon the slumped shoulders of his son. His father's left palm caressed the back of his son's head. "That is enough for today." Steve Song slowly rose from the adjacent couch and walked into the kitchen. The sound of pouring water echoed into the living room.

Trevor left the living room and entered his dark room. Without turning on the lights, he lay on his bed, staring at the ceiling. His father's words swirled out of his head and bounced against the corners of his all-too-familiar room. "Find a technique." Trevor closed his eyes as a series of words crossed his inner eyelids.

"How can I find a technique if there is nothing that I like to do?"

Trevor's eyes opened once more and the darkness of the room seemed brighter. His eyes adjusted and fell upon a small notebook upon his desk. It was his black Moleskine notebook. He opened it and felt the pages as he flipped through them. He remembered Gabby's avid interest in his writing and the way her eyes seemed to bulge out of their sockets at the treehouse at Aunt Marie's. But his father's words and the reminder that he was not good enough haunted his soul again and he put the notebook down with a sigh. He lay back down on his bed and stared at his ceiling for many hours. He thought of all the things he didn't do, and all the things he failed to be.

Gabby had texted Trevor while he was talking with his dad, but Trevor wasn't replying; this alarmed her. She knew that something must be wrong. She finally called him, and Trevor, not wanting to worry Gabby, answered the phone. Gabby was shocked and perplexed by his quiet, muted voice.

"Hello?" he said, lifelessly.

"Hey, Trevor. What's wrong?" Gabby asked frantically.

"Nothing," he answered.

Gabby never heard him sound so lifeless.

"I'll go to you," Gabby said.

Quiet. Trevor did not speak for some moments.

"Okay," he finally said in his mouse-like voice.

Gabby raced over to his house, and after waiting for about five minutes, Trevor came out of his house and came into her car. His face was pale and expressionless.

"Do you want to go to the swings?" Gabby asked tenderly, referring to the little park near their neighborhood.

"Sure," Trevor said, sounding really tired.

On the swings, Gabby continued to look at Trevor, but he just looked straight ahead, as if in a daze. Gabby's mind searched all of her mind's filing cabinets for an answer to Trevor's condition. She knew that his dad was home from work that night so she asked Trevor, "Did your dad say something to you?"

Trevor jumped, shocked that she found the truth so quickly. For some long moments he just looked at the grainy sand in front of his feet.

"My dad wants me to be more like my cousin who's going to be a doctor," Trevor finally admitted in a meek tone.

Gabby peered into his face. In the darkness she could not see that his eyes were glistening with tears. She held his hand and stopped swinging, listening intently. But Trevor said no more.

"Trevor...I'm sorry," she said quietly. "But not everyone's meant to be a doctor. Remember you told me, "Be who you're meant to be." Trevor, you don't have to be anyone else except yourself."

At that moment, tears streamed down Trevor's face, but he continued to look straight ahead and not at his girlfriend. Gabby got off her swing and hugged Trevor as he stayed seated on his swing. She stroked his hair and held him nurturingly.

Trevor wiped away his tears, not wanting Gabby to see this part of his heart that was so painful to talk about.

Just then, Gabby sang a song.

I wanna sing while the ocean sleeps

I want to feel what it's like to be free

I want to see what you see in me

I want to know what it's like to believe

Cuz I feel lost

Somehow drifting away

Was almost gone, You brought me to life again

So let me be your lighthouse

And I'll help you find a way out of here

~

Listen to "Lighthouse (Hope cover)" on Gabby's blog here: www.gabbysmelody.com

~

Somehow the sound of Gabby's sweet, warm singing voice and the words of the song comforted Trevor and he rested his head against Gabby's stomach as she continued to hug him. Gabby stroked Trevor's back and, when the song was done, she finally looked at his face. His eyelids were puffy and he continued to look down. She made her face level with his and looked into his clear brown eyes.

"Trev, look at me," she said. "You are the most talented writer and communicator I have ever met. And you are incredibly creative. There is a path for you," she said.

These words penetrated the webs that entangled Trevor's heart and ripped off some of the cords of his dad's words.

"Thank you," Trevor answered. He hugged her tightly, burying his head in her stomach again.

That night, after she arrived home, Gabby texted Trevor:

~

Dear Trevor,

I know it hurts a lot when our parents want us to be someone we're not. I've been there, too. My mom expects me to go to Harvard. But I want to go to UCLA. It fits me better. Our parents care a lot for us, and they know us very well, but the only person who knows you the most is you. No one else knows you like you know you. I believe that you know the gifts that are inside of you, and no one can take those gifts away. They are so precious and beyond any worth that can be given to them by the

249

world. One of your gifts is writing and I know you love it. I hope you will cherish this, cherish the love you have for writing. I once heard a quote that said your passion is linked to your purpose. I truly believe that for you, Trevor. When you speak, when you write, you move me in ways that no one has been able to move me. Your words don't just impart life–they seemingly raise the dead. They have raised the dead places in me. They have made me into a bigger, better Gabby Choi. This is the power that you wield. Don't ever let go of that Aragorn sword. Wield your sword– your pen. I will always support you in your dream to be a writer. You are already the most phenomenal one I have seen.

I adore you!

-Gabby

~

Trevor was lying on his bed on his back with his arm resting over his forehead, when his phone suddenly vibrated. He quickly looked at it to see if his girlfriend had texted. A smile of relief spread across his saddened face as he opened up a long text message from her. Trevor loved long texts. Quickly turning over on his bed, he read the text as if it were a rare treasure. The fiery passion and genuine kindness in her text flooded his soul and his heart seemed to come alive again after a long, dead winter.

"She believes in me," he said aloud to himself, softly, in the darkness of his room.

"She believes in my writing," he thought.

Eyeing his Moleskine again, Trevor felt a spark of hope inside his darkened heart as he drifted off into a sleep made peaceful by Gabby's text.

G&T

With Trevor by her side, Gabby felt encouraged and took on her studies with great determination and passion like before. Even though her dad was still ill, now she had hope and faith that he would get better by a miracle of God. She had this newfound faith because God had gifted her with Trevor, who, to her, was a walking miracle in her life. With Gabby's constant encouragement and presence in his life, Trevor started to feel more motivated. But, their college applications were already done, and nothing could change the outcomes. On the last day of March, they received their fateful envelopes in their mailboxes.

Gabby and Trevor decided to go to the new boba shop in Toccoa, Sharetea, to open their letters from the colleges at the same time.

Trevor warily eyed the bustling, raucous teenagers that crowded the small cafe. He scanned each face, hoping that no one he knew was there, so that they wouldn't see which colleges he got into, or didn't get into for that matter. Loud K-pop music blared exuberantly from the cafe speakers. The back wall of the establishment was covered with fake green ivy and dozens of small polaroid photos of customers were taped on here and there with colorful tape. Trevor wondered if he and Gabby should take a couple's photo as well.

Meanwhile, Gabby clutched her college letters close to her side. Trevor's palms were extra sweaty, and he wiped them on his faded jeans over and over again. Finally, it was their turn in line. Gabby ordered her favorite drink, Mango Milk Tea, and Trevor got the Green Apple Slush, the sweetest drink on the menu. After receiving their drinks, they finally started the task of opening their envelopes one by one. Gabby grabbed the UCLA envelope first since it was her dream school, her heart beating tumultuously in her chest. She ripped the envelope, not caring about the jagged edges. Her eyes grew wide as she read the first sentence of the letter.

"Oh my gosh!" she shrieked. She swallowed a boba ball whole.

Trevor scanned her letter and hugged her. "Congratulations!" he boomed. "LET'S GOOOOO!"

Four high schoolers sitting at the table behind them stopped drinking their boba and stared at them. Trevor and Gabby grinned together as Gabby stared at the letter in her hands with awe and glee. She wanted to get up and dance, if there weren't so many people around her.

"Oh my gosh, oh my gosh, oh my gosh!" she squealed in her little girl voice. She quickly got out her phone to text her parents the great news.

Trevor opened his letter from UC Santa Cruz and found out that he had gotten in.

"Wow! Congratulations, Trev!" Gabby shouted, clutching his shoulder and shaking it.

Trevor smiled sheepishly, but then his heart thudded to the floor. As they scanned his other envelopes lying on the table, they noticed they were all small, meaning he didn't get in.

"Isn't UCSC like five or six hours away?" Gabby asked her boyfriend, her heart sinking. Her stomach twisted into knots.

"Yea, it is," Trevor acknowledged.

Gabby stopped drinking her boba and stared down at the table, saying nothing. Trevor mustered up a smile and looked into Gabby's eyes that remained glazed over in melancholy. "I'll visit you, Gabby. I'll ride the train to you," he spoke warmly and reassuringly. He tried to sound strong for the both of them, though his heart felt drenched in sadness, too.

Gabby looked up and met his gaze. Trevor quickly drew her into his arms, placing her head close to his chest. She buried her face in his red polo shirt. He was silent for some long moments and it seemed like he was deep in thought as well.

"I don't want to be long distance," she moaned.

"There is no distance between us," Trevor said romantically, stroking her hair.

"But still," Gabby whimpered.

"I'll write to you every day," Trevor responded, trying to be optimistic.

Gabby giggled a little at what he said. Trevor's face grew serious and he stayed quiet, his brow furrowed.

After a while he spoke. "I'll study really hard my first year at UCSC and then try to transfer to UCLA," he promised.

Gabby lit up at the idea and beamed widely. She hugged Trevor tightly, putting her head against his chest again and smelling his sweet, clean scent. She tried to be mature about it and said no more. She then held Trevor's two hands in hers and felt his soft palms against her own. As she admired his majestic, pale hands, she silently promised herself that she would do all that it takes to maintain a great relationship with him.

Needing some fresh air, they left the boba shop. Gabby held Trevor from the side as they walked across the parking lot. She kept peering up at his face. He looked down into her eyes with a gaze of sincere love and care.

Once he got home, Trevor wrote her a long text:

~

Dear Gabby,

I know you're worried about how we will be once we become long distance. I promise you that I will do everything possible to make you happy. I am devoted to you with all my heart, mind, soul, and spirit. You are my one and only eternal love. Just as God has blessed us and changed our lives for the best, I know He is still our God and will help us when we are long distance. He will make our love only grow stronger and brighter. I will work hard at UCSC and try my best to get to UCLA by our second year. I adore you so much. Don't worry about a thing.

~

Gabby was lying flat upon her bed in a starfish formation, her face willingly being smothered by her blankets. When Gabby received the text from Trevor, she jumped. As she hungrily read his loving words, a great comfort flooded her soul, but she also felt uneasy as she shifted her legs at her bedside. She asked God, "Why?" Her worries became magnified like a great beast in the growing darkness of the evening. In the indigo blue twilight, she wrote Trevor this text:

~

Dear Trev,

I adore you and will adore you for the rest of my life. With every breath I breathe, I adore you. I will try my best to make you feel loved by me every day you are at UCSC. I know that God will help us. God loves us and I know He has a good plan for us.

Thank you for being so brave and helping me feel positive about our situation.

I adore you so much! I treasure you!

~

A sob stayed stuck in her throat, begging to be released. Gabby buried her face in her blankets again, wishing this were all just a bad dream. Just then, her phone lit up with a text. She reached for it, thinking it was Trevor again. But it was Rochelle: "Hey Gabby! Did you get into UCLA?"

Gabby shed tears of gratefulness. She hadn't talked to her friends much for a long time because of what she was going through. God knew she needed a friend at this very moment.

Wiping away her tears, she grabbed her phone and texted Rochelle back. "Hey, yea, I did. Are you free to talk on the phone?"

"Yea!" Rochelle replied immediately.

Gabby called Rochelle and was relieved to hear her friend's calming, nurturing voice. Rochelle was always so mature in difficult situations.

"I got into UCLA but Trevor is going to UCSC. So we'll be five hours apart."

"Oh my gosh…" Rochelle replied, truly sad for her.

"I know…" Gabby felt another sob forming in her throat.

"You guys are gonna make it through, though. You guys have such a strong bond."

Gabby smiled at Rochelle's words. "Thank you."

"I'll pray for you guys," Rochelle continued.

"Thanks!"

Knowing that Gabby felt very down, Rochelle thought of something encouraging to say. "I've never seen a guy more crazy about a girl. You are Trevor's whole world, his universe."

They both laughed loudly at Rochelle's last statement.

"He'll definitely make a way to see you. Definitely."

Gabby giggled sweetly. "Knowing Trevor, he would make a way," Gabby pondered.

"What college are you going to?" Gabby asked Rochelle.

"Cal State Long Beach!"

"Oh my gosh! You wanted to go there!"

The two girls chatted excitedly about their approaching college adventures, about the boys they liked, and about their families.

"You know, my mom told me not to tell anyone, but my dad has been ill." Gabby was startled at her own honesty. It seemed that Trevor had opened up a part of her heart that was so reluctant to open up to others.

"Oh my gosh. Are you serious?" Rochelle said. She didn't say anything to let Gabby talk more.

"Yeah, it's been really hard." Gabby finally felt the release of all her emotions before her best friend and she began to cry quietly.

"I'm so sorry I didn't know sooner," Rochelle said comfortingly. "What kind of illness does he have? Is it trauma from the war?"

Rochelle was always quick to perceive things about people. Gabby started from the beginning and told her everything, and asked her not to tell anybody, although she knew she wouldn't.

After their phone call, Gabby felt much better and, for the first time in a long time, dozed off into a restful sleep.

G&T

On the phone the following night, Gabby said, "Trev, I always wanted to go kayaking with you." She always spoke faster when she was excited. "I went kayaking with Girl Scouts at Catalina and it was so fun!"

Trevor gulped. How could he tell Gabby that he was afraid of being eaten by sharks? He had watched numerous Youtube videos of gigantic ferocious-looking sharks devouring arms, legs...He covered his face with one hand.

But wanting to look brave, and wanting to make Gabby happy, he said with all the brightness he could muster in his voice, "Let's go!"

Gabby squealed and then screamed with delight. She laughed a belly laugh. "Oh my gosh! Yes!"

Trevor quickly began searching up survival techniques and emergency procedures in the case he came face to face with a man-eating fish on his phone as Gabby continued to giggle with glee over speakerphone.

"I'M SO EXCITED!" she squealed again. "Hug," she said, to signal a virtual hug through the phone.

Trevor sighed with relief and happiness. "Hug," he said warmly, smiling into the night. Suddenly, all his fears had disappeared at the sound of Gabby's strong, comforting voice.

That night as soon as Gabby said good night, Trevor looked up the best kayaking experiences around them. After comparing the ones at Manhattan Beach, Hermosa, Redondo, Marina del Rey, and Long Beach, he decided Marina del Rey would be best. It would be their first date outside of the South Bay. Trevor grinned and lay back with a happy sigh upon his pillow, picturing Gabby's smile as he announced they'd be going kayaking at the best kayaking place ever, the Marina Aquatic Center. He also planned a romantic date afterwards in Westwood, Gabby's soon-to-be college town.

"Yeah!" he yelled into the silence of his room as he imagined their date night and Gabby's happiness.

Saturday came quickly and Trevor drove them to Marina del Rey. Gabby kept profusely apologizing for making him drive since she didn't drive on the freeway.

"It's okay, Gabby," Trevor said warmly like an older brother. He shot a glance at Gabby, his eyes squinting as the afternoon sun shone straight at them through the windshield as cars whizzed by. He admired Gabby's profile as she looked outside her window in peaceful silence. Suddenly, she looked at him with her big brown eyes and he quickly looked away.

"What…?" Gabby asked with a voice she never used. She was usually always so sweet and gentle. But now she was looking at him with an inquisitive, demanding look.

Trevor guffawed and grinned widely, still looking straight ahead and paying attention to his driving.

Gabby started laughing too. She was so happy to be going on this adventure.

"Trevor, is it okay if I sleep a little?" Gabby asked Trevor sweetly in her normal voice.

"Of course, darling," Trevor said in a deep, manly voice.

Gabby smiled at him with her deep, twinkling doe eyes again and then turned to her side and, holding her arms, tilted her head toward the window to sleep.

Trevor looked over at his girlfriend who always looked so peaceful and graceful. Suddenly, Gabby stretched out her hand and reached for Trevor's arm which rested on the center compartment of the car. Her hand gently held his arm, her eyes closed the entire time, and she settled herself into her nap.

Something moved inside of Trevor's heart and soul, and he felt something he never felt before. He felt like Gabby was his girl, and he wanted to be the one to protect her all of his life.

About fifteen minutes later, they arrived at the parking lot of Marina Aquatic Center, and Trevor looked over at Gabby who was still asleep. Always a light sleeper, Gabby awoke suddenly as she sensed Trevor looking at her face. She looked shocked and confused for a second, and then she quickly hugged Trevor, burying her face in his chest. Trevor's heart leapt. He froze for a second and then wrapped his strong arms around her but gently and

261

reassuringly. She just lay there for a while with her eyes closed and it looked as if she would fall asleep again, but then suddenly she opened her eyes wide and exclaimed, "Let's go!" Trevor laughed loudly again, and Gabby smiled a sleepy smile, still holding onto him and looking into his handsome face, her eyes level with his eyes. They just smiled into each other's eyes for a while.

As soon as they got to the small white building, a tanned man in his late-twenties wearing sunglasses and bright red swimming trunks approached them out of nowhere with a clipboard. He greeted them with a hearty handshake and said, "Welcome to the Aquatic Center!" with a wry smile. Trevor looked at Gabby who was all smiles as she flashed her bright, cheery smile at the employee. Trevor smiled too, but he secretly felt nervous. He scanned the area for life jackets, and at just that moment, the employee, whose name they learned was Frank, took them into a small, old-looking, dark shed and grabbed a blindingly yellow life jacket for each of them.

"Do you need help?" Frank asked Gabby, and Trevor shot him a jealous glance. Luckily, Gabby said, "No, I'm good, thank you," as she gently positioned her life jacket on her body.

Trevor fumbled with his life jacket, which he had never worn before, and Gabby, so quick to notice things about Trevor, lovingly came and pulled the various straps on the life jacket. "Is it nice and snug, Trevor?" she asked so sweetly, looking into his eyes with concern. He just smiled and nodded.

Gabby usually never wore shorts but that day she had worn light pink board shorts that said Roxy on the back and a Track and Field white t-shirt over her bright orange swimsuit that showed a little above the neck of her t-shirt. Trevor marveled at this new "athletic look" of his girlfriend that he never saw before.

Gabby confidently followed Frank's lead and Trevor followed close behind, keeping a wary eye on Frank.

The sun shone upon them with blinding brightness but friendliness, as if it were smiling upon this joyful day they were about to have. The asphalt lot was surrounded by the bay on three sides and was fairly empty. Trevor sighed peacefully as the beach breeze blew against his face and tousled his hair.

They turned a corner and came face to face with the kayak docking station. There about a hundred yellow, sturdy-looking, new kayaks with dark grey rubber paddles attached to the side of each one. Gabby and Trevor admired the neat rows of identical kayaks.

Trevor's heart beat a little faster and faster as Frank grabbed them a kayak and started to tell them the procedures.

"Have you guys kayaked before?" Frank asked. Trevor concentrated on Frank's overly white teeth against his extremely tan, orangish bronze skin.

Gabby spoke for them. "I have once, but Trevor–it's his first time." She smiled at Trevor, thrilled that they were on the brink of their adventure.

Frank placed the kayak on the pier and sat in it, demonstrating the motions of rowing for them to see. Trevor watched him with great focus and scrutiny, memorizing the motions. Frank then had Trevor and Gabby sit in the kayak and show him that they got it. Trevor was a natural, and Frank said with a hearty laugh and a blow of his whistle that hung around his tan, lean neck, "You're good to go!" "Remember to keep your life jackets on at all times!" he repeated. Then, he shoved the kayak onto the water, and held it down with his foot as he helped Gabby and Trevor step in. "Have fun!" he said as was his custom and stood, watching the two glide into the ocean waters.

Bobbing up and down on the ocean waves was an interesting sensation Trevor had never felt before and Gabby had forgotten. Squealing, Gabby started giggling. Trevor looked at her face which emanated pure glee. He internally vowed to himself to keep Gabby safe on this entire trip. Very quickly, they were rowing in rhythm and steadily traveling into the open sea beyond the bay, because Gabby said she "did not want to be stuck in a bay." Gabby looked across the sea, surrounded by very light blue sky, the gleaming sun, and a wonderful refreshing breeze and Trevor smiled at his adventurer and the freedom that overtook Gabby's soul at the moment. Trevor began to relax, feeling like kayaking was a cinch, much easier than he expected.

Their eagerness to row may have driven them too far; their arms began to get sore and they put down their paddles for a moment and let the kayak drift. Gabby playfully scooted toward Trevor a little to hug him, and as she smiled, looking past his shoulder upon the sea, she yelled, "Trevor! THERE'S A SHARK!" Trevor jumped and nearly fell backwards off the kayak. He grabbed Gabby closer to his body and swiftly turned his head in all directions around them, but nothing was in sight. Feeling Gabby starting to shake and giggle loudly against his chest, he realized it was a joke.

"Sorry, Trevor," Gabby said. "I didn't know–I didn't know it would scare you so much," she said in between giggles. "Hahahahaha," she kept laughing. Trevor still looked grim and a little pale but then he grinned.

"I never saw you laugh so much before Gabby," he said, observing this newness in his girlfriend. He hugged her again, to make the fear melt away completely from his body.

Her laughing slowly subsided and she looked up at Trevor's face. "Sorry," she said again, as she with both hands began to pull strands of hair off of his forehead and out of his eyes. He smiled lovingly at her two shining eyes, that to Trevor, shined brighter than the very turquoise waves that day.

"Let's go toward that cove," he told Gabby, his courage mounting.

Gabby looked in the direction in which Trevor was pointing and noticed a sea cave next to a cove. "It's a cave!" she yelled. She had always wanted to go into a sea cave.

"Let's do it!" she yelled, and the two began to eagerly and skillfully paddle toward the alluring spot that was about seventy yards away. Now and then Trevor would scan all their surroundings to make sure the coast was clear.

They were making great progress and Trevor was starting to really enjoy the feeling of his arms exerting force upon the paddle and against the push of the water current underneath. They were the perfect team.

"We're almost there!" Trevor boomed like a ship captain.

Just then, Trevor heard Gabby say, "Oops." He looked at where Gabby was looking at upon the water and saw that her hair tie had bounced off her head as she was tying her hair and landed upon the water. It was a scrunchie hair tie with a small white fabric hibiscus flower sewn onto it that Gabby often wore and Trevor knew she liked.

"I gotchu," Trevor said reassuringly and reached for the hair tie that was at arm's length. Just then, a wave carried the hairtie away from Trevor and he lost balance and crashed overboard.

What Trevor and Gabby did not know was that Trevor's life jacket had a tiny slit in it that the Aquatic Center had never noticed or fixed.

His life jacket began to fill quickly with water and Trevor, not knowing why he wasn't floating, began to panic and try his best to tread water. But he had never properly learned how to swim and he was being pulled down into the ocean.

Gabby, always very alert during emergency situations since she was young, dove into the water and made her way toward Trevor with quick strokes. She didn't know how her body remembered how to swim so well when she hadn't swum in years. Trevor was sinking fast and he swallowed large gulps of water as he continued thrashing around and kicking his legs as fast and as hard as possible. After seemingly endless moments he felt Gabby's hand around his arm. Gabby decided she had to do something drastic. Since she was a good swimmer, she pulled her lifejacket off herself with amazing speed and quickly draped it around Trevor's body from behind him and tried to secure it. Trevor had already pulled off his own jacket since the weight of it was dragging him down. At this point, Trevor's eyes were closing as he was unable to take in enough air. Gabby was holding him from behind and as soon as she felt the vest buckle click against Trevor she pushed his body up out of the water. Reaching the surface Trevor started spitting water out of his mouth and coughing. He became more alert.

Gabby quickly got into the kayak first and pulled Trevor with all her might, helping him climb onto the boat. She grabbed his back and pulled his body in with all her strength. Trevor lay against Gabby's lap, his head resting upon her legs as she sat cross-legged. Gabby searched his face in a panic. Trevor just lay motionless with his eyes closed, embarrassed about what just happened. Gabby placed her ear over his nose and listened for his breaths.

"Trevor, I think I need to do CPR. Should I do CPR?" Gabby asked urgently, not knowing how to do CPR. Just then, Trevor opened his eyes and started to laugh, imagining Gabby do mouth-to-mouth CPR on him.

"Trevor!" Gabby screamed and hugged him. Overwhelmed that he was alive, Gabby placed her face against his cheek as she hugged his neck and her lips pressed against his wet cheek.

Trevor's eyes grew wide and he knew he was fully alive and okay now.

"Trevor!" Gabby screamed again. And then she started to cry. Everything had freaked out Gabby.

"I thought, I thought you almost…died," Gabby said between little sobs.

Trevor grinned as he held the wet Gabby in his arms, smiling away into the horizon, having not known that his girlfriend was so brave and so awesome. Kissing her wet, cold cheek sprinkled with freckles, Gabby jumped a little.

"Do you know you kissed me on the cheek Gabby?" Trevor asked playfully and warmly, looking into his adorable girlfriend's face.

Gabby stopped wiping away tears and started to smile a very cute smile that widened more and more. She felt her cheek where Trevor just kissed her and looked down for a moment.

Her shyness disappearing in that moment, Gabby came up to Trevor and kissed him on the cheek again, with all her love. She felt she had almost lost him.

They both started giggling and the sun began to set at the horizon to celebrate their love that was brighter than the flames of the sun.

The two quickly made their way back to the Aquatic Center because Trevor noted that they now only had one functioning life jacket and it was too dangerous. As Trevor rowed back with Gabby, he kept looking at her with a look of wonderment but Gabby did not notice. She was too busy rowing. "She's so brave. She's so clutch," Trevor thought to himself.

Once they got changed, they piled into the car and were once again on their next adventure. "TO WESTWOOD!" Gabby boomed, with a giggle of delight. She looked over at her handsome boyfriend, and shot him a big sneaky smile. Trevor started laughing again, thinking his girlfriend was so funny and fun to be around.

It was both their first time in Westwood, and their eyes grew wide in admiration over the sights. There were long, tree-lined boulevards that were wide enough for both cars and people to travel through comfortably. Boutiques and restaurants they had never heard of lined the blocks and everything looked both chic and elegant but also friendly and casual. College students roamed around, some in groups and some in pairs, and they looked relaxed and happy to be there.

Gabby sighed, looking out the window. Trevor intuitively sensed she was feeling much more at peace about being long-distance for college.

As they strolled hand-in-hand along the sidewalk after parking, Trevor asked Gabby, "What made you like UCLA so much?"

Gabby smiled a peaceful smile at just the thought of UCLA. "When I first went on the campus with my parents, I just felt at home. The campus is so beautiful. When I visited UC Berkeley, the kids were carrying these HUGE backpacks." She acted like a UC Berkeley student trudging down a hill with a heavy backpack with a curmudgeonly face. "They looked like these sad turtles. And I did not want to go there," she said.

Trevor chuckled at her description and tone of voice.

"Oh!" Gabby suddenly said, looking through a store window. There was a large blue and white sign that read BRANDY MELVILLE and the shop window had ivory mannequins clad in chic girls' clothing.

"That would look better on you, Gabby!" Trevor said, pointing to an outfit on one of the mannequins.

Gabby grinned, feeling lucky that her boyfriend was always full of compliments for her. Grabbing Trevor's hand, she said excitedly, "Let's go in."

Watching Gabby in her feminine element, walking swiftly in and out of clothing racks, gave Trevor another view of his girlfriend.

Gabby eyed a pink knee-length dress with wide straps that had gold buttons going down the front. She waited until Trevor was paying attention to the dress under which she stood. "Ever since we started dating, I'm starting to like more girly stuff! I was such a tomboy when I was younger," she said.

Gabby laughed. "Actually, I was a baller wannabe in middle school! All the boys said I had "big guns." And I was like, "What are guns?" And they said, "MUSCLES!"" She guffawed and Trevor did too.

"You do have big muscles, Gabby! You pulled me out of the ocean with your bare hands!" Trevor said playfully, his eyes open wide for comic effect.

"Haha!" Gabby laughed. She stayed silent for a moment, rummaging through some other clothes. But then what he said sank in and she smiled to herself. Turning around to face Trevor she grew serious for a moment, imagining what could've happened out there if things had gone bad.

"What?" Trevor asked. Then he held up one of Gabby's arms and told her, "Flex, Gabby! OOH, show 'em those muscles!"

Gabby started laughing again and hugged Trevor amidst the clothes.

Trevor eyed the pink dress again and asked Gabby kindly, "Do you want that Gabby? I'll buy it for you."

Gabby smiled widely but then said, "Nooooooo…"

"Why?" Trevor asked, studying her face.

"I'll buy it," she said.

"No, I will," he said, reaching for the hanger on which the dress hung.

Gabby tried to chase him down before he reached the cashier counter, but it was too late. He had swiftly taken out his wallet and presented cash to the cashier. Gabby realized it was too late and just smiled at the cashier, a stylish woman in her late twenties.

"Thank you, Trevor," she said quietly from behind him as he made the transaction.

It was the first time he had bought her something while they were shopping together.

Gabby's heart leapt and warmed as Trevor handed her the shiny pearly white bag that contained her new dress. Embracing him, she said, "Thank you Trevor," feeling very thankful for him and his generosity.

As twilight descended upon the city, the trees along the boulevards lit up with stringed lights and the mood was great, or so the romantic Trevor thought.

But Trevor did not know that when night came, Gabby tended to think less optimistically and more fearfully about her future. She had gone through too much in her family and felt kind of shaky when it became dark every night. But Gabby did not tell him this.

Studying Gabby's face carefully, Trevor noticed she looked a bit more tired, even older, in the fading sunlight. Although she smiled at him, when her face was resting, she looked a little distracted and worried.

Reaching for her hand, Trevor asked, "Are you okay?"

Gabby looked at him, a little startled. She mustered up all her hope and bravery and, not wanting to worry him and not wanting to feed her fears, said, "Yea! I'm okay," in a cheery voice.

Trevor did not ask any further to not intrude upon her, but naturally held her hand gently.

"We're almost there," Trevor said reassuringly as they turned the corner to reach a brightly lit Diddy Riese, the most famous cookie ice cream sandwich shop in LA. Gabby's face looked in amazement at the line of twenty people outside the door of the small shop. The rich smell of baking cookies wafted out the front and filled the whole stretch of the block.

Upon entering Diddy Riese, Trevor and Gabby's bodies were in close proximity with college students crowding the tiny, madly popular business.

Trevor drooled at the sight of huge ice cream sandwiches that people were carrying in small paper trays. Trevor loved ice cream almost as much as basketball. The ice cream looked so rich and creamy and Trevor and Gabby read all the flavors with amazement–Butter Pecan, Chocolate, Chocolate Chip, Cookie Dough, Cookies & Cream, Espresso Chip, Mint Chocolate Chip, Peanut Butter Cup, Rocky Road, Strawberry, Strawberry Cheesecake Chunk, and Vanilla Bean.

Trevor noticed Gabby looked free of her worries and just enraptured by the ice cream. He placed his arm gently over her shoulder.

"Trevor, what are you gonna get?" she asked, still studying the ice cream flavors.

"Mmmm...Espresso Chip!" he said resolutely. "How 'bout you?"

"I'm gonna get Cookie Dough. But can I try your Espresso Chip? I like coffee ice cream," Gabby said.

"Of course!" Trevor replied, still studying Gabby's youthful face to make sure she was okay.

After choosing their cookie flavors, they each held their gargantuan ice cream sandwiches with glee and, at the same time, took a huge bite out of them. Gabby had gotten red velvet cookies and Trevor had gotten white chocolate macadamia. Swapping sandwiches, they took a bite out of each other's, wiping ice cream that had smeared across their faces with an embarrassed giggle.

"This is mmm…delicious!" Trevor squealed with huge popping eyeballs.

Gabby looked up from her sandwich for a second and saw that Trevor only had two bites left of his.

"You ate it so fast!" she laughed, "I didn't know you liked ice cream that much!"

Trevor gave a cute surprised look and then chuckled and continued to gobble down his cookie-ice cream morsel like it was just air.

Gabby continued staring at him and laughed loudly again when she saw the remaining ice cream sandwich disappear like smoke into his mouth. Grabbing her napkin, she gently wiped a little cookie crumb off Trevor's side of his mouth and he sweetly stayed still like a baby with his mama.

Stepping out of the shop and onto the sidewalk again, Gabby, overcome by peacefulness and happiness, spontaneously embraced Trevor and began swaying, wordlessly asking him to dance. Clasping his hand in hers, he placed his cheek softly against

Gabby's and they began swaying in the middle of the sidewalk, not noticing any of the many people crowding around the storefront. They only felt the singular moment of being in each other's arms and only saw each other. There was no music, only the din of the city, but they heard the music flowing out of their souls.

The whole universe stood still for a moment, and they heard the song of the galaxies, celebrating the two, celebrating their love, celebrating their courage in coming this far.

"Trevor," Gabby said softly as their dance came to a stop. "I adore you."

Trevor looked into her eyes and said with every ounce of his heart, "I adore you."

They didn't even realize that passersby were turning their heads to watch the pair and observing the rare connection between them.

G&T

The next day was Sunday, and Gabby was at home with just her dad in the next room. He stayed in his room the whole day and didn't say a word to her. The entire house was as silent as a mausoleum. It didn't affect her at first, but as the hours ticked by, Gabby grew more and more frustrated. She tried to distract herself by looking at fun things on her phone, like videos of cute puppies, but as soon as a video would end and she'd return to the silence of her home, she felt she would implode. She didn't want to burden Trevor so she didn't tell him, but she felt so bad inside that she finally texted him. She didn't tell Trevor how she felt, but Trevor already knew just by the way her texts sounded.

"Where do you want to go?" Trevor asked as he opened the car door for her in front of her driveway.

"I don't know," Gabby said in a defeated tone, looking down. Trevor studied her young face that now appeared aged and strained.

"Do you want a green tea frappuccino?" Trevor asked in his funny booming voice, elongating the "o" in "frappuccino," knowing that that was her favorite Starbucks drink.

Gabby lit up a little at the thought of food. "Okay!" she answered, getting into the car.

After they swung by Starbucks, Trevor drove them to Wilson Park where they could sit amongst the lovely pear blossoms that were in bloom. They found an empty bench near the pear blossom trees and Trevor wiped the place where Gabby would be sitting swiftly with his hands. Gabby smiled widely and said thank you. As soon as they sat, she leaned her head against his shoulder.

As she stayed quiet next to him, Trevor took out his phone and said, "Gabby, I have a quote I want to show you." He read aloud from his phone: "Be soft. Do not let the world make you hard. Do not let the pain make you hate. Do not let the bitterness steal your sweetness. Take pride that even though the rest of the world may disagree, you still believe it to be a beautiful place."

"Hey! I know that quote! I like it too," Gabby said excitedly.

Trevor held Gabby warmly. After a while, he spoke. "Do you think you can find it in your heart to forgive your dad?"

Gabby stayed silent, the scar on her cheek shining in the sun. Trevor read the lines of pain in the scar, and looked down, wondering if he should've asked her that.

"I don't know if I'm bitter at him, or if I'm just upset...that both my parents aren't...great," Gabby said, squinting and frowning at the sun. Suddenly her green tea frappuccino in her hand didn't look so appetizing. The chill in the wind was felt by her bones as it traveled through the trees of Wilson Park to the bench where they sat side by side. She silently beheld the little white petals flying from the pear blossom trees. They looked like snow to Gabby's winter soul.

"We've got to love the people who are hardest to love," Trevor said gently, his warm, soft hand taking ahold of Gabby's. He said it as if it was something he had told himself many times before. She loved how he never sounded like he was judging or preaching to her.

The truth of those words hibernated in her ears; Gabby grew quiet again, and then looked down, holding in a sigh.

Trevor noticed the glint of the golden sun in Gabby's brown pupils. "That way you'll feel free," Trevor added quietly, as if he had once been trapped by bitterness as well.

Gabby looked up at the sky, as if looking for some way out or inspiration. She saw a couple ravens lift off a branch, and wished she could fly far away too. But at that moment, a Bible verse entered her heart: "A house divided cannot stand." She then realized that she didn't want her family to fall; she wanted her family to stay standing, stay together. She searched the gray grains in the sidewalk for a moment, exploring the corners of her mind and heart. After her search, she decided to take the difficult stand. But she pictured herself as a baby horse trying to get up on its feet at the size of the feat.

"The only way I could forgive my parents is if God helps me. I can't do it on my own," she answered Trevor truthfully, finally looking up and studying his handsome, haggard face with a smile. She suddenly realized that he appeared so old and wizened, perhaps from carrying her burdens. She hugged him tightly and lovingly to give him back some of the energy she had taken and kissed him sweetly on the cheek.

Trevor smiled and looked at Gabby, surprised by her change in attitude. Just a few months ago, Gabby would run away whenever he'd discuss her family with her. He remembered how she walked toward the dark forest in the middle of the night at Aunt Marie's. They were making great progress.

Stroking Gabby's long hair gently, Trevor said reassuringly, "I'll pray with you. I know it's not easy, Gabby." His warm, tender voice soothed Gabby's heart and she closed her eyes, resting against Trevor's comfy shoulder. Gabby let her mind drift with the white petals that were floating around them.

Just then, she thought about how God had saved her, how Jesus died on the cross and forgave all of her sins. She had received so much grace and mercy from God. Then, she, too, could forgive her parents.

"Trevor, can you help prepare me to talk to my dad?" Gabby asked with a new clarity and joy in her voice, her eyes still closed. She opened her eyes. "I want to show him that I care for him, and–ask him to get therapy."

"If you think God will help me," Gabby added.

Trevor beamed and almost chuckled with joy and disbelief. "Of course God will help you. God is for you." Trevor thanked God in his mind with a small excited grin.

Tenderly hugging Gabby, Trevor rested in the miracle that had just happened. Something new was growing in Gabby's heart. Trevor silently prayed that God would give him the right words to prepare Gabby for the big moment of talking with her dad. Later, Trevor sent Gabby a text.

~

Dear Gabby,

Sometimes, our key relationships seem to shift and change. We get afraid that we'll never get back what we lost, that we won't ever be the same with the people we love. But our family ties are stronger than you think. Even though you may not feel loved at times, you are. Your parents sometimes feel lost and small, just like you and me. So, even though they love you, they might not be able to express it during their hardships. They are just human.

You are their beloved daughter.

What you say does matter to your dad. Remember the place that you hold in his heart as his dear, lovely daughter. Remember the good times of laughter and love you had shared with him. Before he experienced war, he was a great dad, right? And right now, I'm sure he's struggling to be beneath the symptoms of his illness. Speak to him truthfully from your heart and I pray that God would open his ears and his heart to listen. That he would hear each and every word. That your words would sink into his heart and he would respond with kindness, gentleness and great love.

I and many others are praying for you, your dad, and your whole family.

I love you and am so proud of you, Gabby.

Do not be afraid. God is with you!

I am with you all the way!

~

Gabby looked at Trevor's text in astonishment. His words somehow helped her recall the good times she had with her dad and the love they shared. She smiled a little as she was imbued with a fresh hope and joy. She grabbed her journal and lay on her bed with it, poised with her pen in hand and her stomach against her comfy mint-green covers. She closed her eyes and earnestly asked God to help her write a letter that would get through to her dad. She opened her eyes. Then, with intense concentration and determination, she started writing all that she really wanted to say to him. Thirty minutes later, she looked upon what she wrote, and was amazed at what God helped her to accomplish.

~

Dear Dad,

I know that right now, all you might see is your illness, and it may make you feel ugly, and broken. But I wanted to let you know that you are not these things. You'll never be a label. You are my dad. You are a person who is inherently worthy and beautiful. You're wonderful. I know that the Lance Choi that we all know and love is still in there. I read in a book once that nothing could touch our soul because God guards it. Things can hurt us, but they can't harm us. Lance Choi is still inside you, unharmed, and I'll wait until he gets to fully express himself. I'm sorry for not being better at understanding you. How much pain you were going through alone. I will pray for you and fight for you until the day you are better. I love you regardless. I will always love you, Dad. Thank you for being the greatest Dad ever. You're our hero.

Love,

Gabby

~

Gabby wiped away a couple tears that had suddenly emerged as she reread it, and with a courage she knew must've come from God, grabbed her phone swiftly to text her dad.

"Dad, do you want to go to the Palos Verdes Botanical Gardens with me?" she asked. She felt he would feel most at peace at the Gardens since he loved flowers and nature, and if he felt comfortable, there was a better chance he would listen.

"Okay," he replied briefly, but to Gabby's relief. She continued to pray in her head.

As Gabby drove them up Hawthorne Boulevard, the father and daughter remained silent, but she noticed her dad was smiling with that pensive smile of his outside the window. He even turned up the classical music on the radio.

"He's in a good mood," Gabby thought to herself, glad but nervous.

Gabby led them up a winding path to the top of the hill where an old white wooden bench sat, overlooking the stretch of rose gardens below. Her dad slowly sat down; he seemed weary, but Gabby was not sure if it was a weariness of the body or of the soul. She peered at her dad's face, tracing the wrinkle lines beside his eyes with her eyes, studying his steady smile and furrowed brow. He was there, but not there, as if his soul were somewhere else at the same time. As if she could reach out her hand and touch only a phantom.

Gabby looked at the rose gardens that her dad was studying, and her eyes caught the sight of yellow roses, their petals as yellow as egg yolks. The warm golden hues felt like a prick in her heart, for they reminded her of the roses her dad had always brought to her recitals...the love that they once shared.

Without realizing it, Gabby opened her mouth and expressed her memory to her father: "Dad, remember when you brought me yellow roses…" Before she could finish, Lance spoke.

"Every year," he said, still observing the scenery below and smiling that wry, aged smile.

For a moment Gabby was glad he actually remembered, but then bitterness crept up in her heart because he was no longer that dad. She quickly let out a deep breath, as if to banish the negative thoughts and feelings away.

"Dad," Gabby said, looking at her dad's face again, with more love in her heart. "I wrote something for you today...in my journal."

Gabby handed her treasured leather journal slowly to her dad and opened up to the page with the letter, for him to read to himself. She took another deep breath and rocked her body slightly forward and backward on the bench next to him. She prayed quickly in her head, thankful Trevor was praying too at this very hour.

"Why don't you read it to me Gabby?" her father suddenly said, his voice almost like his original voice, tender and certain. Tears almost squirted out of Gabby's eyes then. Her lip trembling, she knew that she would possibly break apart while reading it, but she sucked in her bravery and she began reading it in the tenderest, most genuine voice she could muster.

When she was done, she noticed her dad had closed his eyes. It looked almost as if he were asleep and dreaming a good dream. For a while he stayed that way, but alarming her even more, he took one of her hands and held it in his dry, coarse one. He cupped his other hand over hers, just like he used to.

Gabby didn't hold back her tears then, and expressed everything on her heart.

"Dad, I want you to go to therapy. I—don't want to see you be like this, suffer, anymore." She wiped away the wetness from her cheek. "I think you can get better if you go."

"Please?" she added weakly, her voice still tearful and snot now emerging from her nostrils.

Her dad chuckled then, the rays of the sunset shining golden on his face. For a moment, his old self seemed to reappear in fullness.

"The season is changing," he spoke as the philosopher he was. "The roses are blooming, and it is time for me to bloom too," her father joked with that sweet smile of his, but sincerity giving weight to his words.

Gabby couldn't believe her ears. She looked at her dad in utter surprise, her tears stopping. He meant yes.

Gabby buried her head in his arm and smiled and then cried some more, and then smiled again, until the sun went down. Her dad held her hand until they got up to go home.

~

Gabby collapsed into Trevor's arms that evening and squeezed her eyes shut against his chest. Trevor hugged her tightly back, asking urgently, "What happened, Gabby?" He had been waiting for the news all day.

Gabby stayed silent for a moment, feeling small in the face of such a titanic feat. "He said he'll go," she said, not believing even her own words coming out of her mouth, her voice muffled with her face pressed against his chest. A smile crept up in her mouth. "He said he'll go!" she said more loudly with a laugh of relief.

Trevor's eyes brimmed suddenly with joyous tears, as if they had been waiting to come out. "Gabby!" Trevor yelled, scooping her up and lifting her a foot off the ground.

"That is amazing!" he yelled so that the whole neighborhood could hear.

Gabby beamed into Trevor's face in the ever-thickening night, feeling very proud of herself all of a sudden. The chilly night air crept beneath Gabby's sweater and she began to shiver. Trevor saw this and quickly led her into the car, opening the car door for her.

"Trevor! It was because you helped me!" Gabby squealed, reaching over to squeeze him tight.

But Trevor quickly shook his head no and took Gabby's hand, saying, "Let's pray to thank God." Closing his eyes, he spoke in a thundering voice that took Gabby by surprise.

~

Dear Father,

Thank you so much. You've heard the cry of our hearts. You saw Gabby's dad and his suffering. You saw Gabby's suffering. Thank you for rescuing us. Thank you that he agreed to go to therapy. We know this miracle is all because of You. Thank you for being so good and mighty toward us. You're the wonder-working God. We love you. We praise you. We worship you.

In Jesus' name, amen.

~

Gabby was speechless in wonder. She wondered at who her boyfriend was–how his heart could love God so much, how he humbly gave all the glory to God. When they opened their eyes, Trevor wiped tears off his cheeks. Gabby searched his beautiful eyes that shone like two gems in the night, her heart moved by how much he cared for her. He quickly embraced her and patted her back comfortingly.

"Good job, Gabby. Good job."

Gabby started bawling and Trevor embraced her. He patted her back, soothing her gently. "It's okay, it's okay," he murmured to her. Trevor kissed her cheeks and stroked her hair until she stopped crying.

The school bell rang to dismiss Mr. Durbin's English class. Lunchtime. In a motion that they had done a hundred times as students, Toad, Cid, and Trevor uniformly swung their backpack over their shoulders as a procession of students staring at their phones all tried to exit through the same door. Unlike his peers, Trevor's attention averted from his phone's siren call in search for one Gabby Choi. She methodically organized her belongings into her backpack, treating each item with the utmost care and attention. Trevor stood still, waiting, as the throng of students adjusted around him. Toad and Cid sensed that their friend was no longer with them and shouted for him from out in the hallway.

"Trevor, you coming?"

Trevor waved his hand to usher them along to go without him.

Soon, they were the only students left in the classroom. Gabby finally looked up and saw Trevor waiting for her. Mr. Durbin, like any busy teacher, sat at his desk, typing away on his laptop.

"Were you waiting for me?" Gabby played coy, knowing full well that Trevor did wait for her, yet still was incredibly touched by the small gesture.

Trevor smiled that smile of his that created a small dimple on his left cheek. Gabby quickly grabbed onto Trevor's arm and laughed with glee. He looked down at her as his once small smile widened as he could not help but smile as big as he possibly could. She held tightly onto his left arm as she too looked at him, adoringly, lovingly, wholly.

A cough from the corner of the room broke the couple's adoring gaze. Mr. Durbin found a chance to look up from his work and with a wide-eyed look gave them leave to exit the class.

The couple, love-stricken, glided through the hallway, passing gawking stares and gossiping peers.

Trevor Song and Gabrielle Choi. Together. Who could have guessed?

They soon found themselves in the school's quad and sat themselves on a ledge of one of the planters. The quad quickly buzzed with excitement. Each group of students cliqued amongst themselves. Gabby's usual group of friends near the band room. A group of freshmen with their large backpacks huddled together around another table, slapping down binders and trading cards against the table. Some sophomores circled on the grass all looking at their phones nearby. Trevor unzipped his backpack. He found and opened a bag of chips to share with Gabby.

Looking afar, away from Gabby for what seemed like the first time today, Trevor let the words fall from his lips. "I've decided what I want to do."

Gabby, in mid-munch, widened her eyes and gasped. Holding his arm, she exclaimed her curiosity, still covering her mouth, careful not to spit anything out.

Trevor turned his gaze toward her. His brown eyes focused upon her. "I've decided I want to be a writer."

Gabby, still wide-eyed, tightened her grip on Trevor's arm and excitedly shook it. Her face turned crimson.

"Gabby, are you okay? Are you choking?" Trevor began to pat her back as Toad and Cid shouted out for them.

As Toad and Cid greeted them, Gabby finally finished her chips and exclaimed, "Trevor is going to be a writer!" Toad and Cid looked at one another then looked at Trevor, who gave them a slight nod and awkward smile.

Before the aspiring writer could respond, Cid sat next to him and patted his back.

"Imagine that. Trevor Song. Writer extraordinaire. What are you going to write? For the newspaper?"

Cid, imitating a newscaster, placed an imaginary microphone in front of Toad, who was busily devouring Trevor's leftover chips.

"Great analysis Theodore. What's this? We have breaking news. There has been an accident on the 405. Trevor Song, acclaimed journalist and reporter, is on the scene." Cid, holding his hand to his ear, moved the imaginary microphone in front of Trevor who played along.

"One moment Cid. This just in. There is even more breaking news. Jim is stealing my chips and eating all of them." Trevor immediately reached for the bag of chips but noticed immediately that Toad had finished them off. Trevor crumpled the bag and tossed it back at Toad.

A satisfied Toad finally felt it appropriate to enter the conversation, "What are you going to do as a writer?" Toad was always the more thoughtful of the two friends.

Gabby, amused by the whole interaction of the three friends, moved her gaze toward Trevor again, waiting for his answer.

Trevor ran his fingers through his curly, brown hair and looked off into the distance. "That's the thing. I don't know yet. I am going to find out what I want to write about. That's the journey."

The three onlookers stared at Trevor for what seemed like minutes. Toad's munching broke the silence.

Cid patted Toad's stomach. "Toad, let's go get some food."

"Where? The cafeteria?"

Cid, too, looked off into the distance and whispered into the air, "That's the thing. I don't know. That's the journey." The two chuckled amongst themselves as Trevor playfully kicked Cid away. Soon Trevor and Cid started wrestling one another with Toad commentating.

Gabby looked on with bewilderment. It was the first time Gabby had seen boys interact with one another up close. There was such joy there. She made sure to remember that moment.

With his curly brown hair in disarray, Trevor returned with a large, boyish grin. Gabby reached out to pat down a tuft of his hair, gently matting the stray strands. She soon noticed Trevor staring at her with amazement. He took hold of her wrist and placed it down to the side of the planter.

Trevor coursed with adrenaline from wrestling. He boldly grabbed Gabby's hands and beamed with determination. "Just to clarify, Gabby, things can change with this writing thing, but for now, I am going to give it my all. I don't know where this will go. It's my senior year. It's too late to make a writing club or whatever. I'm going to find a way to pursue this passion. Whatever I am going to do, I'm going to give it my hundred percent." Trevor took deep breaths between the sentences, making sure the weight of the words felt true to him and to Gabby.

The sun rays reflected in Gabby Choi's usually dark brown eyes, giving them a lighter, softer, chocolate-brown hue. Her eyes focused on his. "I know. You always give your best. I'm a witness to that. And I will support your dreams all the way."

Their intertwined hands pulsed: resolute, fearless, and bold. The bell rang once again, summoning the crowds to their next class and quieting the quad. The two held hands until they were the only ones left, still sitting on that planter's edge.

290

Ever since Gabby's dad agreed to get therapy, Gabby and her mom teamed up to research the best hospitals and centers that her dad could possibly go to. They read testimonials of actual veterans online and called various places. After visiting their top three choices with Lance, they decided on Bridgeport Hospital for Veterans which was two hours east of Toccoa. The ten days leading up to his hospitalization sped by and Lance seemed hopeful but sad that he would be lonely in the hospital apart from his family.

Finally, the big day arrived and Gabby found herself inside the small hospital lobby, which smelled old and felt quaint, but appeared neat. It was a clinic that was founded in the 1950s with a long history of service to veterans. The lobby reflected how old-fashioned it was, with a small registration desk and a single potted plant on an adjacent counter. A few awards from the government hung in gold frames on the wall, proclaiming the clinic's excellent service and assistance to veterans. Both the carpet and the wooden walls were a deep brown hue. No one was around but the Choi family and one other patient seated at the corner of the room in a wheelchair.

Hugging her dad tight, Gabby felt a tornado of emotions flurry around inside of her. Her father stood relatively stiffly but patted her hair three times gently. She looked up into his eyes and saw that they were still distant, but a little less hard than usual. Today, his eyes were drooping like the eyes of an old, lost dog. Trying to imagine that her dad would come back as the strong, cheerful man that he once was, Gabby mustered up her courage to tell him goodbye.

"Dad, I'll miss you," she said. She wanted her voice to come out bright but it cracked a little at the "you." She smiled gently at her dad.

"I'll try my best," he spoke clearly, a flicker of confidence in his gaze toward her, to her surprise. Gabby let out a little gasp. She couldn't believe the change. The miracle that she and Trevor were praying for was perhaps already starting to unfold.

Looking around the lobby, Gabby spotted the young soldier sitting in the wheelchair. He had muscular arms and was wearing a plain white tank top and a bandage around his left eye. Though this place would remind her father of battle, it also seemed like a safe place where he could fully be himself. As she peered at the bandaged eye of the man, wondering what happened, Gabby shuddered. At that moment, it dawned on her how little she actually knew about her father and his experience in Afghanistan. She could not begin to imagine what it had actually been like. She wished she had known more about what he went through and understood him more instead of being impatient and wanting him to change.

Just then, she got a text from Trevor as if God were silencing her worries. "Gabby, I'm proud of you and your great love for your family. Your dad is in good hands. Don't worry."

She beamed down at her phone in disbelief. Just then, a tall, heavy-set, kind-looking African American male nurse approached them and smiled broadly and genuinely at the family. Gabby and her mom hugged Lance one last time. Holding Lance's shoulder gently, the nurse slowly walked away from them with him down the clean corridor. For a moment, her dad looked back once at his family, a look of helplessness and timidity written all over his face.

As they waved at him with bright, encouraging smiles that hid the ache in their hearts, they couldn't help but remember all the times they had to say goodbye to him in the past. He would be wearing his army fatigues and he would look back swiftly to wave goodbye with an unshakeable fortitude in his brown eyes. He had looked so confident and unconquerable back then. Gabby pushed away her feelings of helplessness and grabbed onto her courage to continue to smile at her dad and imbue hopefulness in him, with a power she never knew she had until then.

G&T

S itting in church the next day, Gabby listened intently as her pastor, Pastor Byron, spoke from the stage. Gorgeous natural light streamed into the sanctuary from the tall windows that lined either side of the pews. She sat next to her mom, who was wearing a lilac blouse and cream-colored skirt with dark purple flowers. For a brief moment, Gabby turned her head and studied her mom's face, making sure she was feeling okay. It was their first Sunday attending church without Dad. Her mom appeared a little tired but okay.

Just then, Gabby heard Pastor Byron say her favorite Bible verse: "God works all things together for the good of those who love him." The elderly pastor had deep lines around his mouth from smiling at his congregation for decades with that warmth that radiated from his heart.

"God can take even the messy parts of our lives and create beauty–beauty from the ashes," he said into the mic, tenderly and genuinely.

Gabby's heart started thudding fast. That was her. Suddenly, she remembered the time she sat alone at the beach with her dad's guitar last year. It had been raining, but then a huge rainbow appeared. When she saw it she felt this hope in her heart–hope that something good was coming. "That something good was Trevor," she realized. "Trevor was the answer that God sent me to come out of the darkness I lived in because of my family. He helped me believe that God loves me and is still caring for me. And now, I even have hope that Dad could get better."

Gabby grinned radiantly. "God, you surprised me," she said almost aloud. She gazed at the large wooden cross on the church stage where a ceramic white figure of Jesus hung. "Even though death seemed to have the final say…Even though his suffering was great…Ultimately it saved the world," she reflected. "And he rose again to life."

"Even in your life, Gabby, I transform the darkness into light, the curses into blessings," God whispered into her heart all of a sudden. She rarely heard God's voice so she felt a flutter of excitement and joy in her chest.

After church, Gabby ran all the way to Trevor's house to tell him about what God had done for her. As Trevor jogged toward her out of his house, his handsome hair blowing in the wind, she jumped into his arms.

"Gabby," he laughed, sounding surprised. "What's the matter?"

"You were the answer!" she yelled.

He had never seen her this excited.

"You were the answer God gave me!"

Trevor smiled, tears in his eyes. He was elated to see that she was so happy and free. But he scratched his head, not knowing what exactly she meant. "I didn't do anything," he said, something he often said to Gabby.

Catching her breath, Gabby held Trevor's hand with both of her hands, squishing the softness of his palm. "God gave me you at just the right time, to help me get better! And God will make my dad better too!" She began to dance in his yard, jumping up and down, not caring that neighbors were walking past on the sidewalk.

Trevor pulled her in for an embrace. "Amen," he said, pressing his forehead gently against hers. "Thank you," he said with sincerity.

Heads pressed against each other, they smiled. Their noses touched lightly, and they gave each other an adoring eskimo kiss.

"What do you want to do this afternoon?" Trevor asked, staring at his girlfriend's lovely face. Her face appeared younger because of her joy.

"Umm…I don't know! What do you want to do?"

"Want to go to Mirror Lake? We've never been there before," Trevor suggested.

Gabby giggled and looked at her boyfriend with a suspicious sideways glance. "Isn't that where all the kids…make out?" Her voice got quieter at the words, "make out".

Trevor gulped. "Yes, but I want to go there with you because it's calm and peaceful."

296

Gabby guffawed loudly and unabashedly and playfully hit his arm. For a moment, she thought about it. "Okay! Let's go!"

Mirror Lake was once a lake but was now dried up. Soft, brown cattail plants bordered it and a lone willow tree drooped its long branches over it on one side. Though the lake was dry, the willow tree was beautiful, with fresh green fronds. Under this tree was the precise place many teens of Toccoa had their first kiss.

The young couple made their way to the large grey boulders under the tree. A few smaller rocks surrounded the boulders. Trevor quickly wiped the top of a boulder clean with his hand before Gabby sat down. His girlfriend was beaming brightly at his gesture, and stood up to hug him.

"Thank you," she said into his fresh-smelling shirt.

Trevor's expression said it was only natural for him to do this for her. As soon as they sat down, a warm gust blew across the valley and made the willow fronds move around them. Gabby giggled because it was quite romantic.

"I could see why people kiss here," she quietly thought to herself.

"I heard from my 90-year-old neighbor Joe that there used to be a lot of wildlife here on the lake, like fish and ducks and other interesting bird species," Trevor said contemplatively as he scanned the dry lake.

While Trevor imagined how it once was, Gabby envisioned what it could be once again.

"There's some vegetation here…Maybe one day it'll flourish again, if it rains!"

Trevor smiled his crooked smile at his girlfriend's constant optimism, but a shadow gripped his heart at that moment. As he scrutinized the dry lake, it felt like a mirror of his own soul, his own life.

Gabby's smile vanished as she looked at her boyfriend's eyes, like two pools of clear, deep water. She wasn't sure what to ask him, though, never wanting to probe. She reached for his hand and smiled warmly at him.

He kept looking at Mirror Lake, though. She didn't know he was trying not to cry, a river of tears that could fill up the whole lake. The jokes he made in class, his antics with his friends, were a facade behind which he hid. His insecurities ran deep within his bones.

Gabby felt she needed to say something. "Are you okay?" she asked hesitatingly.

Trevor thought about his father, who was always busy working, and when they did get a chance to talk, it would be about his dad's displeasure at Trevor's academics.

Trevor said nothing. Gabby's heart fell. She felt thick castle walls bordered his heart and she couldn't get through.

"I just…want to feel proud of myself," he finally uttered.

Gabby almost gasped.

"I'm proud of you," she wanted to say, but she didn't want to just "fix."

Gabby put her arm around his torso and cuddled closer to his side. She let him rest in his silence. She silently prayed for what to say. "Do you want to talk about it more?"

Trevor finally looked at her. His eyes had wrinkles next to them and he appeared to be a 120-year-old sea turtle at that moment. He smiled weakly, and he quickly wiped away his tears with both hands. Gabby hugged him tighter.

"It's okay to cry, Trev," she whispered nurturingly into his neck, her nose pressed against his nice-smelling skin.

It seemed he didn't want to say anything more. But Gabby already knew what he meant. She had already inferred it all.

At that moment, it began to rain lightly upon their heads.

Trevor's hair looked so cute, drenched at the tips.

"Want to kiss?" Gabby asked.

Trevor giggled, as his tears got washed away by the rain.

"You want to kiss?" he asked innocently.

"Yeah," Gabby admitted sweetly, but with innocent desire.

Trevor held the side of her face gently, and softly put his lips against her soft ones. They closed their eyes, as Mirror Lake disappeared, all the world faded, and it was just them, lost in this moment together. They kissed over and over again as the music of their passion, of their love, pulsed through their souls. No other music was needed from the outside. Her heart racing, Gabby finally paused and opened her eyes. Trevor's eyes appeared like two huge twinkling stars in a night sky. He grinned sheepishly and pulled her in for an embrace.

"I found her," he thought. "The one I've been looking for all my life."

"I can't believe we kissed!" Gabby squealed, the biggest, brightest grin stretching across her lips.

She leaned in to kiss him again. Trevor started laughing loudly as her lips met his.

"What?" Gabby asked.

"I'm just so happy," Trevor said.

They kissed until the rain stopped thirty minutes later.

Skateboarding home from school, Trevor felt this new momentum in his body, in his soul, in his spirit. The May wind lapped at his hair and he smiled in the cool rush of air against his face. The day couldn't feel better. He wondered what had happened. Usually, his rides home were monotonous. He looked forward to one thing: playing Legend of Zelda for hours on end. But suddenly, now, he had this power in his veins, the power to invent–to reinvent–his life. He started dreaming bigger. He felt nothing was impossible… because he had proven it to himself. He saw Gabby transform in a matter of seven months. He saw the fruit he had borne.

Reaching his room, he left his computer keyboard untouched and instead picked up his *Pride and Prejudice* script from English class. They had just finished reading the Jane Austen novel and they were having a mini-play in two weeks.

Stopping for a second, he imagined he was Mr. Darcy, clad in 19th century garb–stately, elegant, brooding. Then, imagining Gabby standing before him as Elizabeth Bennet, he began his monologue.

He could almost smell a whiff of the moist dirt and grass of the English countryside in his nostrils as he began.

He made a dramatic pause.

"Miss Elizabeth. I have struggled in vain and I can bear it no longer. These past months have been a torment. I came to Rosings with the single object of seeing you...I had to see you. I have fought against my better judgment, my family's expectations, the inferiority of your birth by rank and circumstance. All these things I am willing to put aside and ask you to end my agony."

"I don't understand," said Gabby as Elizabeth Bennet in his mind.

"I love you." Clearing his throat, Trevor started laughing and laughing. "That wasn't too bad!" he congratulated himself heartily.

Leaping upon his bed with his script, he underlined and highlighted and scribbled in notes on the margins for facial expressions, gestures, and body language he could employ. Turning over in his bed, he sighed a happy sigh and grinned at his ceiling. For once, he felt truly alive, more alive than he ever expected to be. Standing up once more, Trevor rehearsed his lines to perfection until the sun went down and it was dinnertime.

After dinner, Trevor entered his bedroom, and, in the growing darkness, excitedly sat at his desk and was about to turn on his computer to play games. But then the thought suddenly hit him. If he kept living this way and not investing in himself more, what would happen to his future? For once he felt he was worthy of a good future, a great life.

While Legend of Zelda enticed him, his mind traveled to lunchtime that day when Gabby handed him a flyer about an upcoming writing contest for high school students across Southern California. At first Trevor had smiled and told Gabby that he would try later. But his girlfriend, being so intuitive, knew he was simply afraid, and told him words that he could never forget.

"God is with you."

Trevor stared at his wall, where a poster of a pug dog hung. He contemplated those four words she had spoken with such gentleness but confidence. Gabby had a unique way of speaking. For such a small and relatively dainty girl, her words had weight, power.

"Trevor, you can do it. I believe you can win." Her eyes sparkled with her sincere warmth, a shining belief in her boyfriend's abilities and talents.

Trevor stood up and brushed his hair from his eyes. Suddenly, the thought of Legend of Zelda had completely vanished from his teenage mind. He moved his neck left and right to awaken his muscles. Eagerly, he stooped down and rummaged through his red backpack, his hands shuffling through papers like a raccoon's paws sorting through the trash. Finally, he found the neon orange flyer. SOUTHERN CALIFORNIA YOUTH WRITING CONTEST. It was time to work.

He skimmed the contest requirements written in small bullet points and he noticed that one requirement was a teacher's recommendation.

"Oh no...Ugh," Trevor said loudly to himself in his room. He heaved a deep sigh, his chest rising and falling. Rubbing his mass of curly hair ferociously, he wished he had tried harder in school.

"Mrs. Rogers. No. Mr. Thompson...He could not care less." Trevor scratched off names on the mental image of his class schedule. Unfortunately for Trevor, many of his teachers had a strong distaste for Trevor's antics and demeanor in their classes.

"Mr. Passe. No, I slept in his class once and he now talks really loudly whenever I look down. Ms. Stevenson. Nah. Mr. Pascal. He hates that I talked with Toad all of class that one week. Damn. I am running out of teachers." He only had three remaining teachers: Mrs. Batista, Mr. Durbin, and Mr. Chung.

"Mr. Durbin is probably my best shot, but you never know. Gonna try Mrs. Batista, too, just in case."

"Mrs. Batista is first." She was known for adoring breakfast foods like donuts. Trevor remembered that Toad once sneezed on her, leaving traces of mucus on her dress. Disgusting. To make up for it, he bought her donuts to be in her good graces again. According to Toad, once she saw the donuts, her eyes seemingly glazed over as if they were frosted with the same sweet sugary goodness that the donuts were coated in. All was forgiven with one bite.

Remembering this, Trevor begged his father to buy some donuts early in the morning to give to Mrs. Batista. His father shook his head and sighed. The very next morning, the donuts were on the kitchen table, fresh and ready for Trevor. "Thanks, Dad." The young boy's gratitude whispered in the early morning air.

It was 7:30AM and Trevor, fresh donuts in hand, knocked on the donut-loving teacher's door. His ears were met with a grunt and a hurried "Come in." Upon entering, Mrs. Batista quickly pressed down her blouse and shuffled papers in a somewhat organized manner. Trevor flashed his brightest smile. It must have been one of the most unsettling images that Mrs. Batista had ever seen in her short teaching career. Her face, battling the signs of an early morning and that of outright surprise to see such a random student in Trevor, looked as if two invisible fairies were pulling it in two separate directions.

Unhindered, Trevor smiled even bigger. "Good morning, Mrs. Batista. I wanted to ask you a favor. I am entering a writing contest and I need to have a teacher's recommendation. I was wondering if you would be interested and willing."

Mrs. Batista snorted, smelling the sweet whiff of the fresh donuts. "Good morning, Trevor. Are those donuts for me?" She pretended to be nonchalant, but her green snake-like eyes were fixed intently on the white Krispy Kreme box.

Trevor handed her the box with a little bow. "My dream is to be a writer. I know I wasn't the best student in your English class last year, but since then, I've done a lot of reflection and recently I've been trying my best. I want to pursue this new dream full-force and I think entering this writing contest is the first step in a positive direction. Would you be willing and able to write me a recommendation?" Gabby helped him with that statement and he felt it was the best statement he had made in all four years of his high school career.

She eagerly opened the box and quickly bit into a glazed twisted donut. The rush of sugar must have immediately flowed through her body because she smiled, dispelling the air of awkwardness that pervaded through the room before.

"My my. Thank you. That was delicious." Mrs. Batista wiped her mouth and glanced at her former student, who suddenly appeared more mature and adult-like. "Trevor, I think the idea you have is a wonderful idea." Trevor's heart began to soar. It was going to happen. "But, I am afraid that I am uncomfortable writing a recommendation letter for you. Not to sound harsh, but your grades did not reveal much effort or dedication. I'm sorry." In a matter of seconds, Trevor's once soaring heart sank into the mire of regret and disappointment. Mrs. Batista wiped her overly pink, shiny lips gently and innocently.

"Thank you for the donuts though, Trevor." Trevor weakly nodded and, without a word, left the classroom. The rush of the cold morning's air battered his cheeks and trampled through his hair. The poster that hung outside Mrs. Batista's room read in bold letters, "Believe and you can achieve!" He slammed his palm onto the poster and sighed. In the breeze of the empty hallway, he muttered a profanity under his breath and mentally crossed a name off his list. "On to the next one."

The pattering of feet began to echo through the hallway. The students were filing into school, ready to start the day.

"I'll talk to Mr. Durbin after our third period class." Trevor thought as he gathered his thoughts. "But I have to come to him with the right strategy."

In what seemed to be mere seconds, Trevor's first two periods passed. He scarcely remembered what happened in them, because he was so focused on what he was going to say to Mr. Durbin. He formulated a nice opening line to hook him in. "I will talk about basketball. Mr. Durbin loves basketball." Then he introduced three key examples of his leadership, passion, and drive to succeed. He could already see himself elegantly stating his points in front of the awe-inspired teacher. "Then I will hit him with my conclusion: I want to be a writer who helps people become informed, compassionate citizens!" He smiled at his last line like a child conqueror on top of a molehill of dandelions. The bell rang for the end of second period and Trevor walked boldly out of the class, ready to face Mr. Durbin.

Mr. Durbin was the English teacher for the senior class. Rather than having them do worksheets, he encouraged conversation and discussion. "Everyone, we are going to do Socratic seminars today!" Mr. Durbin's voice echoed through the room as the seniors, just beginning to wake up, took their seats. "Form a circle." Groans and grumbles could be heard from the students as they screeched their chairs across the linoleum floor into an oblong shape.

"Today, we are going to dedicate our time to the character study of Kurtz, the ivory trader, in *Heart of Darkness*." Trevor could hear the collective stomachs of most of his classmates twist into knots. He saw his friend Toad's face scrunch, his brow furrowing as if he were frantically searching through his brain for snippets that he could regurgitate into somewhat coherent sentences. Mr. Durbin began to scan through the room, looking for the first patsy to start the discussion. As his eyes went left to right, he could see the faces of dread. He smiled as he saw, from the corner of his eye, one hand shoot up. It was Michelle, the one student who always volunteered.

"Michelle, go ahead. What about Kurtz did you find interesting?" She straightened her posture and coughed to clear her throat.

"Throughout Conrad's work, Kurtz represents the harshness of Western imperialism. He sees the natives as pawns to his rise to power in the Western world. He controls them as if he were a god figure and is held in that esteem by the natives. Conrad displays how, for Westerners with an imperialistic philosophy, that the subjugation of people is thought of as a way to power and societal climb during the time of the book."

Mr. Durbin's lower lip puckered out and he nodded his head. "Impressive! Anyone want to add to Michelle's thoughts of imperialism in the book?" Mr. Durbin began to look around once again, but this time, Michelle did the same, seeing if anyone could challenge her in terms of literary knowledge. Her eyes darted to the left and right.

Wanting to promote discussion, Mr. Durbin shouted, "Toad! What do you think about Marlow's opinion on Kurtz?" Toad's eyes widened. Trevor could almost see an expletive cross over his face. "Good," he weakly muttered. Mr. Durbin blinked twice. Trevor's hand covered his mouth, trying not to laugh.

Seeing the discussion was stalling, Mr. Durbin began talking rapidly and calling out more people. Each student began spouting out terms and quotes that they either had read from the assigned book or from other forms of media. He could have sworn one of his classmates quoted a cereal commercial.

Finally, Mr. Durbin's eyes met Trevor's. "Mr. Song, what do you think about Kurtz's final words: "The horror! The horror! What is Kurtz referring to when he says this?" Everyone's eyes turned to Trevor, awaiting his response. They knew that Mr. Durbin's question was a softball that Trevor could knock out of the park, but Trevor had no answer. He frantically tore through each cabinet of his mind, trying to find an answer that was like Michelle's, but to no avail.

"He was scared." Trevor let those words out slowly as if he were a child weakly tapping a tee-ball. "Of what?" Mr. Durbin

308

was trying to pry more words out of him. Trevor drew a blank. "What would Gabby say?" he thought. Trevor had no answers.

Mr. Durbin's once cheerful face showed a tinge of disappointment. Before he could call on anyone else, the bell rang.

Trevor's thoughts swarmed him like ants upon roadkill. "What a dumb answer." "He is never going to write you a recommendation now." "Better save yourself from embarrassment and not ask him." Trevor's carefully crafted plan was thrown out the window. To Trevor, no talks about basketball could save him in the eyes of Mr. Durbin. He walked out of the room without a word. Gabby was absent from class that day, because she was doing interviews for Journalism.

Trevor's mind was enveloped in a thick white fog. The words echoed through his mind again and again. "You messed up. You messed up. You messed up." Any semblance of hope died amid the ceaseless barrage of the mental arrows. Mrs. Batista's words returned with malevolence. "But, I am afraid that I am uncomfortable writing a recommendation letter for you. Not to sound harsh, but your grades did not reveal much effort or dedication." To Trevor, they translated to: "You'll amount to nothing." His heart sank into the precipice of darkness.

However, like a sharp whistle that cuts through the deafening silence of discontent and discouragement, a new set of words rang true. "Trevor, you have a gift for writing. The world needs exactly what you have."

Trevor quickly rummaged through his backpack to find his treasured hand-written letter from his supportive girlfriend and best friend:

~

Dear Trevor,

When you speak, and when you write, you move my soul. There were times I was sitting in a dark pit of despair because of my family, but your words lifted me out. Your words instilled hope in me. It blew a fresh wind through my lifeless heart and I found myself running again, smiling again, living again. This is the power that your words have.

Trevor, you have a gift for writing, and the world needs exactly what you have. The world needs what's in that caring and brilliant mind of yours. The world needs your wisdom and compassion. The world needs you.

I adore you.

-Gabby

~

He remembered how Gabby smiled as she read his short story about his mother. In his memory, her face was as vivid and brilliant as the breaking dawn. Those words brought him back, not to a complete state of self-confidence like he was in the morning, but to a state of leveled "It is worth a shot." The final school bell rang and Toad and Cid waited for him at the doorway.

"You guys go ahead. I have to talk to Mr. Durbin real quick." Toad and Cid shrugged and walked away. As they grew distant, Trevor could see them punching each other in the arm.

At the door of Mr. Durbin's room, Trevor took a deep breath. In two swift steps, he walked through the doorway into a seemingly different climate. The classroom was distinctly hotter and more humid than the breezy hallway. Mr. Durbin, with a receding hairline at around the age of 38, was seated at his desk, writing his final notes for the day. His face was clearly drained from a day of teaching high school English. His eyes, now sunken and half-opened, slowly greeted Trevor. Trevor's forearms tingled with regret.

"Hello. How can I help you, Trevor?" Trevor's name crept out of Mr. Durbin's mouth like a snake from the underbrush.

"The world needs exactly what you have." Gabby's words echoed in his mind.

Trevor's heart swelled as his opening words torrentially rushed out of his mouth. "Mr. Durbin, I have the answer to your question about Kurtz's last words."

Mr. Durbin's eyes flickered with a flame of interest. "Really?" In anticipation, the seasoned teacher stopped his writing.

Trevor's mind spun ideas, spider legs crafting a seemingly intricate and delicate web. "What would Gabby say?" The tensile filament of the web swayed up and down with the arrival of the new idea. His fingers opened and quickly closed.

"Kurtz is the heart, metaphorically, of Western imperialism. Marlow slowly discovers who Kurtz is through other people. And to Marlow, Kurtz starts off the ideal. He is the ideal imperialist. But as Marlow discovers, Kurtz is actually the symbol of the dark-hearted nature of imperialism: how one can have power over another people. That is the horror that Kurtz realizes."

Mr. Durbin stared at Trevor, speechless.

Quickly seizing the opportunity, Trevor flashed the writing contest flyer in front of Mr. Durbin. "I want to enter a writing contest and I would be honored if you could write my recommendation." Trevor wanted to push those words out as quickly as possible.

"I know I may not be the best student, Mr. Durbin. But I believe that I finally found my passion. And I think that by pursuing this passion, I can help make the world a better place, a place where people are more open-minded and insightful and compassionate about what the people around them are going through. That is what my dream is about. That is what I am about."

In that moment, Mr. Durbin's hazel, bloodshot eyes burrowed into Trevor's very soul, searching every nook and cranny for conviction, for hope, for passion. He flashed a quick grin. "Finally. Passion!" His loud voice resonated off the corners of the empty classroom. "FINALLY! FINALLY! FINALLY!" The seasoned teacher threw his hands into the air in raucous jubilation. Trevor stood there, in shock.

"I will only write this recommendation, if you show even just a flicker of passion that you showed me today." His eyes gleamed at Trevor, awaiting his response. Trevor, still shaken, nodded in reply. The next few moments were a blur. He remembered thanking Mr. Durbin with a sweaty handshake, a shy smile, and even a bow. He found himself in the hallway once more. The breeze felt cool upon his face.

"I cannot wait to tell Gabby."

At that moment, he heard footsteps coming up the stairwell, and his heart leapt when he noticed a familiar figure–his girlfriend in a beautiful, flowy white blouse and her Journalism badge swinging around her neck. For a moment, he lingered in the magic of the moment as her perfect, wavy brown hair flowed in the wind. Knowing Trevor would be asking Mr. Durbin at this very moment after third period, Gabby had rushed over to meet him. Trevor found himself running down the stairs. Gabby's eyes lit up and she giggled, seeing that they had coincidentally run into each other at that exact moment.

"What happened? Did he say yes?" she asked breathlessly, her eyes searching his deeply.

Trevor just embraced her wordlessly for some long moments.

"What happened? Are you okay?" Gabby spoke with alarm.

"I got the recommendation, Gabby," Trevor admitted quietly, but with a new confidence in his warm voice.

"What? Oh my gosh!" Gabby yelled and screamed. She jumped up and down and hugged him again and again.

"You did it!" she congratulated her boyfriend.

"No, we did it!" he said. They smiled into each other's eyes for a few seconds. Seeing the admiration, respect, and love flow out of Gabby's big brown eyes made Trevor's heart expand a million times.

He scooped her into his arms, lifting her a foot off the ground. Gabby laughed and hit his shoulder, saying, "Let me down! Let me down!" He quickly let her down like a gentleman and stood proudly before her.

She leaned toward his face and gently kissed his cheek. Trevor's eyes grew comically large, and he kissed her back sweetly.

When she was growing up, Gabby's happiest times with her dad were when they would play basketball in their backyard. In the backyard was an oval-shaped cement "court" surrounded by shrubbery, and at the top of the court was a basketball hoop that would tower over Gabby like a mountain to be vanquished. With her dad, that towering seven-foot basketball hoop was nothing, because he was confident in her.

Passing the ball to her, her dad would encourage Gabby to shoot. After making a shot, Gabby would pass the ball to her dad with a great smile, but he would automatically pass it back to Gabby, wanting to give her chance after chance.

They delighted in each other.

Gabby still remembered the way her dad would excitedly approach the hoop from the right side and shoot with his right arm over his head, almost looking like a swinging monkey, his mouth wide open. She would giggle and giggle, amazed at his various shooting styles. When Lance was with his daughter, his spirit soared; he was free. Gabby thought he was the best person ever, and that meant everything to him.

Watching Trevor dribbling the ball up the court in their school gym, Gabby longed for that connection she had once shared with her father. Stuck between the place she had once shared with her father and the place she was now with Trevor, Gabby stood up and tentatively took the ball that Trevor passed to her.

"This doesn't feel too bad," Gabby thought. Positioning herself at the free throw line, she aimed with steady and intent concentration. The ball looked as if it would go in, but then bounced out of the basket. Trevor, in one swift, sweeping movement, scooped up the ball and did a rebound. Satisfied, he looked over at Gabby with the grin of a high school boy who wanted to impress his girl. Gabby's dad used to do "monkey rebounds" just like that, and Gabby stood there, faking a smile but realizing that nothing would be able to take her father's place in her life.

Trevor continued to smile his goofy grin, and walked up to Gabby. Immediately sensing that something was bothering her, he looked at her face with alarmed, concerned eyes and Gabby giggled to hide her sadness.

"What happened?" he asked, still with a look of worry in his eyes.

Gabby didn't pretend anymore because she realized Trevor didn't like being left in the dark. She decided to just tell him.

"I miss the times I spent with my dad…playing basketball. It was really…great."

She crossed her arms, looking away. Letting go of the ball, Trevor came in for an embrace, placing his hand protectively behind her head.

Enveloped in his arms, Gabby felt like she was in a snug nest and that nothing could get to her there. Snuggled against his chest, Gabby smiled and her fears and worries melted away from her body. Trevor was her saving grace in times like these.

~

That Saturday morning, Gabby finished eating a buttery croissant and some slices of salami for breakfast, when she decided to get creative and make herself a matcha latte. Grabbing her favorite large red-and-white mug with dog faces all over it, she got the small bag of matcha powder and carefully poured about a spoonful of the lovely green powder into the mug. By then, her water had boiled and she poured the steaming water into the cup, quickly stirring the dark green concoction with a small spoon. She swiftly made her way to the refrigerator and took out the carton of oat milk. Unscrewing the small white lid, she poured the oat milk into the matcha tea and delightedly watched the white and green liquids swirl until the color became a nice light green. Then, she drizzled honey into the matcha latte and mixed it one last time. She eagerly took a sip and a smile formed in her mouth; it tasted perfect. Holding the warm mug with both her hands, she slowly wandered into the living room.

Feeling content from having taken several sips of her sweet, milky matcha latte, Gabby put her mug down on top of the grand piano and sat peacefully on the piano chair. All her muscles felt relaxed as she breathed in and out deeply. The sun gave the mahogany brown piano a lustrous sheen, and with two of her fingers, she caressed the unbelievably smooth wood. Placing her delicate two hands upon the keys, Gabby wondered what kind of sound would come out today. Birds sang their jubilant song amidst the trees outside as she got ready to play her own song.

She stared down at the piano for no longer than a moment, and then began to play without any intentional thought. She grinned at the sounds that she heard. There was a freshness in her tune and a new kind of beauty that wasn't there before. They reflected her light, buoyant heart and the peace that filled her life. She paused for a moment and grabbed her phone so she could record her music.

Gabby continued to play. Wonder filled her soul at the sound of victory and wholeness which sprung from the keys. Her music taught her that she was not the same Gabby as a year ago. She recalled how she felt last September when her dad came home; darkness crept into her soul just from thinking about it. She had been fearful, hopeless, dark, and depressed. But since then, she had transformed into the girl she was now: strong, joyful, courageous, bold, and so loved. Gabby had changed. Gabby had been restored.

She decided to call this new song "Gabby Rises."

~

Listen to "Gabby Rises" on Gabby's blog here:
www.gabbysmelody.com

~

"Dedicated to God and Trevor, who helped me to rise," she thought to herself. She turned around on the piano chair to behold her backyard that was stunning in the luminous sun. The shrubs and the trees were a vibrant, glowing green. Her eyes lingered upon the orange tree heavy with fruit and foliage. The white puffy clouds in the clear blue sky matched the lightness she felt in her heart. Just then, the Toccoa breeze blew in through the screen door and licked her face, a refreshing feeling flooding her whole being.

"God, thank you for transforming me," she said softly, knowing no one was around. She paused for a moment, not being able to believe how much God had done for her in such a short span of time. "Thank you for saving me from the pit and for giving me new life. You are so good." She let the wonder of the miracle sink in for some long moments as she continued to behold the beautiful nature. For all her life, it had been hard to believe in God's goodness and blessings. But now, she felt it deep within the sinews of her heart, in the whisper of her spirit. She knew that God indeed loved her.

Wanting to also thank Trevor for what he had done in her life, Gabby went out to buy him a card. At Target, she scanned her eyes across card aisle after card aisle, never settling for something less than perfect for him. Suddenly, her eyes rested upon a simple white card with a green T-Rex in front. She giggled at its goofy grin. Gabby remembered that the T-Rex was Trevor's favorite dinosaur growing up and excitedly grabbed the card.

~

Dear Trevor,

Thank you for being the one to resurrect me—like the phoenix. I know it wasn't always easy. What I wanted to say was, you're perfect. :)

You're perfect.

Remember that you're not who you think you are—you are much, much more.

To me, you're the best person I have ever met. You are a walking miracle.

You are evidence that God exists.

This is who you are to me.

Thank you for making my world brighter...the world brighter.

Because you live, I want to live on. I want to dream on. I want to build a beautiful future with my hand in yours, and only yours.

Thank you, Trevor!!

YOU'RE THE MAN.

-Gabs <3

~

Sealing the envelope with a satisfied, sweeping lick, Gabby waited for Trevor to pick her up so they could go to their favorite place—Yami Teahouse.

When they arrived at the boba shop, high schoolers filled every beige wooden table along the perimeter of the large cafe, their noisy, excited chatter filling the air. Large windows let the afternoon sun stream in on all four sides of the shop. To the left of the cash register counter hung a large pink neon sign that said "Boba is Life". Six people stood in line, eager to order their drinks. Holding hands, Trevor and Gabby also studied the menu on the TV screen together. As Trevor continued to study the various drinks, Gabby sneaked behind him and sweetly hugged her boyfriend from behind. She felt she would melt in the warmth and love that emanated from his body to hers.

Once they placed their order, the two lovebirds scooted into one side of a table together. Snuggling for a moment, they gave each other an eskimo kiss. All the world vanished and all they saw was each other. Gabby's heart fluttered as Trevor rubbed his nose against hers. At that moment, Gabby remembered the card. She reached into her purse and handed it to Trevor. Upon seeing it, his eyes gleamed with happiness and expectation. He quickly turned the turquoise envelope over and with utmost care, slowly opened the envelope flap little by little to not tear the envelope. Gabby giggled and grinned at his cautious, loving care. Looking at the funny-looking green T-rex on the front of the card, he laughed loudly. Gabby cleared her throat as Trevor began reading it. She had just written what was on her heart and wasn't sure what he'd think of it. Trevor radiated glee and smiled a big toothy grin as he read the card. Beneath the din of high school students talking at Yami Teahouse, the words on the card spoke so loudly to his heart.

He beamed, awestruck at what Gabby had given him, and Gabby giggled, looking at the look of surprise on her adorable boyfriend's face. She gave him a tight, sweet hug, and he thought he might melt into a puddle of cheese.

"GABBYYY!" he exclaimed. "Wow!"

At that moment, their order number was called. Gabby swiftly kissed his cheek before getting up to grab their boba drinks. Quickly returning to their table, she looked down, smiling, and sipped some of her milk tea boba before speaking with her mouth full of boba balls.

"It isn't much," she said. "But I'm so glad you like it!" She laughed with relief.

Trevor straightened up in his chair, his shoulders less slumped, looking more like the Trevor that Gabby saw in him—more confident, bolder, and strong. The true Trevor.

"Trevor, I could say a million things in a million cards...and it still would not be enough," Gabby said, not knowing this would make Trevor wild with joy.

Trevor laughed heartily, unable to believe that he found Gabby and that Gabby was his girlfriend. He sipped his green apple boba smoothie with great satisfaction, knowing that he had found what he had been looking for all his life.

"There's a second part to your gift," Gabby said breathlessly with excitement.

Trevor's eyes popped open wide, eager for the surprise.

"But we need to go to a quiet place, because it's...a song," Gabby said excitedly.

"Okay! Let's go back to my car," Trevor said happily.

They headed out of Yami Teahouse holding their boba cups and each other's hands, and crossed the street to Trevor's car which was parked in the adjacent neighborhood. Trevor walked over to Gabby's side of the car to open the door for her. She smiled with appreciation at this small but kind act he had done so many times.

In the stillness of the car, Gabby got out her phone to play "Gabby Rises." But first she wanted to tell Trevor sincerely what he had done for her. For a few seconds, she gathered her thoughts. Finally, she spoke, honest and brave.

"Trevor, when I met you, I was really broken. But somehow, you helped heal me and I transformed so much since then. I'm not who I used to be. I'm more whole and happy, thanks to you and God," she said with a sweet, appreciative smile.

She pressed play as she looked up and saw that Trevor's eyes had moistened. He embraced her in his arms, enveloping her in love. As the song began, Trevor sat very still and tuned his ears and all his attention to the precious music.

~

Listen once again to "Gabby Rises" on Gabby's blog here: www.gabbysmelody.com

~

Gabby watched Trevor's eyes, which were full of sincerity and a veil of tears as the song played on. When it was done, he hugged her once more and stroked the back of her head, but stayed silent. Coming out of the embrace, Trevor brushed away his tears and tried to stop crying.

"What?" Gabby asked with a curious smile.

"Gabby, you truly rose. You conquered. You overcame," he said with pride in his voice.

Gabby smiled a shining, emotional smile at what he said. She let his words sink into her heart and she received the affirming power of them deep within herself.

She hugged him close and whispered into his ear, "Thank you so much, Trevor."

eanwhile, at Bridgeport Psychiatric Hospital, Gabby's father's heart was changing as well. The medication was starting to work after repeated attempts to find the right ones for his condition. His daily routine included group sessions with other veterans, who were encouraged to talk about how they felt and what had scarred them during their wartime experience. For seven weeks straight, Gabby's father only listened, his arms crossed, watching the other soldiers describe their weaknesses with almost a contempt for them. He would come back to his room and sit in the dark, hunched over, feeling even more contempt for himself for being there.

"A psychiatric hospital," he muttered one afternoon. "I am in a psychiatric hospital. What the hell happened to me."

He would lay in his bed silently day after day, refusing to open up about what was really bothering him. He could not put it into words at the time, anyway, and he did not want to show any sign of weakness.

But one thing kept him going: the memory of playing with Gabby. Her laughing face. The way they would play basketball together. Watching her grow up and do well in school. Feeling proud of being a good father to her. Until now.

Then like an angel visiting him at his window or a bright yellow light streaming into his room from heaven, a gift arrived that changed Lance's hardened heart, from stone, to flesh.

A CD arrived in a bright turquoise CD case; turquoise was his daughter's favorite color. He grinned, looking down at the CD, but with cynicism to the brim in his heart.

Lance nonchalantly asked his nurse for the communal mini stereo, which he took back to his room. His hall was so quiet. "Everyone must be taking an afternoon nap or something," Lance muttered, as the echoes of his solitary footsteps rang shrilly through the empty, eerily clean and dimly lit hallway.

He sat down on his bed, which had become his home; he spent the most time there. His hands which lacked human touch held the CD, and he tried to feel its connection to Gabby, to other humans, to the outside world in which he had once belonged. With a sigh that no one heard except him, startling him because of the loudness of it in his room, he quickly inserted the CD into the stereo.

With a moment's hesitation, he pressed play.

Lance didn't expect much, but his heart unknowingly beat wildly, as if it was afraid to feel too much, as if afraid to feel love—something he hadn't felt at all in this hospital for wounded men.

At the sound of his daughter's voice, his heart jolted as if with electric shock; she sounded so sad. He expected her to be cheery like her usual self; he was almost certain life without him at home would make both his wife and Gabby happier.

~

Listen to "ptsd" on Gabby's blog here:
www.gabbysmelody.com

~

His heart beat fast; it stirred with feeling. A feeling he had never felt. Empathy. The empathy in her voice.

It was as if she had felt every single thing that he did.

Feelings he never told anyone.

Feelings.

Just then the army's strict disciplinarians' voices bombarded his mind: "To show emotion is to be weak. A soldier must stay strong, resolute. Always look to the mission, not to the self. We don't have time to feel. We do." His younger self ran through the rain and mud in his memory, committing these words to memory as his superiors yelled them, feeling a sense of pride in his duty as his dog tags jangled against his chest.

Lance lay back in his bed as if the memory stabbed his face, his mind reeling from the chasm between the young, brave, admirable soldier he once was, and who he was now—a useless invalid who let down his family. But then the song called to him, reached for his heart that was victim to these tenacious, unrelenting thoughts.

The sound of his daughter crying overpowered all the other thoughts and he could now only hear her voice.

"She...knows," he realized then.

He realized he was not alone in the struggle.

At that moment, he felt his pride crumble and fall to the floor. His need to feel self-sufficient tumbled down into ruins. He only heard one thing: his daughter's hurting heart.

And that was all it took for him to wake from his stupor. He ran down the hallway, wildly looking for the nurse who was in charge of phone calls and demanded that he be allowed to call his family. His hand shook violently as he held the receiver against his ear, but he couldn't complete the call as he broke down in sobs. The sobbing broke forth as a wail, as the wailing of a child who hurt his knee for the first time and needed the help of his parents immediately. The nurse next to him realized that Lance, the one patient who never talked in group therapy, was finally free, and embraced him in a warm and loving embrace, giving him the compassion that this lost soldier needed. The elderly Black nurse stroked his back with maternal comfort and power and spoke reassuringly to him in low murmurs as he continued to cry for an hour.

Waking up the next morning, Lance first noticed the sunlight glimmering golden through the curtains by the sliding door, which was slightly open. Someone must've opened it. Next, he noticed his face was tear-streaked and that a stereo was on his bed, beside his thigh. A nurse promptly came in with breakfast and she pressed play on the stereo.

Gabby's second song promptly came on.

~

Listen to "Waiting for God" on Gabby's blog here:
www.gabbysmelody.com

~

"Your daughter has some talent, being able to make her daddy heal with just one song," she chided in her strong, maternal voice.

Lance smiled, unknowingly. Not knowing it was his first smile in two months. He suddenly remembered how he had cried the night before and he looked away from the nurse, suddenly embarrassed.

"You're a good dad," the nurse observed, her hands on her wide hips.

Lance smiled, turning his head to the side against the headboard, looking out the glass sliding door toward the sunshine again. He smiled with his eyes closed, feeling an immense peace all around. A heavenly, all-encompassing peace.

He heard only quiet in his mind. An utter quiet that he had not experienced in so long. He could finally rest from his battles.

God had fought the war and won. He got the life of His son back. Back from the dead, to fullness of life.

~

Missing her dad, Gabby got up from her bed where she had texted with Trevor for thirty minutes and made her way into her parents' bedroom. She was startled to find her mom standing amidst jumbo pouches of jewelry put on display on a stand in the middle of her room. A wide array of antique necklaces, pendants, and clip-on earrings shone through the plastic-covered bright purple pouches in which they were meticulously organized. Gabby immediately ran over to where her mother stood, studying the jewelry that she hadn't used in forever.

"Mom! These are all yours?" Gabby asked in disbelief with a great smile as her mom handed her a pair of enormous earrings. She didn't know her mom used to be such a fashionista.

"Try these ones on, Gabby," her mom replied, her mind still concentrating on how to organize or get rid of all this jewelry.

Gabby studied the two earrings her mom had placed in her hands. They were bulky, with a small circular white piece at the top attached to a gumball-sized dark bluish-purple ball. The earrings had lovely gold borders and clips. She felt the weight of the precious pieces in her palm, lifting her palm up and down.

"Mom! How can I wear them? They're so heavy!" Gabby exclaimed incredulously while she quickly ran over to the adjoining bathroom's full-length mirror to try them on.

"If your Aunt Lauren could wear those, you can too," her mom replied in a matter of fact, funny tone which she never used. "Aunt Lauren wore those in her early twenties," she added.

"Aunt Lauren…" Gabby reflected upon her most stylish aunt who supposedly would attract all the men's stares when she'd ride the elevator at her fashion company. She was a fashion designer and model in her single years.

Gabby tried one clip-on on her left earlobe, and she guffawed gleefully at the sight.

"Mom, it looks weird on me. It doesn't match me," she said, turning her head slowly from side to side, eyeing the giant indigo ball hanging off her small earlobe.

Gabby's mom made her way toward Gabby, and for a moment mother and daughter silently looked into the mirror together.

Gabby's mom studied her young daughter's sweet face. She felt a pang of guilt; her daughter was always so sweet and willing to be close with her mom. Her mind drifted to her talk with her therapist that she hadn't told Gabby about. She had been waiting for a good moment.

"Gabby, why don't you sit down," Gabby's mom nervously asked as she patted the bedding next to where she had just sat down herself.

Gabby's first reaction was to feel afraid because her mom might want to scold her for something. Her pulse quickened as she searched her mom's eyes, face, and overall demeanor. She looked calm but Gabby still held her breath. Sitting about a foot away from her mom, she felt her butt sink into her parents' plush white comforters that were always perfectly laid out.

Gabby continued to look intently into her mother's face; her mom wouldn't look at her and only looked down at her slightly wrinkled hands. Gabby never saw her mom look so uncomfortable. She was always so self-assured, haughty even.

Gabby's mom then did something that made Gabby's heart drop in sudden shock: She took one of Gabby's hands and placed it in between hers, gently, in an unaccustomed fashion, rarely having done this.

For a moment or two her mom just gently caressed her hands. Gabby's hands were kissed by the glow of the early afternoon sun and the room bright with the color white in the walls, drapes, and bed. A breeze traveled into the room and soothed Gabby's senses.

Gabby felt her heart beat more slowly and she looked at her mom for some sign.

"When you ran away from home, I went to see a therapist because I wanted to get some answers," Gabby's mom spoke, looking straight ahead, her voice clear and resolute. "I asked her why my daughter ran away," she said, looking at Gabby.

Gabby noticed tears emerging in her mom's eyes and her nose getting slightly red at the edges. Gabby couldn't believe what was happening.

"My therapist asked me all these questions including whether I abused you...She asked me if I was harsh toward you."

Gabby shrank in the immensity of what was being said.

"Until that moment I thought I did nothing wrong," her mom said, her face twisted as more tears ran down her white, powdered face. "But when I was about to say no, I suddenly had all these images come into my mind, like God was making me recall how I was—as your mom. I then knew it was my fault. It was my fault you ran away."

Gabby sucked in her breath.

"I'm sorry," her mom said, looking into her daughter's face.

Gabby didn't know what to say, but her heart felt a release, like water flowing freely after a river had been dammed up for years. She had wanted to hear those two words for so long.

Her mom spoke again, in a helpless, childlike voice. "I will try to be a better mom."

Gabby peered at her mom. Her mom's invincible, hardened look was gone, and she looked broken, smaller, and weak. Gabby looked down, still in disbelief. She was still holding the earrings in her left hand, and she felt moisture had gathered in her palm from clenching them too tight. As she turned to carefully lay them on the bed next to her, her mom spoke once more.

"The therapist asked me to remember if I had ever gone through something when I was a child." Gabby's heart stopped. "When I was in high school, I stayed at church late one night talking to a boy about church matters. We didn't like each other or do anything...bad. When I got home it was about 11:30. I thought it would be okay since I was doing work for church. But when I got home, your grandpa took a door and hit me with it."

Gabby grew wide-eyed, never having heard this story. Her late grandpa had seemed like a reserved, gentle man.

Gabby looked over at her mom silently, not knowing what to say. At that moment her mom left the room to blow her nose in the bathroom. Gabby waited for her mom to return but she felt so uncomfortable and it seemed her mom would rather have her private time. Gabby glided next door to her room as if her legs were not there.

"She said sorry...She actually said sorry," she repeated to herself in her head.

And then Gabby wondered to herself if that trauma of getting hit by her dad made her mom the way she had been toward her family.

Her head numb, Gabby looked straight ahead for a while as she sat at the corner of her bed. Then, closing her eyes, she prayed for her mom: "Dear God, please heal my mom's heart of the hurt that she received from Grandpa. Please surround her, bless her, and be near her. In Jesus' name, amen."

Gabby opened her eyes and, dazed, wondered what was happening to her life. Things she thought would never change were changing before her eyes. "Thank you, God," she whispered in the silence of her room, her heart still thudding.

Trevor texted Gabby a little while after her conversation with her mom: "Gabby, want to hang out at my house today? Remember the attic I always wanted to show you?"

"Sure!" she replied, feeling thrilled and relieved to see him.

Trevor promptly arrived at three o'clock to pick her up.

"You walked here?" Gabby gasped, noticing Trevor just standing there, with no car in sight. His back was turned to her, and he seemed to be looking at something, but Gabby sensed he was deep in thought. Gabby admired his red plaid shirt over his faded distressed jeans. She admired the arch in his back and his broad shoulders.

Turning around, Trevor's eyes opened wide and so did his mouth into a smile as he saw what she was wearing. "You look beautiful!" he exclaimed, embracing her gently.

333

Gabby was wearing the pink dress that Trevor had bought her when they were at Westwood. It didn't fit right at first, but she lost a little weight and now it fit perfectly. The light pink matched perfectly with her fair skin and the gold buttons gave it a vintage look. Gabby never wore form-fitting clothes, so she looked around, feeling slightly embarrassed.

"I feel weird," she said, still avoiding Trevor's eyes. Clearing her throat, she put a strand of hair behind her ear. Trevor looked away so Gabby wouldn't feel uncomfortable and held her hand comfortingly as they started walking to his house.

The sun cast its bright yellow light upon Gabby's face, and she squinted and frowned. Trevor, noticing this, immediately shielded her face with his hand. "Man! I should've brought my car," he said urgently.

Gabby couldn't help but smile. She held his free arm and cuddled closer to him. She grinned to herself, feeling lucky to have such a caring boyfriend.

Trevor continued to walk with one hand shielding Gabby's face.

"Haha!" Gabby guffawed, in disbelief. Trevor was walking backwards so he could keep his eye on Gabby's face and make sure his hand was in the proper place.

"It's okaaay!" Gabby said cutely.

Trevor chuckled. Suddenly, he stopped walking and embraced Gabby close, not saying anything. Gabby's heart leapt as her face came in contact with his soft, fresh-smelling shirt. Her eyes looked up, this way and that, wondering what was going on in Trevor's heart. She always wanted to be aware of how he was feeling and what he was thinking about. She wondered if he was feeling vulnerable because he would be hearing the results of the writing competition soon.

She hugged him a little closer in a nurturing embrace and softly kissed his right cheek. Closing their eyes, they just rested in the embrace where they felt their hearts were at home. Everything was all right here.

When they arrived at Trevor's house, Trevor, holding Gabby's hand, led her down the immaculate hallway, and Gabby smiled at the photo frames on the walls that had become so familiar. Trevor's warm, strong voice interrupted her happy thoughts of knowing Trevor's childhood. She stared at the back of Trevor's head—the shaved portion near his pale neck. She realized his hairstyle had gotten significantly more stylish during their short relationship.

Trevor spoke, his voice ringing clearly through the hallway's acoustics. "We turn this corner, and then go up this flight of stairs…" He guided them like a tour guide.

Gabby smiled at this quality in his voice. She held his comforting hand a little more firmly. "Hey! It's my first time going upstairs in your house!" she squealed with surprise.

Trevor motioned for Gabby to go up the steps first, wanting to protect her from behind. Grinning sheepishly, Gabby blushed a little, and, clearing her throat, went ahead of Trevor.

The railings of the staircase were a deep brown wood, old, but polished. Gabby gasped at the sight of forest green ivy and luxurious white blossoms weaving across each railing, on either side of the staircase. They were fake but beautiful and magical, in a way.

Gabby was wondering who had decorated the house like this, when Trevor broke into her thoughts.

335

"My mom did this. She loved decorating, making things beautiful."

Gabby searched his eyes for some long moments. His eyes looked joyful and peaceful, to her relief. Still, Gabby reached out her hand and gave his arm a squeeze.

Gabby spoke in a quiet, gentle voice, "It's so lovely," as she admired the decor on either side of them once more. At the top of the staircase was a little door. Gabby giggled because it looked like a door that the seven dwarves from Snow White would go through.

"Watch your head," Trevor said, and, opening the door slowly, he guarded Gabby's head with his other hand.

Gabby gasped at the sight of the attic. It looked like someone's room, with a wooden desk in the corner and matching wooden shelves of books next to the desk. There were three small windows that allowed the bright sunlight from the outside to stream in, casting a golden glow upon the room.

"Who used this as their room?" Gabby found herself asking.

"My mom came up here whenever she wanted to pray or spend time with God," Trevor answered.

The ceiling of the attic was A-shaped because it was at the top of the house, so they couldn't stand all the way straight.

Trevor grabbed two cushions and placed them on the wooden floor for them to sit on.

"Hey, this reminds me of when you gave me your cushion to sit on in Aunt Marie's treehouse," Gabby reminisced with a dreamy, playful grin.

Trevor chuckled.

After they got comfortably seated on the beautifully embroidered, colorful cushions that Trevor's mom had made, Trevor grabbed an old photo album from the shelf next to his mom's desk. Gabby leaned over to look at the pictures in the album as Trevor flipped through the album. She spotted a photo of Trevor on his fifth birthday about to blow out candles. His cheeks were puffed up cutely and he was donning a colorful cone-shaped cardboard birthday hat. Gabby giggled.

"You were sooooo cute!" she said as she gave him a tight side hug.

Then, Trevor showed Gabby a picture of him holding a huge rainbow trout that he had caught in fifth grade. He was staring at the fish and not at the camera with a huge grin stretching his mouth out wide.

"Oh...so that's where your fishing skills came from!" Gabby joked.

"Nah, I'm not good at fishing," Trevor replied, always humble. Then he encountered a photo that made him pause.

Gabby wonderingly peered at what had caught his attention. It was Trevor on a stage holding an award at an award ceremony.

"Wow!" he said. "I forgot about that!"

"What?" Gabby asked, studying the young Trevor in the photo more closely.

"In middle school, I won a poetry contest," Trevor replied.

"Wow!" Gabby exclaimed.

Then, they noticed Trevor's mom had written a little note under the photo: *Trevor wins poetry contest in 6th grade. So proud of his writing talent.*

Tears immediately emerged in both Trevor and Gabby's eyes. Gabby quickly reached over to give Trevor a hug. She knew he was thinking about how his dad would never approve of him being a writer.

Gabby held him in her arms and rubbed his back gently for a while. To inspire Trevor and cheer him up, Gabby exclaimed chirpily, "My mom said sorry to me today! For the first time in my life."

"What?" Trevor said.

"Yeah, she said sorry for being harsh to me." Gabby paused a little, as if swallowing down her throat all the sadness of her past. But then she smiled, thinking of the miracle that had just happened.

Trevor hugged Gabby and stroked the back of her head. "Finally. I'm so glad," he said, honestly and reassuringly.

Gabby smiled in his embrace. He held her for a long time, and she sensed that he was feeling emotional about what had happened.

Just then, a notification sounded from Trevor's phone. He checked his phone and saw that an email had arrived. Upon opening it, Trevor looked frozen in shock.

"What is it?" Gabby asked urgently.

"Oh my gosh," he said. "I won first place in the writing contest."

"Oh my gosh!" Gabby shouted. "That is amazing!" she yelled, squeezing him tight with glee. "Let me see the email!"

Gabby's eyes raced across the email and she grinned widely. She started laughing loudly with joy.

Trevor shed tears of relief. This was the one thing he really wished would happen so that his dad would let him be an English major.

"Let's tell your dad right now!" Gabby squealed, tugging at his arm.

But Trevor hugged Gabby. Muffled against her shoulder, he said, "Thank you so much for helping me."

Gabby's heart leapt a little. She hugged him back and, closing her eyes, cherished this awesome moment with Trevor. Rubbing his hair gently, she whispered, "You're phenomenal. I knew you could do it."

After some moments, Trevor said, "I want to tell my dad I want to be an English major, but..."

Gabby searched the frown lines on Trevor's forehead. She held his hand. Just then, she got an idea. "I'll pray for you, Trevor."

Trevor looked a little more at ease when he heard that. "Okay," he agreed.

Still holding his hand, Gabby closed her eyes and began praying in a sweet but strong voice, full of intense conviction.

"Dear God, today Trevor is going to tell his dad that he wants to be an English major and pursue writing. He won the writing contest and we thank you; we give you all the glory. Please give Trevor peace because you gave him the gift of writing, Lord.

You created him to be a great writer. So please go with him as he goes to his dad and speak through him. Please give him strength and boldness and open up Trevor's dad's heart to listen and to accept what Trevor is saying. Thank you for your love toward us. Thank you. In Jesus' name, amen."

When Gabby finished, she opened her eyes and saw that Trevor had opened his eyes, too. He smiled and embraced Gabby tightly.

"It's going to go great," Gabby said into his ear, with great faith.

Trevor searched Gabby's deep brown eyes. Within them he could see two flames aglow. Her conviction imbued his heart with a fresh strength and confidence.

~

That night, Trevor found his dad seated at his desk in his study. In his right hand, Trevor was holding his phone so he could show his dad the congratulatory email. Sweat moistened his palms and he rubbed them against his pajama pants.

Trevor cleared his throat as he continued to watch his dad busily paying his bills at his desk.

"Dad," he said. "I have some, uh, good news to tell you." He couldn't believe the words actually came out.

His dad stopped working and looked up at his son with a look of surprise in his eyes. He turned his chair to face Trevor.

"What is it son?" he asked intently, looking into Trevor's eyes.

Trevor inhaled deeply and opened up the email on his phone to show his dad. He lifted the phone up to his dad's face.

"I won first place in the writing competition I told you about," he said with a mature sounding, confident voice that even took him by surprise. Trevor didn't look into his dad's eyes just yet.

His dad read the email intently and a grin grew upon his tired face. Trevor looked up and spotted his dad's smile. Trevor sighed a little sigh of relief. Suddenly, Trevor's dad gave him a great embrace. He held him for some long moments. Steve Song had always wanted to see his son try and go for something wholeheartedly. It didn't matter what it was.

"That is so awesome," he said warmly to Trevor.

Trevor stood woodenly in his dad's embrace, not expecting a reaction like this. Trevor stood tall again and got ready to tell his dad what he wanted to say all along. He looked him straight in the eye and took a deep breath.

"Dad, I think I have a talent for writing, and I want to pursue it. I want to be an English major at UCSC."

For a moment Steve's forehead crinkled up. He rubbed his face once with his right hand, looking toward the wall in front of his desk. He inhaled deeply but didn't say anything to Trevor. He thought long and hard about how Trevor won first place. He recalled how his son had won first place in a poetry contest in middle school, too. Miranda had smiled with such great warmth and a sparkle in her eyes. "Our son is gifted," she had said in that soothing voice of hers. Finally, he turned to Trevor and looked at his son as if for the first time. He had always wanted Trevor to pursue medicine because it would give his life stability, but as he studied Trevor in this moment, he suddenly realized how different

Trevor was from him. He knew he had to let go and trust Trevor, trust God's purposes for Trevor's life.

Holding his teenage son's shoulders and looking at him square in the face, Steve paused, studying his son's deep, sweet brown eyes.

He then opened his mouth and replied, "Go for it. If it is your passion, give it your all. I'll support you."

Trevor's heart jolted. He didn't expect to hear those words at all. Tears begged to be released from his eyes, but he made sure he didn't cry in front of his dad. For a while, Trevor just stood there, not sure how to respond.

He hugged his dad suddenly, and then the tears came. "Thank you...so much,"

He sniffled. He held onto his dad's back, feeling like a vulnerable little kid.

His dad patted his back, feeling ever so proud of his son.

Trevor walked out of his dad's room and toward the attic to call Gabby and tell her about what happened in private. The inner dork in him also wanted to relive that afternoon he spent there with Gabby. As he walked through the ever-darkening attic, he vividly recalled the way she hugged him and held his hand and prayed for him. He couldn't believe God answered their prayer!

Trevor quickly called Gabby and, when she picked up, Trevor's excitement became full-blown. "My dad said yes!" he squealed.

"What?" Gabby answered. "I knew it!"

"What?" he asked emphatically with an incredulous grin.

"Yea! I trusted in God!"

Gabby and Trevor both laughed and laughed.

"Thank you so much!" Trevor said. "Thank you." Just then, Trevor got an idea to do something to thank Gabby.

"What are you doing right now?" he asked spontaneously.

"I'm just chilling with my phone," she answered.

"Can you meet me at the swings in thirty minutes?" he asked eagerly.

"Sure!" squealed Gabby, full of glee that she could see him once again.

"Okay! See you."

Trevor drove over to Ralph's as fast as he legally could. There, he was pleased to find that they had a small but nice collection of fresh, pretty roses. He studied every single bouquet, and then chose the classic: red roses. He asked the nice florist lady if she could add some baby's breath in the bouquet, since he knew Gabby loved baby's breath. She wrapped the roses with a deep pink paper and tied the ensemble with a beautiful silver ribbon. Looking at the completed bouquet, Trevor sighed a satisfied sigh.

Trevor drove over to the neighborhood park, tears streaming down his cheeks but also a wide grin stretched across his lips.

"Phew," he said, glad that he had arrived earlier than Gabby.

He sat on one of the swings and started swinging. For once he had no troubles, worries, or woes in his heart. He hadn't felt this refreshed in a while, or, ever. Looking up at the ever-white full moon, he felt an all-encompassing contentment. For the first time in his life, he felt like he didn't have to justify himself and that it was fine to just be himself. He even felt a little proud of himself.

"Thank you, God," he said quietly to the huge white moon.

Just then, Gabby jogged over and breathlessly hugged Trevor as he stood up from the swings.

"Come with me," Trevor said, and, holding her hand, he led her to his trunk where the bouquet lay. He had quickly cleaned up his messy trunk so that the display of roses would look more attractive and majestic when he opened the trunk.

As she saw the flowers, Gabby gasped and her eyes smiled ever so brightly. Trevor eagerly grabbed the bouquet and presented it to Gabby.

"I thought of getting you other color roses, but I ended up just getting red. I know it's kind of boring."

"I love them!" Gabby said, her mouth wide open as she studied the stunning, flawless roses enveloped by soft, white baby's breath.

She hugged Trevor tightly. "Thank you so much," she said, feeling a great warmth fill her heart. She couldn't stop beaming.

Trevor studied his girlfriend's glowing face and felt a surge of satisfaction in his chest.

"Thank you, Gabby," Trevor responded, kissing the top of her head.

"I'm so happy for you Trevor!" Gabby said.

"It's because you prayed for me," Trevor said.

"No," Gabby replied cutely. "It's because God loves you, Trevor!" she said, full of passion.

Trevor put his forehead against Gabby's and smiled. He then gently took her hand in his and began swaying.

Gabby giggled that they were doing this in the neighborhood park where lots of cars pass by. "You're becoming like me," she told Trevor between giggles.

They both felt giddy. Gabby jokingly fast danced, her hand still in Trevor's. Trevor laughed a youthful laugh, which Gabby rarely ever heard.

"I'm so happy for you," she said again, putting her forehead close to his. "So, what did your dad say?" Gabby asked, wanting to know all the details.

Trevor could not forget his dad's words. "He said, 'Go for it. If it is your passion, give it your all. I'll support you.'"

Gabby looked at him, her mouth wide open in disbelief. "Just like that?"

"Yea!" Trevor replied.

Gabby placed both of her hands around Trevor's face and looked him in the eyes. "So how do you feel?"

Trevor looked into her eyes, then looked up at the sky for a moment. "I feel like I'm born again."

"HAHA," Gabby laughed. "I feel like I'm born again, too," Gabby admitted with a sweet smile and giggle. She hugged him again and swayed with him slowly back and forth.

"You did an amazing job, Trevor," she whispered into the night.

"Thank you for everything, Gabby," Trevor whispered back, kissing her cheeks.

G

Two months had passed since her dad entered the hospital, and Gabby missed him a lot more than she used to. The house felt strangely big and cavernous, and when she was about to sleep, she felt afraid that someone might break into her home and that she and her mom would be defenseless. Even though her dad had been quiet and rarely smiled, she still missed the comforting feeling of him sitting in his study and quietly reading on his laptop. She missed the sound of his slow but measured footsteps around the house.

Just mulling over and contemplating the thought of missing her dad made the aching feeling worse, so Gabby decided that every time she missed him, she would make something for him and the many veterans that were in similar situations. While her dad was gone, she researched post-traumatic stress disorder and veteran care. She learned that veterans with PTSD were a group of people that were suffering intensely but silently, with little help or attention. She also learned that veterans had poor access to healthcare. But what broke Gabby's heart the most was that many veterans struggling with mental illness were facing divorce and great brokenness in their personal lives. An urgency stirred in her heart to take a stand and be a voice for her dad and other veterans.

"Should I make a piano song dedicated to them?" Gabby wondered on that quiet Saturday morning.

She sat at the piano. Her fingers masterfully produced a melody, but the notes flew up into the air and echoed eerily throughout her large, uninhabited house, coming back into her ears with an unpleasant metallic edge. Her house would never feel the same without her dad. Quickly grabbing her purse, she rushed out to her driveway and got into her car. She turned left onto Hawthorne Boulevard and kept driving, as quickly as possible away from home. Soon, she was ascending the hill of Palos Verdes.

The sight of tall, lush pine tree groves lining the street filled Gabby with peace and she breathed with more ease. She rolled down the windows and breathed in deeply with great satisfaction as the wind rippled across her face. She had the sudden idea to drive all the way to Terranea Resort, the beautiful oceanfront resort at the tip of Palos Verdes.

As she turned into the huge, grand entrance of the resort, she admired the majestic cacti and exotic orange-and-yellow flowers that grew abundantly on either side of the street. The panoramic view of the deep sapphire ocean made her mouth curve into a great smile, her mouth muscles being stretched because she hadn't smiled all morning. The sky above the horizon was a refreshing light blue and wispy white clouds streaked the sky lightly here and there high above the horizon. She turned left into the public parking section and parked her car.

All was quiet around Gabby and there were no people walking around. It was just her, and the breeze softly flowing in through the window.

She felt it was the perfect moment to make a song. Closing her eyes, she put herself into the mode of how veterans would feel. She wanted to capture the chaos and darkness that mental illness put veterans in, and also their inability to feel love, which she read was sometimes an effect of the trauma they suffered. She opened her eyes, and pressed "record" on her voice recording app on her phone. She began to sing whatever flowed from her heart.

The night raged on

The night raged on

The night rages on inside my soul

Never-ending war, never-ending fear

I don't feel love anymore

Don't feel love anymore

I'm all alone

I don't know what to do

I don't know what to do

About my family

I reach for them

But my heart feels nothing at all

I don't feel anything at all

Save me Lord

She pressed the "stop" button on her recording app, then replayed it. The haunting feeling in her voice gave her a visceral reaction, even to her surprise. It was kind of weird, but she liked it. She saved the song and named it "Soldier Cry."

~

**Listen to "Soldier Cry" on Gabby's blog here:
www.gabbysmelody.com**

~

After listening to the song intently two more times, Gabby decided to make a second song. This time, she wanted to inspire people to rally together to support veterans in their recovery from PTSD. She gathered up all her compassion in her heart for veterans, then pressed record.

~

**Listen to "We Will Stand" on Gabby's blog here:
www.gabbysmelody.com**

~

The war is over

But you're still fighting alone

Alone

With no one to understand at all

How horrible it was

How horrible it is

To live inside your mind

But you're not your illness

And you are more than all this going on

You gave your life for us

We give our lives for you

We will stand shoulder to shoulder

We will stand heart to heart

Giving our hearts to you

Till the fight is over–

Till the fight for your soul is won

We will fight

When Gabby replayed it, she was amazed at how heartfelt it sounded. She also liked how the song built up to a triumphant-sounding ending. Holding her phone in her palm, she wondered how she could use these songs to make positive change for veterans.

Looking out the window, she sighed as a breeze came in and played with her long chestnut hair, the sun making small diamonds across her locks. For some moments, she thoughtfully studied the tall grass and the unique mustard-yellow flowering plants surrounding the parking lot. Just then, she got the inspiration to sing these two songs at her school's end-of-year spring concert. This would allow her to raise awareness on the issue of veterans before a larger audience. Her heart began to beat rapidly at the thought of performing before her entire school. Playing each song once more, she tuned her ears to carefully study each nuance and note. The concert was three weeks away, so she resolved to make the best use of her time and practice diligently every day.

"I think I'll say a short speech about veterans before I start," Gabby said aloud to herself in the stillness of her car.

Looking out toward the ocean, she wished her dad could be there to hear the dedication she was going to make to veterans. She pictured him sitting before her in the sea of seats in the audience. But how would he look? Would he be whole again? Would he be the strong, cheerful dad that she used to know? For a moment, her heart faltered, and the image of her dad vanished from the imaginary audience in her mind. She was tempted to fall into a whirlpool of doubt, but then she quickly shook her head and firmly decided to keep hoping and waiting in faith.

Playing "Soldier Cry" again, she began practicing for her performance, with all her heart and all her being.

"*The night raged on / The night raged on / The night rages on inside my soul...*"

G&T

Spring was turning into summer, and the balmy weather inspired Gabby and Trevor to go on a picnic date.

"It's our first picnic!" Gabby squealed as Trevor drove them over to Trader Joe's, their favorite store, to grab some yummy foods. Gabby had always imagined a picnic date would be very picturesque and romantic, and she sighed happily with hopeful expectation.

Going down the chilly refrigerated aisle together with a bright red basket on Trevor's left arm and Gabby clutching his right arm, they couldn't be more gleeful.

"It's like we're married!" Trevor exclaimed cutely.

Gabby guffawed at his girly remark, but inside she was oozing with happiness. Though they were surrounded by a sea of bustling shoppers, it felt as if it were just the two of them. All she could see was Trevor. She admired the way his navy blue polo draped across his broad shoulders. Just then, Gabby started shivering from the chill coming from the refrigerated section. Trevor, noticing this, held her tightly from the side with his free arm and they walked snugly side by side.

As they passed by the cheese section, Trevor picked up a large, triangular block of cheese and exclaimed with a goofy French accent, "How about we have some charcuterie?"

Gabby's eyes grew wide. She never made charcuterie by herself before. Her tongue salivated at the thought of salami and cheese. "Yea! Let's do it!" she exclaimed.

They picked up salami and brie cheese and then browsed the rest of the aisles of Trader Joe's. They loaded their cart with some crackers, cobb salad, double chocolate chip cookies, macarons, kettle corn, and penguin gummies. They wondered what would be the last thing that would finish off their ensemble. Trevor held up a bottle of sparkling pink lemonade triumphantly; it was encased in a lovely, curvy glass bottle and it was perfect for their romantic date. Gabby squealed with delight. After making their purchases, they piled into the car and headed to El Retiro Park.

When they got to the peaceful park, Trevor opened his trunk and began rummaging through it like a raccoon. Gabby's eyes grew wide in amazement as he began taking out blankets, a mat, cups, plates, napkins, forks, and knives.

"Wow! You prepared all this?" Gabby said, gulping in shock.

Trevor smiled as if it were a given.

Gabby was impressed at how prepared her boyfriend was. "Thank you so much," she said as she hugged him, smiling in his embrace. She thought of how lucky she was to have a guy like him.

Trevor carried all the heavy items and Gabby took the lighter ones as they headed into the park. Gabby looked over at her boyfriend admiringly as he lugged the heavy items effortlessly.

The park was expansive, with a set of tennis courts and a basketball court to the left and a small playground in the front. Large hilly stretches of grass and trees rolled before them. The sun shone upon the park, highlighting the fluorescent hues of the grass, and a balmy afternoon breeze traveled through the park, soothing Trevor and Gabby's senses. A few parents played with their cute little toddlers, going down the yellow slides in the playground, and a young man played frisbee with his collie on the grass.

"What a cute dog!" Gabby squealed as she pointed at the excited dog.

After choosing a nice, shady spot under a large maple tree, Trevor and Gabby carefully laid out the mat and blankets together and unpacked the food. Trevor began slicing the salami, while Gabby sliced the brie. Gabby carefully placed a piece of cheese on a cracker and lovingly fed Trevor as he sliced the salami. She grinned, feeling the picnic was indeed romantic. She watched as he crunched on the cracker and thought the way he ate was adorable. Trevor then piled a cracker with salami and cheese and fed Gabby with a sweet, tender look upon his face. He watched her attentively as she shyly crunched on the snack.

"Trev, you want to listen to the songs I made for the spring concert?" Gabby asked after taking a gulp of her sparkling lemonade. The fizz tingled on her tongue, a mix of sweet and tang delighting her taste buds.

"Yeah!" Trevor exclaimed.

"Okay," Gabby said excitedly. She put her cup of lemonade down on the mat.

She cleared her throat and sat tall, straightening her back. She squinted her eyes for a second, trying to overcome her nervousness and focus on the emotion of the song. She had sung many times in the car in front of Trevor, but this was the first time she was actually trying her best to sound good.

"The war is over / But you're still fighting alone / Alone / With no one to..."

Trevor listened, rapt. He was hypnotized by the wistfulness in Gabby's voice. He never saw the performance side of her. He observed how she closed her eyes, her eyelashes fluttering at times. Her voice, which was usually so sweet, sounded deep and mature. When Gabby finished, Trevor stared at her, his mouth hanging wide open.

Gabby opened her eyes and giggled at Trevor's expression.

"What?"

"That was...amazing!" Trevor replied. "How did you make that?" he asked, incredulous.

"I don't know. It just came out!"

"Wow! You are so talented!" Trevor scratched his head, wondering how she could produce something out of nothing.

Gabby giggled with glee. "Thank you."

"I could really feel your heart for veterans, and it made me want to do something to help them out," Trevor said with genuine warmth.

Gabby just smiled at Trevor adoringly for a while, like a girl who had found the best guy in the world, then leaned in to kiss him on the cheek. Trevor grinned and kissed her on the lips. His girlfriend's heart fluttered wildly like the flapping of a dove's wings. He drew her in for an embrace and her heart pounded loudly.

"Here's my next song," Gabby said with a growing grin. She straightened her posture again and looked far away to the other side of the park.

"The night raged on / The night raged on / The night rages on inside my soul..."

A chill traveled up Trevor's spine. His heart admired the soulfulness of her voice.

"I don't feel love anymore / Don't feel love anymore..."

Trevor smiled in awe at his girlfriend, having not known she was so talented. When she was done with the song, Trevor clapped loudly and emphatically. Gabby laughed, embarrassed.

"Isn't it weird?" she asked, putting her hair behind her ear.

"No! It's perfect. It felt kind of eerie, which is good because veterans with PTSD feel a lot of fear and uncertainty. It was as if you knew exactly how it feels to be a veteran! That was spectacular, Gabby!" he hollered, giving her a big, warm hug.

Gabby smiled, satisfied, not expecting to get this response.

"You're going to move the audience," Trevor said with all sincerity, that beautiful sparkle in his chestnut eyes.

Gabby lit up and smiled.

"Really?" she said, embracing Trevor. She gave him a kiss on the nose. Trevor kissed her nose back. They looked deeply into each other's eyes for some long moments.

"Thank you," she said sweetly. She sighed a happy sigh, relieved that Trevor liked the songs. They held each other for a while, resting their souls and delighting in the serenity of the greenery surrounding them.

"I'm also planning to say an intro to tell the audience about the plight of veterans and how we should help them. Can you help me?" Gabby asked, knowing that Trevor was very eloquent and could provide a lot of good insight.

"Sure!" Trevor quickly said.

They discussed what Gabby could say and ate their snacks until sundown. The grass and the trees were now soaked in a deep golden glow, and the park took on a magical presence. As the sun set, Trevor held Gabby in his arms, her back leaning against his chest, and they beheld the beauty of the nature around them in contented silence as a gentle breeze traveled to them. By then, the park was empty, so it was just them two.

"It's as if we're in the Garden of Eden," Gabby whispered to Trevor sweetly as she held his arms that held her. Gabby enjoyed the sweetness of being close to him and so did Trevor. Resting peacefully together, they felt utterly joyful and complete.

~

The three weeks leading up to the concert sped by. As soon as Gabby opened her eyes the morning of the concert, she jumped out of her bed and ran to her mom, who was thoughtfully looking at mail in the kitchen.

"Did you get a call from Dad's hospital?" she urgently asked. Her heart beat wildly with hopefulness.

"No, I didn't," her mom replied apologetically. She studied her daughter, hoping she wasn't let down.

"Okay," Gabby replied, refusing to let go of her hope. She ran back to her room to prepare her concert outfit and practice for her performance.

She asked her mom three more times throughout the day whether she got a call from the hospital saying that her dad was coming home, but her mom shook her head each time. Gabby's heart sank but she knew the show must go on. Gabby came back to her room and faced her full-length mirror hanging on her wall. She placed her hands on her hips and inhaled deeply. In her reflection, she noticed a glint in her eyes that hadn't been there in the past. There was a fire in her eyes. She cleared her throat loudly in the silence of her room. Then, she said out loud to herself with conviction in her voice, "I am an advocate for veterans." She said with even more confidence, "I'm going to do a great job today." She then did some vocal exercises that her voice teacher taught her and practiced her songs several times each until they sounded perfect to her ears. Gabby was going to drive over to the concert herself, but then Trevor texted, saying he would drive her.

At four p.m. sharp, Trevor arrived in front of Gabby's house. When he saw her in her concert attire as she strode down her driveway, his grin stretched from ear to ear. He covered his mouth, bashful about his reaction at her beauty.

"You look glorious!" he exclaimed, unable to contain himself, as he took her hand and opened the car door for her. The car was gleaming because he had gotten a car wash to match the occasion.

Gabby flashed him a bright smile like that of a celebrity on the red carpet, and Trevor continued to marvel at her look. She was wearing makeup, which she usually never did. Her eyelashes looked longer and darker with mascara on, and her eyeliner accentuated her lovely brown eyes. She also had on a classy shade of plum red lipstick. Her navy-blue satin dress came down to her knees and had a simple, sophisticated cut, paired with an elegant pair of simple black heels. Trevor never saw her look so ladylike.

Gabby beamed at Trevor and then her mouth dropped open, because he was wearing a suit and had gotten a fresh haircut, and his sideburns had a great fade.

"You look so amazing!" she shrieked as she hugged him tight. She admired his dark blue suit and light blue tie. Her heart fluttered at her boyfriend's brand new look. "You look so great in your suit!"

Trevor grinned a shy grin, a glow expanding golden in his heart.

On their drive to school, Trevor kept looking over at Gabby from time to time and smiling.

"What?" Gabby said with a smile, feeling flattered, fully knowing why Trevor was smiling.

Trevor fumbled over his words. "You just–you look–so beautiful today!"

"Haha, you never stumble over your words!" Gabby noted. She felt even more flattered, and smiled a shy but satisfied smile to herself.

She held onto his right arm affectionately as he drove, and continued to look out the windshield thoughtfully, mentally preparing herself for her performance.

Trevor reached for her hand and held it supportively. His soft, plush hand gave her comfort.

Soon, they arrived at the parking lot of their school auditorium, and Gabby looked into Trevor's face and smiled at her boyfriend as he parked the car. She knew he would pray for her.

"I'll pray for you," he said, sure enough, with bold conviction.

"Okay," Gabby said cheerfully, flashing him a mesmerizing smile again. Trevor felt he would melt to the floor.

Trevor got ready to pray and situated himself in his seat like he always did before he prayed for her.

"Dear God, today Gabby is going to sing for the cause of suffering veterans. She worked so hard to prepare and we pray that she would sing as beautifully as she always does. We pray that the audience would be moved to help veterans as a result of her performance. Please be close to Gabby and steady her heart. May you be glorified today. We love you. We thank you. In Jesus' name, amen."

Gabby hugged Trevor after he said "amen," and Trevor stroked her head, kissing her forehead. He fixed her hair adoringly after kissing her. "It'll go great, Gabby," he reassured her. "You are amazing."

Gabby smiled brightly at Trevor, wanting to kiss him on the cheek. "I would kiss you but then my lipstick would get messed up," she said shyly and coyly.

"It's okay," Trevor replied.

Gabby looked into his eyes, overflowing with gratitude for him. "Thank you," she said, embracing him again and putting her head against his chest.

Trevor opened the car door for her, and hand in hand, they strode to the auditorium with all the confidence in the universe.

~

Holding her father's photograph tightly backstage, Gabby felt sweat forming in her warm hands. She wiped them against her dress. Looking at her dad's young smiling face and her two-year-old self with pigtails squealing from atop his shoulders, Gabby smiled a little. "Dad would've been proud of me tonight," she thought, feeling some strength from looking at the photo.

"Gabby, you're up in one minute," the stage manager said.

Walking up to the great wine-colored curtain, she took a deep breath, reminding herself of the reason she was going up there. Finally, she heard the audience bursting into applause for the previous performer and Gabby knew that was her cue. Taking her guitar, she walked confidently toward the mic and into the spotlight. Silence blanketed the room. Sitting on the stool with her guitar, Gabby began to speak to the audience with a boldness and sureness she didn't expect to come out of her.

"These next two songs I'm going to sing are dedicated to my father and to all the veterans who are suffering from PTSD and their wartime experiences. To be honest, I didn't do a good job of understanding my dad when he would show symptoms of his illness. I just wanted him to get better, to change. But then I realized that the one who needed to change was me. We, as a nation, need to be prepared to receive our veterans with compassion and understanding and insight so that we can help them recover. The things that they have gone through are unimaginable and horrific. I made these next two songs to let veterans know that we are standing with them and that we will support and love them in their recovery to wholeness. My first song is called "'Soldier Cry.'"

~

Listen to "Soldier Cry Finale" on Gabby's blog here: www.gabbysmelody.com

~

Gabby took a deep breath and sang her first note. Immediately, she got into character and she closed her eyes.

"The night raged on / The night raged on / The night rages on inside my soul"

The haunting feeling in her voice made a hush come over the entire audience.

"Never-ending war / Never-ending fear / I don't feel love anymore / Don't feel love anymore / I'm all alone / I don't know what to do"

The atmosphere of the audience was thick with thoughtfulness and suspense. Some members of the audience held their breath.

"I don't know what to do / About my family / I reach for them / But my heart feels nothing at all / I don't feel anything at all / Save me Lord"

She held the last note for "Lord" and then slowly opened her eyes. For a moment, she forgot that she was on stage because she had been so into the song. The entire audience burst into thunderous applause.

"Now I will sing my second song, which is called "'We Will Stand,'" Gabby said as the audience's applause died down. She gathered up her deep compassion for veterans before she began.

~

**Listen to "We Will Stand Finale" on Gabby's blog here:
www.gabbysmelody.com**

~

"The war is over / But you're still fighting alone / Alone / With no one to understand at all / How horrible it was / How horrible it is to / Live inside your mind / But you're not your illness / And you are more than / All this going on / You gave your life for us / We give our lives for you"

She crescendoed as she got ready for the culminating part.

"We will stand / Shoulder to shoulder / We will stand / Heart to heart / Giving our hearts to you / Till the fight is over / Till the fight for your soul is won / We will fight"

She held the last note and finished off the song with a feeling of immense triumph and determination.

Strumming her last chord, Gabby looked up at her mom, who sat in the second row. Tears were streaming down her blush-covered shimmering cheeks. Gabby smiled at her, happy that her delivery was flawless. Looking around the room, she noticed many audience members wiping tears from their eyes.

Just then a shadow moved in the way back of the auditorium. A silhouette had been leaning against the wall but stood straight and began clapping mightily. He was holding a huge bundle in his hands. As he moved toward the light emanating from the

365

stage, she noticed the yellow in the bouquet—yellow roses. Her heart began to race. The light moved from his bouquet to his arms to his shoulders to finally his face. It was her dad.

Dropping her guitar onto the stage, Gabby jumped off the stage, her tomboyishness she learned from her father coming out, and ran down the center aisle into the arms of her father. He no longer stood rigidly and no longer felt like he was somewhere far away though in the same room as her. His body looked relaxed and his smile was easy. His eyes were soft again, making his face look twenty years younger. Jumping into his arms, Gabby squealed and cried bucketfuls of happy tears. By then, her mom had noticed and rushed over as well, and the entire audience began getting up and crowding around them, most of them clapping. Trevor appeared out of nowhere and began snapping photos like a hired photographer, wiping happy tears from his eyes.

"Dad! What are you doing here?" Gabby screamed and giggled.

Her father just pulled her closer and held her for a while. "I'm so sorry," he cried into her shoulder.

"Dad, no, I am sorry," she responded. Then, lifting his face with her two hands, she looked into his eyes and laughed again. "You're back!…Good job, Dad!"

The three Chois hugged, and Mrs. Choi welcomed Trevor into the circle as well. The four of them hadn't felt that happy in a while, perhaps in all their lives.

"Dad, I thought you weren't coming home yet!" Gabby said to her dad as the four of them walked out of the auditorium.

Lance winked at Trevor. "Trevor and I made a special arrangement," he said.

"Sorry, Gabby, that I couldn't tell you sooner," Trevor said.

Gabby hugged him from the side. "It's okay!" She couldn't stop smiling and looking at her dad in disbelief. He walked with an easy gait and confidence was in his eyes. Tears kept wanting to come out of her eyes.

"Dad, what did you think of the songs...and my dedication?" she asked excitedly.

For a moment Lance looked at the ground and gathered his thoughts. He took her hand in his and said, "I felt so moved and touched...and so proud."

Trevor piped in. "We recorded your entire performance. We're going to send it to your dad's hospital so that the people there can watch it too."

"What?" Gabby exclaimed. "Wow!"

Gabby realized her parents didn't get a chance to reunite because she was doing all the talking. Gabby's mom held her dad's hand and they gazed into each other's eyes for a long time.

Gabby held Trevor's hand and let her parents have their time. Tears emerged from her eyes then, as it fully sank in that her family was now okay, and together at last. She quickly hugged Trevor tight, burying her face into his shoulder. He patted her back, knowing that she was going to cry.

"Thank you so much," Gabby said in between her tears.

Trevor embraced her even more tightly.

ather and daughter, arm in arm, walked into Toccoa Creamery, a place that Gabby and her father used to frequent because her father loved ice cream. Gabby couldn't keep her eyes off of her dad's shining face. His tan and weathered face had a golden glow as if it were the very sun. She wondered how he could look so young, so vibrant, so new.

Gabby couldn't wait to sit down and have their first father-daughter conversation, the first in a long time.

Together, they peered at the flavorful ice cream lined up in rows with exotic flavors like Lavender Lily, White Chocolate Red Velvet, and Pumpkin Chocolate. They looked at each other for a moment with a knowing smile because they were both thinking the same thing. They were going to go for the Pumpkin Chocolate.

"Two double scoops of pumpkin chocolate, please," Gabby's dad said in his good-natured voice, looking into the eyes of the cashier with that genuine smile of his.

Gabby's heart fluttered. She was always so proud of this magnetic quality of her dad's. They were the only ones in the ice cream shop at the time and Gabby liked how they could exclusively focus on each other.

They sat in the round corner table, which was white with matching plastic white chairs. It was next to the large window facing the street.

"Trevor is an amazing young man," her dad said as he took a big bite of his orange-colored ice cream.

Gabby's eyes widened in shock. She didn't expect her dad to think so highly of Trevor already, although she thought of him very highly.

"Dad, why do you think that?" she asked in an excited, high-pitched voice, quickly swallowing her ice cream.

He chuckled, seeing that his daughter was so nervous and excited about talking about her boyfriend. He reached over and rubbed her hair at the top, his spoon still stuck in his mouth. Gabby grinned, and tried to hold back tears, since this all felt so familiar to her, yet also felt like ages ago. Gabby felt playful and rubbed her dad's hair back, just like he did. They laughed and laughed, their laughter echoing off the walls of the empty ice cream parlor.

"So what do you like about him?" he continued in his playful voice.

Gabby's cheeks turned red, but then she was also thrilled to be able to share all the wonderful things about Trevor to her dad finally.

"Well, where do I start?" Gabby said breathlessly. She grinned widely, knowing she knew exactly what she wanted to say. She wanted to tell her dad about the random acts of kindness and Trevor coming all the way to Aunt Marie's cabin.

"There was this one day I felt really...discouraged, and when I reached my locker after class, there were three daisies stuck in the crack between my locker and the next one! That was the first time Trevor did something nice for me so that I could feel uplifted," Gabby said with that sweet smile of hers spreading across her face.

Lance studied his daughter's brown hair which shone bronze in the sun and her big brown eyes which hadn't changed at all since she was just a toddler. He studied her freckles which graced her cheeks and he realized she had grown up so much, yet was still his little girl.

"So Trevor liked you from the start!" Lance joked.

"Nooooo!" Gabby retorted. "He was just being kind!" she exclaimed vehemently.

"Okay, okay, Gabby," her dad replied with a mischievous smile.

She continued. "Yeah, he kept doing these nice things for me, but I of course had no idea who was doing it. But I felt really happy every time it happened and I looked forward to the next day because of it. One time, I was really sick with a fever and body ache and when I got home, Trevor had dropped off this huge pot of chicken noodle soup!"

She giggled. "I mean, how did he make it so fast after school?" She guffawed as she put her hair behind her ear.

Her dad crossed his arms across his chest and smiled, but slightly jealous that Trevor had stolen his daughter's heart. "And he then followed you all the way to Aunt Marie's?" her dad asked with a quizzical brow.

Just then Gabby smiled the hugest, dreamiest smile, just thinking about their time at Aunt Marie's. Lance laughed, so happy that there was someone to take care of his beloved daughter the way he cared for her.

Gabby described how Trevor was standing behind a tree ready to surprise her at Aunt Marie's house, and how they explored the forest together, and how he made strawberry pies with her. But then when it got to the part where he confessed his feelings to her, she paused. Gabby looked down at her melting ice cream with a secretive, embarrassed smile, not sure if she wanted to tell her dad about how they got together.

"How did he ask you out?" her dad asked, interrupting her thoughts.

Gabby's eyes grew wide, realizing dads knew everything. "Ummmm...That, I will tell you later," Gabby said quickly, giggling a little.

She stirred her ice cream with her spoon and took a lick. She used to stir her ice cream until it was like soup and then slurp it up when she was a child. She felt so happy that it was just like the old times with her dad.

Gabby looked up, and caught her dad looking intently into her eyes.

371

"I approve," he said, making her heart expand three thousand times with bliss.

"Thanks, Dad!" she exclaimed, and then got up to hug him, the pleasant scent of his cologne filling her nose.

"I always hoped and prayed you'd meet someone like him," he said sincerely into her ear.

"He's the best, Dad," Gabby said.

"No, you're the best," he answered.

Gabby guffawed, loving how her dad was always full of pride over her.

As father and daughter left the ice cream shop arm in arm, Gabby looked up at her dad's face and said, "Want to grab Chinese food on the way home for dinner?"

"Sounds great!" her dad replied.

Gabby smiled up at her dad, her hero.

Lance smiled down at his loving daughter, his saving grace, his everything.

~

After swinging by Seafood Town to to-go some flat rice noodles, walnut shrimp, and salt and pepper pork, Gabby and her dad entered the house, holding giant bags of food in each hand.

Gabby's mom, always quick to smell things, exclaimed, "Wow, that smells like some good food! And thank you, that means I don't have to cook tonight!"

She went up on her tip-toes to peck her husband on the cheek.

Gabby looked from her mom to her dad, then her dad to her mom, smiling at their adoring gaze toward each other.

Gabby's mom would've usually nagged at them about how they spent too much money on food, or asked why they didn't use coupons, but today, she seemed content. Gabby studied the peacefulness that had overcome her mom's face, and she wondered if her mom looked that way because her dad was now himself.

Lance started to unpack the bags, placing the styrofoam containers of delectable Chinese food on the dining table.

Gabby gulped and looked at her mom again. Her mom didn't approve of storing hot food in styrofoam containers because styrofoam released bad chemicals. But luckily, her mom didn't say anything, once again.

The three of them gathered around the table, and Gabby couldn't help but hold back tears because it was their first real meal together after her dad had returned from the hospital.

"Let's hold hands," her dad said in his warm, confident voice.

The three of them linked hands, and closed their eyes, knowing Lance would pray.

"Dear Father, Thank you for keeping my family safe and well while I was away. Thank you for healing me and for letting me be reunited with my lovely wife and daughter. May we be a family that is always thankful to you and tells the world about the wonders that You have done for us. We love you. In Jesus' name, amen."

Lance opened his eyes and saw that his wife was blowing her nose into a napkin from Seafood Town, and that Gabby was looking up at him with glistening eyes.

As they started ravenously digging into their food, Gabby wondered if she should ask her dad about what it was like in the hospital. Then, she thought of the perfect question.

"Dad, what do you think really helped you to get better while you were at the hospital?"

Lance paused for a moment as he chewed his flat rice noodles. He studied the light green tablecloth for just a moment. He took a sip of his water.

"Gabby, remember the music you sent me?"

Gabby's heart jumped. She didn't think the music was that great, and plus, she hadn't heard back from her dad about it.

"Your music was what started me on the path to healing," her dad admitted with a weak smile and eyes sparkling with tears.

Gabby paused in shock. "No way, really?" she asked him. "How?"

"Just like it moved the entire audience at your spring concert," he boomed with pride and joy in his eyes.

Gabby giggled. "Nah…" she said.

Her mom chimed in. "Gabby, your music really moved the entire audience. A lot of moms and dads came up to me afterwards and told me that your performance was so special."

Gabby squirmed in her seat, but then it sank in. She started smiling a broad smile as she looked shyly down at her plate.

Lance stretched out his arm across the table and took his daughter's hand softly in his. "Your music comes out of your heart and that is why it can move and heal people the way it does," he said with a reassuring smile in his eyes.

Gabby was still speechless. "Thanks, Dad," she said, still unable to believe that her music had helped heal her father.

"As Trevor told you, I'm going to send your music to my hospital so the veterans there could listen to your tribute, too. I know they will love it and feel very valued and honored by it."

"That's what I wanted, Dad! I wanted to help a lot of veterans," Gabby admitted with a huge, lightning bright grin.

Lance couldn't believe his little girl had grown into a young woman of such great character, into a person whose heart cared for so many people.

He put his fork down on the table and just stared in wonder at Gabby.

Gabby just kept smiling, so thrilled that all her work had not been in vain.

"I'm so proud of you," her mom said warmly, looking into her eyes.

Gabby looked at her mom in disbelief, because her mom never said things like that. Gabby had always felt she wasn't enough for her mom.

The life of her dreams was unfolding right in front of her.

All of this emotion was a little too much for Gabby, and she switched the subject to something lighter.

"Dad, how did you and Trevor plan the surprise? I totally didn't expect it," Gabby said excitedly as she bit into a big piece of fried pork.

Her dad guffawed.

"You have a very clever and very thoughtful boyfriend," he replied, and he described how they hatched the plan together.

After dinner, Gabby asked if she could go see Trevor for a bit, and they met at the neighborhood park.

Gabby leapt into his arms with a happy sigh. Trevor scooped her up and held her for a long time, smiling into her hair. They looked into each other's eyes with shining smiles, Gabby holding his cheeks in her palms. Trevor could read the happiness in Gabby's eyes, and in them he read the story of her family. He could tell that her family was now reunited and very happy.

"I'm so happy for you," he said warmly, hugging her close again. He stroked the back of her head in the way that she loved.

"My dad and mom both love you so much," Gabby said to him, knowing that he'd love to hear this.

Trevor laughed. "No, they love you, so they love me because you love me," he said.

Gabby was used to hearing things like this. "Nooo, they love YOU!" she responded. She kissed Trevor playfully and passionately so he could feel the truth of her statement.

They made their way to the yellow rubber swings and sat down.

"Want me to push you?" Trevor asked, always so sweet.

Gabby giggled exuberantly. "Sure!" she agreed.

He got off his swing and went behind Gabby and began to push her gently. Gabby soared higher and higher and she started giggling louder and louder. Gabby imagined she had grown wings; that was how she felt at this point in her life.

Suddenly wanting to thank Trevor, she said to him, "You can stop pushing me," in her sweet, clear voice.

Trevor helped her swing slow down by grabbing the swing chains with both hands securely. He held Gabby from behind and he kissed the top of her head. Gabby melted into this moment and grinned to herself.

She then got off her swing and hugged Trevor with all her love being transmitted from her heart, to her arms, to his chest, to his heart. "I adore you," she said.

Trevor remained silent, knowing she wanted to say more.

"Thank you for helping my family. Thank you for helping me and supporting me through it all," she said, her heart full of appreciation. She rested her head against his chest.

Trevor held her and said, "You did it, Gabby. You are the strongest person I know."

"No, we did it together," Gabby replied softly, feeling the comfort of his presence against her face. "Thank you so much," she said again.

They stood there, holding each other for a long time, exchanging affectionate, adoring kisses again and again in the moonlight.

G&T

The two lovebirds spent that summer before college making more unforgettable memories together. They went kayaking one more time; this time, Trevor did not fall into the ocean. They went on a few more peaceful, romantic picnics at local parks. They wandered the famous museums of LA. But for their final date before they went off to their respective colleges, they wanted to do something special.

One Saturday as the couple lay in the shade of a maple tree in their little private corner of El Retiro Park, Trevor turned his head and gazed at his girlfriend who had closed her eyes in the immense peacefulness of the afternoon spent out in nature with Trevor. As he gazed at her loveliness, he thought about all the months that had gone before and all they had been through together. He gently took her hand and placed it lovingly on his cheek.

Gabby opened her eyes and smiled into his lovely eyes that reflected his pure spirit. "What?" she asked with a short giggle. She turned to her side and held his hand and stared deeply into his eyes for some long moments. Then she leaned over to his face and kissed him on the cheek.

Trevor drew her hand close to his mouth and kissed the top of her hand. Gabby's heart fluttered whenever he did this sweet, cute gesture.

"Gabby, how about for our last date before college starts, we can go up north to Aunt Marie's?"

For a moment his girlfriend's brow furrowed as she recalled the dark period of her life at Aunt Marie's. But then she smiled again, thinking of all the wondrous memories they made there, and how it led to their confession of their feelings for one another.

"Why do you want to go to Aunt Marie's?" she asked quizzically.

Trevor paused for a moment and then pointed up at the tree above them.

"Looking at that tree made me think of how strong our relationship has grown, just like a robust, evergreen tree. I thought we could buy an evergreen tree and plant it in the forest of Aunt Marie's place to symbolize our eternal and true love."

Gabby smiled, shocked as always at her boyfriend's ingenuity and romantic soul. She thoughtfully looked up at the maple tree again. The sun rippled across the bright green leaves. The little yellow spots of sunlight danced across the leaves and boughs, mesmerizing her.

"That's the best idea, Trev," she said with an excited grin. She embraced him, and for a moment they relished in the romantic moment of holding each other on the picnic blanket.

Gabby smiled to herself as she breathed in his calming, clean, sweet scent. "When do you want to go?" she asked sleepily.

"How about the first week of September?"

"Okay," Gabby replied, and she drifted off into the most peaceful sleep of her life, cuddled close to his chest.

As September approached, Gabby and Trevor's hearts grew heavy at the thought of not seeing each other except for during school holidays. They looked forward to their special day trip to Aunt Marie's the weekend before their freshman orientations.

Early in the morning on September twentieth, they each woke up at 5:30 a.m., got dressed, and packed their backpacks for their six-hour journey to Aunt Marie's cottage. This time, they got onto the Greyhound bus together, and as Trevor held her hand to help her get onto the tall vehicle, Gabby smiled a genuine smile, relieved that she had Trevor by her side from now on. As they scooted into the moss green leather seats, Gabby's mind flashed to the memory of her leaning her face against the window, her cheek cut and in pain. For a moment she frowned, but she quickly shook the memory away, and squeezed Trevor's hand. At the same exact moment, they opened their backpack front pockets and took out some Hot Cheetos.

"Hahaha," they giggled, seeing how they were so alike.

Crunching away at their Cheetos and chatting together, their trip was off to a lively start, as other passengers snored and slumbered all around them.

Excitement mounted in Gabby for their romantic date where they would commemorate their love in a permanent way–by planting the evergreen. She faced the window to her right, and in the cold morning air, she blew her warm breath at the glass and then spontaneously drew a heart with her index finger. Trevor noticed and leaned over and drew a heart too. Then, Gabby wrote, "G&T". Trevor's face lit up like the morning sun and he kissed the top of her head, her soft brown hair always smelling freshly of shampoo.

The hours flew by, as they always did when they were together, and for most of the ride, Gabby slept soundly against Trevor's comfy shoulder, her favorite pillow. Trevor mostly stayed awake, studying the interesting sights along the way and imprinting each moment to his memory.

Five hours and forty minutes into the journey, Trevor noticed Gabby shifting her head, and he whispered gently, "We're almost there." Gabby smiled a dreamy grin, having forgotten during her slumber that she was with Trevor. She hugged him tightly from the side.

"Are you hungry? Want more snacks?" Trevor asked, always so quick to take care of her.

Gabby paused, feeling touched every time by his kindness. She hugged him again. "Do you have more candy?" she asked softly.

Trevor quickly rummaged like a raccoon through his backpack and took out a new pack of Fruit Roll-Ups. They both giggled loudly, since these were both of their favorite childhood snacks, which their mothers only allowed on rare occasions, making them want them even more.

They quickly opened the wrappers, and Trevor proceeded to twist his fruit roll-up and yank a piece off with his mouth vigorously.

"Hey! I used to do that, too!" Gabby squealed. She twisted her fruit roll-up too and imitated Trevor's yanking a piece off with a ridiculous expression on her face.

Trevor guffawed and kissed his cute and funny girlfriend's soft cheeks one by one.

As the stately redwood trees emerged, they both gasped and gazed at the magnificence of the towering forest together. The branches seemed to reach upward to the very sky, and no matter how much they craned their necks, they couldn't see the tops of the trees. A silence overcame them as they couldn't help but feel the solemnity and sadness of the previous time they had seen this sight.

Gabby leaned her cheek against Trevor's shoulder. Trevor, being so intuitive, stroked her head comfortingly.

"Trevor always knows exactly what to do to make me feel better," Gabby thought with gratitude.

As the bus swung into a parking lot, Gabby noticed Aunt Marie because of her bright red matching blouse and skirt. She was holding a bouquet of sunflowers.

Gabby ran down the stairs of the bus, jumped off, and hugged Aunt Marie with all her being.

"Sweetie, I missed you so much!" Aunt Marie cooed in her high-pitched but pleasant voice. "Hey, Trevor! How've you been?" she asked with a huge smile, as she ruffled up his curly hair.

Trevor grinned, feeling like he had a new family member.

"Are you guys hungry? Want to eat at home or want to pick up something on the way?" Aunt Marie asked chirpily.

~

After making some turkey sandwiches with fresh tomatoes from Aunt Marie's garden, Gabby and Trevor were left alone in the kitchen.

Gabby peeped out the kitchen window to see if Aunt Marie was out of sight, and then, seeing her far off, she went over to Trevor and quickly hugged him. Trevor melted into her arms and they gazed longingly into each other's eyes for a moment. Suddenly feeling nervous being alone together in the big, quiet house, Trevor cleared his throat.

"Want to go to the arboretum now?" he asked.

Gabby grinned at how wise and God-honoring her boyfriend was.

"Yea, sure!" she replied.

They got into Aunt Marie's car, which she had lent them, and they headed to the local arboretum, where they could pick out an evergreen tree seedling.

At the front of the arboretum was a large tree nursery. Gabby's eyes grew wide with wonder and excitement at their adventure of finding the perfect tree to symbolize their love.

"Red Mulberry, Bur Oak, Sweetgum, American Beech, Quaking Aspen, Sandbar Willow," she read aloud as they walked slowly along the neat rows. "Their leaves are all so different and each of them are pretty in their own way!"

Trevor admired how his girlfriend always saw beauty in everything and everyone, and thought it was cute how she would feel a leaf between her fingers as she passed by each tree.

Just then, Gabby read one label aloud that made them pause: "Laurel tree."

"Hey, isn't that from Greek mythology?" Gabby asked Trevor curiously, since he had an answer for her every question. "Oooh, I think that the winner of the Olympics would get a laurel wreath in ancient Greece," she added.

They stared at the tree's leaves, which had sharp, clean edges, making the tree seem strikingly stately and noble.

Trevor nodded and grinned. "Greek heroes would get crowned with laurel wreaths, too."

Gabby looked at Trevor and Trevor looked at Gabby. This was what they wanted.

"Trevor, like an Olympic champion, let's run this race of life for God, and for His glory alone."

Trevor's heart expanded at the enormity of her words, admiring his girlfriend's devotion to God and humility.

"I also like this tree because you deserve a crown for how you helped me, Trev," she added sweetly, with a sparkle in her eyes, as she looked deeply into his.

"You helped yourself, Gabby," Trevor said immediately.

Gabby giggled briefly. She held onto his arm and nuzzled her head against his shoulder. "You're my hero," she added.

Trevor's heart glowed, and he felt larger than life, a feeling only Gabby could give him. "You're my hero," he responded.

Gabby smiled, feeling a sense of accomplishment in her heart. "Let's get that one!" she exclaimed, pointing at a robust-looking young laurel tree. Trevor admired how the long, stately leaves were fresh and there was not a hint of dryness or wilting on the tree. He grabbed the burnt-orange clay pot and lifted it up and they oozed with glee as they rushed over to the cash register.

Soon, they were in Aunt Marie's red Chevrolet El Camino again and heading back to the cottage.

"Trev, remember when we played basketball one-on-one last time we came here?" Gabby said, loudly laughing.

"Yeah, you were on fire! So competitive. I didn't expect to see that side of you."

Gabby looked at him sideways quizzically. "What was your first impression of me?" she asked with a hint of slyness.

"I thought you were a very kind and demure girl."

"That's it?" she asked in a jokingly demanding tone.

Trevor fumbled for some moments.

"I'm just kidding," she added sweetly, holding onto his arm. "Well, what do you think of me now?" She giggled that giggle that made Trevor high with happiness.

Trevor beamed. He was always brimming with compliments for Gabby. "I think you are the most daring, boldest person I have ever met."

Gabby looked up, her eyes wide and her mouth wide open. She laughed happily, leaning her head dreamily against his shoulder.

When they got to the front of the house, Trevor carefully took their laurel tree out of the car. They then made their way to the backyard, where they grabbed a shovel with a red handle, along with a green plastic watering can with a sunflower imprint on it.

After filling up the watering can to the brim with a hose, Trevor carried the watering can and the tree, while he let Gabby hold the lighter shovel.

Giggling and chatting as the birds chattered high above them in the trees, the pair walked into the cool, shaded forest—the forest that held their secrets, the forest that held their friendship, the forest that echoed their love.

They walked past the large logs where they had pretended to fight as knights and met a curious and feisty raccoon. They walked past the train tracks where Gabby had rested from a sweaty, tiring hike and Trevor had fanned her face with a hat.

They hiked all the way to the clearing at the top of the hill, where they had lain and watched the passing clouds together, feeling at home for the first time in their lives. The clearing was still covered with long grass, bright yellow mustard plants, and brilliantly vibrant poppy flowers. In the radiant afternoon sun and the gentle breeze, the field was brushed with gentle yellows, royal purples, and fresh greens. It was all new, all sun-kissed, just as they had remembered it. The whole field seemed to celebrate the magic of Trevor and Gabby's love, and how far they had come.

Putting down the shovel, tree seedling, and watering can, they held hands and ran through the field, yelling joyfully and triumphantly. After their spurt of energy, their breaths slowed, their chests calmed, and they faced each other. Trevor scooped Gabby up in his strong arms, lifting her two feet off the ground. She laughed and laughed.

"Put me down! Put me down!" she squealed, playfully hitting his shoulders.

"Where do you want to plant the tree?" he asked as he gently put her back down.

At the very same moment, they thought the same thing. They would plant their evergreen tree at the center of the beautiful clearing. They walked to the middle of the field together and Gabby pointed down with her finger. "I think this is the perfect spot!"

Trevor quickly got the shovel and began creating a hole the size of the seedling pot. He huffed and puffed as he kicked downward against the shovel, sprays of rich, dark soil flying about.

Then, together, Gabby and Trevor gently lowered their lovely tree into the hole and eagerly filled the hole with dirt, using their bare hands. After patting down the earth many times, leaving their unique handprints all around the tree's base, Gabby held up the watering can, indicating that she and Trevor should water the tree together.

They paused.

"You ready?" Trevor asked her, a sincere seriousness written across his young face.

Gabby nodded.

Their hands overlapped on the watering can handle, they watered their evergreen tree for the first time.

Afterwards, they stood in silence, watching the small but sturdy tree and its long green leaves that had crowned victors in ancient times.

Trevor found Gabby's hand and held it. Trevor's fingers interlaced hers lovingly and they grinned at each other widely, tears in their eyes.

~

Listen to "Let Me Be Your Lighthouse" on Gabby's blog here: www.gabbysmelody.com

~

Epilogue

7 months later...

Gabby's mother held her dry hands in her own soft ones. Carol lay peacefully on the bed as Gabby sat beside her petite body. In that moment, her mom looked so small and frail like a weak, helpless child. The comforting scent of her Korean skincare products wafted through Gabby's nose.

"What did it feel like to grow up with me being so harsh?" her mom asked humbly, genuinely curious about Gabby's experience.

"Dad would just go into his room and not protect me so I felt like I was all alone in the world."

Her mother's eyes glistened with tears. "I feel so bad," she said remorsefully.

The dam in Gabby's heart got punctured and water rushed through the hole.

"Mom actually feels bad," she thought. "She actually wants to know about my experience."

The mother and daughter murmured to each other deep into the quiet night as Gabby's dad slumbered upstairs. Gabby had been away for college and they were treasuring this opportunity to chat.

"How's therapy been?" Gabby asked.

Her mom smiled so brightly; Gabby had never seen her look like that.

"I love my therapist. Her name's Shirley. She's an angel on earth…like you."

Gabby lit up.

"She made me feel…seen, noticed, heard…for the first time. I didn't realize I was carrying so much."

Water rushed from Gabby's eyes then. She had wanted this for her mom since she was young.

"That's so great, Mom," she said, wiping away tears and suddenly embracing her mom's small form.

"Gabby, be free now. You lived in fear for so long."

A door swung open in Gabby's soul. The door led to a lush, green garden. She stepped inside. She ran. Gabby understood that her mom would be easier on her now, now that she knew what her daughter had been through.

For a moment, Gabby was speechless. All that she had hoped for, for nearly twenty years. It was happening…now. It was all so beautiful, it was like staring at the sunrise without sunglasses on. Blindingly beautiful, you just keep basking in it.

"Toccoa."

Gabby remembered being at the bookstore and reading about the meaning of their city's name, Toccoa.

In Cherokee: "Beautiful"

In that moment at the bookstore she had felt her life was far from beautiful. But now, she could feel God's fingers masterfully creating beauty in her life. She thought her mom would never change, not in Gabby's lifetime.

"Gabby, what are you thinking about?"

Gabby wondered if she should explain all this to her mom, but she was tired from all these overwhelming emotions.

"Nothing," she said with a grin. "Wow! It's almost 1 a.m," Gabby exclaimed as she looked at the clock.

Gabby and her mom embraced one more time.

"I love you, Mom."

Her mom kissed her on the cheek, like the gentle, nudging peck of a mother hen, something she had never done before.

"I love you, Gabby."

Gabby made her way down the hallway. The lights were off, but it was as if she was in the light of day.

~

Stephanie Cho & Paul Jeon

Acknowledgements

We'd like to first thank God, who has given us the rare and precious opportunity to use our gifts to serve the world. We would then like to thank our family and friends who supported us and encouraged us every step of the journey. A warm thank you to our parents, Kun Hyung Cho, Sung Hi Cho, Ik Soo Jeon, and Myung Hee Jeon, who supported our book writing journey from beginning to end and cultivated our writing talents from a young age. Special thanks to Esther Cho for reading the whole manuscript and giving valuable feedback. Also, a special shoutout to Jessica Iida and Mina Chang who lifted up prayers for us whenever we needed it and rooted for us. Moreover, we'd like to thank Bronwyn Harris, our caring editor, Karine Makartichan, our wonderful book cover designer, and Elijah Feyisayo, our amazing formatter. Lastly, a thank you to Mitali Perkins for giving kind and exuberant advice at the start of our author's journey.

About the Authors

Stephanie Cho and Paul Jeon dated for nine years and got married in 2023. Stephanie Cho is a private tutor, and Paul Jeon is a high school English teacher. They both love God, kids, and family. They live in Torrance, California, and they enjoy trying new boba shops together. You can follow Stephanie Cho on TikTok @stephanie.s.cho and follow the book on TikTok @flyagainphoenix! You can also visit their website here: www.flyagainphoenix.com.